THE PRICE SHE PAID FOR LOVE

She glanced around the brightly lit room. "Might we extinguish the lamps?"

"All but one," he conceded.

She put her hands on his shoulders and stood on tiptoe to brush a kiss on his lips. "I am not afraid, or reluctant in any way. Please don't worry about me. Tonight is for you."

"For us," he corrected, with a smile that touched her heart.

"Lynn Kerstan's *Lady in Blue* steals your heart with its dynamic story and unforgettable characters. It is a very, very fine and unusual book. Great job!"

—*Romantic Times*

"Sexy, sassy, and altogether unique, Lynn Kerstan brings an exciting new voice to the romance and intrigues of Regency England."

—Kasey Michaels

Lady in Blue

LYNN KERSTAN

HarperPaperbacks
A Division of HarperCollins*Publishers*

This is a work of fiction. The characters, incidents, and dialogues are products of the author's imagination and are not to be construed as real. Any resemblance to actual events or persons, living or dead, is entirely coincidental.

HarperPaperbacks *A Division of* HarperCollins*Publishers*
10 East 53rd Street, New York, N.Y. 10022

Cover illustration by R. A. Maguire

First printing: March 1995

Printed in the United States of America

HarperPaperbacks, HarperMonogram, and colophon are trademarks of HarperCollins*Publishers*

❖10 9 8 7 6 5 4 3 2 1

For Alicia Rasley—superb writer, perceptive critiquer, sometimes collaborator, always friend.

Prologue

Wales, 1799

The howling broke into his sleep just after midnight.

Bryn clutched a blanket around his shoulders and buried his head in the pillows, but the sound persisted, ever louder and more tormented. He knew from experience there would be no end to it this night. Nor any other, until his father died.

With a low moan, he swung his feet to the cold floor and lit a branch of candles from the single taper on the bedside table. Sundown to dawn, all responsibility for the earl was his.

Two servants remained at the castle, an elderly couple with nowhere else to go. During the day they attended the sick man as best they could, with Bryn's help. The other staff had fled when there was no money to pay them. Only Mr. and Mrs. Dafydd remained at the once-flourishing estate of the Earl of Caradoc, along with the earl himself and the boy who would be heir to the ruins and the debts—if the end ever came.

After stuffing his feet into worn hose and slippers, Bryn shrugged into a threadbare robe. He picked up the brace of candles and padded grimly down the long dark hall.

The howling grew louder, echoing against the stone of the fortress that had stood for centuries between England and Wales. Like a great wounded mastiff, the Earl of Caradoc cried his desolation into the night.

As he opened the door to his father's bedchamber, Bryn was assailed by the stench of putrefying sores and excrement. He took a moment to breathe heavily, knowing he'd soon become accustomed to the smell. After a while, almost anything became tolerable when there was no choice.

He lifted the candleholder. Across the room, the earl rolled back and forth across the bed. He'd flung off the covers, and his skinny, naked body gleamed ghostly in the light. The room was icy cold.

Bryn closed his eyes briefly, gathering strength, and crossed to the fireplace. Wood was stacked, awaiting his arrival. It wasn't safe to leave the earl alone with a fire, not since the night he had stuck his hand into the flames, seeking warmth, and burned his numb fingers to stubs. Laudanum gave him peace for a few hours, but always, near midnight, he came to life with a vengeance.

Methodically, Bryn stuffed kindling under the logs and lit it with a taper. A stack of linens was set nearby, along with a basin and a kettle of water. He hung the kettle over the hearth and broke the ice that had crusted on top. Moving from habit, he spread towels across the flagstones to warm before lighting a lamp on the mantelpiece and another on a sideboard. It would be several minutes before he could bring himself to approach the bed. Pulling up a footstool, he sat down to wait for the water to heat.

The nightly exercise had become a ritual, no less terrifying for its familiarity. As always, he turned first to the enormous portrait of the earl that hung above the sideboard. In the dancing light of the fire, the Earl of Caradoc was a glorious apparition. Elegant in rich blue velvet, Dresden lace at his throat and wrists, the tall handsome man he had been mocked the shell of a man he'd become.

Bryn had adored his father, the rare times he saw him. Owen Talgarth swept in from his travels for the hunting season, usually with a horde of friends, always with boxes of presents for his lonely wife and child. Between the hunting parties and revelries, he took his son fishing and taught him to tickle trout and tie exotic lures. He told wonderful stories, too, about his exploits, and promised that they would share those adventures when the boy was old enough. Bryn lived for these visits from the man he idolized, but they ceased when he was ten years old.

That year his father had come home alone and ill. He stayed a few months, seemed to recover, and disappeared again. Soon after, his wife drowned in what everyone politely called an accident.

The earl did not return for her funeral. He was in Italy, some said, or Paris. Bryn, left to fend off his father's creditors, told the estate manager to sell one after another of the castle's treasures to pay the debts.

But there was no money to keep servants, and within a short time even the kindly manager took his leave. In spite of his youth and scanty education, Bryn learned to keep the accounts and strike deals with tradesmen and tenants.

When Caradoc finally returned, his face marked with sores, his mind uncertain, it was to die. So far the process had taken three years. Bryn had begun to expect his blind, maddened father would outlast him.

He dipped his hand into the kettle, found the water acceptably warm, and with a sigh of resignation came to his feet. The earl had begun to sing, his voice remarkably strong and the words of the bawdy ballad clear as daylight. Now and again he spoke, words of flattery and courtship or a challenge, as if he were playing at dice for high stakes.

At such times, Bryn imagined his father's mind had separated from his body and was living again the glories of the past. He profoundly hoped that was true. No doubt the old man merited hell, but surely he was enduring that now. If there was an afterlife, perhaps he'd be admitted to paradise, all his sins paid for with this terrible agony.

Old man. Bryn glanced again at the portrait across the room. It had been painted when Owen was thirty, a vibrant, lusty, devil-may-care rake. His gaze lowered to what was left of his father. A few straggles of hair sprouted from the blotched scalp. His glazed eyes were sunken above high cheekbones red with fever. He looked eighty years old. He was thirty-four.

As Bryn gently bathed the skeletal body, careful of the open sores, he murmured meaningless words of encouragement. It helped to concentrate on better times. Two years ago, the Earl had still possessed most of his faculties, though by then he had gone blind. Bryn became his father's eyes, leading him on walks through the overgrown gardens, sometimes coaxing him all the way to the river. They sat in the sweet grass, talking about fishing and the future. About the countess.

The earl never accepted that his wife was dead, even when he was lucid. He spoke of his beloved Mary as though she'd gone away for a time, as he'd so often gone away. Even now he talked to her, long speeches of love and fidelity.

But he had never been faithful. And that had destroyed them both.

Bryn had long since learned to shut his ears to the ceaseless babble, but suddenly he heard his name.

"Brynmore?" croaked the earl. "Is that you, boy?"

Startled, Bryn dropped the basin. It shattered on the stone floor, and lukewarm water soaked into his slippers. "Yes, Papa." He stroked the fevered forehead. It had been months since the earl knew who he was.

"Where's your mama?" His voice sounded oddly strong. "Where's Mary?"

"She's . . . paying calls in the village," Bryn improvised.

An emaciated hand seized his shoulder. "You're getting big, son. Like me. What are you now? Nine years old? Ten?"

Bryn swallowed hard. "I'm fifteen, sir."

"All that." The hand let go. "How did I miss your growing up?"

"You were in Vienna, Papa. And Paris. And Rome. You sent letters."

"Ah, yes. I met the pope last week. Did I tell you? We drank cognac. Or was that the Duke of Brunswick?"

"It was Brunswick," Bryn replied, not sure if popes drank spirits other than sacramental wine.

"Let's go fishing tomorrow, boy. Long time since we've cast for salmon, eh? Mayhap your mother will come along, with a picnic lunch. Like the old days."

"I'd like that, Papa." Bryn felt tears streaming down his cheeks, although he'd thought it impossible to cry any more. "We can catch our dinner."

The earl frowned. "Too late. We should go to London if you are fifteen. Had a woman already, boy? One of the housemaids?"

Bryn gulped. "Not yet, sir."

"Past time, then. See to the carriage and pack up your best clothes. I know just the place. Lucinda will still be there. Pretty Lucinda. Not so beautiful as my Mary, but she knows all the French ways."

Bryn shuddered and took a moment to calm his voice before responding. "Whatever you wish, sir. But you should sleep now." He tugged the sheet over his father and plumped the pillow under his head. The earl closed his eyes, and for a few moments it appeared that he'd drifted off.

Suddenly he sat upright, jabbing a finger at Bryn's chest. "Don't listen to 'em, boy. Do what you want. They tell you not to enjoy yourself, damn their eyes. What do they know?"

"Nothing, Papa." Bryn gripped his father by the shoulders and lowered him gently to the bed.

The earl released a long sigh. "Be a little careful, though. Careful. Careful. Careful. . . ."

Bryn gritted his teeth. Often the earl fixed on a word and muttered it for hours. Tonight it was the same. *Careful careful careful* echoed in his ears as he tugged nearer to the hearth the pallet that was kept ready for him. He extinguished all but one of the lamps, unfolded the blanket, and wrapped it around him, settling his long body on the thin mattress. Then he reached into the pocket of his robe and drew out lumps of wax, rolling them between his fingers until they were soft enough to stuff in his ears.

The wax dulled the sound, but he could still hear his father singsonging *careful careful careful.*

Damn right he'd be careful. If ever he escaped from this nightmare, he would make sure it did not repeat itself. Dully, Bryn gazed into the dying fire, remaking the promises that sustained him. The promises that kept him from despair.

That night the earl sank into a restless sleep from which he never emerged. Two weeks later he died.

Shrouded in fog, the bleak funeral was attended only by Brynmore Talgarth, now Earl of Caradoc, and the Laceys, a neighboring family. Bryn gazed at them across the open grave as the vicar muttered insincere prayers for the repose of a soul he obviously considered beyond salvation.

The Laceys had sustained him all his life. Robert, his best and only friend, was away at school, but the others were there. The viscount and his wife had provided food and clean linens the last few months. They'd have done more if he'd let them, but the Laceys were not wealthy. Isabella, only ten years of age but wild as an eagle, grinned at him. She knew how relieved he was to be free of his burden.

Even Aunt Ernestine, the most eccentric of the Laceys and the only one with money, had come up from London. It was she who paid for the coffin and the burial. Ernestine Fitzwalter was impervious to protests and did exactly what she wanted. Bryn envied her for that.

They expected him to move into their home, since the castle was all but unlivable, and Ernestine had offered to provide for his delayed schooling. He'd refused her offer, with the same pride that had characterized his father, but expected he'd stay with the Laceys long enough to settle what he could of his father's debts and discover if there was anything remaining of his inheritance to sell.

To keep his vows, he'd need a stake. His wits and determination would do the rest. One day he would be rich, independent, and true heir to the centuries-old name he bore. From almost nothing he would create a legacy for his children and restore the family reputation.

At the vicar's impatient gesture, he picked up a handful of damp earth and tossed it into the open grave. "I loved you, Papa," he murmured under his breath, "and I fear that I'm too much like you. But I swear this will never happen to me."

London, 1819

A devilish nuisance, this business of hiring a mistress.

The Earl of Caradoc had put it off for several weeks, dreading the awkwardness of the first meeting and, worse, the first night. But when he snarled at his valet for no reason and spent too many late hours at the gaming tables, it became clear that he could wait no longer.

By now Florette knew he was on the prowl again. She had an uncanny way of knowing everything. Doubtless she'd already procured a replacement for the fiery Marita Sanchez, whose departure had been as explosive as it was unexpected. Until then, no woman had ever walked out on him, and he didn't like the experience one bit.

As his fingers tightened on the reins, the grays

broke stride and the curricle lurched. "Sorry," he said over his shoulder to the tiger, who grinned cheekily at him. All his staff, including this groom, knew he was out of temper. They endured his frequent bad moods because he paid them well. Money, he had learned, could buy almost anything, even loyalty. And in the next hour it would purchase another woman for his bed.

He found the thought eerily discordant. By now he should be married, with children in the nursery and some purpose to his life. Already he had outlived his father by seven weeks. When had he lost sight of the goal?

Owen Talgarth's son, he reflected dourly—addicted to pleasure and his own whims. One of these days he'd pull himself together, keep the last of his promises, and close the account. He'd marry, sire an heir, and restore the castle at River's End. By now it must be a pile of rubble. He'd not been there since the day he buried his father, twenty years ago.

As Bryn pulled up in front of Florette's Hothouse, the door opened and a woman stepped out. She paused at the top of the wide marble stairs. Aloof and somber, she seemed to be staring at him although he could not see her eyes.

Not an inch of flesh was visible. Swathed in blue, from the veiled hat obscuring her face and hair to her dark half boots and gloves, she put him in mind of the sybil. Only her veil moved, fluttering in the early spring breeze. Her stillness unnerved him.

Lord, everything spooked him these days, even a whore on her way to the shops. What else could she be, emerging midday from London's most fashionable brothel? Probably she was assessing the quality of his clothes and horses, weighing the advantage of doing a little business before going out.

The acute discomfort of being appraised by invisible eyes raked the ashes of his foul mood. Tossing the reins to his tiger, Bryn swung from the curricle and advanced up the stairs until he stood directly in front of her. Something about her provoked him, and he never declined a challenge.

All the girls in Florette's bouquet were named for flowers. This one was tall, slender, and serenely composed. He lofted his hat and flashed her his most devastating smile. "Iris?" he guessed. "Or is it Lily?"

Her head lowered slightly, and again he felt her study him like a diamond cutter examining a flawed stone. He heard a coach pull to the curb. Without a word, she swept gracefully down the stairs, deliberately arcing in a smooth curve to avoid him.

Moving swiftly, he beat her to the sidewalk and planted himself in her path. She went utterly still.

"Is the hackney yours?" he asked with a bow.

The veil bobbed.

His smile widened. "I am sorry to hear it. Would you not prefer to stay indoors this afternoon?"

The *yes* to his first question turned quickly to a *no* as the heavy silk swirled around her face and shoulders. "I must go," she said, in a low, husky voice. "Please."

"This is no way to make your fortune," he chided, fingers itching to raise the blue curtain so he could see her face. "I suggest you reconsider."

The heel of her boot slammed down on his toe.

"Bloody hell!" He got out of her way immediately.

She darted past him to the cab, but he caught up in time to cover her gloved hand on the door latch with his own. Bryn heard her sigh, as if resigning herself to an obnoxious fate. When he offered his arm to help her mount, a feathery touch at his wrist was all he felt as she lifted with the grace of a seabird riding an updraft. Then, in a singularly swift motion, she yanked the door shut, the hard edge clipping his shoulder as it whizzed by.

Witch. He swore under his breath. Folding his arms across the bar of the open window, he peered into the dim coach. She could see him clearly through that veil, while he could see nothing of her at all. He resented her impertinence. And was annoyed with himself for his bad manners even as he persisted. For no reason he could explain, he wanted to prolong their encounter. "Shall I give the coachman your direction?" he inquired silkily. "Or join your expedition?"

Head tilted slightly, the Blue Lily raised her hand toward his cheek. For a second he thought she was going to touch him, but she reached higher, and with a sharp crackle the window shade snapped down in his face. A rap of her knuckles against the wood panel set the cab in motion, and the great back wheel barely missed rolling over his Hessian boots.

Repique, he thought, watching the hackney lumber down the street. Apparently he was not to her taste.

He chuckled. Nor she to his, of course. Like the other blossoms in Florette's bouquet, the Blue Lily must long since have been plucked. And if she knew who he was, she had no reason to encourage his feigned advances. The Earl of Caradoc's requirements were met by special order. This full-blown flower, however lovely she might be under all that rigging, could expect no more from him than flattering male appreciation—from a distance.

He was amazed he'd even touched her.

Bryn mounted the stairs, handed his gloves to the burly footman, and proceeded without ceremony to Florette's private salon. After that public and rather embarrassing display, no doubt she was fully aware that he'd arrived.

Seated before a delicate curve-legged table, Flo beamed at him with unconcealed amusement. Steam wafted from the antique Chinese porcelain teapot on the tray, clouding her gold-rimmed spectacles. "As you see," she greeted him, "there is shortbread." She held up a blue-and-white plate. "I was expecting you."

"I daresay." Lowering himself onto the fragile chair across from her, he gathered several of the buttery sticks in his hand and popped one whole into his mouth. Flo knew all his weaknesses.

She poured him a cup of tea and laced it with thick honey. "How very late you are, *chéri.* Marita has been gone these last few weeks. Never tell me you've been ill?"

The earl stretched his long legs across the Aubusson carpet. "Shall I assume Miss Sanchez reported to you"—he grinned wryly—"everything?"

Florette shook her head. "Ah, my dear, a chamber pot? What did you do, to make her so angry?"

"Devil if I know. She told me she was leaving, I said *adiós,* and that set her off. Threw everything at me she could get her hands on. The chamber pot was empty, by the way."

"*Tsk-tsk.* A quarrel with your mistress, on your birthday. 'Twas a night to celebrate, *je crois.*"

He shrugged. "That was certainly my intention. I'd anticipated a wild Spanish *corrida,* as only Marita could stage, but she claimed ears and tail before I got into the ring. Mad because I didn't take her to the birthday dinner at the Laceys', I suppose. My back-alley Spanish isn't what it used to be." He leaned back and crossed his ankles. "No mistress, whatever her charms, is welcome at *ton* affairs, *ma fille.* I trust you'll find me a replacement somewhat less encroaching—not to mention volatile. That little chili pepper nearly took my head off with a candlestick."

Selecting a thin cucumber sandwich, Florette regarded it thoughtfully. "I am afraid," she said slowly, "there will not be a replacement. Not one I can supply, at any rate." She nibbled at the soft white bread. "As of Wednesday last, I am retired from the trade."

The earl gazed at her blankly. "Tell me you don't mean that," he said in a dark voice. The consequences, for him, were disastrous. When she failed to reply, he levered himself from the spindly chair and aimed for the mahogany sideboard where she stowed his special vintage brandy.

Bryn took his time fixing the drink while the implications sank in. He'd never had a woman Florette didn't find for him. What the hell was he going to do now?

Florette LaFleur was about as French as the Prince Regent. When her accent slipped he detected a faint Yorkshire drawl, but that was the only clue to her origins he'd deciphered in the years he'd known her. Like everything else between them, his attempts to penetrate her disguise turned into a game they both played for the delight of matching wits.

She must be well into her fifties by now, still attractive although her lush figure had ripened to plumpness. She'd been a spectacular beauty when they first met, to transact the sale of this very house. Lost in memories, he rummaged on the sideboard for a corkscrew and dug the sharp metal point into the cork.

She'd managed to take him royally on that deal. Bribed his solicitor, he suspected, and made off with the only thing of value he owned for half its worth. Smiling, he recalled her dismay when a skinny adolescent showed up to sign the papers. Florette concluded the sale without upping her offer, but her conscience prodded her to invite him to dinner. He jumped at the chance for a rare good meal, and the friendship forged that evening had endured for twenty years.

Swallowing two fingers of brandy in a single gulp, he refilled the glass. What would he do without Florette? She was the best thing that ever happened in his life. The afternoon they'd closed the deal on this house, with a knowing glance at his straining breeches, she'd offered him a night of pleasure to compensate him for a loss he wasn't downy enough to recognize.

He had refused, necessarily, regretting it then as he did now. Just once, he would have liked to make love to Florette LaFleur.

Swirling the amber liquid in his glass, he remembered the first time he tasted brandy. It was in this room, that same evening, when he drank too much too fast and blurted the real reason he couldn't touch her. After what happened to his father, he did not dare take any lover who'd ever been with another man. He expected Flo to laugh, but she drew him into her arms and hugged him warmly. Now that he thought about it, another first. A good day, all in all. He had immediately acquired a strong taste for hugs and brandy.

The night was even better. Florette obliged him

with his first virgin, free of charge, a shy, petite girl only a bit more ignorant than he. She had light curly hair, he recalled fondly, and her name was Polly. Thank the stars she had a sense of humor and few expectations.

There had been three mistresses since, each one provided by Florette. She was the only one he trusted. Virginity was easily faked, and while he was expert enough by now to discern a fraud, the proof was in the taking. By then, too late for safety. He *needed* Florette! At any cost, he couldn't afford to lose her.

"Don't do it, Flo," he barked over his shoulder. "If this is one of your games, it's not funny."

"I have already sold out," she said calmly. "To Rose."

"The devil you say!" Pivoting, he glared at her. "I can't stand that woman. She'd filch pennies off a dead man's eyes."

"A good businesswoman, though." Flo tapped long nails against an ivory-handled fan. "For all purposes but your own, she will do well."

"And what *about* my purposes? I'll have no woman that strumpet dredges from the stews." He paced the room with one fist clenched behind his back and the other wrapped around a glass of brandy. "Tell me you are staying in London. No reason we can't do private business."

"I'm packed, all but gone already, and nothing will change my mind. The fact is, you are to all extents and purposes back on the streets. I'll provide the names of my competitors, should you require their services, but you'd do better to find yourself a wife." She flicked open her fan and studied the painted goldfish swimming over crisp folds of heavy parchment. "Indeed, I've likely done you a disservice all these years, dealing out one mistress after another while you put off the inevitable. You must marry, Bryn. You're thirty-five years old, you know."

Groaning, he plucked another hunk of shortbread as he stalked past the tea tray. "Don't remind me. By now I should be dangling an heir on my knee, but things got out of hand." He shot her a sideways glance. "The war didn't help."

"Five years in the army," she pointed out, "does not account for three times as many spent catering to your own pleasures. No, no," she protested, waving her fan when he spun on his heel. "Don't snap at me. You must do as you wish, and Lord knows you will. The thing is, I shall no longer be here to stock Clouds with a supply of suitable mistresses. It is time you think about settling down. The Season is barely under way, and a fresh crop of debutantes awaits your inspection."

"You might have given me some warning," he grumbled. "I can't look over the field with nothing to go home to at night. Even if I fix on a bride, it will be weeks before the wedding. And the wedding night."

Did he look as pathetic as he felt? Bryn wondered. He'd come here with the familiar twinge of anticipation and dread he always experienced when replacing a mistress, but never had he imagined the roof was about to cave in. As he bit ferociously into the crisp biscuit, his eyes suddenly narrowed. In fact, Florette would not leave him high and dry. He'd bet everything he owned that she had something up her sleeve.

His prowl eased into a languid, graceful stroll around the room, ending at the chair across from her, where he settled with his arms folded across his chest. "A wife," he mused, gazing at the ornate ceiling. "I've done the pretty every season these many years, but each crop of eligible females is more insipid than the last. Don't think I haven't tried. Come to think of it, didn't I offer for the Berrington girl?"

"Fifteen years ago, when you couldn't afford a decent settlement." Wickedly, Flo plucked the last chunk of shortbread from the dish. "Now your tastes are too fine. Nothing suits you."

He grinned. The first three mistresses she'd provided had suited him very well, although Marita Sanchez had been a rare aberration from the type of woman he preferred. While the bed sport had been unparalleled in frequency and variety, her temperament was even worse than his own. Marita was a good argument for finding a demure English bride and settling down, which Florette damn well knew. More than likely, she'd planned it that way.

Her smile revealed nothing as she fluttered her fan and regarded him through the spectacles perched on her nose. "You will miss me, *sans doute.* I expect to be gone within the week."

Recognizing a lure, he swam past. "Off to France, are you? The Loire Valley, as I recall. Near Blois."

Flo acknowledged his swift dodge with a wink. "*Exactement, chéri.* To my family home, in a village so obscure I doubt it can be found on any map."

And he was Queen of the Nile. Bryn raised an eyebrow. "You'll provide me an address?"

"But of course. When you send word of your nuptials, I'll ship a case of the best champagne to be had."

Leaning forward, he propped his elbows on his knees and templed his hands. "And what has all this to do," he inquired tranquilly, "with the Lady in Blue?"

"Ah." The fan wagged appreciation. "I knew you would not fail me, Bryn. When did you suspect?"

"Not soon enough. But this is the last place I'd expect to troll for a wife. No wonder she was wrapped up like a mummy."

"Wife?" Looking startled, Flo shook her head. "Oh, no, *mon ami.* No woman suitable to become Countess of Caradoc would set foot in this place. When Marita took her leave, I cast about for a young woman to replace her. Not an easy task, considering how very particular you are of late. But . . . well, you must judge for yourself. This one is on the house, by way of a parting gift, if she will have you. She insisted on seeing you first."

"Indeed." A muscle jumped in his cheek. "Aspiring mistresses don't vet me, *poupée.* Rather the other way around."

"Generally true," she conceded. "But times change."

Didn't he know it. "And what is the name of this gift?"

"Well, perhaps gift is not the right word," Flo said meditatively. "For myself, there will be no commission, but Clare has requirements of her own." She cast him a smug look. "Expensive requirements."

"Clare what?" He winced at the impatience in his voice. "And how much?"

"Clare whatever-she-tells-you. And if she approved of what she saw, which I cannot know until I speak with her again, one night will cost you ten thousand pounds."

"The devil it will!" Lurching to his feet, Bryn towered over the graceful tea table. "What in hell makes that rapacious female imagine I'd pay out a fortune for one night? And don't tell me you led her to believe it was possible."

"You can afford it," Flo said imperturbably.

"Which is nothing to the point. I *hate* the first night." Bryn felt the tips of his ears go hot. "What in blazes does she think I am?"

"Clare reveals nothing of what she is thinking, ever. Pray do not loom over me that way. It is most annoying."

Firing her a look of pure malice, he stomped to the sideboard.

"Bryn, the real point cannot have escaped you. Clare is the last virgin I shall provide. If she agrees to meet you, perhaps you can negotiate better terms for the future. However, her price for the first night is inflexible. As a matter of fact, I don't expect you to accept her. She is lovely, untouched, and available, but otherwise she'll not suit you at all."

He swung around. "And why is that?"

When Flo lifted her eyes, he saw the flash of cunning. "Clare is . . . not the usual young woman anxious to enter my profession. But she is determined to do so, however briefly. Her innocence fulfills your primary requirement, and your wealth satisfies her own. Beyond that I have little hope. Shall I tell her you are not interested?"

Bryn ran a finger under his starched collar. The mysterious Clare did not sound a suitable mistress, but Florette was deliberately trying to interest him by making the girl sound like forbidden fruit. He was well and truly hooked, he thought savagely, with Flo enjoying every minute of this. She was bent on victory in their last game and knew she held a winning hand.

"I am curious," he allowed, "as you intended. And less interested than you hope. Now give over. What makes this one special?"

"Why, nothing at all. In bed, is not one woman much like the next? I doubt Clare found any fault in your appearance, for you are too handsome for your own good. But she may reject your offer nonetheless."

"A offer I've not made," he pointed out. There were wheels within wheels in this plot, and he was as anxious as she knew he'd be to trace it to the center. Damn Florette, and damn Clare, and loneliness, and lust.

And damned if he'd agree to anything until he'd inspected her the way she inspected him. If she wasn't the most desirable woman on the planet, he would bloody well discipline his raging body the way he'd done, painfully, the years he'd spent attached to Wellington's staff. On the Peninsula there were none of Florette's virgins to ease the lonely nights. Surely it wouldn't take another five brutal years of celibacy to find himself a wife.

"How much," he asked acidly, "will it cost me to see her?"

"Why, nothing at all, assuming she agrees. For ten thousand pounds, she will expect to provide an audition. By sight only, of course. She won't let you touch her until you've paid up in cash. As a personal favor, Bryn, I would ask you not to meet her out of trifling curiosity. If you've no real interest, let it go."

His spine tickled a warning. "Just what is she to you?" he asked warily.

Flo tossed her head. "Goods. Wares. I'd market her carefully, with an eye to profit, were I not leaving the trade. As it is, I offer her to you without any charge of my own if you promise to treat her fairly. In honor of our years together."

"Our friendship," he corrected with a lopsided smile.

"Exactly." Florette adjusted her spectacles and gazed fondly at the tall earl. He was combing his long fingers through the thick straight hair that must have defied his valet's best efforts to control it. One swatch gravitated inevitably over his right eyebrow, giving him a boyish look at odds with the arrogance so natural to him it was more amusing than offensive. In a peculiar way, she thought of him as her son, although he'd be horrified if he knew that. Never had she met a man so determined to avoid emotional entanglements of any sort.

In most ways, he'd grown up too soon. But in others, he'd yet to mature. She had decided it was past time to shake him up and by good fortune had found the means to do so. "You have made me a wealthy woman, Bryn," she said in a complacent voice. "Once you were able to pay, you more than compensated for my generosity in the early days. I could not possibly retire so young if not for your lavish commissions and your advice about how to invest them."

"Had I anticipated the consequences, pernicious woman, you'd not have done so well by me." His eyes were shuttered. "I'm going to miss you."

"I'm retiring," she assured him tartly, "not sticking my spoon in the wall. When things have settled, I'll be in touch. Shall I send Clare to you?"

"Tomorrow morning," he replied gruffly. "Eleven o'clock. Send her to Clouds." He frowned. "No, better not. The place is a shambles after Marita's theatrical exit. Make it St. James's, and have her come in through the servants' entrance. I won't eat her up, Flo, but for that amount of money I'll damn well find out what's under all those veils before making up my mind."

"Fair enough. I'll tell her so, and she will come to you if it suits her. Clare is my goodbye gift, or my last mistake, but under no circumstances do I wish to be responsible for anything that happens once you meet."

"That sounds rather ominous."

Rising, Flo held out her arms, and he walked straight into them for a last hug. "Ah, you are a beguiling thing, Caradoc," she whispered against his neck. "Alas that I took my first lover long before I met you." Setting him back, she brushed the hair from his forehead. "Still, *je ne regrette rien.* The profession has been kind to me, and I shall retire in comfort with memories of the most delightful sort to keep me young. Along with a dalliance or two, *tu comprends,* for one is never too old to dance." Her eyes, which she'd once told him were greener than emeralds, shimmered with tears. "Take care, my friend. And look to the crossroads."

As he drove away, Florette stood at the door and waved, feeling a tightness in the vicinity of her heart. On instinct alone, she had begun something that might well lead to disaster. Bryn was curious about the mysterious veiled lady, as she'd hoped. And resistant because he could not bear to relinquish control of any situation to someone else. But she knew him, and understood him better than he could imagine. The man needed exactly what she'd given him. All he had to do was realize it.

With a sigh, Flo closed the door. She had gathered the players and dealt out the hand, but the outcome was unpredictable. Clare was the wild card in this game. The Lady in Blue, as Bryn called her, was not what he expected. Nor what she wanted to be.

When they came face-to-face, anything could happen.

2

Bryn waited for Clare in the library of his townhouse on St. James's Square. He'd thought to pass the time between breakfast and her arrival by catching up on some paperwork but found himself unable to concentrate. Turning his back on the papers strewn over the enormous desk, he gazed into a lovely garden.

It was that view which had inspired him to have a platform constructed, about eight inches high, to hold his desk and chair. Without the added height, his vision was obstructed by a wide ornamental panel halfway up the ceiling-to-floor panes of glass. Into the platform was built a device that allowed him to rotate his chair without standing up to turn it around. He dabbled with inventions, most of them designed to enhance his comfort and pleasure, some more successful than others. The library was unusable for the three months it took to get the revolving chair to work smoothly, and a faint odor of grease still permeated the room.

He did his best thinking in that chair, arms folded behind his head, gazing into the garden. But, unaccountably, today he was too nervous to stay seated. He moved to the large bay window and pressed his forehead against the glass, infuriated by his own eagerness to meet the mysterious virgin in blue and find out what made her think she could demand a fortune for relinquishing the title.

And what made Florette think he was going to pay it?

Did she figure he was in no position to reject Clare whatever-her-name-was? Hell, he wasn't that desperate. And damned if he'd be extorted. He hated the idea of satisfying Flo in her little game. He was tempted to declare the Blue Lady unsuitable at first glance and send her back like an unopened parcel.

Which fine display of temper and ego would net him precisely nothing. Given the alternative—celibacy—he was in no position to thumb his nose at Flo for the brief satisfaction of bettering her. The Lady in Blue was the last virgin, until he found another reliable source—or a bride.

It was unlikely he'd agree to her outrageous price, but he found himself wishing the chit would somehow find a way to convince him otherwise. He pulled out his watch. Where the devil was she anyway? It was five minutes past eleven. No woman kept him waiting. He would make that very clear to her.

More time passed before he heard the discreet knock on the door. "Come," he called, his voice unnaturally harsh. He swung around, curled fists planted on his hips, poised for his first real look at her.

She was veiled, gloved, and swathed from neck to ankles in a dark blue gown exactly as before. She came into the room and paused, hands at her sides. Behind her, the butler stood indecisively.

The earl waved his hand. "That will be all, Walters. No interruptions." Walters bowed out, closing the door behind him.

Clare stood without moving. She was, Bryn thought, the stillest creature he'd ever seen. She scarcely seemed to breathe.

"You are late," he said coldly.

"Your carriage was late." Her voice, a pleasant low alto, was expressionless. She crossed the room—he might describe it as a glide—until she stood in front of the desk, head tilted to look up at him.

"Be seated," he said, determined not to give her the satisfaction of asking her to lift that damnable veil.

Two large chairs were angled by the corners of the platform. She chose the one to his left, settling gracefully on its edge with her hands folded in her lap.

He sat too, leaning forward with his elbows propped on the desk, hands templed, chin resting lightly on his fingertips. "And just what is it, young woman," he asked bluntly, "that makes you worth ten thousand pounds?"

She lifted her head. "That, my lord, is for you to decide." Slowly, she drew up the veil with both hands and removed the hat. As if granting a favor, she allowed him to look at her face.

What he saw took his breath away.

She was not the first woman lovely enough to catch a man's eye in a crowded room. Hers was a quiet, marble beauty, all line and shape. A woman to look at for a long time. Her hair seemed to be a pale brown, dusted with gold, very thick and curly where it had come loose from a chignon at her nape. Wisps and tendrils, disturbed by removing the hat, curled at her temples and forehead.

She appeared older than the girls he'd come to expect, but that might have been her demeanor. Clare was ineffably serene.

The hair on the back of his neck prickled a warning. Flo was right. This one was different. He struggled to control his initial reaction, along with the incredible sense of challenge she fired in him. He felt uneasy, as if something crucial was at stake. "Would you care for some refreshment?" he asked, temporizing as he pulled his thoughts together.

"No, thank you." She placed her hat on the corner of his desk.

He shrugged. "Well, shall we begin then? With your name, perhaps."

"Clare. Clare Easton."

"Um. And your age?" Did her lips quirk slightly?

"Three-and-twenty, my lord."

He let out a breath. "That seems a bit old. Under the circumstances."

"I presume you mean a bit old to have any claim to virginity."

"For a lovely woman, yes." He regarded her skeptically. "Shall I assume you have spent the past six or seven years in a nunnery?"

"My background can be of no interest to you, so long as your conditions are met." Her chin lifted. "I assure you, they are."

"Ah, but you do not know all my conditions. Only the first, and you cannot blame me for being suspicious. Innocence is not likely, considering your age, beauty, and chosen profession. And virginity is easily faked."

"You would know better than I. But with your own experience, could you not unmask a deception?"

"Only when it was too late. How can I be sure you are not lying to me?"

Her eyes flashed, like lightning out of a clear sky, so unexpected that he wasn't sure he'd seen it. "Integrity," she said in a chilling voice, "is not confined to the aristocracy. Even a whore can tell the truth."

That word, whore, seemed altogether out of place on her lips. He bristled. "I do not tolerate insolence, Clare."

She bowed her head and said nothing.

For some perverse reason, he was annoyed that she didn't strike back. Bryn folded his arms across his chest. She was too calm. Too controlled. Were she truly virgin, it could only be because she was frigid. And a passionless woman, however beautiful, held no interest for him. "You will not do," he said in a businesslike voice.

"As you will." She reached for her hat.

He swept it away. "Why do you wear this? Are you afraid someone will recognize you?"

Her lips curved slightly. "I have only one thing to sell, my lord. Were I seen leaving your house, all London would assume I'd relinquished it already."

The earl regarded her with new interest. He almost thought she was laughing at him. Rejected women, and he had rejected a few, rarely found the situation amusing. He placed the hat near his elbow, out of her reach. "I would not have expected you to have given up so easily," he said with sudden insight. "Men interested in your peculiar temporary attribute and able to afford your outrageous price don't grow on trees."

Clare stood. "Indeed not. I expect they are hatched in ponds, under rocks."

He found himself laughing, and swung his chair around to gaze into the garden. If the white rosebud, just beginning to open, had poked through the glass and bitten him, he could not have been more surprised. She had a temper, that cool-eyed young woman, and concealed it extremely well. "Sit down," he directed. "I'm not finished with you."

"Indeed? It seemed a clear dismissal: *You will not do.* Have I misunderstood, my lord?"

He grinned at the white rose. Impertinent baggage. But he'd always loved the bite of iced champagne and felt a shiver of anticipation. "It pains me to admit it, but I seem to have changed my mind. At least for the moment. *Please* sit down, Miss Easton. What have you got to lose?"

"That would appear painfully obvious. The same thing I walked in this room with, although you seem to doubt it."

He heard the rustle of taffeta and glanced over his shoulder to see her settling on the edge of her chair. He hoped his relief didn't show.

"How do you manage to spin around like that?" she asked.

He lifted his knees and made a complete circle, then leaned back and crossed his ankles on the desk like a satisfied boy. "Physics, grease, and a clever carpenter with a blacksmith brother."

"Most impressive. Did you design it?"

"Yes and no. The idea came from something I saw at the theater. Part of the stage revolved, and what had been a drawing room was suddenly a tavern." He chuckled. "The audience liked it so well that the stage manager had to repeat the trick three times before the play could go on."

She nearly smiled. "Have *you?*" she inquired. "Swung around, I mean. Shall this play continue?"

"Let us say I am willing to hear more. Ten thousand pounds is an exceedingly high price for a woman of no experience, however lovely."

"I had thought a woman of no experience was precisely what you wanted."

"Not really."

She blinked. "Can a woman be experienced *and* a virgin?"

His brows lifted. "Not in that order, of course. But after a few hours of instruction . . ."

At last, he thought with fiendish satisfaction, he had ruffled that disturbing composure. At least to the point where one gloved hand fiddled with her skirt.

"I have no experience," she said flatly. "If you are willing to exchange ten thousand guineas for my virginity, let us come to terms. If not, please give me my hat."

He opened a drawer and put it inside. "I see the price has gone up, from pounds to guineas. An outlandish sum, Miss Easton, for such a trifle."

"A *trifle?* It is not so to me, my lord, nor to you. It was my virginity, and only that, which admitted me to this interview. It is what you advertised for, and what I have to sell."

"You must need the money badly. What you *really* want to do is tell me to go to the devil."

She paled. "Not that. Never that."

His brow furrowed. "Is someone compelling you, my girl?"

She stiffened. "No one. I have . . . debts, that is all."

"Where is your family?"

"Dead. I've no relations, not by blood. Be at ease, Lord Caradoc. No outraged protector will show up on your doorstep to avenge the loss of my virtue."

"You relieve my mind." Bryn swung his legs from the desk and leaned forward, chin propped on his fingers. "Miss Easton, I've no intention of prying secrets from you, but you cannot expect to enter my employ without answering a few pertinent questions. Even footmen are interviewed at length and expected to provide references."

"That would be a bit difficult, don't you think?" She flashed him an annoying little smile. "A reference could only prove me unsuited to the job."

Your point, he admitted with a nod, but she wasn't looking at him. Her gaze floated around the room, taking in the bookshelves lining both walls. "Do you read?" he asked with some surprise.

"You have a wonderful library," she said, a touch of awe in her voice. "And yes, I love to read above all things."

"Your vocabulary indicates some education," he observed, "as does your accent. Clearly you were reared among the upper classes."

She cast him a sly glance. "Like integrity, my lord, a love of knowledge is not restricted to the peerage. By good fortune, I have been educated. I can also embroider and play the pianoforte. But what is that to the point? It cannot be conversation or drawing-room entertainment for which you want me."

The earl was not accustomed to being rebuffed, but the surge of resentment he felt was not for her words, only for the poised way she delivered them. "Then let us get to the point, my dear. On the matter of your virginity, I accept Madam LaFleur's assurance that you are qualified." She didn't flinch. "For the rest, I would like to see for myself." His gaze caught hers and held. "If you are still interested in the position, you will now remove your clothes."

Clare looked at him without expression for a long moment.

He thought she was stunned. He was wrong.

Gracefully, as if she'd done it a thousand times, she stood and began to unhook the row of buttons that ran down the front of her dress to below her waist. One by one, slowly because she did not remove her dark kid gloves, the buttons opened. Her gaze was fixed on his face, but he suspected that she didn't see him at all. He followed the path of her fingers, down her long neck to the hint of flesh at the gradually widening vee, which had reached the edge of a plain cotton chemise. His eyes blurred.

How must he seem to her at this moment, leaning forward, practically slobbering over his desk? The awareness hit him like a harsh light, as if shutters were suddenly raised in a dark room. As if someone had turned over a rock and exposed him.

Clare was removing her dress, but she was clothed in a peculiar light of her own. Suddenly *he* felt naked. Uncomfortable. Shamed. He felt, dammit, all the things he'd expected her to feel.

Pretending boredom with the slow proceedings, he swung his chair around and stared into the garden, hearing the faint swish of taffeta. The white rosebud seemed to mock him. His mouth felt dry. How far had she got? Would she tell him when it was done? He came to his feet, almost missed his footing as he stepped off the platform, and let his glance fall on her briefly as he walked to the marble fireplace and leaned his elbow on the mantel. He caught a glimpse of white shoulder.

Why didn't she take off those stupid gloves?

She hadn't seemed to notice that he'd moved. He stared, brooding, into the empty hearth, for what seemed like a week. Finally he heard the dress fall to the floor. Glancing up, he realized that he could see her reflection in the mirror that hung above the mantel.

She bent slightly, grasped the hem of her chemise, and began to pull it over her head. The fabric caught, momentarily, on a hairpin, and then it was loose and gone. She let it drop to the floor and turned to face him.

Bryn looked back at her, from the mirror. If his hands were not gripping the mantel, he'd have sunk to his knees.

She was perfect. Flawless in every detail. He saw long legs in dark stockings which reached to mid-thigh, tied with simple ribbons, no spare flesh above the binding. And then the curve of hip, a soft nest of gold-tinged hair, smooth abdomen, and narrow waist. Her breasts were full but high, beautifully formed.

The palms of his hands, tightly clenched on marble, were sweating. His breeches stretched against his uncontrollable arousal. And her eyes lifted, catching his in the mirror. The tiniest hint of a smile curled her lips.

He recognized contempt.

Then, as smoothly as if she'd been poised on his

revolving chair and with exquisite slowness, she turned around. In profile she was breathtaking: the svelte arc of her back, the slight rounding of her belly, the sleek flanks. A tiny birthmark, shaped like a quarter moon, was raised just over the dimple on her right buttock. It was the only flaw—no, jewel—on skin like rich fresh cream.

She still wore her gloves. Bryn had a sudden vision of long legs in black stockings wrapped around his waist, hands in leather gloves caressing him.

Clare came around full circle. She stood with her arms at her sides, still as glass.

"Take down your hair," he said huskily.

Her arms lifted, and she pulled the long hairpins from her chignon. Her gaze pinned him in the mirror. She combed her fingers through her hair until it hung thick and softly waving over her shoulders, reaching to her waist. A thick swath concealed her left breast. With the folds of blue dress and foam of white chemise at her feet, she looked like Venus born of the sea.

Only iron-hard control kept him in place. His gaze dropped to a porcelain shepherdess on the mantel, and he picked it up with determined fascination. The figurine was sleek and cool and smooth. He wished he hadn't touched it.

Inexplicably, what he wanted to do most was apologize.

But who was to say she even minded? Clare had performed with the serene grace of a prima ballerina. Did she know he would have her, at any price? That she undervalued herself when she demanded a fortune?

If he looked up, he might find the answer in her eyes. For certain, she would recognize her victory in his. He had challenged her and lost. “Get dressed,” he ordered harshly, fingering the shepherdess.

The soft sounds of cotton and heavy taffeta tickled at his ears and skin. There was a long silence then, and he glanced into the mirror. She was turned away from him, gloved hands fumbling with the buttons near her waist. It was more difficult buttoning than unbuttoning. He considered pointing out how much easier it would be if she took off her gloves. He even thought to go help her but didn’t dare turn around.

She had the courage to face him naked, but he lacked the nerve to let her see him swollen with urgency. At all costs, she must not see that. It proved him the lust-driven, slimy thing she already thought him and put him at an awesome disadvantage for the negotiation to come.

It would be that, he reflected with a mixture of dread and excitement. He would not count the cost, even as he demanded more of Clare than her elegant body. Money could not buy what he desired from her.

He wanted her to want him. To writhe under him with passion in her eyes and words of need on her lips. He wanted all the fire she held so coldly in check.

Above all, he wanted her to stay with him. The idea shook him. He set the figurine carefully on the mantel. It was the cool finger on the trigger that made the best shot. Bryn realized he had to control his rising excitement at the prospect of a challenge. He must not leap into fantasies of a long relationship with a female he’d barely met and scarcely knew. Most of all, he had to control her. And he knew, with the edgy excitement of a born gamester, that it would not be easy.

As she fastened the endless line of buttons, he

probed for her weakness. What he found unnerved him. She had no weaknesses, save her need for money, and that was trivial in comparison to his own vulnerability. He wanted her more than he wanted the game. Until now he'd never gambled with any real concern about the outcome, and even losing brought a new challenge—the rematch. He never lost twice.

This time, winning was more important than he was ready to admit. Bryn sensed the imbalance and knew he was overcompensating with the arrogance of a born aristocrat with money to spend.

"Very nice," he said in a deliberately impassive tone.

Clare abandoned the last two buttons at her neck when he gestured for her to sit down. She did, wrapping her long hair into a chignon and securing it with pins.

Somewhat awkwardly, he sidestepped onto the platform and settled into his chair, relieved at her failure to look at him. Safely concealed behind the desk, he leaned back and folded his arms. "Yes, I believe we can come to terms, Miss Easton." The formality seemed odd, in light of what had just transpired. "Naturally I regret the uncomfortable exercise, but you could not expect me to—"

"Buy a pig in a poke?"

At first he could not believe he'd heard it.

"You have not examined my teeth," she continued. "Please do so if you wish and have no concern about my comfort. I expect we shall deal better if there are no misunderstandings."

His fingers dug into his ribs. Exactly when had he passed the reins to this astonishing creature? "Do you understand, young woman, what I expect of you?"

"Not in detail. I believe there is some pain, and a little bleeding."

"That's not what I meant!" Regretting the outburst, he schooled his voice. "But while we're on the subject, it's true the first time is rarely pleasurable. I shall most certainly endeavor to cause you as little discomfort as possible."

"I have told you, my lord, that you need not trouble yourself about my comfort."

"Devil take it, lady!" He raked his fingers through his hair. "Forget the first time. It's not important."

"Not important!" Her eyes blazed, only for a second. "You will pay dearly for that one night. What else could possibly matter?"

He sighed. "We have a grave misunderstanding, my dear. I will not pay you ten thousand guineas . . . no, not even ten guineas . . . for the dubious satisfaction of claiming your virginity. Did Florette not explain to you?"

She made a helpless gesture.

"I want a mistress, Clare. A woman exclusively mine for as long as we choose to stay together. The fact that our relationship must begin with your innocence is my personal predilection, which I need not explain, any more than you are willing to tell me any of the things you seem determined to conceal. This is not a matter of one night, the taking of a virgin and a payoff in the morning."

There was a tense silence. "How long then?" she asked falteringly. "How many . . . nights?"

"Until I am finished with you."

"I see." Clare smoothed her skirt, considered for a moment, and rose. "Please, may I have my hat?"

"Not until you hear me out." He grinned. "Sit,

Miss Easton. You have come so far already. How can it hurt to stay the course?"

"The course," she said acidly, "has become very rocky." But she perched on the edge of her chair and gazed at him with admirable calm.

Again he marveled at the control of this woman. She had confronted, he knew with a shot of insight, challenges worse than this. And lost, or she would not be here now. His voice softened. "I am finding all this difficult to explain. To be honest, I've never had to explain it before. Did Florette tell you nothing about me?"

"Almost nothing." Her lips sloped in that enticing, elusive smile that intrigued him. "But I insisted on seeing you before we met."

"Indeed? At the time, I thought she staged that encounter so that I could see *you.*"

"Florette's knives," Clare said wisely, "have a double edge. She told me nothing but your name."

"Likewise." He laughed and caught a responsive gleam in her eye. For a moment they were united against Flo's conspiracy and the sting of being caught in her trap.

"I would ask more of you, Clare," he said softly, "than what you had thought to yield. And I shall, of course, pay you accordingly. There is a small house, on Half-Moon Lane, fully staffed, for you to live in. I wish to settle you there, today if possible. I hope that you will come to me freely, ready to agree to certain other provisions, which I shall explain later, and prepared to work out a comfortable and mutually enriching relationship."

"Not today," she said quickly. "I had not understood the terms of your contract, nor truly met you before this morning. I must have time to consider." Standing, she held out her hand. "My hat."

With reluctance, he took it from the drawer and came down off the platform to stand in front of her. She gazed at him, her eyes smoky with unhappiness. His heart sank. Gently, he placed the hat on her head and let his fingers linger for a moment against her smooth cheek. "You have not truly met me even now, Clare Easton. I very much regret how I . . . what I . . . oh, damn! Just give me another chance to set things right. Please."

She stepped back and lowered the veil. "Florette will send word," she said ambiguously. For a moment she regarded him through dark blue silk. "Should you not summon the carriage?"

Swallowing an oath, he went to the bell cord and gave it a vicious tug. Clare was already at the door when Walters opened it.

She turned her head slightly. "I must say, Lord Caradoc, that this has been a most interesting morning."

Before he could think to respond, she vanished down the hall.

3

"The man is insufferable." Clare paced the salon with short jerky steps, her gloved hands fisted into balls.

Florette stirred honey into her tea. "But will he have you, my dear?"

"I'm not surprised he has to pay for a woman. You should have seen him, Flo. The peacock actually built a stage for himself. He was poised there, with his hands on his hips just so." Clare spun around and assumed a languid, sardonic pose, chin tilted, eyebrows arched, nostrils flaring slightly. "Insolence personified, he was, with light pouring over him through the windows. It was all I could do to keep from laughing. He looked down on me, a *long* way down his nose, and said something obnoxious. Then he got worse."

"But will he have you?" Flo repeated patiently.

"I daresay. Only because he can't read my mind. If

he knew what I thought of him, he would turn his disgusting attentions elsewhere. But it would not occur to him that any woman might find him lacking."

"None has ever done so, to my knowledge."

Clare glared at her.

Flo lifted a negligent hand. "Present company excepted, of course. Obviously he made a cake of himself, which does not surprise me. You are not what he expected."

"And what was that? A simpering twit? A lecherous barmaid? What exactly does a vulgar libertine expect when he opens his wallet to buy a virgin?"

"A good deal less. I have provided the earl with every woman he has taken under his protection and can tell you that he never encountered a situation like the one he faced today. You ought to spare him a little sympathy, knowing what it is to founder in deep water."

"So I do." Clare ceased her pacing and rested her hands on the back of a chair. "But *I* am desperate, and he is not. In any case, he is willing to see me again, to negotiate the terms of our arrangement." Her teeth clenched. "He has a great many terms."

"And you do not feel you can agree with them?"

"Perhaps I could. At this point, I'd agree to almost anything. But what I cannot do is tolerate that vain, degenerate rakehell. You'll have to find me someone else, Florette."

"He's handsome enough—"

"And doesn't he know it! Whenever was any man so incredibly arrogant? Can you imagine what I'll do when he starts ticking off rules like a headmaster?"

"I wish I could see it," Flo said with a laugh. "But since you've taken his measure, what have you to lose by hearing him out? Perhaps he'll be more amiable when next you meet. In any case, I suspect he was a bit nervous this morning."

"Nervous! That one? He hasn't a nerve in his body." Clare frowned. "Although, for just one moment, he seemed almost . . . but no. I must have mistaken him. From beginning to end his behavior was insupportable."

Florette sighed. She'd expected Bryn to be much kinder to the girl. Clare was fragile as thin glass, for all her poise. Had he not seen that? Perhaps this tangle was her own fault. She'd wanted to make him curious, but it seemed she'd only made him defensive. Or offensive, from all accounts. The earl had not begun well, that was certain, but he'd accomplished something important. Clare was angry. Furious. Stomping the salon like a provoked bull. That was, Flo thought, very very good. Worth the risk of sending her back into the arena with Bryn Talgarth.

"Sit down, my dear," she said pacifically. "Have some tea and tell me all about it."

"I can't sit down. Which reminds me, he's got this chair, all carved wood and gold brocade padding, that whirls around in a circle. He uses it like a throne. And he leans forward with his elbows propped on the desk and his hands like this"—she templed her fingers under her chin—"and says, *Well, Miss Easton, what is it that makes you worth ten thousand pounds?* I wanted to tell him, *You do!*" She chuckled. "Actually, I did tell him that, in a way. What I really wanted was to double the price. Triple it. There must be someone else, Florette."

"Probably so. Many would pay a fortune for you, although few could afford it. And those who could—"

She shivered delicately. "I do not allow such men in my establishment. Come here, Clare. Sit down and listen to me very carefully."

The serious tone sent Clare obediently to a chair across from Flo, who gestured at the tea tray. Clare shook her head and folded her hands in her lap.

"My dear, the same . . . taste . . . that convinces a man to pay a high price to bed a virgin is often mated to cruelty. I will not entrust your safety to such a man. Such is not the case with the Earl of Caradoc. And no matter how angry he makes you, nor how angry you make him, he will never do you harm."

Clare stared at her folded hands for a long time. When she looked up, her eyes held the same controlled blankness that first drove Flo to try and help her. "The truth is, I haven't many choices, have I? I must get the money, and there is no other way."

"You know there is."

Clare smiled and shook her head. "Let us be frank. You were acquainted with my mother, many years ago, and for the sake of that friendship you wish to assist me. I am grateful beyond words. But you've lost money on the 'Change, too much to consider making me a loan I'll never be able to repay unless I do later what I am trying to do now."

"And you are too proud to accept a gift." Flo clucked into her teacup and set it on the tray. "I have more than enough money from selling the Hothouse to retire comfortably. In the country, far from temptation, I shall not be so eager to take flyers on tips from my patrons. Playing the 'Change is like gambling, if you do it the way I have done. Somehow the money never seemed real, and I never understood it was gone until too late. Away from London, pottering in my garden, I shall let my banker invest for three percent and dwindle into a cozy old age."

Clare looked mulish. "Whatever your financial circumstances, I'll not become your dependent. Good heavens, you know better than anyone the circumstances that drive a woman to sell herself. And I'm not planning on a career. I've only to endure one man's lust, take his money, and fulfill my obligations."

Flo regarded her steadily. "Then you will meet the earl tomorrow?"

"I suppose so." Clare spoke in a resigned voice. "But don't be surprised if he turns me away. I suspect he is playing with me, like a little boy taking apart a watch to figure out what makes it tick. Once he does, I'll be out with the rubbish."

"It is possible," Flo said, "that he can put you back together again. He has a way with inventions, I hear."

"You are doing nothing," Clare said between tight lips, "to win your case for him. Whirling chairs indeed!" She picked up an almond biscuit. "Just why is it, if he is so different from the men you won't let me meet, that the lofty Earl of Caradoc insists on bedding a virgin?"

"Ah, that you must ask him."

"Don't you know?"

"Of course I do. But as you made me promise I would tell him absolutely nothing about you, not even your real name, I owe the same discretion to him. Whatever you discover about each other, or choose to reveal about yourselves, is not my concern."

"Not even a tiny little hint?" Clare's dimple winked.

"Oh, perhaps one or two, between women. We do start at a disadvantage in most ways, although we control the greatest power of all. As for the earl, I can tell you that he will never break his word or fail to honor an agreement. He will also"—she reached for the teapot—"see to it that all agreements go his way. He has snares concealed in his traps, and pits dug underneath."

"Then I shall stay airborne at all times. What else? You said *two* hints."

Flo grinned. "Not precisely. Only this: If you are bound on the course you've set, you will do no better than Caradoc. And if you won't see him again, I cannot help you unless you accept the money I've offered. It is your choice, my dear."

Clare brushed crumbs from her skirt. "I have lived too long on the kindness of those who could not afford it, Florette. And I tried too long to make my own way, without success. Had I only myself to consider . . . but you know how things are. And if you say that odious coxcomb is the best you can produce, so be it. At the least, I'll meet with him one more time. Better to get it over with, so let's set the encounter for tomorrow morning. Will you let him know?"

"I'll ask him to send a carriage for you at eleven o'clock. Would you care to stay here tonight?"

Clare shuddered. "No, I'll return to the post house and come back in time for the appointment. You needn't get up so early. Just be sure someone will let me in."

Flo laughed. Even the servants rarely stirred before noon in this house. "Come at nine, and we'll have breakfast together."

"I don't dare eat anything before I see him again," Clare said with a grimace. "The Earl of Caradoc turns my stomach."

4

When Clare was gone, Bryn went to the place where she'd stood and turned to face the mirror. He could see himself clearly, as Clare must have seen her own naked body. As she must have seen his eyes, looking back at her.

What had possessed him? Even now, with the results limned on his memory, he wasn't sure why he'd ordered her to unclothe herself. He'd never done that before, with any other woman. Nor was he certain how Clare felt about it. From her tranquil expression and fathomless eyes, she might well have been proud to show herself. She had every reason to be.

More likely she thought him a degenerate goat.

His gaze lowered and caught sight of a small button on the carpet. It was blue, like her dress, with a tail of dark thread. He picked it up and rolled it between his fingers. Already the ten minutes since she left seemed an eternity. In another hour he'd be climbing the walls unless he found something to distract him.

Stuffing the button in his pocket, he went to his desk and scribbled a note on the back on an engraved card. Robert Lacey always had interesting plans for the evening.

Bryn had just abandoned an untouched luncheon, served on a tray at his desk, when the viscount's reply was delivered. He prepared himself for an exercise in cryptography. Lacey's handwriting had been the despair of Wellington, who frequently summoned Colonel Lord Talgarth to decipher an obscure dispatch. This one appeared to say *Frog Wetherford's balls. Ten. Pick me up horse in Claridges. Claws too. Sorry. Lazy.*

No challenge at all. He was to pick up Claude and Lacey in his carriage at ten o'clock. *Horse* had to be *house,* presumably Lacey's, and apparently Lord Wetherford was hosting a ball.

He groaned. High-stakes gaming better suited his mood, but for some doubtless compelling reason Lacey had to do the pretty tonight. Damn right he ought to be sorry. But they could look in on the ball and escape early to one of the clubs. No one expected Lord Heydon or the Earl of Caradoc to remain long at a society affair.

Midafternoon, another messenger arrived. Clare had agreed to meet with him again, tomorrow morning at eleven, and would await his carriage at the Hothouse. After her signature, Flo appended a postscript: *Behave yourself!*

He nearly shouted for joy. Tomorrow! He would see her again tomorrow. Immediately he wrote a letter of instructions to Mrs. Beales, the housekeeper at Clouds, and spent the rest of the afternoon selecting books to take with him.

He suspected there were no books at Clouds, and Clare liked to read. It was oddly pleasant, choosing a small library for her, guessing what she would enjoy. He wound up picking his own favorites, thinking how relaxing it would be to have her read to him in her low, husky voice.

Tomorrow she would be his. With his own fingers he'd undo her buttons. Take down her long hair.

But first he had to dispel her first impression of him and convince her to stay.

"Sorry to keep you waiting." Robert Lacey swung into the carriage, grinning at Bryn's impatient expression. "Brummell here couldn't tie a knot."

Claude Howitt settled beside Lacey, placid as always. "I'm no hand with a cravat. Hate the damn things."

Bryn tapped the overhead panel with his cane to signal the driver. "I suppose you have an explanation for this outrage, Lace. Why are we wasting a perfectly good evening at a bloody ball?"

"No escape," Lacey said in a mournful voice. "And don't think I didn't try. Isabella put the screws to me."

Bryn chuckled. Isabella had covered her brother's tracks during a notably wild childhood, being possessed of a bedroom with a window that could be accessed by means of a large tree for predawn sneaking home. She'd been calling in favors ever since. "What stake has the fair Dizzy in a *ton* ball? And what did you mean by Frog Wetherford? The marquess has a beak like a toucan."

"*Frau,* fool. Frau Wetherford. German, don't you know. She's bringing out a chit tonight, and Izzy likes the girl. Said I was to show up and dance with her or else."

"We're going to a bloody come-out? You might have warned me."

"You wouldn't have come," Lacey said amiably. "Snagging you for this party has put me in Izzy's good books for a change. She is hellbent to see that Elizabeth Landry makes a splash tonight."

"Landry? You can't mean the baron's whelp. Why the devil would Wetherford sponsor a girl of no breeding?"

Lacey chuckled. "Wetherford is the only man in England stupid enough to owe money to Giles Landry. I expect Izzy arranged the deal. Frau Wetherford likes to play hostess, Elizabeth is treated to a grand ball, and Landry doesn't get his hands on cash he'd gamble away. Smart woman, Izzy. She's fond of Elizabeth and says the chit is nothing like her father. You are expected to dance with her."

"The hell I will," Bryn said crossly.

Claude spoke up. "You could be wrong, Lace. Giles Landry is so deep in River Tick that nothing can save him. Perhaps he is trying to secure his daughter's future before he's clapped in Newgate."

"Claude, you'd make excuses for Attila the Hun." Lacey crossed his arms behind his head. "Landry plans to sell her off. A rich son-in-law is his last chance to stay out of prison."

Bryn nodded. "But what does Izzy expect *you* to do about it? Surely not marry the girl. Your income wouldn't dredge a minnow out of River Tick."

He laughed. "I am by way of a decoy. Or maybe a lure. I dance with Elizabeth, and first thing you know she has that cachet only the attention of London's best-looking bachelor can provide. One can only imagine her success if London's richest—"

"Forget it." In his present mood, Bryn didn't think he ought to come within touching range of female flesh. "I'll make my bow for Izzy's sake, but no more than that."

"Well, *I'm* going to dance with her," Claude said staunchly. "Can't be easy, standing there all by herself like she's up for auction. What's worse, only a rich old deviant would pay a fortune to have her."

Bryn went cold.

"Unless she becomes the fashion," Lacey pointed out. "And that's where we come in. We'll stay an hour or two, Bryn. Then we'll have a late supper at Watier's and you can head out for Clouds. How is Marita these days? Still a wild woman?"

"She's gone. Took herself where—let me see if I can translate this for polite company—where all the men are hung like stallions and she doesn't have to ride the same one every night."

"That filly was born to run," Lacey said with a laugh. "Is she back at the Hothouse? I wouldn't mind a steeplechase."

"As I understand it, Marita will be playing *corridas* in the south of Spain. And I've bad news for you, coxcomb. The estimable Florette is going out to pasture. She has retired."

"What?" Lacey sat up. "She's closing shop? What

the hell are we going to do? More to the point, what are *you* going to do?"

"Find someone else, I suppose. Any suggestions? You're on terms with every madam from here to Bayswater."

"There is only one Florette. Damn. I'm going there tonight and talk her out of it."

"Flo can't afford to retire," Claude put in. "Lost a bundle on the 'Change."

"Did she?" The Earl regarded him with interest. Claude did not patronize the Hothouse or any other establishment, but he had his finger on much of importance in London. "I wouldn't put it past her to bait me, just to watch me squirm."

"That must be it." Lacey *whoosh*ed in relief. "She wanted to see your reaction when she threatened to cut off your supply of vir—"

Bryn's cane hit his knee.

"Ow!" Lacey scowled at him. "I need that leg for dancing."

Shrugging, Bryn fixed his gaze on Claude. "Use all your mysterious sources and see what you can find out. By the way, what if I want to trace someone's background? Family and all that?"

"A Bow Street Runner, I expect. Want me to put you on to a good 'un?"

"Do that. Talk to my secretary first thing tomorrow."

Lacey leaned forward, still rubbing his knee. "Trouble, Bryn?"

"What do you think? Florette is, as she so chipperly put it, throwing me back on the streets. Meantime, I'm in a coach with the two most boring individuals of my acquaintance, on my way to a schoolgirl's first ball." He raised his cane in a salute as the coach pulled up behind a long line of carriages, two blocks from the Wetherford mansion. "Cheers, gentlemen. Let's get out and walk."

Few things, Bryn thought as he edged his way down the receiving line, were as dampening to lust as the stench of a crowd in a closed ballroom. He made straight for the terrace and fresh air.

He'd been there several minutes before realizing he wasn't alone. Concealed behind a potted tree, huddled on a marble bench, a small shape was trying to make itself invisible. "I didn't mean to disturb you," he said. "Did you wish to be alone?"

"I rather wished to breathe." A young girl with dark hair, small and slender in her white dress, moved gracefully toward him.

He bowed, hoping she would leave him to his solitude. "Are you enjoying yourself this evening?"

"I must be," she said lightly. "This is my come-out ball."

The top of her head scarcely reached his shoulder. A pretty girl, he thought, smiling at her. "Then you must be Miss Landry. Iz—Isabella's friend."

"Yes, I am Beth Landry. And Lady Isabella has been most kind. I cannot think why, since she scarcely knows me. We became acquainted by accident at the British Museum."

"Elgin marbles?" Bryn guessed.

Her laugh was delicious. "How did you know?"

He lifted her white-gloved hand and brushed his lips across her fingers. "At the moment, Isabella is obsessed with Greek antiquities. It won't last. Within a month she'll be on another tear. I have known Isabella since she was in pigtails, so perhaps we need not be formally introduced. I am Caradoc."

"Oh." She looked a bit flustered. "I have heard much about you."

"Believe little that you hear, Miss Landry, in *ton* ballrooms. And less if you hear it from eccentric widows with more impertinence than sense. Isabella does not confine herself to tormenting family, but stretches her claws to encompass the innocent friends of her brother."

"Innocent," Miss Landry said with suspicious demureness, "was not the first word that came to mind when you introduced yourself."

He grinned. The chit had spark. Not so timid as he'd first thought, when he saw her clutching her arms around her chest on that bench like a lost little girl. He regarded her with more interest. "If this is your debut, Miss Landry, why are you not dancing?"

She gestured to the card dangling from her wrist. "I expect I shall not be missed for the next hour or two."

He didn't have to look to know the card was empty. "As a matter of fact, I know of two gentlemen scouring the ballroom, their toes positively itching to dance with you."

She giggled.

Bryn despised giggling women, but for some reason this one didn't irritate him. "Would you allow me to partner you before you are besieged with offers? I have no taste for country dances, though. Do you waltz?"

"I know how, but—"

"Of course. This is your debut, and the despotic

dowagers have not granted permission. Come, let us beard them together. I have a sudden uncontrollable urge to waltz."

Lady Jersey, with a lifted eyebrow and vast curiosity, nodded approval before speeding away to share the news with her cronies. The Earl of Caradoc, who rarely attended balls and never danced, had fixed his interest on the Landry chit.

Bryn was fully aware of the gossip and slanted glances as he led Elizabeth to Lacey and Claude. Each leapt hungrily for her dance card, and several other men added their names. By the time he swept her onto the parquet floor, her card was nearly filled and her eyes were shining.

Her inexperience was obvious from the first steps, but she was graceful and yielding. "You are lighter than dandelion fluff," he said.

Elizabeth gazed up at him happily. "Until now I've waltzed only with my dance master, who is even shorter than I and rather fat."

To his surprise, Bryn enjoyed the dance and her company. She chatted engagingly about Isabella and school, treating him, he began to discern, much like an older brother. Older than that. Like an uncle. To his relief, and somewhat to his pique, she didn't seem to consider him a potential suitor.

An idea hit suddenly, and he stumbled. Tightening his hand on her small waist to cover the misstep, he swept her into an elaborate series of whirls that left her breathless.

When the waltz came to an end, Elizabeth thanked him politely, clearly unaware of the signal honor he'd done her. A moment later, he was forgotten completely as Lacey stepped forward to claim her hand.

Women were invariably dazzled by the viscount's startling good looks and the twinkle in his eye.

Bryn seized a glass of champagne from a passing waiter and leaned against a marble pillar. Why not marry the girl? As Florette had taken care to remind him, it was past time he found a wife and produced an heir. Elizabeth was pretty, certainly innocent, and he could give her a better life than she was likely to have otherwise. Few men in this room could afford to bail out her reprobate father, and fewer still would marry into that family.

Bryn scowled at his champagne flute. A busy day, my boy, he thought sourly. After some twenty years on the town, he'd nearly despaired of finding the perfect mistress, let alone a tolerable wife. Today he'd met both, assuming either would have him. And the fact was, neither woman was in a position to refuse should he make an offer, proper or otherwise. Money was a wonderful thing. It could buy almost anything.

But Miss Landry would have to wait. By dancing with her, he had propelled her into fashion. Now she'd have a chance to make a desirable match. If she did not, he would give more thought to the matter.

More immediately, he wanted Clare. Until she was permanently installed as his mistress, he could not propose to anyone. Marriage was a business arrangement, and a prospective bride had every right to know the terms. His were fairly simple, and certainly reasonable. The Countess of Caradoc would bear his name, remain faithful until she produced an heir, and tolerate his mistress with good grace.

Things would be different, of course, if he'd ever met a woman he could love. But Elizabeth Landry was only the second female to arouse even the slightest thought of matrimony, and he knew instinctively that he could never share with her the encompassing, passionate love he craved. Naturally he would be kind to her. Already he liked her. If she found no one else, perhaps he'd marry her.

And perhaps he was an arrogant, overweening, selfish buffoon.

He downed the last of his champagne. Yes, it had been a busy day. He'd met a potential wife, an irresistible mistress, and a part of himself he wasn't altogether glad to have been introduced to. The man who looked at Clare Easton's body in a mirror. The man who bought women because there was no woman, not one he wanted, to give herself freely.

Most of the women in the ballroom would come to his bed if he beckoned. Most of the men would join him at any pursuit, just to be in company with the Earl of Caradoc. But in that pressing crowd, his ears pounding with voices and music, he felt very much alone.

5

Bryn arrived at Clouds an hour before Clare was due to appear.

There was no trace of the shambles Marita had produced with her dramatic exit. The last time he was in this parlor, he stood ankle deep in shattered glass and broken pottery. A wild woman, Marita. He would not miss her, even in bed.

Mrs. Beales offered him a mug of coffee, which he refused. Even after a sleepless night, he felt too jittery for stimulants of any sort. She regarded him apprais-ingly through narrowed eyes, chuckled when he growled at her, and vanished into the kitchen.

Maude Beales knew all his moods. She'd served him twelve years in this house, named Clouds by the first of his mistresses to live here. Angela had asked that all the ceilings be painted sky blue and adorned with fluffy clouds. They had long since been painted over to fit the taste of her successors, but the house retained its name.

At his instruction, the young footman unloaded the books from the coach and arranged them on a window seat. The small house boasted not a single bookshelf. Bryn decided to line one wall of the parlor with shelves and make sure they were filled. Considering the amount of time he spent here, it was amazing he'd never thought of it before. But then, he was never at Clouds to read.

Shortly before eleven, Mrs. Beales directed the footman to place a large tray on a table in front of the sofa. Bryn saw all his favorites: cream-filled cakes, slim finger sandwiches of rare roast beef, peach tarts, and a large pot of steaming coffee. Best of all, a plate of shortbread. He took a handful of small squares and chewed with pleasure while examining the furniture, planning strategy.

Clare would be placed on the sofa, directly in front of the table. He would settle to her right, in the winged chair. No, that was too far away. He directed the footman to move the chair closer, then to the left, then directly opposite the tray. Mrs. Beales stood with her arms folded, a smile quirking her thin lips.

Damn but he was nervous, and he didn't need her smug face to tell him so. "Get out," he said. "You too, Cassidy. Go shopping or something. Come back in . . . two hours."

"Charley, you have two hours to get into trouble," said Mrs. Beales with amiable nonchalance. "I shall be in the kitchen, milord. Do call if you need me."

He eyed her balefully as Charles Cassidy made his escape. "I will introduce you to Miss Easton when and if necessary, Maude. Don't come wandering in here with some excuse about warming the coffee."

"As you wish, milord." From the door, Mrs. Beales

turned and gazed at him down a sharply pointed nose. "Don't take her upstairs."

"Out!" When she was gone he began to prowl the salon, checking his watch every few seconds. Did the woman think he planned to consummate this arrangement immediately? Within two hours? Not a chance. Clare had yet to agree to anything beyond another meeting, and even if she accepted his offer he would not rush her to bed in the middle of the day.

Tonight, with wine and candlelight and slow seduction, he would draw her willingly into his arms.

The palms of his hands were damp with sweat. He'd not felt this apprehensive since the night he huddled under a leaking tent in the pouring rain, just outside a flyspeck on the map called Waterloo.

At precisely eleven o'clock, the knocker sounded and Bryn hurried to open the door. Once again Clare was swathed in veils, wearing the same blue dress as before. They stood awkwardly for a moment, and then he backed up to let her enter, unable to summon even a casual welcome.

Offering his arm, he led her to the parlor and gestured to the sofa. She sat, gracefully, and removed her hat, placing it beside her.

His memory had not failed him. She was regal as a princess, demure as a nun—quietly, enchantingly beautiful. He mustered a smile. "Thank you for coming, Miss Easton. I was afraid you would not."

"Indeed?" Her head tilted. "I rather thought you expected it."

"Not after the way I behaved yesterday." He regarded her moodily. "If I apologize, will you forgive me?"

"If?"

"Very well," he said, shifting on his feet. "I was a boor and a snob."

"Not at all," she responded in a cool voice.

He understood exactly. He'd been much worse. "Shall I grovel?" he asked, heat rising to his ears. "Offer my cheek for you to smack?" Take off my clothes, he thought, and let you stare at me the way I stared at you? The notion was wonderfully exciting.

"I would like some coffee," she said, pouring herself a cup. "And you?"

He shook his head and lowered himself onto the chair across from her, so tense that a muscle in his left calf cramped painfully. Longing to shake it out, he stretched his legs across the Axminster carpet, determined to appear at ease. "Miss Easton—Clare—I know this is impossible, but could we pretend we'd never met before? I very much want to start over, without the events of yesterday looming between us."

"Pray, think no more about it. You had every right to examine your purchase." She lifted a square of shortcake, studied it intently, and set it down again. "Shall we discuss terms? You indicated requirements, other than those I'd been given to expect. May I hear them?"

"Dammit, I want us to be friends!" His exclamation surprised them both. At least it broke her awesome composure for a bare, nearly imperceptible moment.

Her brows lifted. "Friendship, my lord, cannot be bought. At least, not at any price I am aware of. I had thought our arrangement to be more . . . straightforward. If we are to speak frankly, more exclusively carnal."

"The one," he said between clenched teeth, "does not rule out the other."

She must have sensed his dry mouth, because she poured a helping of coffee, added a generous dollop of honey, and held out the cup. He took it gratefully, wincing as the hot liquid seared his tongue. The pain, coupled with that in his leg and groin, brought an edge to his voice.

"If you insist on a ledger of terms, I shall provide them. In writing, should you wish it."

"That will not be necessary. But this is a matter of business, and I should like a clear explanation of what you expect from me."

Business? Despite his overheated body and whirling mind, that word sent a chill down his spine. He tried to match her matter-of-fact tone. "Very well, Miss Easton. I require a mistress, preferably one who will remain with me for a considerable time. She will live in this house, be available to me when I send word, and remain exclusively mine. She must—*you* must—take precautions, at least until I have married and sired an heir."

His gaze lowered. "In your case, the usual means will not suffice. I doubt my own ability to be responsible and will expect you to take instruction from Mrs. Beales, unless you are acquainted already with a method you prefer. She is my housekeeper, probably lurking at the keyhole right now although she has heard most of this before."

"How delightful," Clare murmured, sipping her coffee.

"Excuse me for a moment." Bryn came to his feet. "I'll make certain we are not disturbed."

When he returned, Clare was leaning over the

window seat, reaching for a book. She jerked up and spun around, hands clasped guiltily behind her back. As if she'd been caught pilfering the silver, he thought. "Mrs. Beales has suddenly remembered an errand across town," he said, moving to the window. "I brought these for you. I've no idea what you like to read, but if it cannot be found in my library, we'll spend an afternoon browsing the bookshops."

Her gloved fingers reached out to stroke the leather bindings. "Truly? Anything I want?"

Bryn wondered if she would ever caress him as lovingly as she touched those old books. Suddenly jealous of paper, glue, and ink, he was relieved when she pulled herself away from the small library and resumed her place on the sofa.

"I have—a few questions," she said in a stoic voice.

"Be free with them." He lowered himself onto the chair and folded his arms. "Things will go better if there are no misunderstandings."

"When do I get the money?" she asked bluntly.

"Not in advance," he replied with equal bluntness.

"The next morning?" she persisted. "In full?"

"My dear, this is haggling. Do you imagine I will not honor my end of the agreement?"

Her eyes flashed. "Do you imagine *I* will not?"

"I cannot be sure—of anything—until the arrangement is consummated." He bit his tongue. Devil take it, he was doing it again: attacking when he meant to conciliate. And she was reaching for that damned hat. "Clare, if you accept my offer I shall proceed to Child's bank first thing tomorrow and secure ten thousand pounds—"

"Guineas."

"*Guineas.*" Mercenary little witch. "But it will be a

draft, not cash. That is too much money for either of us to carry around. And I'll present it to you, with a great flourish, when next we meet. Agreed?"

"So long as the draft can be negotiated when and where I choose. How long will it take for me to earn it?"

He sat up, hands planted on his knees. "What do you mean?"

"What I asked," she replied with a touch of impatience. "I understand now that you do not mean this to be the simple exchange of my virginity for payment, and that you expect me to remain with you for a period of time. I want to know how long."

"I damn well don't want an indentured servant, marking off a calendar and counting down each night before she can pack up and disappear."

"But there must be a limit, don't you see? I need to know how soon I can leave without cheating you."

He stiffened. "The terms of our agreement end when I say so."

"Then you must say so now."

Devil take it, who was in charge here? "If you insist on some arbitrary date, I shall provide one. Let us say, ten years from today."

"That is not reasonable," she chided. "And if I irritate you as much as I obviously do, it would be a very long ten years."

Laughing, he took a square of shortbread and waved it in the air. "I'll not bargain with you, Clare. Your forced servitude is done when you expected it to be, after the first night we make love. If you choose to leave after that, I'll not hold you."

For once, he seemed to have unnerved her. "That is . . . remarkably generous," she said.

"So it is. But if you stay, you'll discover exactly how generous I can be. Bloody hell, lady, I've made concessions that weren't demanded of Bonaparte after Waterloo. Perhaps you will keep that in mind." Leaning forward, he gazed at her solemnly. "You have a low opinion of me now, and I suspect I deserve it, but allow me time to make everything up to you. At the very least, enough time to make you very rich."

For once, she did not meet his eyes. "This is not what I expected, and I am not altogether sure I can give you what you want. More than likely I shall wish to leave immediately."

"Then I must contrive to change your mind." Cold sweat pooled at the back of his neck. Already he was fiercely jealous of any man who might succeed him. "What will you do after you leave me?"

"I've not thought so far ahead." She sliced him the hint of a smile. "In truth, I've not been certain of getting past the first night. Will you accept a promise to do my best?"

"If it includes forgiving me when I'm impossible, I accept your promise with gratitude. And I hope you will always speak your mind without fear of the consequences. There will be none, although my friends would tell you that I am often insufferable."

"I shall take your word for that," she said, too sweetly. "Do you expect me to live here?"

"Yes." The change of subject, implying her consent to stay, sent his blood racing. "The staff is not large, but you may add to it as you wish. Mrs. Beales is cook and housekeeper. Two of her nieces assist her, although they live at home. There is a footman, Charles Cassidy, and we must find you a maid. You are to consider the house your own and may fix it up any way you like. There is an allowance for that, and I'll increase it because more than a few things were destroyed . . . in a recent storm." He stood and held out his hand. "Come. Let me show you the other rooms."

Only when he opened the door to the larger bedroom did Bryn remember Mrs. Beales's warning not to take Clare upstairs. By then it was too late. He groaned to see the enormous bed, set on a pedestal and draped in filmy silk. Marita was partial to the color red, and he'd been told the curtains and counterpane were vividly scarlet. Everything else was done up in black and gold.

Even worse, two walls and the canopy over the bed were mirrored. A lump the size of an orange settled in his throat.

Clare stepped into the room and examined the furnishings with slow deliberation. "Oh, my," she said. Strolling to the bed, she fingered the drapes.

Once again, as if in a nightmare this time, Bryn found himself staring at her reflected image, their gazes meeting in the mirror. He stood stiff as a pillar, helpless with embarrassment. "You'll want to redecorate," he said.

"Not if you like it," she replied serenely.

"I don't! Really. Mari—er, the previous occupant . . . oh, damn." He managed a lopsided grin. "Clare, I forgot what this place looked like. I ought never to have brought you up here."

She pointed to the platform. "You are partial to stages, I gather. Do you build one whenever you perform?"

Longing for a trapdoor to open and swallow him, he swiped his wrist across a hot, moist forehead. "No.

Of course not. The elevation you saw yesterday in my library is constructed for the view, so I can see the garden. This one—"

"Is also for the view." Mounting the three stairs, she bent forward, calculating angles and reflections. "My heavens! Well, you must do as you like, Lord Caradoc. I've no skill at decorating, nor am I familiar with the London shops. I wouldn't know where to begin."

"I'll take care of it." He seized her hand and led her firmly out of the room. "Across the hall is a smaller bedroom. The servants occupy the third floor and there is a back staircase, so you will not be disturbed." He met her eyes. "Has that awful room changed your mind about me?"

"Not in the least," she said, with the light ambiguity he was coming to recognize.

As he ushered her downstairs, Bryn wondered, not for the first time, if she was laughing at him.

The coffee had cooled, and he drank his in one swallow while Clare nibbled at the edges of a biscuit. After what she'd seen upstairs, everything he wanted to say to her lodged in his throat. It was lowering to realize this woman was only sitting across from him now for the money. And probably wondering if she'd asked enough.

His stomach twisted in knots. He was the one being tested for approval. He wanted her so badly he'd pay anything she demanded, but she didn't want him at all and could refuse everything he owned. Three other women had sat across from him in this very room, arching and preening or nervous and shy. Never once had he wondered what they were feeling as he spelled out his requirements and watched them fall all over themselves to agree.

The truth was, he'd thought they were lucky to get him.

"What do you wish me to do now, my lord?"

With a show of indolence, he leaned forward and took a sandwich. "Well, for one thing, stop calling me *my lord.*"

"I don't know your name," she said with a smile.

"Do you not?" He bit off a hunk of bread and roast beef, regretting it instantly. His mouth was too dry to chew. "Surely Florette told you all about me." Swallowing hard, he reached for the coffeepot and swore under his breath to find it empty.

Clare passed him her half-full cup. "Not a word, my lord. Beyond the obvious."

He lifted an eyebrow as he drank.

"I meant, the size of your fortune. And that you only employ virgins."

He set down the cup. "Seriously? Nothing more than that? If you are telling the truth, Flo has been ominously secretive. I'd expected her to prepare you, if only to give you the advantage. Had she done so, what you've seen of me thus far would not surprise you."

"I am not," she informed him, "in the least surprised." Then she brushed her skirts with an uncharacteristically nervous gesture. "That is not strictly true. Before I saw you, I'd imagined you would be old, with skinny legs and thick wet lips and cruel eyes."

Had all his mistresses been so terrified? he wondered with a painful shot of awareness. Did they expect him to be cruel, even perverted, because he took only virgins under his protection?

"You have not told me your name," Clare reminded him gently.

He regathered his wits. "I have rather too many,

and you may choose the one you prefer. I was christened Brynmore Evan Anthony Owen Morgan Talgarth and hold the title Earl of Caradoc. My friends call me Bryn."

"You are Welsh?"

"In part. The Caradocs have a long tradition of playing both sides against the middle. Our holdings march the border, crossing into Wales for water or the best pastureland. In early days we stood as a buffer between warring factions, but my ancestors shifted with the wind and always allied themselves with power and money. Nothing to be proud of."

"My lord—Bryn. . . ." She hesitated, as if finding it difficult to say his name. "I have one more question."

He bit into the shortbread. "Yes?"

"I'm not sure . . . that is, what did you mean about Mrs. Beales teaching me?"

"When you are settled here, she will explain everything. Mrs. Beales tells me it is never a comfortable lesson, but it is truly necessary, my dear."

For the first time, she blushed. "I intended to ask Florette. Would that be acceptable?"

"She would know, of course. I've no objection. But you must tell Mrs. Beales what method you have chosen, and she'll see that you are supplied."

Her gaze shot up. "Method? Is there more than one?" She was decidedly pink now. "I fear I am woefully ignorant."

Light dawned. "I suspect," he said dryly, "that we are talking about two related but entirely different things. And since Madam Florette is pulling far too many strings for my comfort, let us cut her off. Mrs. Beales will teach you what you need to know before we begin our relationship, and from then on I shall, with great delight, teach you the rest." He smiled. "For now, let us attend to more immediate matters. Where are you staying?"

"At an inn. Please do not ask me which one. I prefer to meet you at Florette's."

"As you wish. You can move into Clouds on Sunday. That will give me a week to get the place in order." He templed his hands. "I mean no insult, but is that the only gown you own?"

She lowered her eyes. "The only good one."

"Then you need a wardrobe, my girl, top to bottom. My carriage will collect you tomorrow morning at ten o'clock. Plan to spend the entire day, and the one after that, in the shops. Mrs. Beales will assist you. She knows which modistes I favor, and the bills will be sent to me. No skimping, Clare. If you don't spend my money lavishly, I shall personally drag you through the stores and ogle you while you are being fitted. It will give me pleasure," he added more genially, "to see you clothed as befits your beauty."

"Surely I need very little," she protested. "I shan't be going anywhere—"

"On the contrary. You'll need gowns for the opera and the theater, for drives in the park, for picnics and"—he winked—"for the bookstores and circulating libraries."

She looked downright horrified, not at all like a woman who'd been offered *carte blanche.*

"Clare, buy anything that strikes your fancy. Mrs. Beales will see that you come home with everything you require. And try to enjoy yourself." He grinned. "I never met a female who didn't love to shop."

"Perhaps I will," she said thoughtfully. "I've never actually done it before. It seems wasteful, though."

"Indulge me," he said. "And let me indulge you. All your fancies. Anything you want."

"Are you trying to bribe me?" she asked suspiciously.

"Absolutely. I want to please you, and thus please myself. How can you find fault with that?"

Her brow knitted in a frown. "I'm not sure. But I won't stay with you for trinkets, however expensive—and that is a foolish declaration, since I come to you for money and a great deal of it. This is much more complicated than I ever imagined, my—Bryn."

"I like that," he said. "*My Bryn.* Hold that thought, lovely Clare. And tell me we have come to terms."

Standing, with the fluid grace he loved to watch, she put on her hat and pinned it into place. This time she did not lower the veil.

He stood, too, and reached for her hand. "What color are your eyes?" he asked, watching them widen in confusion.

"Light brown, I suppose. Sometimes almost gray."

"Like smoke. Good. I wasn't sure. And your hair?" A tendril curled at her ear, and he drew it between his thumb and forefinger. This close to her, he was aware of her subtle fragrance, like soap and powder.

"No color, really," she replied. "Brownish, rather like fog. City fog, not clean country mist."

Warming to the concern in her wide, curious eyes, he fingered her hair, relishing the texture. "My vision is perfectly fine," he assured her, "except that I cannot discern all colors. Mostly reds and greens, I'm told. To me, they look like mud, so I wasn't certain if I was seeing you as you really are."

"Truly? But how do you know which colors you can't see? Have you ever been able to distinguish them?"

"You are wearing a blue gown. Too dark for you, I think. Yellow is very clear, which is why I like daffodils. Mrs. Beales told me the curtains in the bedroom are crimson, but to me they appear a dull brown. I've always been this way, as was my mother's father. Likely I inherited it. Some years ago I consulted with John Dalton, the scientist, who also experiences color deficiency, and he thinks it may be caused by fluid in the eyeballs. In any case, nothing can be done about it. My valet sees that I don't wear clashing colors, and I shall never be able to appreciate the Old Masters, but otherwise it is merely an inconvenience. You mustn't mind if now and again I ask you what color you are wearing."

Her face was alight with fascination. "But if I answered green, and you cannot see green, what difference would it make? Have you any idea what green looks like?"

"None whatsoever," he replied cheerfully, "although I am informed there is a lot of it around. Trees and shrubs and grass are green, I understand. Friends tell me I see the landscape, even in spring, as it appears to them in winter. Most of all, I miss red. In poetry, it is the color of passion."

He regretted saying that immediately. The light in her eyes shaded and she backed away, wincing a bit when his finger caught in her hair. Carefully, he unwound the long tendril and lowered his arm.

"Then we are agreed, my lord," she said, as if negotiating the price of a cut of meat, "I shall spend your money recklessly, be schooled by Mrs. Beales, and move into this house when you are ready to bring me here." She glanced wistfully at the window seat. "Could I select a book and take it with me? I'll bring it back."

Those damn books. He'd offered her freedom to buy anything she wanted, and all she asked was the loan, for a few days, of a book. "Take them all," he said. "Choose what you can carry now, and I'll have the rest sent over."

"This will do." She picked up the heavy volume of Shakespeare's plays and clutched it to her chest. "With all that shopping, I won't have much time to read."

"I'm beginning to think you agreed to be my mistress only to get your hands on my books."

Clare smiled at him, the first bright, open smile he'd yet seen. It took his breath away.

"Yes. But mostly because you were kind enough to bring them to me." She reached up and swept the veil across her face. "Until Friday." In a gesture he knew was without conscious thought, she tilted her head to the ceiling as if imagining herself upstairs, in bed with him. She stumbled slightly when she turned toward the door.

It was the first ungraceful move he'd ever seen her make. "Clare?"

Pausing, she turned her head.

"I will not make love to you Sunday," he said gently.

She went completely still.

"We'll take it slowly, my dear. A bit at a time, until you feel comfortable with me. Contrary to what you saw upstairs and the way I behaved yesterday, I shall not jump on you the minute we are alone. We'll do nothing until you are ready, however long that takes." He smiled. "Well, however long, within reason. Now wait here for a moment while I see the carriage brought around."

She nodded, still clutching the book to her chest like a shield.

6

It was time, Bryn decided ruthlessly, to call in a few debts, and no one owed him more than Robert Lacey. That evening, as they relaxed over cigars and brandy at White's, he informed the viscount of his intentions.

"Clouds is a mess. I want the place decorated, top to bottom, and you, Lace, are the man to do it."

"Got a new one, eh?" Lacey rounded his lips and puffed a smokeball.

"Flo's parting shot, and a direct hit." There was no point fabricating with Lacey, who had known him since they were children. "The young lady and I came to terms this morning, but I can't move her in until you've worked some magic. Go over there tomorrow morning, make some plans, and get things started."

"*Morning?* This must be serious."

"So it is. Money is no object, and chances are you can pick up commissions for yourself from the suppliers."

"You'd do better to hire a professional, old lad. I know pretty much what a place ought to look like, but as for the rest—"

"Consider it a challenge. You have a good eye and ought to put it to better use than squinting at a deck of cards."

"Across the table from you," Lacey pointed out. "Which is why I shall attempt to refeather your love nest. Damn, but I wish you'd let me pay you off in cash. This business of crooking your finger every time you need something done you can't be bothered to do yourself is a bloody nuisance. At dawn, no less."

Since Lacey's notion of dawn was eleven o'clock, and because his small inheritance couldn't make a dent in what he owed, Bryn was unimpressed. "I'll settle for cash any time," he said amicably. "Meantime, one of the rooms downstairs should be a library. Shelves floor to ceiling."

Lacey coughed on cigar smoke. "A library! At Clouds? You *are* getting old."

"I want everything simple. Nothing flamboyant. Fashionable but comfortable. Clean lines, but soft."

"*Be thou familiar, but by no means vulgar,*" drawled the viscount. "*Rich, not gaudy.*"

Laughing, Bryn refilled both glasses from the crystal decanter. Lacey was the only friend he could drag along to *Hamlet* who would actually watch the play. "Make it special, Polonius. To suit Clare."

"Ah." Lacey wafted a long-fingered hand. "*That he is mad, 'tis true.* Does a slight difficulty present itself to your befuddled brain? As in: I've never seen her?"

Bryn took a long drink. Clare was so vivid in his own mind it was unimaginable that Lacey could not picture her. Contrarily, he was loath to share that vision. "She looks good in blue," he said finally.

Lacey chuckled.

"Yes, I know. Half the world is brown to me. But I asked her to describe herself, and what I see appears to be accurate. Her hair is . . . not exactly a color. Light, something like parchment held up to the sun. And her eyes are smoky gray." He gestured to the smoke ring floating up from the viscount's pursed lips.

Puffing a breath, Lacey scattered the smoke. "What will you do with her while Clouds is uninhabitable? Not good for her to stay at Flo's that long."

Stretching his legs, Bryn contemplated a polished boot. "I want her under my protection immediately, but devil if I can figure out the logistics. She can't move in with anyone respectable, and I won't let her move in with anyone who isn't. Probably she should go to a hotel, but I hate to coop her up in one room."

Lacey drained his brandy and settled back with his arms crossed behind his blond head. "As it happens, and assuming enormous shall we say *condescension* on your part regarding my debts, I have an idea that will solve both our problems."

"Is that so?" Bryn didn't care two beans for the money Lacey owed him, but his friend's pride demanded some kind of equable payment. "And just what *is* your problem?"

"Insatiable curiosity. Damned if I'll lift a finger until I've seen this mysterious Clare."

"You can't afford her," the earl said icily. "And I'll kill you if you make a move in her direction."

A wickedly arched brow lifted in denial. "Perish the thought. And hark to a brilliant notion, however devoid of propriety. As it happens, the redoubtable Ernestine Fitzwalter is currently nosing out Egyptian artifacts in, of all places, Egypt. Wouldn't you have thought all of them to be in London by now? Nevertheless, her house is vacant for at least a month, with a small staff to keep it up. She left me a key, and what dear old Auntie doesn't know—"

Barking a laugh, the earl shook his head. "She'd string you up by your balls, Lace, if she ever found out. And then she'd come for me."

"Is this the man who led a cavalry charge that cut Boney's finest to mincemeat? And now you fear retribution from a seventy-year-old battleax, just for commandeering her house? Nosey would be ashamed of you."

Bryn stiffened. "Installing my mistress in Grosvenor Square, at a duchess's mansion and without her consent, is bad *ton.*"

"And you are a hypocritical, aristocratic boor. That comes of inheriting the title when you were barely out of short pants. Dammit, who's to know? Well, the servants will tattle, I suppose, but I can dispatch them on holiday while you send a few of your own people over. We can work it out. And I will personally face Ernie when she returns, tell her part of the truth, and shoulder the blame." Lacey clapped his hands in satisfaction. "It's a perfect plan. Hell, when this business is done with, you'll be in debt to *me!*"

"I expect so, but that unthinkable state of affairs won't last through our next face-off at piquet." In fact, Bryn could well picture Clare in Ernie's mansion. It would suit her, unlike the vulgar bedroom at Clouds. And he wanted to give her a taste of something elegant, to prove he could offer it with a flick of his wrist. "Lace, if you bring this off we'll call things even. I'll meet you at Clouds tomorrow morning at nine so you can look things over. Then we'll collect Miss Easton and take her to Ernie's house. You'll get your chance to see her, but I want your word you won't set foot there once she's settled in."

"You needn't spray every rock and tree in London like a tomcat, Bryndle. No man who values his life would trespass on your territory. And since when can't you trust me?"

"Since Clare." He looked over in surprise when Lacey didn't respond. The viscount's gaze was fixed on a burly, puffy-eyed man with a large red-veined nose, ringing a peal over one of the waiters. Bryn recognized Giles Landry.

"Devil take it," Lacey swore. "Why hasn't he been blackballed?"

"Old family. And why bother? Almost no one plays with him at White's. He games in the hells."

Lacey's face was grim. "He's worse than a gambler who doesn't pay off. He's a brute."

"Yes? I hadn't heard that. More bark than bite, I'd have thought."

"He's brave enough when his opponent can't fight back. Took a horse whip to his tigcr last week, Isabella told me, and beat the boy senseless. I've half a mind to go pick a fight with him."

"You've half a mind, anyway. And you can't call him out until you've decorated Clouds. Nine o'clock, Lace." The earl stood, stretched, and stabbed out his cigar in the ashtray. "By the way, did you drop by the Hothouse last night?"

Lacey grinned.

"Well?" Bryn glared at him. "What's the story? Is Florette really leaving?"

"Within the week. Rose bought her out." The grin widened. "Saw the contract myself. I do hope your new mistress pleases you, because she's the last one Flo will ever provide."

And the last I'll require, Bryn thought as he left the club. Things were rapidly falling into line. The bank draft was locked in his safe, Lacey would see to the restoration of the house, and Clare had a place to stay until it was ready. His secretary had begun inquiries for a suitable girl to maid her, and Bow Street Runners would be tracing her background. He wanted to know where she might go when the terms of their bargain were fulfilled. She'd not escape him easily. He would leave her no place to hide.

Behind that cool poise and those impenetrable eyes, a passionate, fascinating woman waited to be claimed. He was sure of it. He'd had glimpses, but he wanted it all. There was nothing he could not arrange, nothing he would not give her, at least within the boundaries of mistress and—

He frowned.

The porter muttered an apology as he handed over his lordship's hat and cane, clearly wondering what he'd done to offend.

Bryn scarcely noticed. As he swung into his carriage, he tried to think of the right word for his position with Clare. Protector, yes. He would guard her with his life. Lover? Oh, yes. Friend? That too. Scarcely knowing her, confused as to his own uncharacteristic possessiveness, he realized there was no word to describe what he wanted to have with Clare. And so far as he knew, she didn't even like him. There was no sign, not the slightest, that she was attracted to him.

All he had was her promise to try.

His staff was astonished when the earl arrived home before midnight. He ensconced himself in his study, making lists and detailing orders. A big business deal brewing, they muttered among themselves over a late cup of chocolate in the kitchen.

Long after he'd sent them off to bed, Bryn leaned back in his chair, facing the dark garden, remembering. Strange how every detail was etched in his mind. Everything she'd said. Most of all, how she had looked, draped in her long hair, naked and remote, yielding and proud, with nothing to give or withhold except herself. He was still there when the first light of dawn filtered through the trees, lost in a fantasy of their first night together.

7

Three days after coming to terms with the earl, Clare sat in the music room of Ernestine Fitzwalter's mansion, absently picking out the melody of an old hymn on the ebony pianoforte.

Whatever was she doing in this bizarre house? The walls, hung with wooden African masks, war hatchets, and objects she could not identify, seemed to be closing in on her. And all the tables and chairs had paws, like animals. Bellpulls dangled everywhere. She had only to give a tug and a servant appeared, so proper and aloof that she took care never to touch the cords.

This was her first day alone, at loose ends. Until now Mrs. Beales had kept her occupied, towing her through an endless number of shops where she was tugged at and measured, draped and pinned, until her head spun and her feet ached. A tiny portion of her new wardrobe was stored upstairs, while seamstresses completed the rest, but already she had more clothes and fripperies than any one person ought to need.

The earl appeared to have lost interest in her. Since bringing her here, in the company of a charming man named Robert Lacey, Lord Haydon, he had virtually disappeared. She had a note from the earl this morning, saying he would call on her at his earliest convenience, and since reading it she'd been unaccountably nervous. For a short time, she'd almost managed to convince herself that he didn't exist.

Lost in thought, she was startled when the door swung open and a Vision in Lavender swept across the polished floor. Clare came to her feet, heart thumping in her chest.

The woman was beautiful, with blue eyes, pale blond hair, and a bright smile curving a wide mouth. Except for the gold settings on her necklace and earbobs, she was done up completely in shades of violet.

"You must be one of Aunt Ernie's friends," said the vision in a light, cheery voice. "How nice to meet you. I am Isabella Marbury, her most disreputable relation. But I expect she told you about me. She makes it a point to warn everyone in advance. And you are—?" She extended a gloved hand expectantly.

Clare stepped back, flushing hotly. She didn't think women in her new profession ought to shake hands with ladies. "C-Clare Easton," she stammered.

Isabella colored too and dropped her hand. "Oh," she said, her eyes a little hurt.

Clare hurried to explain. "Truly, I don't mean to be rude. It's only that I have never met the duchess and ought not to be here at all."

"But how delicious! An authentic mystery, and I so longing for one. Will you have lunch with me?"

The startling invitation rendered Clare mute again. She had no idea in the world how to deal with this awkward situation.

It quickly became apparent the matter was out of her hands, because Isabella Marbury was the violet personification of an irresistible force. "Come," she said, already on her way to the door. "We'll have Mrs. Halley fix us a bite and a dish of tea."

"Mrs. Halley?" Clare trailed in her wake. "But the cook is a man. Mr. Lyle."

"Hendly Lyle?" The vision paused. "How odd. I thought he worked for . . . well, never mind." She took off again, heels clicking on the marble floor. "At least we'll have a fine meal."

Isabella maintained a steady flow of chatter while the servants dished up lobster salad, veal medallions in cream sauce, gingered carrots, and asparagus soufflé. Clare pecked at her food, little being required of her but an occasional nod. The woman was Isabella Marbury, Countess of Hogge, she learned. And because she despised being addressed by her proper title, Lady Hogge, she insisted that everyone call her Lady Isabella. Even the High Sticklers had finally agreed to do so. She was Robert Lacey's sister and a widow. Her bridegroom's regiment had been dispatched to the Peninsula three days after the wedding, where he was almost immediately killed in battle.

"How sad," Clare murmured.

"Dear me, no. Not that I wished him dead, but I scarcely knew the man. Henry Marbury has been gone these eight years, and all I remember of him was how splendid he looked in his regimentals. I was very young and immature, you understand."

"But you are still in mourning."

Isabella look puzzled. "Why would you think . . . ah! My clothing. This is merely my lavender phase, Miss Easton, which I sense drawing to an end. Perhaps you'll help me select a color for my next wardrobe. I've wanted to try shades of orange, but with blond hair I might look too much like a summer sunrise. What do you think?"

"Blue would suit you perfectly." Those were the last words Clare spoke during the meal. After a dessert of raspberry pudding, Lady Isabella led her to a small sitting room, where she examined the furniture meticulously before choosing a silver brocade chair.

"So many colors clash with lavender," she explained, settling herself gracefully. "Sometimes I am compelled to stand for an entire evening. Why don't you sit right across from me, so I can look you in the eye while I quiz you. You do have the most spectacular eyes."

Unable to muster a response, Clare sat obediently and folded her hands in her lap.

"Have you had sufficient time to recover yourself, Miss Easton? When I first came into the room I thought you would swoon dead away. Actually, I've never seen anyone swoon who wasn't pretending—not that I wanted you to demonstrate, of course. But you were so pale I thought perhaps you ought to eat something." She cocked her head appraisingly. "You do look better. Or at least more composed. I would not turn you over to the authorities, you know, even if you were a housebreaker. And that is impossible, because Hendly Lyle would never prepare luncheon for a criminal."

He would if you told him to, Clare thought, wanting to smile. "I was admitted with a key," she said, answering the real question before launching a small surprise of her own. "By a relation of yours, I believe, since he also referred to the duchess as—"

Lady Isabella raised both hands, which sparkled with amethyst rings. "No, no. Let me guess." Then she frowned. "It's too easy. No one but Robert would even think of using Ernie's house while she's gone, let alone have the nerve." She looked directly at Clare, her gaze frank and not unfriendly. "Have I stumbled upon a difficult situation, Miss Easton? Is my brother keeping you here under his protection? It's a clever idea, I must say, though Ernie will have a fit. Good heavens, what a lark. I'm glad to see old Lace is still up to snuff. Never think I'll give you away, because Robert and I have been covering for each other all our lives. And I should be able to let you know when Ernie is on her way back to England, for we are in frequent correspondence. Indeed, I only came by to sort through her post and forward anything important."

Clare could barely keep up with her. "I am not your brother's mistress," she said after a moment.

"Oh, dear." Isabella wrinkled her pert nose. "I *have* blundered."

"Not . . . precisely. Lord Heydon is doing a favor for a friend. I am *his* mistress."

"No, no, don't tell me. Let me guess." She stomped her foot. "Botheration! This is all *too* easy. The chef gives it away. Bryndle must have sent him."

"B-Bryndle?"

"I expect he hasn't told you his nickname. Doesn't like it, which is why we take pains to use it at every opportunity. Considering your relationship, Miss Easton, you might do well to refrain, but then one always blurts out the exact words one is trying *not* to say. Bound to happen. Just don't tell him where you first heard it. That will be our secret . . . one of many, I expect. You have a great many secrets, do you not?"

For once in her life, Clare was unable to repress her amusement. It gurgled up, past her embarrassment and self-control, past both hands pressed over her mouth, erupting in a laugh so light and charming it found an echo.

Countess and mistress giggled like two schoolgirls, neither quite sure what they were laughing at. At last, wiping tears from her eyes, Clare found her voice. "Do you know *everything?*" she asked, awestruck. "I daresay you do. I feel I'm being pried open like a clamshell. Does anyone manage to withstand your inquisitions?"

"Not if I persevere. It's rather like fencing: a bit of dancing around, now and again a partial engagement, and then *voilà*—ze lunge for ze throat!" This was accompanied by a dramatic swoop. "You see, you've dropped your guard. May I call you Clare?"

"Yes, of course." When she sniffled, Isabella opened her reticule and passed Clare a lace-edged handkerchief. It was lavender, and scented with lavender water, which set Clare laughing again. It was years since she'd laughed so long and so loud, and oh, it felt good. "But you ought not be speaking to me at all, Lady Isabella."

"Why ever not? Don't think to stand on ceremony with me, Clare. I shan't permit it. In the normal course of things we are unlikely to meet, but if good fortune brings us together, as it has today, it would be a crime not to enjoy each other's company. I will ask you to call me Isabella, though I really wish you'd call me Izzy. But by all means choose an address you feel comfortable with. Bryndle prefers Dizzy."

Feeling dizzy herself, Clare leaned back in the chair and smiled weakly. Friendship with this comet was impossible, but she had never been so instantly drawn to anyone. Except Florette, she thought, her smile fading. You are a whore, she reminded herself. You will burn in hell.

A warm hand touched her forearm. "Have I offended you? I don't mean to. It's just that I've known Bryn all my life, and he's nearly as much a brother to me as Robert."

"As Lord Caradoc's sister or his friend, you can scarcely approve of me."

"But no one has called on me to approve or disapprove, except you. In truth, were you not such a snob, I could like you enormously."

Clare sat forward. "A snob?"

"My, yes." Lady Isabella shrugged prettily. "Likely I am not respectable enough for you. Or perhaps you are offended because I too have seen Bryn naked as a newborn babe."

"But I haven't se—" She clamped her lips shut.

"Truly? Excuse me, but how can that be? The man is never shy, and why would he be with that glorious physique?"

Clare's cheeks felt hot enough to roast potatoes. "I have not yet . . . taken up my duties."

"*Duties?*" It was Isabella's turn to whoop with laughter. But when she spoke again, her tone was remorseful. "In that case, I have embarrassed you and I apologize most sincerely. My tongue has a mind of its own, and not a very wise one."

"You mustn't apologize to me, Lady Isabella. And

truly, I am not a snob. But everyone I meet seems to take my position so . . . nonchalantly."

"Except you."

"Yes. I am not sure how to behave, or what to say, or to whom I ought to speak at all. Mr. Lyle scares me to death."

"The hauteur of otherwise excellent servants with irreplaceable skills can be most annoying," Isabella agreed. "And no one is more temperamental than a chef. But never allow yourself to be intimidated, Clare. We all came onto this earth naked and squalling. The next time anyone dares look down his nose at you, just imagine him a baby with a soiled nappy."

Clare tried, and failed, to picture the Earl of Caradoc as an infant.

Isabella pulled out her fan. "I ought to explain that when I saw Bryn in the altogether, I was four years old. He and Lace had been riding and chose to take a dip in a small lake where I happened to be playing." She grinned. "Naturally I purloined their clothes and left them two miles from home bare-bummed as the day they were born. It is one of my fondest memories. Their revenge is not such a fond recollection, but we'll save that for another day. May I quiz you a bit more, Clare? Why are you here and not at Clouds?"

"It is being decorated," she answered, welcoming the change of subject. "Your brother expects the work to be completed soon, and meantime Caradoc has stored me here."

"Robert has excellent taste," Isabella said. "I'm sure you'll approve the results. And Bryn is color-blind, of course. I expect he didn't choose that gown, which is very becoming. Is my brother supervising your wardrobe too?"

Clare fingered the soft apricot muslin, quite the nicest dress she'd ever worn. "I've been turned over to a dressmaker with a French accent more phony than—" she almost said "Florette's" and bit her tongue. "Tomorrow I am scheduled for a dancing lesson and a trip to the circulating library, if his lordship has time. This afternoon I am to select a maid." She shook her head. "As if I'd know how."

"Choose a girl you like," advised Lady Isabella. "Maids are always underfoot, and a companionable maid can be taught skills while a skillful one cannot be grafted with a pleasing personality." She glanced at a clock, set incongruously in the forehead of a primitive mask hung over the fireplace. "I must be off," she said briskly, drawing a small gold case from her reticule and pulling out an engraved card. "This is where I live. If ever I can do something for you, please send word or come to me directly. I mean that, Clare Easton." Her blue eyes narrowed. "I mean that," she said again.

From instinct, or desperation, Clare seized the offer. "You can help me now," she blurted, "if it can be a secret."

"I *knew* we'd have secrets," Isabella exclaimed with clear delight. "And I sniffed a mystery from the moment I saw you." She leaned forward eagerly. "What can I do?"

Clare's hands twisted in her lap. "I need something delivered to a friend that cannot be trusted to the post, and no one must know about it."

Frowning, Isabella shook her head. "I can do nothing to betray Bryn."

"Of course not. I would never ask such a thing of you."

Isabella studied her intently for a long moment and

nodded. "In that case, I'll be glad to see it delivered. Shall I take it with me now?"

Clare popped from her chair. "Oh, yes, if you will. Just let me get it and write some directions. I'll be back in a moment." She sped upstairs, returning minutes later with a large envelope. "You cannot go yourself," she said, handing it to Isabella. "My friend is at a postinghouse on the outskirts of London. But please send someone you trust completely." She stared at the envelope, watching Isabella fold it in half and place it in her reticule.

"I shall deliver it personally," Lady Isabella informed her. "It will be a small adventure, and you have my word I shall tell no one. Naturally, you'll owe me a favor in return. Shall we say another of Lyle's excellent luncheons, perhaps Thursday next, during which I shall regale you with the success of my mission? Send word when you know your plans, Clare. I am counting on it."

Clare gazed at her self-consciously.

"Use a footman, my dear. If you are to remain any time with Bryn, you must accustom yourself to luxury. He can afford to provide it, and it gives him pleasure to do so."

With that the improbable vision took her leave, carrying in her purse a bank draft representing ten thousand guineas of the earl's pleasure.

8

Later that afternoon, Bryn entered Ernestine's house through the back door. It had been three long days since he delivered Clare, with equal stealth, to the mansion on Grosvenor Square, and he was wild to see her again.

A servant led him to the music room, where Clare was seated at the piano plunking a discordant tune. She was wearing gloves, he noticed, but when had he ever seen her without them?

She stood immediately when the butler announced him. God, he'd thought her lovely wearing that heavy blue dress, but in a pale muslin gown with puffed sleeves that left her arms bare, she was breathtaking. Her long hair hung in a thick braid down her back, soft tendrils drifting over her ears and forehead.

"I've missed you," he said simply.

"My lord," she replied, her gaze focused on the carpet.

Not sure what to do next, he gestured to the piano bench. "Please go on. I am partial to music. Play a bit myself, actually." When he moved closer, she resumed her place on the bench with her hands folded in her lap.

"I've not touched a piano for many years," she said. "This is a wonderful instrument."

He sat next to her, deliberately moving close. Her thigh felt warm and tense. "Do you like music then?" he inquired, rippling his fingers over the keyboard. "I learned to play as a boy but have forgotten what little I knew. We can have a piano at Clouds if you like. In fact, that's an excellent idea. I'll find a teacher for you."

Flushing, Clare said nothing.

"Lacey tells me we can move you over on Saturday next. Several of the downstairs rooms will not be finished, but he expects the bedroom to be ready."

She erupted from the bench and fled to the bay window, arms clutched around her waist.

A woman condemned to the gallows might react like that. In silence he watched her take hold of herself, and when she turned around, her smile was pleasantly impersonal. He sighed.

"Excuse me for a moment," she said. "I'll arrange for tea. Unless you prefer something else?"

"Tea will be fine." She might have pulled the bell cord inches from her hand, but he knew she was only looking for an excuse to leave the room. When the door closed, he let his fingers move over the keyboard, falling naturally into a haunting folk melody.

Was he handling this all wrong? He'd been so busy setting her up and rigging her out that he'd scarcely spent five minutes alone with her since their meeting at Clouds.

In part, that was essential. It was dangerous to be with her until he reclaimed control of himself. From experience he knew that virgins were inevitably nervous, even apprehensive, about the first night. But Clare was downright terrified, and growing more so each day the final accounting was delayed. Ought he carry her upstairs and have done with it? He banged a loud chord and stalked away from the piano, combing his fingers through his hair. Part of him thought it a good idea. All of his body thought so.

She wouldn't want to do it in Ernie's house, of course. She didn't even like staying here. And he could not repeat the mistake of taking her into his own mansion at St. James's Square. That part of his life must remain separate.

A hotel, perhaps. He knew an elegant and discreet establishment frequented by gentlemen and their lovers, although he'd never been there himself. But the idea of making love to Clare on mattresses and pillows used by others disgusted him. He could imagine her repulsion if they slunk into a hotel for an afternoon tumble.

Clare deserved better. The first time should be special. Memorable. So good it would make her want more. If he escorted her upstairs, or to a hotel, she'd be gone by sunrise, and there had not been time for the Runners to trace her background. Worse, Florette had disappeared, without so much as a goodbye. Whatever she knew about Clare had gone with her.

No, the first plan was best. He would ease her gently into an enduring relationship. Past time he learned how to court a woman, he reflected. He'd never done so before, but why should an expensive mistress require wooing and seducing? He was an attentive lover, which ought to suffice.

But Clare was . . . Clare. And worth any degree of trouble. He had five days to entice her into his bed, more if necessary, but she'd be expecting him to claim her Saturday night. By then it was unlikely he'd be able to resist.

Bryn heard the door open and returned to the piano, trying to play the song that had come so effortlessly to his fingers when he wasn't thinking about it. This time the results were not so good.

A maid placed a tray on a table near the piano and left with a curtsy.

"I prefer tea without milk and with a great deal of honey," he told Clare, stealing a glance at her as she followed his instructions. She added nothing to her own cup, he noted. "Tonight," he said, after tasting the tea and nodding approval, "we shall go to the opera."

Her cup rattled in its saucer. Deliberately, she set it on the tray. "I do not wish to appear in public, my lord. That was not part of our agreement."

Standing, he held out his hand. "Come here, Clare." He led her to a small divan and sat beside her at an angle, so he could see her face. "We must talk," he said gently. She stared back at him, her gaze somber. "Tell me what is troubling you, my dear. Have I said something, or done something, to make you afraid?"

"You have been all that is kind," she said in an expressionless voice. "I simply do not wish to go where people can look at me."

"Do you think to hide away at Clouds twenty-four hours a day?" He regarded her speculatively. "Or is it that you expect to be there only twenty-four hours?"

Her lips tightened.

"I realize," he said carefully, "that you have made me no promises beyond the first night. Perhaps you are unable to think any further, and for that I am sorry. Things have not been as I hoped, and the delay is unsettling to us both."

"Yes."

So guarded, he thought, massaging her palm with his thumb. So many barriers between them, like these damned gloves. She never took them off, not when she stripped naked for him that morning in his study, not even when she played the piano. Curious, he began to peel the supple leather from her wrist.

She recoiled, snatching her hand from his grasp as if he'd burned her.

He raised a quizzical brow. "Only your glove, princess. No more than that."

"Please don't," she said, clearly distressed.

After a moment, he held out his own hand. "I rather think I must. Come, my dear, let me see what you are hiding."

In the long silence that followed, he thought she was going to refuse him—and wondered how he would react if she did. But finally, her arm trembling, she placed her hand in his and allowed him to remove the glove.

Her fingers were long and slender, the nails clipped short. A lovely hand, he was thinking as he turned it over and caught sight of the palm. "My God," he whispered between clenched teeth. "Who did this to you?"

She stared at a spot over his shoulder, her face impassive. "I was punished, for insolence and disobedience.

Mostly for my ungovernable temper. It was a long time ago."

"By your father?" he demanded.

She shook her head. "Papa was the sweetest man ever lived. He could not step on a spider."

"Tell me, Clare. I'll persist until you do."

She released a sigh. "It was my stepmother. And she had been hurt, by someone she loved before she married Papa. I suspect she went a little mad."

"Bloody hell, how could any man let a child be whipped like this? Why didn't your father protect you?"

"He died soon after they were married, Bryn. And she's dead too, so what does any of it matter now? Besides, I deserved to be punished. I could do nothing to please her, and after a while I stopped trying. She never beat me unless I defied her openly." She met his gaze steadily, as if they were discussing the weather. "I should warn you, my lord. The bottoms of my feet are marked in the same way."

Her face became a blur. Gripped by a fierce rage, he lowered his head and kissed the webbing of scars on her hand. Then he pressed her palm to his chest, over his heart. "I would avenge you if I could, butterfly, and comfort you if I knew how, but I feel as helpless as you must have been when your stepmother took a cane to you. Only remember, you are not responsible, in any way, for her cruelty. I forbid you to blame yourself." His lips quirked. "If insolence and bad temper merited a whipping, I would be scarred from head to toe by now."

"Perhaps you will be," she replied with a touch of spirit. "Later in this life, or the one hereafter."

"That's my girl," he said appreciatively. "From

now on, I hope you'll not wear those gloves when we are alone together." Once again, he pressed his lips to the scars. "And since you have gifted me with a confidence, in all fairness I should return one of my own. What would you like to know?"

"*Gifted?*" she inquired with a delicately arched brow.

"As you say. I forced the issue. But this is your chance to do the same, so fire away." He leaned back and folded his arms behind his head, prepared for the worst.

"Very well," she said primly. "I should like to know precisely why you will only bed a virgin."

He winced. "I ought to have expected that question. And you have a right to know, I suppose, although I don't like explaining the reasons. Especially to an innocent girl. What do you know of the pox, Clare?"

Her eyes widened. "I've heard of it, or perhaps read about it. Is it like smallpox?"

"No. I refer to syphilis, which is contracted by having carnal knowledge of someone who has the disease. Any man or woman who is profligate gambles with the devil. Prostitutes, and the men who seek them out, risk their lives every time money changes hands. Even one encounter with an infected lover can be a sentence of death. For that reason I take only virgin mistresses and demand fidelity while they are under my protection." He gazed at the ceiling. "Does that answer your question?"

She took a moment to answer. "In part. But my God, how could *anyone* chance becoming ill for a few minutes of—well, whatever one experiences when . . ." Her voice faded off.

He sat forward, propped his elbows on his knees, and buried his chin between his hands. "Ah, Clare. I cannot explain in words why I need a woman in my bed, or why a woman desires a man. You will understand when we are lovers. And you can be assured that you are safe with me, as I am with you."

She put her hand on his thigh. "You have a deeper reason for taking such care. I hear it in your voice. Do you want to tell me?"

He managed a wry grin. "Not until you answer another question about yourself, my dear. One confidence at a time, in equal measure. Agreed?"

"Perhaps it is better that way. But if it's now my turn to share a secret, we'll make no further progress."

"Have you so many secrets, butterfly?"

"None to speak of," she said tranquilly. "Shall I enjoy the opera, do you think?"

Recognizing submission, Bryn came to his feet. "You'll either like it or hate it, but you must judge for yourself."

"Will everyone stare at me?"

"I have a prominent box, Clare. We can't help but be noticed. Still, it is not my intention to flaunt you in public. I love the opera, even the silliness and high theatrics, and wish to share it with you." He didn't give her time to change her mind. "I shall collect you at nine o'clock. We needn't arrive for the preliminary concert, which is always terrible, nor stay for the afterpiece. Will you wear the gold silk? Lacey told me it had been delivered."

He kept track of her wardrobe? Clare studied his face, reading nothing there but sincerity and something that looked like friendliness. "As you wish, my lord."

"Until tonight," he said with a bow. "And please, call me Bryn. Or any name you choose that does not set us at distance. You cannot hold me away with words, Clare, however hard you try."

"I don't mean to," she confessed. "But you are so . . . *lordly.*"

He laughed. "You won't think so when you know me better."

If Bryn expected gratitude, he was disappointed.

"I don't want it," Clare told him flatly when he opened the satin-lined case and held out an exquisite gold-and-topaz necklace.

"Someday perhaps you will. And jewelry is *de rigueur* at the opera. Do you wish everyone to think me a pinchpenny?"

"Perish the thought," she said, as he fastened the clasp at her nape. His hand lingered there until she deliberately swung around.

"It suits you," he remarked before she could speak. "As does your gown. You are always beautiful, Clare, but especially so tonight."

And so was he, she reflected, while he hooked a matching bracelet around her wrist. The earl was rigged out in evening dress, all black and white except for the pale gold lining of his cape and the darker gold of his brocade waistcoat. A diamond stickpin winked from his cravat.

"I am quite put in the shade by my escort," she said a little breathlessly. "You are altogether magnificent."

He stepped back, an astonished look on his face. "Was that a compliment?"

"I'm afraid so." She tilted her head. "It pains me to

flatter you, for you are too vain as it is, but I could not help myself."

He looked absurdly pleased. "Thank you. That may be the first kind thing you ever said to me. I shall contrive to remember *magnificent,*" he added with a wink, "and forget the retraction that followed."

"I daresay you always ignore what you do not wish to hear," she said crisply.

Chuckling, he draped a fur-edged satin cape around her shoulders. "If all your evening gowns are so modest, I must employ another mantua maker. It is the fashion to reveal a bit more flesh above the waist."

"The dressmaker is not to blame." She tugged the cape over her breasts. "I modified her designs. But perhaps I do not comprehend the distinction between fashionable and unseemly."

"Just as well. The loveliest sights are best reserved for my own eyes."

As the earl escorted her out the back door to a coach waiting in the alley, she wondered what he expected in exchange for the necklace and bracelet. If sold, they would keep her in frugal comfort for some time. Perhaps he was being kind, providing for her future, but he was also damnably controlling. The necklace felt like the collar of a leash around her throat.

They had traveled only a short way when the coach pulled to a stop on a narrow side street. Bryn swung out immediately and held out his hand. "Come along, princess. Your chariot awaits." He pointed to an enormous carriage with crested panels, drawn by four matched bays.

A liveried footman lowered the steps and assisted her into a lamplit compartment paneled in rich wood.

Settling across from her, Bryn stretched his long legs so that his calf rested against the side of her leg. "A bit of subterfuge," he explained. "I cannot be seen coming and going from Ernestine's house, and damned if I'll show up at the opera—"

"Without the accompanying splendor," she finished with a smile. "A wonder anyone bothers going into the theater at all, when they could simply line up outside and look at you for entertainment."

"They are waiting inside, Clare—to look at *us.*"

Her amusement fled.

"You are too beautiful not to draw attention," he said quietly.

She felt her cheeks go hot. "Will they all know I'm a virgin?"

"They will know that you were so when you came to me. My requirements for a mistress are no secret in London. But I expect they'll assume we are already lovers."

The necklace tightened a notch around her throat, blazing a surrender that had yet to occur. She didn't know which was worse—having everyone think her still a maiden, or certain the thing was already done.

"I've tried to make this as easy for you as possible," he assured her. "We shall arrive just before the opera begins, to avoid the crowd, and leave early. There is one interval, during which we are likely to be the main attraction, but except for those twenty minutes, you need not fear prying eyes."

Twenty minutes on the rack, she thought glumly.

"You'll enjoy the performance more if you know the story," he said. "It's a minor work, by a composer with great skill at music and no sense at all of drama."

Clearly trying to put her at ease, he proceeded to weave a tale so outlandish that she was scarcely aware when the carriage drew up in the Haymarket. But she was very aware of the other latecomers pausing to watch as he led her through the gilded doors of the Opera House.

From the foyer, they turned down a dim passage and ascended two flights of stairs. "This is the back way," he said, drawing her into an alcove. "Now we'll wait until the promenade is clear." When the orchestra was midway through the overture, Bryn guided her down a mirrored hall to his box. It could seat eight people, she saw, but two padded chairs were set apart, near the railing. The curtain opened just as they settled in.

Angling his chair so that he could see both the stage and her lovely profile, Bryn gave a tiny sigh of relief. Almost immediately, Clare seemed entranced by the color and pageantry.

He had orchestrated the interval with the same care he'd made all the other arrangements for this night. Only Lacey and Claude would be admitted to the box by the servant guarding the door.

Clare liked the music, he noted with approval. He often took his mistresses to the theater, but seldom to the opera. Not one had really enjoyed it. Perhaps at last he'd found someone to share his fascination, to talk with afterward about the performance, to compare impressions. Even Lacey, who loved theater, was bored by opera and was only making an appearance, under duress, to help the interval pass smoothly.

Too soon, the first act finished, to loud acclaim from the audience. After an interminable series of bows, thc singers left the stage.

Clare sat like a stone, hands clasped in her lap, staring at the velvet curtain.

"Smile at me," Bryn said between his teeth. "Or if you cannot, at least open your fan and hide that martyred expression."

Mechanically, she obeyed, fluttering it before her chalk-white face while he laughed as if she'd said something amusing.

"The fat tenor gets the girl," he informed her, "although it's just as well she kills herself in the final scene. Better a knife to the breast than slow death by suffocation."

Her eyes widened, and then she smiled. "I didn't think he'd be able to waddle all the way across the stage for that last embrace."

"Wait until you see him in the sword fight. Ubaldo fences with the grace of a rhinocerus."

She managed to fix the smile on her lips, but he couldn't miss the frantically whipping fan and the terror in her eyes. "They are all l-looking at us, aren't they?"

"Clare, they are looking at the most beautiful woman they have ever seen. The women are curious or jealous. The men wish they could trade places with me. Try to relax. Do you want them to see you are afraid?"

"I am none of their business," she said, with a welcome return of spirit.

"How sad they've nothing better to do than ogle us," he agreed. "Shall we ogle them in return?" He pulled out his quizzing glass and swept the audience with an arrogant, assessing gaze. Then he pointed to a box directly across from them. "Look, my dear. There is Arthur Wellesley, Duke of Wellington. The one with the long nose. One of these nights, if he's lucky, I'll admit him to the box and introduce you."

Clare could not resist stealing a glance at the hero of Waterloo. She saw an attractive man lift his hand in a gesture of greeting. Flushing, she raised her fan and turned away. "Bryn! He smiled at me!"

Unaccountably jealous, Bryn was relieved when the door to the box swung open to admit Claude and Lacey. A servant followed with a tray, glasses, and a silver bucket holding a chilled bottle of champagne.

It was like a small private party, Clare thought, witnessed by hundreds of strangers. Robert Lacey greeted her warmly and complimented her lavishly until the earl pulled him aside. She couldn't help but eavesdrop, and her heart sank when Bryn asked how soon Clouds would be ready. Not yet, she wanted to beg.

The other man, rather short and pudgy, lowered himself onto the chair vacated by the earl. "May I join you without an introduction?" he asked with a sweet smile. "They forget I'm around. Claude Howitt, ma'am, at your service."

"Clare Easton," she said, drawn to him immediately. "Are you enjoying the opera?"

"Been asleep the past half hour," he confessed. "Alice would like it, but she won't come. We live all the way t'Richmond, and she'd have to stay in the city overnight."

"Your wife does not care for London?" Clare asked, startled when he flushed beet red. "Oh, dear. Have I said something wrong?"

"Not at all," he assured her. "We are wed in our hearts and in the sight of God, I do believe, but Alice ain't m'legal wife. My father won't approve the marriage because he thinks her too common, and I can't support her if he cuts me off. Devilish thing, but there it is. We have three children and another on the way. Hope I haven't shocked you, Miss Easton."

"I am scarcely in a position to be shocked," she observed dryly.

"Things are not always as we want them to be," he said with a nod, "but they can change. Bryn lets me manage some of his investments and gives me a generous percentage of the profits. More than he ought. One day I'll have enough cached away to do without my allowance, and then Alice can come to the opera as m'wife. Hope she don't make me come with her," he added forlornly.

She laughed.

At the sound, Bryn turned to her and caught a look of genuine affection on her face, directed at Claude. He clenched his fists. Why was it Clare responded that way to his friends and not to him? Was it because he would bed her and they would not? Or did she just not like him?

"Sunday," he snapped at Lacey. "Have Clouds ready by then or answer to me."

Clare chuckled when the rotund tenor practically fell over his own feet in the sword fight, but she marveled at his last aria and seemed wholly enchanted by the second half of the opera. Bryn watched her every move, delighting in the play of emotion over her expressive face. He ushered her from the box just before the final chorus, anxious to get on with his plans for the evening. Although he would not bed her tonight, it was past time for a little dalliance.

As they came into the foyer, joining the scatter of

men and women leaving early to avoid the crush, he became aware of a disturbance near the door.

"There you are, Caradoc," a man bellowed. "Been waitin' for you."

An elderly couple was shoved aside and Bryn saw Giles Landry stumbling in his direction. Swiftly, he moved Clare behind him.

"S-swine." Landry hiccuped. "Four nights ago you raised h-hopes in m'daughter's heart. Danced a waltz with her, you did. Saw it m'self. Not the thing to sport your whore in public after that. Ought to call you out."

Bryn drew back as the man's rancid breath assailed him. "You're drunk, Landry."

"Not so foxed I can't recognize a philanderer. It's one thing to take a mistress when your wife is breeding, but until then have the decency, b'God, to show my sweet Elizabeth some respect."

"I am not wed to your daughter," Bryn said coldly, "nor promised to her. Now get out of here before I lose my temper."

"You're promised, all right," Landry slurred. A cluster of people gathered around them, avidly observing the confrontation. "Everybody who saw you at L-Lady Wetherford's ball knows that. I expect to hear your offer in the morning, Caradoc."

With one hand, the earl gripped Landry's neckcloth and lifted him onto his toes. "Get this straight, fool. I'll meet you with pistols or swords after a sober challenge, but take yourself out of here now or I'll pound you into sausage."

"Come along, Giles." A tall man with bronzed skin and tawny hair emerged from the crowd. "I'll take you home." Seizing the baron's elbow, he propelled him toward the door.

Bryn watched them disappear, wondering who the man was. Impressive, at any rate. Releasing a small sigh, he turned to Clare. "I am very sorry about this, my dear. Landry is in his cups and speaking nonsense."

Clare took his arm. "It seems the theatrics are not confined to the stage this evening," she said calmly. "Shall we go?"

"Well done," he said, leading her past the gawking observers to the street where his carriage waited.

When they drew up a few streets from Ernestine's house, he looked out the window and swore softly. "Jenkins is late with the unmarked coach, I'm afraid. It seems we must wait awhile."

With a delicate shrug, she leaned back against the squabs. "The opera was lovely, Bryn. I only wish I spoke Italian so I could understand the words."

He drew the velvet curtains and snuffed the lanterns, plunging them into darkness. "We'll talk about the opera tomorrow, Clare." Before she could think to resist, he lifted her onto his lap. "For now, let us take advantage of a few minutes alone."

The sound she made was indeterminate, like a low moan.

He tilted her chin with one finger. "Don't worry, princess, I will not make love to you tonight. Only a few kisses." He felt a shot of pain when her taut body relaxed. How she dreaded the consummation he so hungered for. "Have you ever kissed a man?"

"N-no."

He'd assumed that from her naïveté but was wildly relieved to hear her confirm it. He wanted to be first with Clare, in every way. His erection pressed against her hip, and he wondered if she felt it or understood its significance. He could not tell, she was so still. In the black silence, he lowered his head and brushed her cheek with his lips. It was hot, and he knew she was blushing fiercely. Tenderly, he moved to her lips. They were cold as ice. "Clare," he murmured, "please. Let me."

She held his shoulders in a death grip. "Let you what? I don't know what to do."

"Trust me. Come with me. Go soft wherever I touch you." He clasped her neck and lowered his mouth again. This time he could feel her trying not to fight him as he kissed her for a long time. His lips caressed her chin, her cheeks, her closed eyelids, the delicate lobe of her ear, and finally the corner of her lips. When his tongue sought entrance they parted—in surprise, he knew—but he seized the advantage. For only a moment he touched her closed teeth and then nibbled at her lower lip. "Open your mouth," he said huskily. "Do it, Clare."

With a tiny sigh, she obeyed.

Her mouth tasted of champagne and honey, more sweet than he'd ever dreamed. After a while her arms reached around him, her fingers pressing into his back through the heavy cape and coat and silk shirt. Through all the layers of fabric, he felt her hands as if they were on fire. Hungrily, he sought her tongue, promising her delights she had never experienced with the anxious thrusting of his own.

Bryn's mind struggled to control his body, but everything of him that was rational surrendered to everything that was male. His hand reached under her cape, molding a full, firm breast, and then moved inside her bodice to fondle her warm flesh. When his thumb stroked her nipple, he felt it harden.

"Ah, Clare," he whispered, nuzzling her neck as he tugged her dress down to free her breasts. They were full and lush, fitting perfectly when he cradled them in his hands. He lowered his head to tease a nipple with his tongue, rubbing his hardened sex against her soft bottom.

Then, to his horror, someone rapped on the carriage door. Hastily, he moved to shield Clare from the intruder.

"Sorry, m'lord," came a familiar voice. "I'm a bit early."

Behind him, Bryn felt Clare adjusting her clothes. Damn Jenkins, who was not supposed to arrive for another half hour.

"Wretch," Clare whispered in his ear. "You arranged this."

"I tried to," he admitted. "Are you—?"

"I am covered and decent," she said. "You may open the door." For a precious moment, after Jenkins lowered the stairs and moved away, she rested her cheek against his shoulder. "It was nice, kissing you."

Torn between murdering Jenkins and taking Clare directly to bed, Bryn helped her alight and settled her in the other coach. "I'll call on you tomorrow afternoon at five o'clock," he said. "Be ready to go out."

With a swift hard kiss, he slammed the door and returned to his own carriage, still thinking of Clare's last words. *It was nice, kissing you.*

A pity the Thames was fouled with garbage. Right now he could use a long swim in very cold water.

9

The door hit the wall with a loud crash. "Get up, man!"

Dimly, Bryn recognized Lacey's voice. He rolled over and saw two murderous eyes glaring at him.

The butler appeared, a large footman at his side. "I was unable to stop the gentleman, milord. Is everything in order?"

"Certainly." Bryn swung his legs off the bed. "Coffee, Lace?"

"Just get rid of the palace guard. We need to talk."

"That will be all, Walters. Close the door, will you?"

The viscount paced between bed and windows, beating a fist into the palm of his hand. "Why the devil are you still in bed at this hour?"

Bryn peered at the ormulu clock on the mantel. It showed two o'clock. "What of it?" He grunted. "Are we at war again?"

"Dammit, get moving." With a hard swipe of his hand, Lacey flung open the drapes.

Bryn glanced past Lacey's rigid back into a gray afternoon. "Where am I going?"

"To a duel. Wear anything."

"Don't be absurd, Lace. If I'm to be laid out, it must be in proper attire. Final impressions are so . . . lasting."

Pivoting, the viscount bared his teeth. "This is no joke, Brynmore. I want you with me when I call the bastard out. If I confront him alone we'll never make it to Hounslow Heath."

This was serious, Bryn realized through his usual sluggishness after waking up. "Neither of us is going anywhere until you explain yourself," he said levelly. "Exactly which bastard do you plan to dispatch?"

"Giles Landry. He beat his daughter. Badly, with his fists."

"Christ."

The room was silent for a long moment. Finally Bryn padded naked to the bellpull to summon Walters and into the dressing room for a towel. He wrapped it around his waist and studied his reflection in the mirror, mauling a dark-bristled chin with a hand that still shook. In his own eyes, he saw the reflection of Lacey's fury.

Yes, someone was definitely going to kill Giles Landry.

When Walters answered the summons, Bryn snapped instructions and within minutes coffee was delivered. His valet began laying out shaving gear and clothing in the dressing room.

The viscount stared moodily out the window, not moving except to take the cup Bryn passed to him. Side by side, the two men regarded the gloomy sky.

"Isabella found out," Lacey began in a monotone. "She and Beth planned to go shopping this morning, but when Izzy went to pick her up the servants said Miss Landry was unwell. You know m'sister. She plowed right on upstairs. At first Beth wouldn't unlock the door to her room, and her voice sounded funny, as if she couldn't open her mouth. She almost can't, her jaw is so swollen."

Bryn choked on his coffee. "I take it Landry wasn't there."

"If he was, no one called him. Izzy took Beth to her house and got word to me. The doctor says there's no permanent damage, but she's pretty banged up."

"She told you Landry was responsible?"

"No, and that's the devil of it. Says she tripped on her skirt and fell down the stairs. And she won't be budged. Izzy and I said flat out we didn't believe her, but she just mumbled about stairs. I know the mark of a fist, Bryn. He might have threatened her with a worse beating, or maybe she's being loyal because he's her father, but she's lying for him."

"Both, I suspect. Have you heard what happened last night after you left the Opera House?" When Lacey frowned, the earl described the incident, wondering if he sounded as guilty as he felt. In a way, he was responsible. Everyone in London knew the Earl of Caradoc would tolerate no outright scandal, which left him open to blackmail for the slightest indiscretion with a girl of his own class. He'd only meant to bring Elizabeth into fashion, and one dance scarcely constituted a declaration of intent, but Landry was desperate enough to exploit the opportunity.

For all his rage, Lacey quickly put the pieces together. "You think he attacked Beth because you refused to marry her?"

Bryn felt very cold. "Probably. But he'd no plausible reason to imagine I would. Hell, *you* told me to dance with her."

"Danced with her twice myself. But I'm not the one up to my ears in money, Bryn. Not your fault, any of it, but I expect you won't mind coming along while I put a bullet in the man."

"Robert," the earl said carefully, "because Landry went berserk is no reason to make things worse. Shoot him and you'll have to leave the country."

"If you could see Beth, you wouldn't lecture me like a pompous ass. I know bloody well what I'm doing. The only thing that matters is making sure Landry never gets his hands on her again."

"Yes, that is certainly true. I'll see to it."

"The devil you will! This is my fight."

Bryn regarded him with an unblinking gaze. "How is that, Lace? Have you a particular interest in the girl?"

He lowered his eyes. "No. This is not personal. It's simple justice."

At the edges of his concentration, Bryn was aware he didn't quite believe that. But whatever his motives, Lacey couldn't hit an elephant at three paces with a gun, which made pistols the obvious choice of weapon for Landry. If it came to a duel, Bryn would have to fight it himself.

He swore fluently. Because of one innocuous dance, everything he'd worked for all his life could go up in smoke. Returning to the tray, he poured himself another cup of coffee.

"You could marry her," Lacey said from nowhere.

Faintly aware of coffee overrunning into the saucer, Bryn set down the pot with unsteady hands. "That is one choice."

"Why not? It solves everything. You get a wife and an heir for the empire you're trying to build, and you could add a clause to the settlement requiring her father to keep his distance. Meantime Beth gets everything a girl could want, and somewhere between the wedding and Landry's departure I'll beat the stuffing out of him." He squared his shoulders. "Do it, man. That, or I'll kill the maggot."

"We'll rule that out right now. I'd break your right arm before letting you at him. And keep in mind his creditors will close in to scavenge everything he owned when he's dead. Where would that leave Elizabeth?"

"In the poorhouse." Lacey grimaced. "Hadn't thought so far ahead. So, will you marry her?"

"If it comes to that. I'm not averse to the idea, Lace. It occurred to me when I met her. She's lovely, intelligent, and rather charming. But now is not the time. Bloody Hell, the timing couldn't be worse. I'm about some other business right now, and it doesn't allow for courting a dewy-eyed youngster."

"Not dewy-eyed," Lacey retorted grimly. "Black-eyed, and bruised, and scared to death. Other business can wait."

Sensing a corner at his back, Bryn cast around in his mind for an escape. Somehow, Elizabeth must be protected, and he was the logical one to do it. But he would not give up Clare. That was not a choice. He could not have said why, but it was absolute. There had to be another way.

At least Lacey was willing to hand the matter over to him. In the next few hours, he would consider every option and make his decision, but at the moment he could imagine no solution that let him come out a winner. And Lacey's bright confidence didn't help one bit. Irrationally, he wanted to plant a fist in his friend's belly for waking him up with this news.

Lacey had another lance to throw. "We couldn't leave her at Izzy's, of course. First place Landry will look when he finds out she's gone, and he's got the law on his side. She's at Ernie's house."

The earl stalked to the nearest blank wall and pounded it with his fist. "Are you insane?" he thundered. "You want me to marry the chit, and you installed her in the same house with my mistress?"

"Where else?"

Bryn sucked his bruised fingers, infuriated because there was no one to blame. Where else indeed?

"Bryn?" Lacey's voice held a note of uncertainty. "You can work this out, don't you think? Dashed awkward, of course, but we had to make sure Beth was safe. Clare will understand. Hell, she was magnificent. Didn't bat an eyelash."

Bryn was sure of that. He could imagine her poise, but not what she must be thinking. Closing his eyes, he felt the same sense of powerlessness he'd experienced when his father went mad.

Not again, he told himself. He was no longer a child, and there was a solution if he could figure it out. He'd made life-and-death decisions before, although a clean war with a clear enemy was little challenge compared to this debacle.

He'd rather lead a cavalry charge unarmed and on foot than face Clare and Elizabeth together in the same house.

* * *

The earl searched every gaming hell he knew, and others Lacey told him about, but Landry was not to be found at his usual haunts. Possibly he'd gone to ground, although Bryn wasn't ready to concede him that much good sense. He decided to try St. James's Street.

Leaving his coach to wait nearby, he wandered through Boodle's and Brooks's and the Cocoa Tree, nodding to acquaintances and resisting the urge for a hefty shot of brandy. He was running out of places to look. White's was the last *ton* establishment on the block, and Bryn didn't expect to find him there. After the confrontation at the Opera House, even Landry would have sense enough to avoid the earl's favorite club.

But he did not. Bryn was astonished to see him seated at a green baize table, tossing dice without an apparent care in the world. Ducking into the hall, Bryn calculated ways to get the blackguard alone without another public scene.

"Lord Caradoc, yes?"

Bryn spun around, recognizing the man who took Landry off his hands at the Opera House.

The gentleman bowed. "Giles told me your name. Well, to be exact, he called you 'that bloody damned Caradoc.' I'm Max Peyton, by the way."

After a beat, Bryn held out his hand. "You prevented a melee last night. I am in your debt."

Peyton's grasp was firm. "As is Lord Landry. Under the circumstances, I could hardly permit you to shoot him."

"Someone will, one of these days." Bryn regarded him steadily. "You wouldn't want to be in the way."

Peyton grinned. "I'm no friend of his, if that's what you are suggesting. Merely a creditor, with a vested interest in keeping him alive. He seems to think you'll make his daughter a rich countess."

The earl barked a laugh. "Even if I do, you'll not collect a shilling from the marriage settlement. Too many others queued ahead of you."

"As it happens," Peyton said with a negligent wave of his hand, "money is not the issue. I have more than I can spend. But Landry bet what he didn't have, which no gentleman ought to do, and should he scratch up a penny I intend to pluck it away. On principle, you understand."

At any other time, Bryn would have invited him to share a bottle of wine and further the acquaintance. Instinct told him they could be friends. It also gave him an idea. "You have done me one favor, Mr. Peyton, and I am presumptuous enough to ask another. One you'll not mention to anyone."

"I think I'm flattered, Lord Caradoc. And I can keep my mouth shut."

"Listen carefully, then. In about five minutes, get Landry away from the table. Tell him I'm waiting around the corner, in King Street. If he asks, I said something about discussing terms."

"And looked friendly. Or, at the least, benign."

"Just so." Bryn chuckled. "Unlike Landry, I always pay my debts. Keep track of what I owe you."

Five minutes later, the carriage door swung open and Landry was tossed inside by the two footmen waiting to grab him when he turned the corner. The lamps were not fired, and Bryn was a dark shadow lounging on the leather squabs, a silver-tipped walking stick resting across his knees.

"What the hell—"

"Shut up, Landry." The coach lurched away. "I wish to spend as little time in your company as possible and won't promise for my actions if you annoy me."

The baron pulled himself up. "If this is about last night, I was drunk. Shouldn't have come at you in a public place. You have my apology."

Bryn ignored that. "This is about your daughter, and what you did to her."

There was a short, tense pause. "I don't know what you're talking about."

The cane lifted an inch. "Think again."

Landry's fingers wrapped around his knees. "Do you mean the accident? Beth fell down the stairs. Damnable thing, but the carpet is worn. Hell, m'luck's been out so long it's all I can do to put clothes on her back. Every penny is going to give her a season on the town. Promised her mother I'd bring her out, but I can't keep the house up too. Dangerous place sometimes, with the chimneys smoking and the carpets in shreds. Easy to catch your foot. The fall bruised her up a bit, but she'll be all right. Told me so."

"The next lie," said the earl with quiet menace, "will deprive you of several teeth. Now listen hard, because I'll say this once. I know exactly what happened, and it will not happen again. There is one way to make sure of that, but for Elizabeth's sake I am going to give you another choice." He smiled thinly. "I rather hope you will not accept it."

"Is this is some scheme to get out of marrying m'daughter? You can't bluff me, Caradoc. I saw you come in with her from the terrace at Wetherford's ball. She says you kissed her. Put your hand up her skirt and cut her lip with your teeth, by God."

"You are digging your own grave," Bryn warned softly.

Landry would not be stopped. "She had expectations after that, and I won't see my little girl unhappy. Not altogether sure I ought to hand Elizabeth over to a disreputable family like the Talgarths, but her heart is set on it."

In a quick motion, Bryn stabbed the knobbed cane into Landry's paunchy belly. He doubled over, groaning.

"I trust that got your attention." The cane pressed under the baron's chin, lifting his head and forcing his mouth shut. "You are going on an extended holiday, worm. This carriage will take you to your house, where you'll have ten minutes to pack. Then to Dover, and I don't give a damn where you go from there so long as it's across the channel."

When Landry tried to speak, the cane pushed harder.

"Naturally, you are wondering what's in this for you. First of all, let me make it clear the alternative is a glove across the face, followed quickly by your unmourned demise. I understand Italy is pleasant this time of year. For that matter, a brief exile under the Mediterranean sun rather appeals to me too, especially when coupled with the pleasure of putting a bullet through your head. But if you'd rather not face me, I shall remain in foggy London while you enjoy a warmer clime at my expense."

Landry's eyes widened.

"Ah, yes, there is good news. I am actually willing to pay an allowance to get you out of my sight. Not a great deal, mind you. Some thrift will be required to keep you the three months I expect you to be gone.

Should you never come back, you'll not be missed. But if you set foot in England before the end of July, I will kill you. Nod if you understand."

Unable to move his head, Landry blinked rapidly.

"Excellent. In the meantime, your daughter will enjoy her season free of your company." With reluctance, Bryn lowered the cane.

Rubbing his chin, Landry kept his eyes on the silver knob poised inches from his torso. "You can't prove anything," he blustered. "Elizabeth will back up whatever I say."

Bryn began to think the man was demented. "You misunderstand, lout. You are no longer in a position to terrorize her or beat her into lying for you. Things have changed. Now it is I who will terrorize *you,* and I won't stop at a beating."

The baron shook his head. "This is all hot air. I knew your father back when he rutted with every gullible female in London. How many husbands did he cuckold? And when they called him out, how many did he dispatch? Five? Ten? You think society will tolerate another Caradoc running wild? I'm giving you the chance to marry Elizabeth without a scandal, but if you refuse I'll spread the word you compromised her. You have a taste for virgins and everybody knows it. For all I know, you've already bedded the chit."

Bryn folded his arms across his chest, the cane dangling loosely from his fingers. "Apparently I've wasted my time, Landry. Consider my previous offer withdrawn. Better we continue to a quiet place along the river and dump your corpse in the Thames. I doubt there will be so much as a cursory investigation."

If Landry could have seen his eyes, Bryn thought in the silence that followed, he'd have given up long ago. As it was, the rattle of the coach wheels was the only sound, that and the clicking of his own fingernails against the cane.

"How much?" Landry muttered. "Maybe I'll take a few months to think things through. But I've nothing to live on."

"Certainly not your wits. You can stretch what I give you to support three months of frugal existence or gamble it away in one night. It's all the same to me, so long as you remain abroad through July."

"And what about Elizabeth? What's to become of her without me?"

"I strongly advise that you do not mention her again. At the moment I want nothing more in this world than to give you a taste of what you've given her." Feeling himself slipping out of control, Bryn rapped on the panel and the coach pulled over. After instructing the footman to locate a hackney, he seized Landry's neckcloth in a wrenching grip. "I'll leave you now in the care of three very strong men who have been informed that I don't like you. Give them trouble, and even I will never know what became of your body."

At the end, Bryn couldn't help himself. The Caradoc temper was legendary, although he'd learned to control it the same way he mastered the vices that destroyed his father. But it coiled inside him, always, and broke loose with one vicious swipe of his cane across Landry's jaw.

Jumping from the carriage, he looked back at the lump curled on the bench, moaning in pain. "*Bon voyage,*" he said, tossing him a pouch filled with sovereigns. "And take heed, Landry. The next time I'll not be so indulgent."

10

It was well past midnight when the hack delivered Bryn to Ernestine's house, where he found Lacey and Isabella pacing the salon.

"Where the hell have you been?" Lacey demanded.

"Is he dead?" Isabella inquired at the same time, sounding hopeful.

"In a minute, both of you. I need a drink." Bryn's gaze swept the room, looking for Clare. She wasn't there, and he couldn't bring himself to ask about her. While Isabella poured him some cognac, he sank onto a sofa and closed his eyes. "How is Elizabeth?"

Lacey pulled up a chair and straddled it, folding his arms across the back. "Asleep, we hope. Clare is with her."

"Wonderful. Just what I wanted to hear." Gratefully, Bryn swallowed a long draught, feeling the warmth course down his throat. For the first time in years he wanted to get stinking drunk. "Landry is on his way to Dover, and from there to a less-than-grand tour from which he will not return for several months. I hit him once, hard. He's damned lucky to be alive."

"I'd have clawed his eyes out," Isabella said flatly.

"I should have threatened to hand him over to you. Might have shut him up. When he gave me the story about Elizabeth tripping on the carpet I was sure I'd kill him. Took me all night to find the cockroach. He was playing dice at White's like nothing ever happened."

"That sort thinks nothing of beating up a woman," Lacey said with a scowl. "And the law backs him up, at least in practice. Whoever said England was a civilized country?"

"Right." Bryn drained the snifter and gave it to Izzy for a refill. One more, and he'd ask about Clare. The odd thing was, in all this mess, it was Clare he worried about. His selfishness, and the determination not to let anything interfere with his plans for her, was not something he liked about himself. But it made no difference. One way or another, Clare was first. Robert and Isabella could deal with Elizabeth, while he concentrated on what mattered most to him.

Before Landry came back three months from now, he would decide whether or not to marry the Landry girl. By then, Clare would either be established as his mistress or gone. Even the thought of the latter made him wince. He studied the amber liquid, warming it between the palms of his hands.

Isabella perched herself on the arm of his chair, the lavender satin of her skirt spilling across his thigh. "Beth will come home with me, I expect. Unless you have other plans for her?"

"Not at the moment. She needs a chance to recover from all this. God, what she must have been through without anybody knowing. Show her a good time, Izzy. Take her to all the best places and introduce her to every decent man with enough money to buy her father off." Bryn's shoulders hunched. "Maybe we can have everything sewed up before he comes back. At the very least, you can give her a season to remember."

"Does that mean," Isabella said slowly, "that you are ruling yourself out? Who could I find for her that would do better than you?"

"Someone nearer her age, for one," he said tiredly. "I can't cope with this right now, Dizzy. If I have to marry her myself, I will. Maybe, in a few months, I'll want to. One way or another, I'll make sure she doesn't wind up under Landry's fist again. But if she ends up marrying me, I'd rather she did so freely and not because there was no other choice." His gaze lifted. "Should she fall in love with a man who can't provide a settlement, I'll provide it. Don't tell her that, but keep your eyes open. The last thing I need is a wife eating her heart out for someone else."

Lacey roused himself from a brown study. "You aren't too old for her."

Glancing up in surprise, Bryn wondered what brought that on. "I had the distinct feeling, the one time we met, that Elizabeth regarded me as something of a kindly uncle. We are almost two decades apart, Lace."

"Thirty-five ain't old," the viscount protested from the position of a man only one year younger. "And you won't find a virgin bride much beyond seventeen or eighteen unless she's an antidote."

"I know you already have me leg-shackled to Beth Landry," Bryn said in a voice raspy with fatigue. "Just don't plant the idea in her head, because I've no intention of considering a wife, any wife, until things are settled with Clare. Do you have the slightest idea how awkward this situation is for me?"

Isabella grinned. "*I* do. And you deserve it. Everybody dances to your fiddle, and you are more spoiled than last week's mutton. It's past time you were set on your ear, Bryndle. But you needn't worry about Clare, because tonight she has taken charge of everything. Lace and I were driving Beth mad with questions because we were so furious about what happened to her, but Clare took her up to bed, fed her soup and a bit of wine, and finally threw the both of us out of the room. In any case, you can leave Beth in my hands. Tomorrow, if she's up to it, we'll move her to my house."

He smiled at her. "Try not to be too outrageous for a while, Dizzy. With Landry for a father, Elizabeth can't afford any more scandal."

"Behold a pattern card of virtue," she said with a laugh. "That *will* set the *ton* on its ear."

Lacey, ominously quiet for several minutes, roused himself. "I'll sleep here tonight, in case I'm needed."

Swiping his fingers through his hair, Bryn leaned back against the chair. "I'd rather you go home, Robert. Landry is halfway to Dover by now, and I want to see Clare alone."

Brother and sister shot each other a knowing glance, mutually agreeing to do as he said. After thirty years of friendship, they recognized when Bryn's mood was dangerous.

* * *

When Isabella and Lacey were gone, Bryn finished his drink and made his way upstairs.

One of the doors along the hall was ajar. He moved into the room and saw Clare seated on a hard-backed chair, a spill of white over her lap. She rose at his entrance, her embroidery dangling from one hand.

A single candle illuminated the bed where Elizabeth Landry was sleeping. Easing to her side, he watched the flickering light play across her bruised, swollen cheek. Dark splotches the shape of fingers stood out against the pale skin of her throat. She looked fragile as gauze. When she turned slightly, moaning in her sleep, his head went back in a gesture of raw fury. Had he seen her first, like this, Landry would be dead.

As he reached to brush Elizabeth's tangled hair from her eyes, a hand settled on his shoulder.

"Let her sleep," Clare whispered. She led him into the hall, closing the door soundlessly. "We finally had to give her a bit of laudanum because she was so restless. But she ought not be left alone, in case she wakes up or has bad dreams."

Bryn leaned his shoulders against the wall. "Can you find someone else to stay with her for a while? I want to talk to you."

"Amy is in the kitchen." She began to fold the square of linen. "I'll fetch her."

Bryn recognized a man's handkerchief and snatched it from her hand, looking for an embroidered initial. "May I hope you are sewing this for me?" Her gaze lowered, and he knew she was not. Suddenly his temper, barely leashed for hours, focused on that swatch of linen. He wanted to rip it to shreds.

"Watch for the needle," she said as he balled the cloth in his fist.

Her warning came too late. With an oath, he sucked at the pad of his thumb. "This has been," he muttered, "a very bad day."

"Indeed, my lord. I'll send Amy to sit with Elizabeth and join you downstairs." With a slight curtsy, she headed for the back stairs.

Feeling dismissed, Bryn removed the needle and stuffed the handkerchief in his pocket. Damned if she'd hem linens for another man. This one, and all the others, would be his.

A few minutes later, Clare came into the salon carrying a tray with two mugs of strong hot tea. Bryn accepted one and added what was left of the glass of brandy he'd been nursing. "I didn't mean to jump on you about the handkerchief," he said, gesturing to the spot next to him on the settee. "Please, sit here with me."

Carefully placing her tea on the low black-lacquered table where his legs were crossed at the ankles, she settled next to him at an angle. He saw she was again wearing the gloves she'd taken off for sewing. Lifting one of her hands, he stroked the palm with his thumb. Even through the soft leather, the scars were unmistakable.

"Is that what happened to you, Clare? Were you beaten for no reason, like Elizabeth?"

She shook her head. "You have asked me this before. I was punished for disobedience and impertinence, and for a temper it took me years to control. I told you the truth."

"All of it?" He stared moodily at their clenched hands, her glove starkly white against the sprinkling of dark hair on his wrist. "Elizabeth lied to protect her father. I cannot help but wonder—"

"Don't." Pulling her hand free, she reached for her mug of tea. "What purpose can there be in speaking ill of the dead? Events that took place years ago cannot concern you, my lord."

Everything about her concerned him. Some day, he wanted Clare to begin with the first thing she could remember from childhood and describe every detail of her life. He could sit for hours, listening to her soft voice, edged with sharp intelligence and sparked by glints of wry humor. At this moment, he could imagine nothing he wanted more, not even making love to her. Just her voice, calm and soothing, talking of normal things like her favorite pet or what kind of music she liked.

He leaned back, resting his neck on the sofa. "Call me Bryn. When you start *my lording* me, I suspect you are annoyed." He smiled wearily at the ceiling. "Are you?"

She sipped at her tea, letting his question hang in the air.

He shot her a sideways glance. "Are you?" he repeated. "I've already apologized for the outburst upstairs. Did I leave anything out?"

"We are both on edge," she said after a moment. "Will you tell me what you have been about? Robert said you intended to speak with Elizabeth's father."

"So I did." He swallowed his reaction at hearing her call Lacey by his first name. "The baron has decided to enjoy an extended holiday on the continent. We won't see him again before the end of July."

"Did you hit him?"

"Only once, if you don't count a hard jab at his

stomach with my cane. I expect he'd have fared worse in a closed carriage with you."

"Pieces of him," she said in a chilling voice, "would be scattered from here to Greenwich. I told you I'm cursed with a temper."

"It cannot be worse than my own. When everything around me is frantic, I remain cool, which served me well in the army. But sometimes, out of nowhere, something hits me wrong and I explode. Usually with sarcasm," he hurried to explain, "not a fist. But for a man determined to avoid making scenes, I am generally on the brink of trouble."

"I've noticed."

He massaged his temples. "You have seen the worst of me, that is certain. And shown me little of yourself." When her brow lifted, he groaned. "Ah, Clare, will you never let me forget that pernicious day?"

Have *you?*" she inquired archly.

"I . . . no," he said, after a moment. "I could never forget the most beautiful thing I've ever seen. But will my offense always lie between us? You *could* forgive me, you know."

"Yes. I know."

"Witch," he said without rancor. "I admire your discipline and poise, my dear, but sometimes you are positively sheeted with ice."

"Will you feel better if we have ourselves a good row? I've had the feeling you want to stomp hard on something—figuratively speaking, of course—ever since you arrived. You can have at me, if you wish."

He grinned. "Thanks for the offer, but I'm too tired to put up a good fight. Women always seize the advantage and pick a quarrel when a man's down and senseless."

Even as he heard the words come out of his mouth, Bryn regretted the lame attempt at a joke. With Elizabeth lying upstairs, almost senseless from a beating, it was the worst possible thing to say.

To his astonishment, Clare reclaimed his hand and held it lightly. That she freely touched him at all sent a lump to his throat.

"Elizabeth will be fine in a few days," she assured him, "although her arms and stomach are badly bruised. I doubt her father meant to strike her face. The doctor thinks he hit her there only once, but very hard. It would not be in his interest to disfigure her."

"If I'd called him out last night, none of this would have happened. So much for the virtue of self-restraint."

"Don't be so hard on yourself. You could not have imagined what he would do to Elizabeth. And she is safe now, thanks to you. Robert said you would take care of everything, and so you have, without violence." She smiled slightly. "Not much, anyway. If it matters, I think you have been splendid through all of this."

His head swung to her in surprise. "It matters very much. But I have another thing to confess, Clare. Anyone who knows me will tell you I am the most selfish man alive, and I would never dispute it. Since Lacey woke me with the news, through the hours chasing after Landry and shipping him off, all I could think about was how this would affect you and me."

He lifted a hand when she began to speak. "Let me finish. In my mind, it was a damnable nuisance that Landry beat his daughter. It got in the way of what *I* wanted. I worried more about how you'd react to the situation than I did about Elizabeth, and I wanted to kill Landry to get him out of *my* way, not hers.

"Do you still think I'm splendid, lady? I assure you I am not. If any man but Lace had come to me with the story, I'd have dispatched him to take care of the business and washed my hands of it. The thing is," he added murkily, "Lacey can't shoot."

"And he hadn't the wisdom, or the funds, to send Landry away." Clare moved closer, gazing solemnly into his eyes. "You need only tell me what you want, Bryn. Nothing has changed between us because of this, unless you wish to marry Elizabeth now and send me away."

He stared back, horrified.

"I cannot return the money, though. It's spent, and I've no way to repay it. Not for a long time, anyway, and probably never. Your gallantry, it seems, was uncommonly expensive."

"Bloody hell, Clare, where did you get the idea I'd send you away? That's the last thing in the world I want. The chit will spend the next few months with Isabella and, if I know Izzy, the two of them will make an appearance at every important function in London. So far as I'm concerned, the matter of Elizabeth Landry is done with in the foreseeable future."

He drained the last of his now-cold brandy-laced tea, aware that several fingers of liquor on an empty stomach had left him mildly foxed. He ought to get up while his legs would still move and make his way home.

Except that he'd no way to get there. By now his carriage was well on the way to Dover, and no hackneys stood for hire in a quiet residential neighborhood like this. He should have told Izzy to send her coach back for him. "It occurs to me that I am stranded here for the night," he muttered sourly. "Short of walking, I've no way to get home."

Rising, Clare gave him a smile. “That is not a problem. I’ll sit with Elizabeth while Amy prepares a room for you. It will take a few minutes, because none of the beds have linens on them.”

With effort, Bryn lifted his cramped legs from the table and came to his feet. “We don’t need another bed, Clare. I’ll sleep with you.”

She went pale.

“Don’t worry,” he said, his voice bitter. “I’m too tired, and possibly too drunk, to molest you.” Swinging around, he stared blankly at the wall. “I only wanted to . . . hold you.”

He heard the soft swish of her skirts, the brush of her slippers on the thick carpet, and the door clicking open. “Bryn?” Her voice was barely a whisper. “Are you coming?”

Blinking against a sudden moisture in his eyes, he followed her to a tiny room next to the servants’ stairs. It was furnished with a plain wooden table and chair, a narrow wardrobe, and a bed he’d never have agreed to sleep on, except that it was small enough to ensure that Clare would be nestled snugly in his arms. A lamp stood on the nightstand, and he saw a voluminous white flannel nightgown laid out across the spread.

Five rooms this size would have fitted into the one where Elizabeth now slept, and he nearly protested before realizing that Clare had chosen it herself. She felt uneasy in this house and had done her best not to impose on Ernestine’s unwitting hospitality. Without a word, he sat on the bed and pulled off his boots.

Clare washed her face in the basin on the table, uncomfortably aware of a man unclothing himself just a few feet away. How was she to remove her dress without a maid? A long row of satin-covered buttons ran down her back, from the high neckline to below her waist. She began to unhook them, the process growing more clumsy button by button.

Glancing up, she saw Bryn, shirt open to his waist, regarding her with a quirky smile. He lifted one hand, languidly, and his forefinger beckoned.

Pretending not to see it, Clare abandoned her struggle with the dress and removed her slippers. It would all be a great deal easier if she could grab her nightgown and finish up in the hall. Turning her back to him, she bent to unroll her stockings, careful not to lift her skirt too high.

When they were off, she straightened and felt his hands touch her shoulders.

"Let me." Skillfully, he loosened the buttons from their tight loops. "I have seen you," he reminded her, one hand resting on her bare shoulder as the other worked its way down her back. "I still see you like that, a hundred times a day, in my mind's eye."

So tense a bullet would bounce off her, she waited for him to finish. And make his next move.

But when he was done, he stepped away. Afraid to turn around, she heard several muffled sounds, the rustle of sheets, and finally the protest of creaky wood.

A *real* gentleman, she thought peevishly, would have passed her the nightgown. She glanced over her shoulder. Bryn had stacked the pillows against the headboard and sat against them with the covers pulled to his waist. His chest was bare. She couldn't tell if he'd removed his breeches. One of his knees was raised under the blanket, and across it lay her nightgown.

White teeth gleamed behind a wide male smile of appreciation at her dilemma.

And then, to her astonishment, he tossed her the nightgown and closed his eyes. "One minute," he said, starting the count immediately. "A thousand-and-one, a thousand-and-two—"

Swiftly, Clare flung off her dress, left on her chemise, and struggled into the mass of heavy flannel. Before he got to a thousand-and-fifty, she was considering how to place herself on the bed. There wasn't much room left, with a tall broad-shouldered man encamped dead center.

"Sixty!" He opened his eyes and spread his arms to invite her in.

The only place to go was on top of him. Her gaze lowered to where the sheet and blanket were folded back, revealing the edge of his navel and hard stomach. She gulped. A narrow line of dark hair stretched up, broadening over his chest and curling around two flat brown nipples. His arms and shoulders, smoothly muscled, glimmered in the lamplight.

Clare had never seen a naked adult male before. Nor imagined anything quite so . . . interesting. She allowed herself one last look at sleek biceps before instructing him to move over. Her voice came out in a squeak.

He obliged, although he couldn't go far on the cramped bed. "I'm not inviting you to the gallows, princess. In that tent, you might as well be wearing armor. I won't be able to feel a thing."

Gingerly, she eased onto the hard mattress, digging her feet under the covers. He slid down beside her.

"Lift your head," he said softly. "You'll need a pillow."

She heard him punch the pillow to fluff it and felt it slip under her neck. With careful positioning, she could just manage to stretch out on her side without touching him.

For a moment he held still, and then he leaned away to extinguish the lamp. The room went black.

Clare huddled like a mummy, so cold and stiff she might well have been dead for centuries. Finally he rolled over, turning his back to hers, leaving a space between them.

At first she was relieved. But gradually the gap between them seemed to widen until it felt like a canyon. Except for the heat of his body tingling against her skin, he could have been in another country. She took a deep breath, catching a faint scent of brandy, sandalwood soap, and male sweat.

Above it all, the subtle odor of loneliness.

So many times he'd reached out to her, and every time she'd backed away. Even cringed, as if she found his touch repulsive.

In the harsh silence, so close to him and so distant, she admitted a truth she could scarcely bear to confront. She *wanted* his arms around her, his hands on her body, the awful pleasures of sin.

Staring into the black emptiness, Clare felt something like the touch of Lucifer's wings. This, then, was temptation. She had always imagined evil an ugly thing, chosen only by weak and foolish souls blind to the consequences. Until now, she never understood the seduction of wickedness.

But understanding was not yielding. She might be forgiven for whoring herself, because God was merciful and her reasons unselfish—so long as she did not enjoy her sin. Above all, she must not do that. She *would* not.

But he had not invited her to immorality. *I only want to hold you,* he had said.

There could be no vice in it, she decided. He'd

confronted a monster, rescued a helpless girl, and for a reward asked only to hold her. A woman he'd paid for.

Turning over, she put a hand on his rigid arm. "Bryn? May I have this again, around me?"

She heard him release a long breath. Then he settled on his back and gathered her in his arms. "Thank you," he said.

In all her dark fantasies about their first night in bed together, she had not considered actually sleeping next to him. For some reason, she assumed he would do whatever he intended to do and go away. Now, more comfortable and relaxed than she'd thought possible, Clare imagined she might even be able to fall asleep like this, her head on his shoulder and her hand at his waist.

His fingertips brushed her cheek. "Princess, I'm afraid you are about to discover a few more things about me you won't like."

"Oh, dear," she murmured.

He gave her a tiny squeeze. "I sleep like a tree stump, and I'm grouchy in the mornings. But tomorrow I want you to wake me up when Isabella gets here, even if you have to hit me over the head with a skillet. And . . . sometimes I snore."

"In that case," she said, "the skillet will be essential."

The bed creaked as he chuckled. "I'll wager you are a morning type."

"Up with the roosters. And invariably cheerful."

"We'll see about that." His thumb made little circles on her back. "In future you'll get up when I do, and I won't mind if you're cheerful. In fact, I intend to give you good reason to be." His hand moved to just below her breast. "Lord, this is one day I never expected to end up feeling so good. Dare I press my luck?"

She tensed.

"I only meant," he said in a hurt voice, "to suggest a drive in the park tomorrow afternoon. A little fresh air."

She touched his chin in a gesture of apology. "That would be wonderful, Bryn. I love to be outside."

He took her hand and pressed it to his neck. "Um, that feels good. What were we talking about?"

"The park. You must tell me what time to be ready and what to wear."

"Half past four. Do you not have a maid to advise you?"

"Not . . . precisely. I am fond of Amy and would not replace her for the world, but we share a mutual ignorance about society wardrobes."

"Any other time and place, we might have a small discussion about that, Miss Easton. But I'm much too excited. About taking you up in Black Lightning, I mean."

"Whatever is Black Lightning?"

"My curricle," he said, with evident pride. "Designed it myself. And you will be the first woman to have the privilege of riding in it."

A ride in Black Lightning sounded like a privilege she'd sooner forgo. But he was in a good mood again, which made her feel oddly happy.

"Be sure I'm up when Isabella gets here," he reminded her through a yawn. "Don't forget."

Seconds later, she was vividly aware that he snored.

11

Clare disobeyed Bryn's order to wake him up. He could not have been thinking straight to imagine Elizabeth would want to be seen as she was, swollen and bruised, by her future husband. Better she never learn he had come to the house at all.

It was clear as the bright morning he intended to marry Elizabeth Landry. Her father certainly thought so, as did Robert Lacey. Last night he had pointed out more than once that their marriage was the obvious solution, since Bryn required an heir and Beth had to be removed from her father's control. Robert wasn't thinking either, to keep repeating that in front of the earl's mistress. Some women might have been offended.

She was only relieved. Bryn's marriage to Elizabeth, or anyone else, marked the end of her employment. Perhaps he'd shed her long before that, but the day his betrothal was announced would absolutely be her last. She had to draw the line somewhere.

Of course, she'd drawn a grcat many lines, only to cross them one by one. But adultery was a barrier no temptation could lure her to pass.

Elizabeth would make the earl an excellent wife. She was sweet-natured, remarkably gallant, and with her quiet dignity had managed to calm Robert Lacey when he badgered her to admit she had been beaten. Men could be so incredibly obtuse, with all the best intentions.

Elizabeth felt a great deal better, or so she maintained as Clare and Amy helped her dress. She insisted on walking, unaided, to the carriage, and made sure to thank Amy for her kindnesses. Then she took Clare's hand.

"I am most grateful," she said, with a valiant attempt at a smile. "We shall meet again soon."

Knowing they would not, Clare nodded and turned to Isabella, who'd been a flurry of lavender all morning.

"I'm so glad to have something *useful* to do for a change," she confided, drawing Clare aside. "Would you believe I'm looking forward to a few months of near respectability while Elizabeth is launched into society? You must help me think of a color to complement Isabella the Chaperone."

"Perhaps all colors," Clare suggested. "It is the last thing anyone will expect."

"Why, that's exactly right. How clever you are. Now I've a confession to make, and it must be our secret. I told Robert to delay the work at Clouds. Only for a few days, mind you, for it's practically finished now. But wholly on my own accord I have determined that Sunday is too soon for you and Bryn to carry on after this repellent business with Landry."

"He will be furious," Clare said at once.

"Won't he, though? But Bryndle always gets his own way, to the point of complacency. A bit of sour medicine will be good for him." Her brow wrinkled. "Will *you* mind, Clare? I own I never thought of that. If you'd rather, Robert can be instructed to proceed at full speed."

Clare lowered her eyes. "I'm not altogether sure. Mostly I want to push it off until the last possible moment, but other times I find this limbo nearly unbearable. Perhaps it would be best to get on with it, if only because I dare not remain here. What if the duchess should come home unexpectedly?"

"Why, then we'd all be in the soup," Isabella said cheerfully. "For my part, I'd prefer you to stay. It will not be so easy to visit you at Clouds."

"No," Clare said with a downturned mouth. "You certainly cannot set foot there."

"Don't count on it. With Elizabeth in tow I must be more circumspect than usual, but there is always a way to spend time with one's friends. And when next we meet, I shall be a walking rainbow."

"I didn't mean all colors at once," Clare protested as Isabella swooped away with a gay wave.

Sighing, Clare went to the kitchen to help fix a tray for the earl's breakfast. She'd not be seeing the newly respectable Isabella again, for all the lady said otherwise. The thought was lowering, and she banished it with one even worse: facing Bryn after disobeying him.

A few minutes later, she entered the bedroom carrying a tray with coffee, sliced strawberries in cream, and hot scones with butter and honey. A great deal of honey, to sweeten him up.

As he'd warned her, the man was virtually impossible to rouse. When poking and shaking him failed, she tried dripping cold water on his face, aiming for the tip of his nose. At last, he responded with a growl.

"Hibernation is over, Bryn. Rise and shine."

"Go to hell," he muttered, rolling over and burying his head under a pillow.

So I will, she thought with a stab of pain. "You told me to get you up when Isabella arrived."

There was no response. She jabbed him in the ribs with a sharp finger and heard a muffled protest. Then his head shot up. "Did you say Izzy?"

"Yes. And it's past one o'clock."

With an oath concerning Bloody Dogs of Doom, he came to his hands and knees in the middle of the bed with the covers draped over him. Head lowered, shaggy hair concealing his forehead, he shook himself awake.

Like a Dog of Doom himself, she thought, wanting to laugh. Grouchy was putting it mildly, but she rather liked him this way.

She changed her mind about that almost immediately. When she'd explained for the third time that Isabella had come and gone, taking Elizabeth with her, and when that information finally penetrated his fogged brain, he came alert with a vengeance.

"What?" he thundered, barely remembering to pull the sheet around him as he surged from the bed.

Again she was hard put not to laugh. Like a togaed Roman senator, one fist lifted to the ceiling, Bryn raged at her. He was not terribly coherent, but the words *obey* and *I told you* appeared frequently. Those were exactly the kind of words apt to send her into a rage of her own, had he not looked quite so silly.

He'd glared at her for several moments before she realized he was finished.

In silence, she took his elbow and turned him until he faced the mirror which hung on the back of the door. "I did not think you would wish Miss Landry to see you this morning. When you've had time to reflect, you will agree she would not want you to see her either. I'll leave you to your breakfast, my lord, and arrange a hackney to collect you in half an hour." With a curtsy, she swooped out.

Damn that woman, he thought, mauling his whiskers. He was getting a little tired of having her show himself *to* himself, in a mirror. He never liked what he saw.

Soothed by a hot bath and the attentions of his valet, Bryn returned that afternoon to collect Clare for the promised drive in the park. This time he came in a hack and hustled her inside it for another rendezvous on a side street with a vehicle everyone would recognize as his.

Black Lightning. The sleekest, lightest, fastest curricle in England.

Clare eyed it dubiously. "It seems awfully . . . frail," she murmured as he lifted her up. When the vehicle swayed she fell back onto the narrow bench with a squeal.

"The hell it is," he said, offended. "Solid as a rock, light as a feather, swifter than the wind. Took me six months to perfect the design, and never mind how much it cost. One of a kind, Black Lightning." He swung up next to her, instructing his groom to make use of the hack to get home. Built for racing, the curricle had no place for a tiger.

"I'm sure it's very nice," Clare stammered as Bryn

feathered the corner and swerved around an oncoming wagon heaped with cabbages.

"*Nice?* I've been offered ten thousand guineas for it, not including the grays."

She clutched his arm as the curricle sped down the street, dodging coaches, riders, and pedestrians with an ease that both terrified and amazed her. "I ought to have more respect," she allowed. "It seems this wagon and I come at the same price."

Bryn whistled between his teeth. "Unfair, princess."

She flushed. "Forgive me. That was a terrible thing to say."

"Apology accepted. But have at me when you will, because I don't mind and you will endure worse from me. You already have. Only, never think I set a price on you. As I recall, *you* did that. To me you are priceless." Without slowing, he maneuvered past two phaetons and a milk wagon. "If you need proof that I value you beyond anything, tomorrow Black Lightning will be broken up for firewood."

"Good heavens, Bryn." She gave him an exasperated look. "What a cork-brained, melodramatic gesture. Sometimes you haven't the sense God gave a goose."

"So Isabella and Lacey keep telling me." He laughed. "With the three of you to put me in my place, I may yet mend my ways."

"I shan't hold my breath," Clare said wickedly. "But when we are not inches from colliding with a milk wagon, I promise to be impressed with your dashing curricle. In the park there will be more room to run."

"Not necessarily." He pointed straight ahead. "There is Stanhope Gate."

Clare looked up in amazement at a virtual parade. One by one, a host of vehicles edged like horse-drawn snails into the press of traffic. She saw riders in top hats and curly-brimmed beavers, aristocratic ladies sidesaddle on delicate steeds, and clusters of women with children in tow or pushing prams. There were gentlemen on foot, gentlemen with ladies on their arms, gentlemen ogling ladies through quizzing glasses. Compared to this, the packed Opera House had been deserted.

Her fingers dug into Bryn's forearm as he managed to pass an enormous barouche and turn onto Rotten Row. "A drive in the park? Fresh air? What a clanker. You might have warned me what to expect."

"Perhaps *drive* was an overstatement, but now and again there is a wisp of fresh air. I failed to explain what goes on at Hyde Park every afternoon because I knew you'd worry about it."

"Any sane person ought to worry about coming here. And it's not as though I could refuse."

He considered for a moment. "Actually, I suppose you could, although no one has ever done so before."

She drew herself up. "What would happen if I refused to accompany you someplace I didn't want to go? What would you do about it?"

"Planning an insurrection?" he asked mildly. "I've no idea how to deal with a refusal from you, on any count, and I rather hope not to find out. We must not be adversaries, Clare."

"We shall be adversaries any time you lie to me."

He nodded. "I did mislead you, by omission, and quite deliberately. But if you prefer, in future I shall provide you with the most gory details of any excursion I plan."

"You have not dealt with the refusing part."

"Clare, I want to go places with you and share

things with you. When you are more comfortable with your situation, you will want that too. For now, you find it awkward to be with me in public, but I'll shield you every way possible."

"You mean I'll get used to it."

"Something like that. It's like swimming in cold water. Some ease in a bit at a time while others jump in immediately. I think you are a jumper."

She thought it over. "Yes, I suppose I am. Although it takes me rather a long time to dredge up the courage."

His eyebrows wriggled theatrically. "There is always one way to escape these outings, m'dear. You can make me a better offer."

She laughed. "You really are the devil's own, Caradoc. And to say you are the most selfish man alive is a gross understatement. You are wholly self-absorbed."

"Not so much as I was before meeting you, princess," he said in a shadowed voice. "But in my defense, there was a good reason for bringing you here today. After the face-off with Landry at the Opera House, followed by his abrupt disappearance, I wanted to be seen carrying on as though nothing happened."

"That makes sense," she conceded. "Am I along to draw a bit more attention to you?"

"In part. Your presence will help dispel the rumors about my attachment to Elizabeth, which have no basis in fact and can only do her harm. She will have a dull season indeed if all the eligible men assume I have staked a claim."

Puzzled, Clare gazed straight ahead, seeing nothing. Why would he risk losing Elizabeth to another suitor? Not that any man could measure up to the Earl of Caradoc, and he was confident enough to know that. But it was generous of him to allow Elizabeth a few months to enjoy herself, free of demands from her father or her future husband. Perhaps he was not so selfish as she'd first imagined.

"Clare?" He cast her a quizzical glance. "Have I offended you again?"

"On the contrary. I was thinking about the care you have taken with Elizabeth, and your kindness to her."

He waved a negligent hand. "I hope she becomes a great success, and I expect Isabella will make sure of it. But her welfare is not the main reason we are trundling through Hyde Park this afternoon. I wanted to be with *you,* princess. It makes me happy."

She swallowed a gulp of surprise. "Then I shall try not to quarrel any more, although wrangling with you is a great distraction from the looks everyone is sending our way."

"Devil take them all," he said. "We've accomplished our purpose, so let's have some fun." With a flick of his wrist, the grays sprang forward, zigzagging around every obstacle until he steered them onto a deserted path just wide enough to accommodate the curricle's wheels. He grinned at her with pure male vanity. "Goes like a dream, don't she? Barely makes a ripple in the air."

Clare released her grip on his arm and straightened her skirt. Seeing Bryn this way, behaving like an overgrown schoolboy, reminded her of Jeremy. She wanted to hug him. "That was quite a display."

"I couldn't resist," he confessed. "Men like to show off for a pretty girl. One day soon we'll drive to Claude's place in Richmond, and you'll have a chance to see how fast Black Lightning really is."

"I can hardly wait. Do watch the road, Bryn. Someone is coming over the rise." She pointed ahead. "What a beautiful horse!"

Bryn's good mood soured when he recognized the rider approaching them on a magnificent bay. Max Peyton was a devilishly handsome man: tan, tawny-haired, and sleek as a healthy young lion. Clare had obviously noticed, because she was smiling at him.

"Caradoc," Max said pleasantly, his gaze focused on Clare as if awaiting an introduction.

Not likely, the earl thought, annoyed that Peyton sat a horse so well. When had he ever imagined he could be friends with this man? "If you are looking for Rotten Row, stay on this path and turn left at the Serpentine."

Peyton laughed. "Actually, I was trying to escape that mob scene, but I got lost on these winding roads. Are you enjoying this fine afternoon, Miss . . . ?"

"Clare Easton," she replied softly.

Bryn snarled.

"My pleasure, Miss Easton," said Max, doffing his hat and regarding her with clear appreciation before returning his attention to the earl. "I say, Caradoc, that is a prime curricle. Never seen its like. Do you race it?"

"Rarely. I have little time for childish games." When Clare chuckled, Bryn cast her a quelling look.

"What a shame." Max raised a brow. "Perhaps you'll allow me to do so when you are occupied with business. She ought to be taken out and put through her paces."

"What the devil makes you—?" Bryn's hand tightened on the reins. "I forgot. You've a claim on me, Peyton, but that's one hell of a favor to ask."

"Forgive our language, Miss Easton," said the lion with a grin.

Bryn lifted his gaze to Clare in apology and caught a wicked glint in her eye. She was enjoying this, the baggage—his own atrocious manners and the unmistakable charm of a man who treated her like a lady instead of a possession.

"Black Lightning is yours when you want it, one race only," he told Max gruffly. "And that is the only thing of mine you can put your hands on."

"But you owe me *two* favors, Caradoc. And you know how I feel about gentlemen who fail to pay their debts. How *is* Landry, by the way?"

"In better health than he deserves, and traveling to preserve it. You'll have no chance to collect from him for several months, and precious little after that."

"Then you see why I must be assiduous about collecting from debtors present and solvent. In your case, I shall consider us even after you buy me the best dinner in London." He smiled at Clare. "Miss Easton, under ordinary circumstances I would invite you to join us, but I plan to use this opportunity to propose a business venture."

"I'll be in touch," Bryn said curtly. Without another word he chucked the grays into a trot.

Clare looked back over her shoulder, and when Peyton waved she waved back.

At that moment, Bryn wanted for the second time in two days to kill a man. He drove blindly for several minutes, so angry he didn't feel Clare's arm steal through his to hold on. Then he heard her gasp and saw a landau coming directly at them. Just in time, he managed to swerve onto the grass.

They sat in silence for a long minute.

"I suppose you think I'm rude," he said, steering the grays back to the road.

"I expect Mr. Peyton thinks so." She let go his arm. "Does everyone know what happened last night?"

"Only you, Lacey, Isabella, and Peyton. I trust you will speak of it to no one."

"Who would I tell, since you've named nearly everyone in London I know?"

"You are not," he said darkly, "acquainted with Max Peyton. I want to keep it that way."

She agreed without expression. "We shall keep everything exactly as you wish it."

Which put him firmly in his place, Bryn reflected as he drove out of the park. By his side, Clare had withdrawn into herself. He signaled a hackney to pull onto a quiet street behind him and found a boy to hold the grays while he settled Clare into the cab. Then he leaned his arms against the open window. She gazed back at him, composed and distant. He felt another surge of helpless anger.

"Tomorrow afternoon, you are to meet with Mrs. Beales at Clouds," he said. "It should not take more than an hour, and the kitchen will do well enough if the workmen have not finished decorating the parlor. In the evening, if you do not object, we shall go to the theater."

Her gaze was troubled. "*What* will take an hour?"

"I explained when we first came to terms," he said, not kindly. "In two days the house will be ready, and this unnatural situation will at last come to an end. There are matters you must know about beforehand, and Mrs. Beales will instruct you. Pay careful attention." His hands gripped the panel. He wanted to say something pleasant and couldn't think of anything. "Get a good night's sleep," he advised finally.

After paying the driver and giving the address, he stood for a long time after the cab disappeared before swinging into the curricle. His precious Black Lightning, soon to be violated by another man. A man Clare had waved to. Smiled at.

Disgruntled, he drove to Watier's for a solitary meal and finally settled himself in a quiet room with a bottle of good cognac to brood.

Clare reminded him of cognac: warm, deep, biting, intoxicating.

When he was younger, he'd imagined falling in love. Even his father's faithlessness and his mother's despair had not rid him of that romantic notion. But as the years went by, he learned how the game was played. Aristocrats married to ally families and fortunes. A wedding was no more than the merging of assets, with love an accidental bonus on the rare occasions it entered the picture.

He'd resigned himself to a marriage of convenience but could never bring himself to make one. Always there was that foolish hope—someday he'd meet a woman he could love, one who'd love him in return. Why had he thought to prove an exception?

Now it was far too late, even for hope. He was thirty-five years old. Suitable brides were half his age, most of them undereducated and likely to bore him within weeks.

Clare would never bore him, but he couldn't marry her.

Bryn poured himself another drink. It was time to face the facts. He required two women: Clare to love and another to bear his name and heir. Elizabeth Landry could do that, unless she was luckier than he had been. She might yet find what he'd dreamed of, but if she did not, he would marry her—so long as she accepted that he intended to keep a mistress.

And Clare would have to accept his marriage.

More air dreams, he told himself cynically. So far she barely tolerated him, and he wasn't even sure he loved her. For all he knew, he was incapable of loving anyone. But God, he wanted to.

So far, all he'd done was make a prime ass of himself. Either Clare brought out the worst in him, or she turned light on what was really there. Repeatedly, he made sure to remind her she was a whore, with duties to perform, skills to acquire, obedience expected. After her session tomorrow with Mrs. Beales, she would despise him all the more.

For the first time in his life, Bryn found himself uneasy in his own company.

"Hallo, Bryndle." Robert Lacey pulled over a chair and helped himself to the nearly empty decanter of cognac. Appropriating the earl's snifter, he refilled it and settled back with a provoking grin. "You appear to be in a bad mood, which is just as well because I have bad news. I'd hate to ruin a good mood—not that I've seen you in one since I can remember."

"Cut line," growled the earl. The last thing he needed was another dose of bad news. "What's happened now?"

"More what *hasn't* happened, I'm afraid. Clouds won't be ready on Sunday. The business with Elizabeth set me back a day, but pretty much everything is in place except the bed. It won't be delivered for another week."

"Bloody hell, Lace, that's the only thing we can't do without. It's not as if we required the Great Bed of Ware. I'd have thought a bed would be the first thing you requisitioned."

"So it was, but I wanted something special. In good taste for a change, elegant and comfortable, hand carved from mahogany. But the woodcarver's been sick from eating bad fish. He'll finish up Wednesday at the earliest, and perhaps not even then." Lacey cradled the snifter between his hands. "Have a dip in the Thames, old boy. You're a blazing fever on two legs."

"You don't know the half of it. And what the devil are you doing here, with Clouds still needing work? I gave you a fairly simple task, and you've accomplished nothing."

Lacey came to his feet. "No doubt I should be hanging wallpaper at three o'clock in the morning, but I had an irresistible urge to be dressed down. Make do with Clouds as is, Brynmore. I resign, effective immediately."

Astonished, Bryn watched him stalk away. Not once in all their years of friendship had Robert Lacey lost his temper for so little cause. His own offensive behavior was nothing out of the ordinary, and Lace had always shrugged it off. Until now.

It occurred to him that he demanded rather a lot of his friends. They deserved his best, but he gave them his worst and expected to be forgiven. Only Clare stood up to him, holding him accountable for his conduct.

So far today, he'd succeeded in antagonizing Max Peyton, Robert Lacey, and Clare. Maybe he should ride on down to Canterbury and pick a fight with the archbishop.

Making up his mind to be exceptionally polite to his valet, who was no doubt waiting up for him, Bryn struck out for home. Tomorrow he would make amends with Clare and Lace. Peyton could wait. That was an acquaintance he did not want to encourage until Clare was content to remain his mistress. At the moment, he wouldn't blame her for turning to a younger and kinder man, but he wasn't ready to give her the chance.

All the way to St. James's Square, Bryn rehearsed speeches to ease himself into Clare's good books after her trying encounter with Mrs. Beales. The housekeeper's lecture had been reviewed for him by previous mistresses, and he felt almost embarrassed, thinking about what Clare faced tomorrow morning.

12

Clare gazed at the large table with some amazement. It was covered with all sorts of things that could not possibly be related: silky paper that looked as if it were oiled, a lemon, thread, scissors and a sponge, vinegar, honey, disks of wax, olive oil, alum, bark, green tea, herbs of every kind, items she could not identify, and a cucumber.

Mrs. Beales looked bored as she allowed time for Clare to examine the display before asking her to take a seat. Obviously she had been through this exercise many times.

Clare settled nervously on the trestle bench, hands folded in her lap, still not altogether certain what to expect. When she arrived at Clouds, the housekeeper led her immediately to the kitchen without explanation. Bryn had told her about this lesson, but she could not figure out what it concerned.

With a thin-lipped smile, Mrs. Beales took up a

position directly across from her. "Today," she said briskly, "I shall introduce you to several methods of preventing conception. As the earl has no doubt made clear, his first son must be born in wedlock. After that happy occurrence, and should you still be under his protection, the two of you may decide to have children together. Until then, all care must be taken. You do understand that?"

Clare stared at her, cheeks flaming. Better than most, she knew the consequences of careless passion and what happened when an aristocrat bred children on a woman he did not intend to marry.

"Very well, then." Mrs. Beales made a sweeping gesture over the table. "This is a mere sample of prophylactic devices, culled from my studies. I have developed rather an interest in the matter and pride myself on keeping up with the latest advances."

"There seem to be a g-great many of them," Clare stammered. "Could you not simply tell me which is the best choice? In truth, I know embarrassingly little about . . . anything."

"My dear, all the young women who have sat across from me at this table were innocent, although few were totally ignorant. However, I shall assume you know nothing at all, and you must stop me if you have a question."

"I do. The same question, actually. In my place, which method would you choose?"

"I would never be in your place, Miss Easton."

Clare stood and regarded her levelly. "Consider yourself fortunate to have been given a choice."

The housekeeper's cold blue eyes held a glint of approval. "Since I lost any claim to beauty before I was out of leading strings, my own choice was confined to

Harry Beales, as ugly-tempered a brute as ever walked this earth until he fell off a horse and hit his head on a rock. I made certain the obliging horse lived like a king for the rest of its life."

She folded her arms across her thin chest.

"Dislike me if you choose, young woman. I have worked for Lord Caradoc these past twelve years, although he tells me I am nosy and insolent. In fact, he has dismissed me eleven times, but always he begs me to come back, with a rise in salary. Should you insist, he'd dismiss me yet again, and I would stay with my sister until another young woman is ready to sit in that chair and learn what she needs to know. It's up to you whether we live in this house together, Miss Easton. Otherwise I shall wait out your tenure elsewhere."

Clare sat, recognizing a force stronger than herself.

Mrs. Beales produced a sour smile. "A wise decision. Now, shall we begin? The only certain way to prevent the birth of a child at an inappropriate time is abstinence. Under the circumstances, we cannot consider that an option, but I wish your understanding to be complete. Your circumstances may change, and what will not do with his lordship may later be your method of choice."

Abstinence would definitely top her list, Clare reflected, once she was free of her debt to the earl.

"Some gentlemen prefer to take the responsibility themselves," Mrs. Beales went on, "whether for lack of confidence in other methods or mistrust of their partners, I cannot say. The earl assures me this will not be possible with you, which is unfortunate. Withdrawal is much the easiest procedure for the female."

"I see." Clare swallowed. "Er—withdrawal of what, exactly?"

Mrs. Beales sat down, regarding her curiously. "Have you no brothers, Miss Easton?"

Her eyes lowered. "No, not precisely. That is, I am aware of certain anatomical differences between the genders and have occasionally witnessed mating between dogs and the like. But somehow I cannot quite imagine how it works." Her gaze lifted. "It all seems exceedingly . . . awkward."

"And so it is, in many ways. When you are more schooled about the physical details, much of what I am about to tell you will make better sense. At that time, I shall be happy to review this lesson. A good argument," she added with a quirked mouth, "for keeping me around. Now"—she drew a small notebook from her apron pocket—"I have written down several recipes, with instructions for everything I am about to describe, so you needn't concern yourself with remembering it all. Just get a general feel for things, and then I'll give you my recommendations."

Clare nodded mutely.

The housekeeper propped her elbows on the table. "We have our concoctions, our insertions, and our barriers. The concoctions, usually brewed into tea or some other liquid, consist primarily of herbs. There are hundreds of such potions, but I have recorded only a few of the most efficacious. To get you started, I prepared a centuries-old gypsy formula." She pushed a small jar across the table. "You must drink a teaspoonful of this mixed into water every morning, but it will take several weeks to become effective. In the meantime, you must also employ another method."

Lifting the jar, Clare held it to the light. The liquid was milky gray, studded with bits of green and globules of black. She set it down, her stomach lurching.

"I cannot recommend the insertions," Mrs. Beales continued relentlessly, "although some have been popular since the Egyptians. On the other hand, Egyptians were especially partial to the use of crocodile dung, which may account for the decline of their civilization."

Clare shuddered. "I believe we can rule out crocodile dung."

"Indeed. But like the Greeks, they also used a mix of honey and gum from the tips of the acacia shrub." She lifted a branch and waved it in the air. "In the absence of fresh acacia, one might substitute olive oil."

"One might," Clare observed glumly, "if one happened to be in a pantry."

Mrs. Beales pushed the exhibit to one side. "Insertions of this sort tend to leave one feeling and smelling like a salad, if not worse. There are, however, some insertions that can be applied immediately after, assuming one has no tendency to fall asleep. Until you are certain you will always remember, I suspect douching is not a good idea. But it carries the added benefit of feeling somewhat fresher, and women often douche in the morning for that reason alone. I recommend a solution of alum, mixed with white oak, hemlock bark, green tea, or raspberry leaves. Should you wish to experiment, I will show you how it is done."

"Thank you," Clare said. "I'll let you know."

"And, finally, the barriers." Mrs. Beales lifted a sheet of oiled, silky paper. "Misugami, from the

Orient. The earl owns ships that trade with Japan, so this is easily come by, but you would require considerable instruction in how to fold it properly. Here is something a bit simpler to manage." Mrs. Beales passed her a disk that resembled a slice of candle. "Beeswax. Easy to get in, not so simple to get out. String may cut through the wax."

Clare was still trying to grasp the concept when Mrs. Beales picked up the large yellow lemon and hacked it in two with a cleaver. Using a spoon, she scooped the pulp from one half and tossed the peel to Clare, who barely managed to catch it.

"This too would require string for removal," Mrs. Beales informed her, "but there is less danger of accident. Casanova swore by the lemon."

Carefully, Clare set it on the table, certain she'd lost her taste for lemonade.

"Now pay close attention," advised the housekeeper. "I expect you'll choose this method until the herb potion takes hold." She picked up the scissors and snipped off the tip of a sponge. "This is about the right size. And make sure to boil your sponges first, Miss Easton. A midwife told me that."

Next she cut three lengths of thread about a foot long and braided them together, tying one end around the sponge. "Dip this in vinegar and insert deeply, making sure the string hangs out. You'll learn to find the moment without destroying the mood, so to speak."

So to speak. In her wildest imagination, Clare could not picture the scene. Like a schoolgirl about to succumb to a fit of giggles in church, she wrapped her arms around her waist, her eyes watering.

"Now, now." Mrs. Beales clucked, shaking her finger. "Nothing to get all worked up about. Keep in mind the earl is well acquainted with this business, and will not be surprised—"

"If I bolt off the bed and start boiling sponges? This is really too ridiculous, Mrs. Beales. Why cannot we use the method you mentioned at first, where I don't have to do anything?"

Mrs. Beales stood and rested her palms flat against the table. "Caradoc does not think he will remember in time." She smiled. "You may consider that a compliment, Miss Easton. Generally, the women are asked to select one of the herbal potions, and he is careful to use preventive measures of his own until they take effect. But it seems that you must take full responsibility, and if that troubles you, pray consider the consequences should you become pregnant before he has sired an heir."

"He would turn me out if I . . . ?" Her voice faded off.

Mrs. Beales gazed at her somberly. "Honor would not permit that. Certainly he would provide for you and the child, but he is most anxious not to complicate the inheritance with scandal. Should a girl be foolish enough to believe she could impel the earl to marry her if she were with child and water a plant with the herbal potion, she would be gone the next day. You seem wise enough to realize he must wed a lady of noble birth and unsullied reputation. You would not wish to put him in a difficult position."

"The last thing I want," Clare assured her vigorously, "is to marry the man. If necessary, I'll even try to figure out what to do with that lemon. Is there anything else?"

Arching her eyebrows, Mrs. Beales picked up the cucumber.

From across the table, Clare stared at it cross-eyed. She took it between her hands when it was passed to her, wondering what was meant by the phrase *as cool as a cucumber.* This one felt hotter than the business end of a poker.

"That," Mrs. Beales said clinically, "is the male member." She held up what appeared to be a sausage casing. "And this is *la capote Anglaise,* as the French would have it. An English riding coat. On this side of the Channel, we call it the French letter." She flapped it in the air. "It is made from the large intestine of a sheep, goat, or calf."

"How very attractive," Clare muttered under her breath.

"In fact, I find it rather clever, although the material is somewhat uncertain. It can split or develop tiny perforations. Before use, it ought to be tested, like this." Lifting the open end to her mouth, she puffed a breath of air and the casing expanded rather like a hot-air balloon. Clare regarded it with awe.

Mrs. Beales came around the table, deflating the odd contrivance and rolling it up. "Once you are certain the device is whole, apply it rather like drawing on a silk stocking, and watch your fingernails." Placing it on the tip of the cucumber, she used the palms of her hands to pull it down snugly. "*Voilà!*"

"Oh, my." Clare held up the sheathed vegetable like a candle. "Is this," she faltered, "a fairly accurate representation of—?"

Laughing, Mrs. Beales removed the casing and tossed the cucumber into the peelings pail. "I cannot say for sure, but women do gossip in this house. From what I'm told, the earl is rather more . . . ripe."

"Oh."

"Just so. But delicious none the less. Now don't you be worrying, Miss Easton. His lordship is not partial to the French letters, and I only told you about them in case you later take a protector who favors such methods. Use the sponge and vinegar for at least four weeks and drink the herbal potion every day. That should do it."

On shaky legs, Clare rose and held out her hand. "Thank you, Mrs. Beales. This has been most enlightening." Her mouth sloped in a forlorn smile. "And mortifying." She gazed for a moment at the exhibits on the table. "Who would have imagined?"

"When the time comes," Mrs. Beales cautioned, "you must remember your responsibility. And that is exactly the time lovers are most apt to forget everything but each other. The earl does not trust himself, so you must take control even when he urges you to forget everything and come into his arms. Men are more . . . *driven* than we, Clare Easton. Always keep your head."

In a daze, Clare climbed into the unmarked coach waiting for her, clutching a packet filled with sponges, thread, vinegar, and the repugnant herbal mixture. She was only grateful that Bryn had chosen not to escort her this morning. It would be impossible to face him right now.

In her mind's eye, he had assumed the form of a large, crisp cucumber.

13

The cat was a bad idea.

From the covered basket on the hackney seat, the outraged feline yowled its own displeasure as Bryn slid another inch away, regretting the impulse that had saddled him with this monster.

The ride back to London, on horseback with the basket nestled between his legs, had been even more unnerving. Sharp claws raked at the woven straw, perilously close to sensitive portions of his anatomy, and the stallion, spooked by his irate passenger, was nearly impossible to control.

Bryn had spent the day at Richmond with Claude Howitt and his family, hoping to distract himself while Clare met with Maude Beales. But everything reminded him of what he'd set out to escape, especially Alice, swollen with her fourth child. He kept looking at his watch, imagining what Clare was doing every minute. Had she arrived at Clouds? Was she disgusted by Mrs. Beales's lecture? Did she despise him for putting her through that ordeal?

The children had played at his ankles and eventually managed to entice him into their games, although he was, as usual, stiff and uneasy in their company. Except for his infrequent visits to Richmond, he never encountered children and had no idea how to relate to them. Still, they seemed delighted when he lost at a game of jackstraws, and even he was laughing when they declared him a horse and took turns riding on his back. He pranced around the room on all fours, now and again rearing up to the sounds of excited squeals while they clung to his neck in mock terror.

Claude watched from his wingback chair, a knowing smile wreathing his face as he puffed on his pipe. Bryn could not help but envy the man. Whenever he visited this house, so filled with contentment and love, he was all too aware how little of either existed in his own life.

After lunch, everyone adjourned to the barn where the children were anxious to show off the newest litter of kittens. Mandycat produced a batch at regular intervals, and the youngsters had strict orders to find homes for them before her progeny overran the small farm—which had given Bryn his bad idea.

He often worried that Clare was lonely, with only servants for company when he was not with her. Perhaps she would like a cat.

When he asked the children to select a candidate, they immediately chose an odd-looking specimen . . . for his personality, they said. The kitten was all white, except for four black paws, black ears and privates, and black splotches above his mouth that resembled an unkempt mustache.

Alice lined a small covered basket with rags and

handed it up when he mounted his horse for the ride home. That was when his troubles began.

He was still amazed that such a tiny creature could make so much noise. When he'd arrived at St. James's Square late that afternoon, he ordered his appalled butler to feed the kitten and adorn the basket with satin and ribbons. Any gift to Clare merited splendid presentation. Then he dispatched a footman to Clouds with a message to expect him at eight o'clock. Tonight he had to win himself back into Clare's good graces, assuming he'd ever been there, after which he would track down Robert Lacey and apologize.

He had skipped dinner, figuring he'd have his fill of humble pie in the hours ahead. And now, as the hackney drew up in the alley behind the house on Grosvenor Square, he felt perspiration gather on his forehead.

Would she appreciate his peace offering? For all he knew, Clare didn't even like cats.

A footman took his hat and gloves, directing him to the salon where Clare was waiting. She wore a simple pale-blue gown and had once again woven her hair into a thick braid that reached to her waist. He could not decipher the glimmer in her eyes as she looked up at him from a deep curtsy.

Not angry, he thought. Nor precisely critical, even after her session with Maude Beales. Her gaze was speculative, perhaps, with a welcome touch of her ironic sense of humor. He bowed in reply and held out the basket. "I've brought you a present."

Immediately her face shuttered. "You have given me too much already," she murmured. "Far more than I've earned."

He stood awkwardly, unsure what to say, and finally set the basket on a table. For once, the kitten was quiet and immobile. "I shall take it back, if you don't like it. To tell you the truth, we are both well rid of the thing."

That seemed to pique her interest. She moved closer, fingering the ribbons that held the lid in place. "More jewels?"

"Open it and see." Then, recalling the animal's belligerence, he held up a hand. "No, allow me." With some effort he untied the ribbon and removed the lid.

Immediately the kitten bounded onto the table, pausing only long enough to rake its claws over the back of Bryn's hand before jumping to the floor.

"Bloody hell!" Bryn stared at the blood oozing from five long welts. Then he looked up to see the demon climbing one of the duchess's expensive Gobelin tapestries. Finally he glanced at Clare, who appeared mildly concerned behind a wide grin.

"Cat scratches can turn putrid," she advised, moving to the door. "I'll be right back."

Bryn used the time to swear fluently at the kitten, which glared back at him from the frieze rail just above the tapestry. The cat was no larger than his hand, but the fur on its back was raised in a gesture of defiance and two malicious yellow eyes challenged him smugly from well out of reach.

The cat, he reflected once again, was a *very* bad idea.

Clare returned with a tray, which she placed on a low table before asking him to sit next to her on a divan. She had removed her gloves, and he was very aware of the scars on her palms as she bathed his hand with warm soapy water.

"This will sting," she cautioned, pouring something that smelled of alcohol over his wounds.

Bryn bit his bottom lip. It burned like hell. When

his jaw unclenched, he managed to say, lightly, "You appear to have some experience as a healer."

"I've treated my share of scrapes and scratches," she acknowledged, dabbing a soothing salve over the throbbing welts. Then she wrapped his hand with a length of soft cloth and tied the ends in a knot. "If you have any serious swelling, and especially if lines of red begin to run up your arm, see a physician immediately."

He studied the bandage for a moment. "Obviously I cannot leave the cat with you. He's a menace."

"I expect he was annoyed after being shut up in a basket. And who wouldn't be?" Crossing to the tapestry, she gazed up at the kitten. "What an absurd little face he has." Immediately the cat began to purr and knead at the ornate rail under its paws.

"You want to keep him?" Bryn asked with some surprise. "I had hoped he might be company for you, but you'll do better with a pet not possessed by the devil. This one has the disposition of a rampaging Hun."

"In that case," she said, tugging a chair to the wall, "I shall name him Attila the Cat."

Bryn helped her climb onto the chair, and she lifted her arms to Attila, still several inches out of reach. In a low voice, she spoke nonsense while the kitten regarded her curiously. After a few moments, he risked a descent down the tapestry until she was able to take hold of him.

Both of them purring, Bryn thought as he watched her gather Attila into her arms. The kitten curled against her breast, altogether content, and for once he respected the fiend if only for its excellent taste. He also wondered if Clare would ever hold him with as much affection.

Thunderation. Now he was jealous of a miserable cat!

Clare returned the placid kitten to its basket, where Attila curled up and promptly went to sleep. Then she placed her hands on Bryn's shoulders, stood on tiptoe, and brushed her lips across his mouth.

"This is quite the nicest present I have ever received," she told him with a smile. "Thank you, Bryn."

Pleased and astonished, he struggled to regather his wits. "I'm glad you like him," he muttered. "But if he becomes too much trouble—"

"I shall deal with it." She chuckled. "I am accustomed to difficult males."

"I expect you are," he said in a serious voice. "Was your encounter with Mrs. Beales altogether repellent?"

Her lashes lowered, but not before he saw the speculative, amused look return to her eyes. "It was most educational. I only hope I remember what to do the first few weeks. After that, so long as I drink the potion she fixed up for me, it seems I can put away the sponges and vinegar."

Her voice grew faint on the last words, and he could tell she found the whole business confusing, and probably repulsive, although she was trying valiantly to hide it.

"Forget sponges and vinegar," he said, drawing her into an embrace. "Drink the herbal mixture, but for the first month or so I shall take responsibility."

She leaned back in the circle of his arms, staring up at him from wide eyes. "But Mrs. Beales said that you could not. You told her so."

"And so I thought. But I will control myself somehow." He grinned. "If nothing else, Clare Easton, you are teaching me discipline. Already I want you so desperately I cannot sleep at night, and my temper . . . well, I have many fences to mend, with all my servants and most of my friends. Nevertheless, until Mrs. Beales tells me there is no longer fear of conceiving a child, I shall do what is necessary."

"But—"

He placed two fingers on her lips. "Let me take care of you, butterfly. I want to. Coping with that demonic cat is difficulty enough. And now I must leave you and go in search of Robert Lacey. If he is still speaking to me, perhaps I can find out when Clouds will be ready for you to move in."

"I had thought Sunday." Her voice quavered. "Tomorrow."

The apprehension in her voice chilled him. How she dreaded their first night together. "There may be a delay," he said quietly. "Don't worry, my dear. I promise not to seize you the moment your trunks are unpacked."

She pulled away. "I am ready whenever you are, Bryn. Do not put things off on my account."

Why else? he thought as the hackney took him to St. James's Street, where he found Robert Lacey at White's, playing whist for high stakes.

A glass of brandy in his hand, he pretended to watch the game until the rubber was done, still thinking about Clare. How ironic, to want her so much that her needs had become more compelling than his own. That had never happened before, with any woman.

After years of tending his dying father, he had quite determined to put his own interests first. Certain sacrifices would be required to keep the promises he'd made, but those he had already accepted. For the rest, he fully intended to enjoy himself.

And so he was, more than ever before. Her pleasure in the cat, her delight with the opera, her relief at being spared the sponges and vinegar . . . hell, one smile from Clare was almost more rewarding than making love to her.

Almost.

Sometimes he had the terrifying certainty that he could only make her happy by letting her go, without ever taking her to bed. Almost, the anticipated pleasure of her joy when he freed her was overwhelming. Now and again he fantasized about it. A part of him wanted to do it.

But in the end, he could not let her go. That much generosity was beyond his strength.

Swearing an oath, Lacey rose from the table and took the glass from Bryn's hand, draining it in a single swallow. "Lost again, damn it all."

With relief, Bryn saw no antagonism in his eyes. "In that case, I'll buy you supper."

"Thanks, but I have to get up early tomorrow. One more drink and I'm off to bed." He drew away from the table as another player took his place.

After signaling to a waiter, Bryn regarded his friend somberly. "I owe you an apology, Robert."

"Belay it. I'd rather keep you in my debt for a while, if only for the free drinks. And here's some good news for a change. Except for the main bedroom and one or two details I'll handle in the morning, Clouds is ready. The bed won't be delivered until Thursday, but meantime Clare could move into the smaller bedroom across the hall. Assuming you are in a hurry to get her out of Ernie's house, of course."

"I am not, but she's uncomfortable there. And anything will be better than the nun's cell she now occupies."

Lacey raised a quizzical brow.

The waiter's appearance saved Bryn from explaining how he knew where she slept. He signed for the decanter of brandy and settled onto a chair.

Lace sat across from him at the small table and clipped the tip from a cigar. "Somebody named Max Peyton is looking for you. Who the devil is he? Never saw him before."

"Just one more rotter I'm indebted to," Bryn said sourly. "Where is he?"

"In the next room, playing backgammon with Alvanley. So, what do you think? Shall we leave Clare where she is?"

Bryn considered for a moment. "No. I'll bring her to Clouds tomorrow afternoon. That will give her time to settle in until the bed—er, the rest of the furniture is delivered. Thursday?"

With a laugh, the viscount lit his cigar. "Why not sleep with her tomorrow night, Bryndle? A smaller bed has some advantages, as I recall."

"Perhaps I will," he said amiably, although he knew he would not. Everything had to be perfect for Clare.

Five days until Thursday. More time to court her, with kisses and flowers. More time to make her want him too.

He came to his feet. "You're a good man, Lace. I'll make this up to you. Finish the brandy while I go find Peyton and see what he wants."

Once again, he found himself watching the end of a game as Max Peyton rolled dice against Lord Alvanley. This time he didn't have to wait long. The baron, his position hopeless, conceded and bowed to his opponent, pausing only long enough to warn Bryn against taking Peyton on at backgammon before moving away.

Feeling challenged, Bryn sat down and arranged the pips in home position. "A monkey?"

"Two," Max replied confidently.

Fifteen minutes later, Bryn had lost a thousand pounds.

"I'm a lucky sod," Peyton said cheerfully as he accepted a scrawled vowel.

"You play well," Bryn acknowledged, forbearing to mention the series of doubles Peyton rolled in the endgame, barely escaping defeat.

"That too. Will you dine with me tomorrow night at Watier's?"

"Have I a choice? As I recall, dinner at my expense was one of your demands."

Peyton brushed a thick wad of tawny hair from his forehead. "So it was, but only at your convenience. Eight o'clock?"

Bryn regarded him curiously. "Any reason you're in such a hurry?"

"Any number of reasons," Peyton responded with a wide smile. "I can scarcely wait for your reaction when you hear them. It should be a most interesting meal."

Bryn would rather spend tomorrow, all of it, with Clare. It would be her first day at Clouds. But perhaps the move would be easier for her if she knew he had other plans for the evening. She could relax, knowing he had no intention of taking her to bed. "Watiers, eight o'clock," he said curtly.

Peyton stood. "Pray convey my regards to Miss Easton."

Bryn looked back at him from the door. "As far as you are concerned, Peyton, she does not exist. Get used to it."

14

Clare had been to Clouds on two other occasions, but this time she felt like a condemned woman mounting the stairs of a guillotine. This time she had come to stay.

She stumbled, and Bryn's arm tightened in support. He drew her to a halt on the stoop and turned to face her, brushing her cheek with his thumb. "Clare, I haven't been here since we . . ."

"Came to terms," she said, when he couldn't seem to finish the thought.

He nodded. "I have no idea what Lacey's done to the house. But when you see it, be honest and tell me what you really think. We can change anything or everything. I want you to feel at home."

He looked even more worried than she felt. "It will be fine, Bryn," she assured him with a smile.

The footman must have been waiting by the door, because it swung open before Bryn lifted the knocker.

"Good afternoon, milord," he said in a lilting Irish accent. "And welcome to ye, milady."

Milady? Her gaze shot to Bryn's in a silent plea.

"Miss Easton will do, Charley," he said, with a touch of amusement in his voice. "Clare, this is Charles Cassidy, in case you haven't been introduced."

They had not, although she had seen the red-headed, freckled young man on her last visit. He was about her own age, with a handsome face, a sturdy physique, and a twinkle in his eyes. She held out her hand. "How do you do, Mr. Cassidy."

Bryn's hand, not Cassidy's, took her own. "Call him Charley, my dear."

Flushing, she looked an apology at the footman, for putting him in an awkward position, and could have sworn he winked at her as he bowed, although his expression was properly deferential.

Bryn must have seen the wink too. In a harsh voice, he ordered Charley to help with the luggage and drew her firmly into the salon.

She regarded the room in wonder. It had been altogether transformed. Now it was warm and relaxing, with wing chairs angled in front of the fireplace and a plush sofa facing a low coffee table. There was also a small desk and chair, a marquetry sideboard, and a rosewood table with an inlaid chessboard. Most of the walls were lined, ceiling to floor, with polished oak bookshelves.

All of them empty.

Bryn muttered an oath. "There should have been books. I failed to see to it."

The duchess's house, although fascinating, had intimidated her, but in this room she felt comfortable. "Everything is perfect, Bryn."

He didn't seem to hear her, apparently still fretting about the lack of books. "We'll fill those shelves together," he promised. "Tomorrow I'll bring over a carriageful. No, I'll send them tonight."

She laughed. "I haven't read all the ones you brought me before. Mr.—Charley is unloading them now."

"Right." He combed his fingers through his hair. "Let's have a look at the other rooms, then." He led her through the formal parlor across the hall, and they peeked into the small dining room before heading upstairs.

Immediately Clare glanced at the closed door of the master bedroom.

"It's not finished," he explained. "The b—the furniture has not been delivered, and I don't expect we can move in for several days. Meanwhile, you'll stay here." He took her into a small bedroom decorated in shades of palest yellow and blue. Fresh flowers were arranged on the dresser and on the table beside the bed.

It was quite the nicest room she'd ever been able to call her own. She rather thought she would sleep here any night Bryn didn't expect her to be waiting for him in the mirrored suite across the hall, stretched out on that platformed bed, wearing one of the flimsy nightgowns Mrs. Beales had insisted on buying. . . .

"Clare?"

Startled from her thoughts, she mustered a smile. "I—"

"You don't like it," he interrupted. "Forgive me. I ought not to have brought you here before checking everything myself."

"The house is beautiful. And have you noticed that all the colors are ones you can see?"

Glancing around, he shrugged. "What's that to the point? Clouds is for you."

"For *us,*" she corrected gently. "At least Robert—Lord Heydon—seems to think so, because the rooms are decorated with both of us in mind. I think he worked wonders, especially with such a limited palette. Has anything appeared brownish to you—except things that really *are* brown, like wood?"

His brow furrowed. "Not that I recall, but mostly I've been looking at your face. And you appear to disapprove."

She crossed to him and gazed into his troubled eyes, reminded of the time Jeremy had coerced Joseph into arranging a birthday gift to her from the both of them and then squirmed when she opened the package because he didn't know what was inside. The Earl of Caradoc was the most commanding individual she had ever encountered, and it never failed to surprise her when he behaved like an uncertain young boy, worried that she wouldn't like what he offered her. He often looked that way, in spite of his incredible generosity to a woman who, so far, had given him nothing in return.

She put one hand on his shoulder. "Bryn, forgive me. I am frightfully nervous. By now I should not be, but I cannot seem to help myself. The house is splendid."

"You are only saying that to make me feel better," he said stiffly.

"As if I would." Her lips curved. "I seize every opportunity to put you in your place, Lord Caradoc. Or haven't you noticed?"

After a moment, he laughed and drew her into his arms. "Indeed I have, hellion."

His embrace led to a kiss, and as it deepened she felt closer to him than she'd ever been, even the night she slept with her head on his shoulder. She wondered if he would take her to bed now, in broad daylight. That was, after all, the only reason she was in this house. Her hands slid under his jacket, wrapping around his waist, and with a low rumble in his chest he pulled her closer.

And then he abruptly set her away, breathing heavily. "I want you," he said.

Unable to speak, she stared back at him.

"But I cannot stay." He turned and moved to the door. "Not even for another minute, or I won't be able to leave." Keeping his back to her—deliberately, she thought—he looked at her over his shoulder. "I stupidly made another engagement for this evening, Clare, to someone who has a claim on me. I owe him a debt and thought to discharge it while you settle in here."

She smiled. "I shall be here whenever you want me."

"Tomorrow I'll take you to lunch, and then to Hatchard's, or perhaps the British Museum. We shall spend the whole day together, doing whatever you like." His expression turned serious. "And we'll we spend our first night together, as lovers, only when you are ready."

Now, she wanted to scream. *Let's get it over with, while you are being so kind to me. While I'm not afraid.*

But he moved into the hall, and she barely heard his last words. "Soon, Clare. I'm not sure how much longer I can wait."

* * *

"I have chosen the wines and the menu," Max informed Bryn at the door of a private dining room at Watier's. "You will be paying, of course."

From the wide grin on Peyton's face, Bryn knew he was in for an expensive evening. And a dull one, making conversation with a man he scarcely knew. But as it turned out, Peyton was capable of maintaining a conversation, or at least a monologue, for the duration of a long, leisurely meal. And to his surprise, Bryn enjoyed his wildly improbable tales about life in India.

"I should travel more," he observed, during a rare break between stories.

"I daresay it would loosen you up a bit."

Bryn lifted a brow.

"Ah, the aristocratic gesture of disdain." Laughing, Max raised his wineglass in a toast. "To British snobbery."

"Someone," Bryn said in a chilling voice, "ought to teach you a few manners."

"It has been tried, with little success. My father eventually shipped me off in the service of the East India Company, with firm instructions not to return until I'd made a man of myself."

"And did you?"

After a beat, Max leaned back and folded his arms. "Most people like me, Lord Caradoc. May I ask why you do not?"

Because Clare smiled at you, Bryn thought immediately. But he couldn't say that. "I am in your debt. It gives you an advantage."

"But once you sign for this meal, equity between us will be restored. Well, not altogether, because I'll still race your curricle when the opportunity arises, but you have already conceded that favor."

"You might have demanded more," Bryn said thoughtfully. "In fact, I expect you intend to do just that. There must be some point to this dinner, besides the dubious pleasure of my company."

"And so there is. I did warn you about a business proposition, although I'd hoped to mellow you first. Clearly my extensive research into your favorite foods and wines has been in vain."

Bryn reached for the port. "Rather too obvious. I resent anyone who pries into my affairs."

"Which I have done," Max confessed without remorse. "To an extent that will put me in your black books for a good long time."

Bryn barked a laugh. "What makes you imagine I'd do business with a stranger, let alone one who admits trying to manipulate me?"

"Perhaps for that very reason. And because the venture I propose will cost you a great deal of money." Max refilled his glass. "Moreover, it will provide no return whatsoever on your investment."

"*What?*" Bryn sat forward. "Are you demented? Why should I spend a minute of my time listening to such an absurd proposition?"

Max shrugged. "Because you are curious, perhaps?"

Bryn didn't bother to deny it. The man knew more about him than his taste in food and wine, to recognize his fascination with the impossible. "I'll hear you out," he said, trying to sound bored. "So long as it doesn't take too long."

With an unsettling look on his face, Max rang for the waiter.

While the table was cleared, Bryn puffed on a cigar and watched Peyton from the corner of his eye. He had come prepared, with a leather case full of papers and maps, and when the waiter was gone he stacked them on the table and resumed his seat. His eyes glowed with enthusiasm.

Bryn felt the familiar tingle a challenge always roused in him and deliberately tried to squelch it. Only a fool entered a business arrangement with no hope of profit. He was curious, nothing more.

An hour later, he was fascinated to an extent that astonished him. Max Peyton's clever, daring scheme had enormous potential, although the early risks were substantial. A large investment would be required at the outset, but that was the least of it.

"As you see," Max explained unnecessarily, "unless we are to wait for years while new vessels are constructed, you will be forced to adjust your current shipping schedule. Radically, I'm afraid."

That was putting it mildly, Bryn thought with an interior snarl. He speculated in land, but much of the Caradoc fortune was derived from trading ventures. Most of the ships he owned outright, although he had established several partnerships in the early days and maintained them for reasons of loyalty. He could never bring himself to abandon the men who helped him get started, even though they'd since become a nuisance.

This new proposal would force him to reorganize nearly every aspect of his business affairs. Peyton wanted more than a financial investment. He was asking him to disrupt profitable enterprises that provided his major source of income.

"Interesting," he conceded, when Peyton had finished his presentation. "If it works—"

"It will, and you know it. John Company is choked by its own bureaucracy, and opportunities go unexplored from sheer inertia. Consider America. It is expanding, with the territory acquired from Bonaparte and most of the continent wide open for development." Max propped his elbows on the table. "Your contacts with markets in the Orient are invaluable. You have both the ships and the access to goods America will be needing in the years ahead. Eventually we'll be cut out, because in my experience Americans prefer to do for themselves, but in the meantime we can make a fortune."

"If so, why did you tell me not to look for a return on my investment?"

"Oh, there will be profits," Max said cheerfully, "but I have plans for them. And that, Lord Caradoc, is the one element of this arrangement you may not take to. In fact, I intend that ever penny be allotted to establish schools for young men and women whose families cannot afford to educate them."

Bryn choked on a swallow of port. "You are setting up a bloody charity?"

"Exactly. Although I do not care for that term." Max reached into the leather case and pulled out another stack of papers. "Part two of my proposal. These you will wish to study in detail."

"The hell I will. As it is, I give a rather substantial amount to worthy causes. I'll not risk everything I've built these last twenty years so you can construct classrooms." His eyes narrowed. "What in blazes made you think I'd even consider it?"

Peyton came to his feet and began to pace the room, hands clasped behind his back. "I have spent considerable time investigating your background, Lord Caradoc. Twenty years ago you came to London, virtually destitute. After selling off an unentailed house and a few family heirlooms, you hired tutors and secured an education. You used your title to ingratiate yourself with merchants, and with daring investments you parlayed a trifling amount of money into a fortune. You were wealthy by age twenty-eight and are fabulously rich at this moment."

"So what?" Bryn leaned back and crossed his ankles on the table.

"Not every impoverished fifteen-year-old comes equipped with a centuries-old earldom to exploit, although many are equally intelligent and resourceful. They only need a chance, and I have set myself to provide it. It will be my life's work, if I can find a partner. Like you, I became rich through my own efforts, but my fortune is a mere tenth of your own. It is not in my nature to start small, Caradoc. To achieve my goal, I require what you have to offer."

"Got religion all of a sudden?" Bryn inquired coldly.

Max came back to the table and leaned over it, palms planted firmly on the waxed cherry wood. "I want something better for myself than I have found so far. In my youth I was careless, and to this day I've no idea how many people I hurt while indulging myself. I killed one man in a duel after he accused me of seducing his wife, which I had. I seduced a great many wives, and ruined any number of young girls. I took callow young men for everything they owned at the gaming tables and spent their money on wine and women. All this, mind you, before I turned three-and-twenty. Then Father exiled me to India, where I realized the uselessness of my former existence."

"Laudable," Bryn said in a drawl, although he was secretly impressed. But why was he still in this room, listening to a confession he didn't care to hear? He looked Peyton in the eye. "For my part, I have seduced no wives nor bedded any woman not already decided on her profession. I've not gambled with reckless young men and have yet to drink myself to oblivion. In short, I feel no compulsion to seek redemption for my sins, as you apparently do, by funding a charity."

Max regarded him levelly. "Did I ever suggest that? You asked about *my* motives, Caradoc, and I explained them. Your own will be quite different."

"So far they escape me. What have I to gain from this endeavor?"

"That is for you to decide." Max pushed the two stacks of papers across the table. "Take these and study them, or leave them here. If you choose to join me in this project, I would ask you to accompany me to Hampshire the day after tomorrow. There are several tracts of land I wish to examine, for the first school. I'll pay for that transaction, and I intend to supervise the—as you put it—*charitable* end of the agreement. But until you see for yourself that I am a competent businessman, you will not be satisfied."

Bryn swung his legs off the table and stood. "For some inexplicable reason, you seem to think I'll buy into your scheme. Tell me why, or I will walk out of here and not look back."

With a grin, Max bundled the papers into one neat stack. "To begin with, you are drawn by the challenge of giving me what I want without losing out yourself. Somewhere in this deal there must be a way to preserve your own steady income while funding the schools. You want to find it. Second, for all your disclaimers, you like me and think we will work well together. Third, you are bored with business as is. You'll enjoy shaking things up and seeing what happens."

His eyes grew solemn.

"Most of all, my instinct tells me you need this project. Examine the proposal and think it over, but go to your heart for the decision."

Bryn cast him a wry look. "That is a ridiculous way to do business, Peyton. I don't aspire to sainthood."

"Nor do I. In theory, you and I will retain the bulk of our fortunes and earn back our losses over time. Although we take financial risk at the outset, the challenge and the goal should more than satisfy us both. Interested?"

"Marginally." Bryn gathered up the papers. "Hampshire, you say? How long would we be gone?"

"Two days at most. As a matter of fact, you need not involve yourself with the schools at all, but I thought we could use the time to become better acquainted. And I expect you'll keep me on a tight leash in early days, until you are convinced I am capable of making decisions on my own."

"Just so." Bryn gazed at him for a moment, wondering why he didn't tell the man *no deal* and walk away. But when Peyton held out the leather case he took it, put the papers inside, and moved to the door. "I hope you know there is little chance I will even consider this proposal, and none at all that I'll accept." He glanced over his shoulder.

Peyton smiled beatifically. "Care to bet on that? Turn me down and I shall hand over what you lost to me at backgammon. In fact, I'll double it."

"Two thousand pounds in my pocket if I say no?" Bryn shook his head. "One hell of a businessman *you* are."

Laughing, Peyton crossed to the door and opened it with a bow. "You have my card. Send word when you've made up your mind. And enclose what you will owe me for losing our wager."

15

"This is an absolute disgrace!"

Bryn suppressed a laugh as Clare stomped around the damp shed constructed alongside the Townley Gallery to house the Elgin marbles.

"How can the government permit these exquisite artifacts to be mistreated in such a way?" she fumed. "I though the whole point of taking the marbles out of Greece was to protect them."

"Not altogether," he said mildly. "Lord Elgin sold them to the government for thirty-five thousand pounds, after eight years of haggling over the price. I suspect his motives were mixed. Don't think to draw me into this controversy, my dear. They are here in England and will probably stay, so get used to it. Greece cannot afford to buy them back, and I doubt the government will give them away in the interests of history."

He took a step back as Clare advanced on him, her

hands curled into fists. "If they remain here, they must be properly cared for. Thirty-five thousand pounds indeed. They are priceless!"

He retreated another step. "I agree. But Montague House is already crammed to the rafters. Until funds are voted to construct a new museum—"

A hard finger jabbed him in the chest. "*You* are the government. Part of it, anyway. Go to the Lords and see that something is done about this travesty. You have influence. Use it!"

He lifted both hands in a gesture of surrender. "I shall make it known that I favor a grand British Museum. But with the war debts, and Prinny squandering a fortune on that monstrosity at Brighton, don't look for anything to happen right away."

"You will make sure that it does," she said with a confident smile. "Come look, Bryn. Have you ever seen anything so beautiful?"

Nothing so beautiful as you, he thought as she towed him from one frieze to the next. They all looked pretty much alike, in his opinion: horses, warriors, assorted goddesses. But he smiled and nodded as she pointed out details he would never have noticed on his own.

They spent another two hours roaming through the collection in the main building. He had visited the museum only once before, royally bored if only because he could not see things as they really were. With his inability to appreciate colors, he had never developed an interest in art or antiquities, preferring books, music, and science. But Clare directed his attention to shape and form, and soon he was captivated by vases, statues, and Roman mosaics.

It was disappointing to emerge from that wonderland into a blinding rainstorm. He had planned to take Clare to Gunter's for ices and pastry but reluctantly directed the driver to Clouds, wondering if she would invite him to stay. Not for the night, of course. He still intended to wait for the bed to be delivered, and for some sign she was ready to welcome him there. But he did not want the day to end.

"What is this?" she asked as the carriage slogged through water-soaked streets.

He glanced where she pointed, to the leather case at her feet. Certain he would reject Max's proposal, he had tossed it into the coach after their meeting and forgotten all about it. "Business papers," he replied. "I'm supposed to look them over."

"Then you can do so before dinner. We shall build a fire, and you can work while I finish embroidering some handkerchiefs for Lady Isabella. Her birthday is next week."

He had forgotten. And how did Clare know so much about a woman she had met only once or twice? But Izzy had a way of making friends, and she would naturally like Clare. He immediately resolved to send a lavish birthday gift.

A few hours later, he leaned back in his chair and stretched broadly, unable to remember when he had spent a more relaxing afternoon. He had stripped to his shirtsleeves and sat at the desk in the salon with Max's papers spread out in front of him, a glass of sherry within reach. By the fire, Clare stitched away on her handkerchiefs, apparently content with the silence and his company.

I could live like this, he thought. I want to live like this, with her.

What would she think of Peyton's absurd scheme? He suspected she would approve of the schools, but the only aspect of the proposal that interested him was the challenge. And the opportunity to increase his fortune. It occurred to him that Max had risked a great deal by entrusting him with these plans. There was nothing to stop him from stealing the idea. On his own, he could realign his trading routes and the products he imported and exported, leaving Peyton and his charities out in the cold.

He would not, of course. But he wondered that Max knew it.

No reason had come to mind why he should gamble his secure livelihood for the sake of educating snot-nosed brats. He ran his fingers through his hair. Who said being rich was easy? The demands never ceased. Clare wanted him to use his influence to finance a new museum. Peyton wanted him to construct schools. And he had yet to restore his own estate on the Welsh marches.

As if reading his thoughts, Clare put aside her embroidery and moved to lean over his shoulder. "What business are you in?" she inquired curiously. "You have never told me."

"Shipping, mostly. But this is a new venture, and I'm not altogether sure what to do. Would you like to hear about it?"

"Yes indeed." She dragged a chair to the desk and sat by his side, her expression eager.

As he outlined the proposal, he was surprised at the pointed questions she asked from time to time—and embarrassed when she pointed out that at one point he had a ship sailing in two directions at once. When he got to the schools, her eyes lit up.

"But that is wonderful!" she exclaimed. "You must do it, Bryn. How can you even consider saying no?"

"I could lose everything I have if this doesn't work," he pointed out.

"It will, with you in charge. And I like Mr. Peyton. He will make you a good partner."

That declaration was almost enough to make him consign the whole idea to the dustbin. He didn't want Peyton anywhere near Clare, especially knowing that she admired him.

But he could not bear to disappoint her. If Clare wanted him to build schools, he would build schools.

"I will do it," he said, "for you."

She went white. "Oh, no. You must not. Not for me."

"You think I am trying to buy you again?" He put his hand on her shoulder. "That is probably true, Clare. I could lie and say I've suddenly developed a profound interest in the education of paupers, but you know better. What I *do* want is to please you, and you will not be be further obligated to me if I decide to accept this proposal. We have already agreed that you are free to walk away after the first night we spend together."

"But you are making it so difficult," she murmured. "Weaving an intricate net, like a spider."

"That is not my intention," he objected. "Or perhaps it is. There is nothing I would not do to make you want to stay. But if I take up this project, I will honor my commitment even if you leave me. Does that help?"

"Not very much. I'd rather you do it because of all the good that will come to so many people."

His throat tightened. "I am not that generous, Clare."

With a smile, she stood and began to gather up the papers. "Whatever you decide, it has nothing to do with us. Mrs. Beales is preparing roast lamb for dinner. Will you stay?"

Did a wolf howl at the moon? He felt like a schoolboy promised a treat. And probably for that reason, he found himself describing his boyhood adventures as they enjoyed a leisurely meal.

Everyone at Heydon Manor had dreaded summer holidays when Robert Lacey came home from Eton and joined forces with Bryn to wreak havoc. Isabella was their usual victim, and with great pleasure he recounted the most outrageous practical jokes perpetrated against her.

Although Clare laughed, it occurred to him that she must secretly disapprove. "I daresay you think me the worst kind of bully, and that I've not changed a great deal in the last twenty-five years."

"Dear me, no. Most boys that age are dedicated to making mischief, although some never outgrow it." She chuckled. "Don't be offended, Bryn. I was not referring to you. Not altogether."

He regarded her balefully. "In my defense, I assure you that Izzy was far from a helpless dupe. She got her own back, and then some. At times her revenge was ferocious."

"Like when you were swimming in the lake and she made off with your—"

Bryn dropped his fork. "Hell and damnation! She told you about *that?*"

Her cheeks white as paper, Clare bowed her head. "I didn't mean to—it just slipped out. Oh, dear."

"Gossipy females," he muttered in a sulky voice. "No man is safe."

Her chin shot up. "As if you had not just finished blabbing tales at Lady Isabella's expense."

He lifted a hand. "Guilty as charged. I yield unconditionally, with humble apologies. Will you throw me out now, or shall we have tea by the fire?"

"Tea," she decided, after giving it enough thought to unsettle him.

Attila, stretched on the hearth, bared his fangs and hissed when Bryn came into the parlor. Clare swept the kitten into her arms and whispered something into his flattened black ears.

From across the room, Bryn watched her closely. She stood straight as a lance, and although her back was turned, he saw the familiar tension return to her body. When she lifted her head to the ceiling, only for a moment, he knew what she was thinking.

Clare assumed he would take her to bed tonight. And while she had apparently resolved to endure his lovemaking, her apprehension heated the air and burned in his throat.

"I cannot stay long, princess," he said quietly. "Tomorrow a business matter will take me out of London, probably for two or three days. Get rid of the cat, if you will, so we can say goodbye in private. And without fear of attack."

Her relief was palpable. He swallowed the pain of it as she shooed Attila into the hall and closed the door. When she turned around, a bright smile wreathed her lips.

"He is generally sweet-natured. I cannot imagine why he dislikes you so."

"I expect he senses your own feelings," he said

after a slight pause. "He wants to protect you from me."

She regarded him in silence for a moment and then shook her head. "Foolish cat. When he comes to know you better he will change his mind. As I have done."

"Have you, Clare? Truly?"

"Truly," she said without hesitation, sweeping across the room into his open arms. "If I seem to be afraid, it is not of you. Never of you."

"Then what? It is not so terrible, even the first time, making love. Sometimes there is no pain at all, or so I am told. Rarely is there pleasure, for a virgin, but I will do everything in my power to make it easy for you."

"I know that," she assured him. "Please, Bryn, take no mind of my private worries. They have nothing to do with our arrangement. If you want to stay here tonight—"

"I do," he interrupted. "I have wanted you from the first time I saw you on the doorstep at Florette's. Every minute I have spent with you since, and every hour I have been alone thinking about you, has only made me want you more. But not tonight, butterfly. You aren't ready. When you are, we both will know it. For now, will you kiss me?"

"Oh, yes," she murmured, tilting her head.

He felt her respond with real desire as their lips met, and then their tongues. So close, he thought, drawing her onto the sofa and lying over her, stroking her breasts as they held each other and kissed for a long time.

So close, but not yet.

After a while, breathing heavily, he pulled himself away. "Sleep well, butterfly. I'll be back on Thursday.

Save the day for me." And the night, he wanted to add, gazing into her beautiful eyes, imagining he saw hunger for him blazing under their smoky camouflage.

She leaned forward and brushed the hair from his forehead. "I shall miss you while you are gone."

Bryn went in search of Max Peyton and found him in a quiet room at White's, reading a newspaper. "I owe you a thousand pounds," he said.

Peyton came to his feet, regarding him for a moment in silence, his expression unreadable. Then he held out his hand.

Bryn took a step back. "I don't have the money with me. Only just made up my mind and took a chance on finding you here."

"I *meant,*" Peyton said with a laugh, "to shake hands on our agreement."

Embarrassed, Bryn obliged. "Don't ask me why I'm doing this," he warned. "I am not sure myself, and more than likely it's because I have taken leave of my senses."

"All the best things are done on instinct. Will you ride with me to Hampshire tomorrow morning?"

"I don't do *anything* in the morning. Make it noon, and we'll take my carriage."

They agreed on plans for the journey and decided to toast their new partnership with a bottle of cognac. But as they stepped into the hall, Robert Lacey met them with a harried expression on his face.

"Gotta talk, Bryn," he stammered. "Now."

Max bowed. "Under the circumstances, I'll be on my way. Until tomorrow, Caradoc."

When he was gone, Lacey seized Bryn's elbow and drew him into the private room. "We've got trouble, old man. Ernestine is back."

"So what? Lucky for us we moved Clare yesterday."

Lacey shook his head. "She knows. How much, and from what source, I've no idea, because Isabella swears she hasn't said a word. But Ernie wants to see the two of us tomorrow afternoon, me at one o'clock and you an hour later. We're in it up to our eyebrows. Got to get our stories straight."

"You think we can bluff her? Not a chance."

Slumping onto a chair, Lacey buried his head between his hands. "Wouldn't be surprised if she knew everything already."

After some consideration, Bryn shrugged. "What does it matter?"

Lacey raised his head, a woebegone expression on his face. "My aunt can slice a roast at twenty paces with her tongue. Easier for you, Bryn. You ain't family. Well, most ways you are, but you never come to the house at holidays, so you don't know what it's like when everybody's mad at you."

"I should think you'd be used to that by now, Lace. But you are right on one count. I have no wish to get on the bad side of the duchess."

"Already are. Thing is, what do we tell her?"

"The truth, I expect. It will be easier to remember. There is no reason," he added pointedly, "to volunteer details."

"Face it, she'll have everything out of me before you get there. At least we can say with a straight face that you never slept with Clare while she was in residence."

Bryn frowned. "As to that, perhaps we need to agree on a definition of terms. The night Elizabeth stayed there, so did I. After you left, I realized I'd stranded myself."

"*What?* You bedded your mistress right under Ernie's roof?" The viscount loosened his cravat. "I might as well sign onto the first ship bound for the Indies. Suggest you come along, Bryndle. We're both doomed."

"I *slept* with her, Lace. In her room and in her bed, but nothing more."

"You think Ernie will believe that? Hell, *I* don't believe it."

"I hardly believe it myself, but that's how it was. A deplorably innocent affair." Bryn sighed. "Don't worry, I'll take full responsibility for everything. I *am* responsible."

"Not for Beth. I did that."

"And Ernestine will commend you for it. Do the best you can and, if she asks, deny being aware I stayed there overnight. I'll confess to that, unless I figure out she doesn't know."

Lacey rose and stared down at him with a grim expression. "Two o'clock, and don't be late. I'll meet you here when it's over, to compare notes. Assuming we are still alive."

16

The duchess kept her nephew well past the allotted hour, while Bryn cooled his heels in the foyer. When Lacey finally emerged, wiping his brow with a handkerchief, he waved a hand in a gesture of futility and stumbled past without a word.

A broken man, thought the earl with some amusement as he headed down the long hall to the library. But nothing Ernestine could do or say would possibly affect *him.* He was not, as Robert had pointed out, family. After an unpleasant few minutes, during which he would apologize sincerely, he'd be on his way.

Everything would be different had the duchess returned one day earlier, to find Clare in this house. He shuddered to think of it. Not for the world would he want Clare subjected to one of Ernie's tirades. But the two women would never meet, thank the stars.

The duchess had chosen to conduct her inquisition from behind an imposing desk of vaguely oriental design. When he came into the room, she glanced up from some papers she was studying. "I'll be with you in a minute, Caradoc. Do sit down."

With a theatricality he admired, she had placed a spindly hard-backed chair directly in front of her desk, to increase the discomfort of her victims. He arranged his long body in a pose of apparent disinterest, with legs stretched out and arms folded across his chest.

He had not seen her for years, but she never really changed. Tall, thin, and angular, her gray-streaked blond hair clipped in a mannish bob, she was the most eccentric of the unconventional Laceys. Decades ago, she'd come to stay at Heydon Manor after her husband was killed at Santa Cruz. Ernie, who freely admitted she married Roger Fitzwalter only for the independence his money gave her, had chafed at the bit while the period of mourning dragged out. That was, coincidentally, the happiest time of Bryn's life, the last year before his father came home to die. He was eleven, Robert ten, and the two of them ran mad together.

Robert's parents rarely disciplined their children, and Bryn privately considered Lace and Izzy a tribute to loose reins. But Aunt Ernestine was less tolerant of their misdeeds, although she never raised a hand to them. A beating would have been preferable to the way she picked a miscreant apart flaw by flaw and left the pieces writhing on the floor.

It was almost twenty-five years since she'd called him on the carpet for some prank, but his mouth felt similarly dry and his fingers twitched. This is ridiculous, he thought, watching her through narrowed eyes as she pretended to ignore him. He was a grown man. Damned if he'd be intimidated.

"If I apologize humbly, and with remorse," he drawled into the silence, "you will be free to read your letters without an audience."

The duchess pushed her round wire-rimmed glasses up her nose. "Still insolent, after all these years. You astound me, Caradoc."

"I doubt that," he replied easily. "But I have offended you and abused your household. For that I am genuinely sorry."

"I intend to make certain you are. Did you actually hope to escape with a few glib words and without an explanation?"

"I assumed you'd have sucked Robert dry by now. Surely there is nothing I can add to the story. But I am curious how you found us out. We took great care to conceal our presence here."

She tapped a finger on the table. "Thank heavens you were not a strategist on Wellington's staff. We'd have lost the war."

"I *was* a strategist with Wellington," he murmured uncomfortably. Did she not know that? But of course she did.

"Indeed? Since you were unable to smuggle one female in and out of this house without the world knowing about it, however did you manage to put anything over on Bonaparte?"

His collar began to feel tight. "Two females. There were two."

"Under the circumstances, Miss Landry was welcome, and that situation is nothing to the point. I am only surprised Robert had the presence of mind to hide her here. My business with you concerns a bit of muslin."

"Clare," he said icily, "is not to be insulted. She did

not want to stay in your house, but I assured her you would not object so long as we were discreet."

Clasping her hands on the desk like a headmistress, she regarded him as she might a schoolboy who had sneaked a frog into the classroom. "And what did you imagine I'd think, returning to find my staff happily recounting an extended holiday while the neighbors carried tales of unmarked coaches and men skulking in and out through the back door."

"Nosey old gossips. The fact is, I'd nowhere else to put her until Clouds was refurbished."

She harrumphed. "Your mistress is too refined for a hotel?"

His eyes flared. "I wasn't altogether certain this house was prime enough for the young lady. But we made do."

"Hoity-toity." Ernestine bit back a smile. Caradoc's arrogance never failed to divert her. She also remembered the brave young man too proud to accept help as he tended his dying father. Bryn had tried desperately to protect Owen Talgarth from humiliation and spare his friends the horrors he endured all those years.

She had respected him then, far more than now, and preferred the boy who struggled to restore the family fortune to the self-indulgent creature he became once he succeeded. Not that she blamed him. She was only sorry for it.

During her long, silent appraisal, Caradoc began to wriggle slightly on his chair. Again, she suppressed a smile. "What should be your punishment, I wonder?"

He sat straighter. "Whatever you decide, your grace, reserve it for me. Lacey is not to blame, because this muddle was all my doing. Tell me how I can make it up to you and I will, although I never imagined you'd give a fig for the scandal."

"What scandal?" she inquired serenely. "I have lived in this house nigh forty years, and my neighbors are as close-mouthed as they are observant. What they saw was conveyed to me only. If word is out elsewhere, it is due only to your ham-handed conduct."

He frowned. "If I understand you," he said carefully, "I am here not because your reputation has been in any way compromised but only so you can ring a peal over me."

"Precisely. And because the neighbors could only report what transpired in the alley behind the house. I want to know what went on behind closed doors. And how it was you and Robert dared to stash a Cyprian in my home. Heydon never did have good sense, but I hadn't thought you'd risk the Talgarth reputation, what's left of it, with a bumble-broth."

The earl studied the tips of his polished boots. "Nor I," he admitted. "The situation was . . . unusual. And I assure you, Miss Easton was not my mistress while she remained in your house. She came here, and left, as innocent as Miss Landry."

"Balderdash. That defies all credibility."

"As I said, the situation was unusual." He chuckled. "And not at all to my liking. So, now that you are acquainted with the facts, what do you intend to do?"

"Make further inquiries," said the duchess with a glint in her eyes. "I shall meet this mysterious Clare Easton and determine if she was a suitable houseguest. If I approve her, you may yet escape my wrath."

Bryn came to his feet and leaned over the desk, his palms flat against the lacquered ebony wood. "Clare is not to blame, in any way, for this tangle. I'll not have her subjected to one of your inquisitions."

"You forget who I am, Caradoc."

"And you forget I am no longer a child."

"Indeed? From where I sit, you have behaved exactly like a randy young buck with no thought beyond the satisfaction of his own pleasures. Brynmore, you are a great disappointment to me. I expected better things, after an admirable beginning, although I do not wholly fault you. Nevertheless, it is past time you consider exactly what you have become."

Straightening, he gave her his most imperious stare. "What I am, or what I do, is none of your damned business."

"Now stamp your foot, there's a good boy. I do so enjoy a tantrum."

Feeling suddenly breathless, Bryn lowered himself onto the frail chair. "I am beginning to admire Lace for walking out of here on his own two feet," he muttered. "But under no circumstances will I introduce you to Clare. It is out of the question."

"Are you ashamed of her?"

He fixed the duchess with a look that would have shattered anything less solid than granite. "Leave her alone," he said in a commanding voice. "She hated staying here and was terrified you would find out. I don't want her to know that you did."

"So that's how it is." With an ominously smug expression, Ernestine leaned back and waved her hand. "You may go now."

He regarded her suspiciously. "What does that mean?"

"Heavens, boy, all words of one syllable. You may go. Now. I'm done with you."

He felt he'd just lost the game without ever knowing the rules. "You'll stay away from Clare?"

She rose and stared down her nose at him. "Like you, impertinent young man, I shall do exactly as I please. And if you've a remnant of good sense you'll hie yourself out of here before I ask why the tapestry in my salon is torn to shreds, and why the carpet smells as if something pissed on it."

Without another word, Bryn made a hurried exit.

A few minutes later, Ernestine stepped into her carriage and directed John Coachman to the house on Half-Moon Street where Bryn usually stored his mistresses.

The harlot, Ernestine decided, was far more poised than Caradoc or her reprobate nephew had been.

With consummate grace, Miss Easton invited her surprise visitor into a tastefully fitted salon lined with bookshelves, requested refreshments, and sat regally on a Sheridan chair with her hands clasped in her lap. She seemed not at all apprehensive, gazing at the duchess with the unblinking calm of a young woman physically in the room but otherwise very far away.

"I trust you enjoyed my hospitality," Ernestine said, reaching for a biscuit.

"Your home," Clare replied in a soft voice, "is vastly intriguing. Like a map of the world in art. I felt everything there had been chosen for a special reason, because it meant something to you. Although I saw only a few rooms, your touch was everywhere. What an interesting life you have led."

Ernestine caught her breath, sensing a blow to the heart. "Liked it, did you? When you come to call, I'll show you the rooms you didn't see. Most everything was under Holland covers, but I've antiquities the British Museum would pay a pretty penny to own, not counting what I brought back from this last trip. Shame to take them out of the country, of course, but they're not being properly cared for now. One day, I hope to send them back."

"Certainly they must be preserved," Clare agreed sedately. "His lordship took me to see the Elgin marbles, and I was horrified to think of them being cut up for building blocks like so many other Greek temples. We are fortunate the war did not reach here and destroy our own heritage. I expect Napoleon would have carted off the Tower of London, if he'd got the chance, and reconstructed it on the Champs-Élysées."

A harlot with an appreciation of history. Ernestine bit her lip. Were she introduced to this young woman at Almack's, she'd have been taken by her intelligence and good breeding.

Clare felt her heart beating wildly and wondered if the duchess could hear it. She had never in her life been so nervous, not even when Bryn commanded her to remove her clothes. For that, she had prepared herself, but the ordeal seemed trivial compared to sitting across from this imperious aristocrat who had every reason to despise her.

"I won't bite you, girl," said the duchess, as if sensing her agitation. "It was fortunate I was from home when you required the use of my house. To be frank, I'd not have welcomed you there, which would have been my loss. But as things played out, we shall now have the opportunity to become friends."

At that, Clare's poise dissolved. "Indeed, we cannot," she stammered. "I never expected to escape easily, whatever Lord Caradoc and the viscount said. Men see only what they wish to see. Of course you must be angry with me, and furious that I violated your home. I only hope my being there will not reflect badly on you, and cannot think what to do except beg your forgiveness."

"For now," said the duchess, holding out a small plate, "you must have something to eat. One is always uncomfortable chewing alone, don't you think? And I cannot resist Eccles cakes. Indulge me, for I've just come from where such treats are unobtainable."

Reluctantly, Clare picked up a cake and nibbled it, her gaze lowered.

"It has been my profound pleasure," Ernestine continued, "to strip a piece from the hides of Caradoc and Heydon. The earl was somewhat less humbled than I intended, but he is a difficult man to stagger. My nephew crumbled immediately and will not make so free with my abode in future. Although he does not know it, he is to inherit everything—with the provision he cherishes my antiquities and sends them home when times permit. I would rather you did not let him in on the secret. The boy is overfond of gaming, and I don't want him wagering on his expectations before I've popped off. If he ever grows up, takes a wife, and sets about a decent occupation, there will be something for his old age and his children. A good man, my nephew, but he's not got his feet on the ground."

Clare regarded her blankly, nonplussed by the confidences entrusted to her.

"As for Caradoc, he has his two feet planted firmly in a rut. It never ceases to amaze me how long a stubborn man will continue on a given road before realizing it does not lead where he wishes to go. Bryn chose his direction when he was barely out of short pants and has never looked back. Now he's stumbled into a mire, which may be his salvation." She took a sip of tea. "I am making no sense to you at all, I daresay, but you must know that all Laceys are passing mad."

Clare had no idea how to respond to that. "I am surprised to hear that you spoke with him today. The earl told me he would be leaving town on business."

The duchess grinned. "My summons took precedence, and rightly so, but no doubt he is on his way as we speak. I expect he will keep his distance as long as possible. In the meantime, we can become better acquainted."

"Surely that is impossible," Clare murmured helplessly. "You must know what I am."

"I do not. Nor does Caradoc, and neither do you. So while we all stumble about in the dark, let us at least hold hands. Come for luncheon tomorrow. I shall invite Isabella, for Robert told me that you and she have become great friends. The three of us will have a pleasant coze together."

Clare rose and crossed to the window, clutching her skirt with both hands. Indeed the Laceys were mad, all of them. Robert and Isabella treated her as an equal, although she was so far beneath them she scarcely breathed the same air. Now this forbidding and oddly charming woman offered her own friendship. To a whore.

It made no sense. She didn't understand. She stared into the small garden, eyes burning.

The duchess came up behind her. "You must learn to trust, Miss Easton. I would not lie to you."

"Of course not." She sucked in a deep breath. "But what am I to do?"

"Whatever I say. Caradoc would tell you that I am relentless. And since he is headed out of town, you are free to spend the day with me tomorrow."

Ever since Bryn told her he might be away for several days, Clare had tried to formulate a plan for a trip of her own. Until now it seemed impossible, but suddenly a door had opened—if she dared trust this remarkable woman.

She whirled around. "Your grace, might I ask a favor?" Her cheeks felt hotter than a stove. "I wish to leave London for a day, without anyone knowing. But if I go, Mrs. Beales will tell the earl. She's the housekeeper."

"I know." Ernestine cocked her head. "Still, if Beales assumed you were with me . . . yes, that would work. Caradoc won't like it, but at least he will not suspect you were off on your own business. I don't suppose you'd care to tell me what that is?"

Clare lowered her gaze. "It is personal. And I shall be back by late afternoon, if I catch a mail coach early in the morning."

"Indeed you will not travel on a common mail coach, Miss Easton. My carriage will be at your disposal." She lifted a hand. "Don't think to argue, for you cannot possibly win. We shall create the illusion that you have spent the day in my company." She chuckled. "And if Caradoc quizzes you, tell him I gave you firm instructions not to discuss the matter with anyone. Considering our last encounter, I doubt he'll apply to me for further information."

Clare could not help but smile. "Does everyone dance to your tune, your grace?"

"Yes indeed. Look how quickly you have fallen into step. We shall deal together famously, and I expect you to make our lie into a truth by spending a day with me in the near future. Perhaps we'll sort through my new acquisitions together. You would enjoy that?"

Clare nodded, suddenly overwhelmed by what had happened in the last few minutes. She had dared to ask yet another stranger, one with any number of reasons to disdain her, for help. Why was everyone so kind—Flo and Isabella, Robert and Elizabeth, and now the duchess? She could never repay them.

It was almost like Heaven was smiling on her, even as she damned herself. Impulsively, she held out her hand and felt it seized warmly. "Thank you," she said. "I cannot tell you how important this is to me."

"You need not. I see it in your eyes. But if ever you want someone to confide in"—the duchess winked—"you know where I live." Releasing her hand, she went to the bellpull. "Now I shall explain to Beales that you are to be my guest tomorrow. Then I'll make sure Caradoc has left town, and send word what time my carriage will pick you up. You are going to . . . ?"

After a beat, Clare replied, "Berkhamsted."

"See, that wasn't so difficult. A tiny confidence, and our secret. We Laceys adore secrets. And we keep them."

A few minutes later, when the duchess was gone, Clare devoured two slices of apricot tart and what remained of the Eccles cakes, her appetite magically restored. Then she sped upstairs to consider her wardrobe.

Her appearance would be important, if the tale she had manufactured about her new job in London was to hold up under Joseph's intense scrutiny. Jeremy, rather like Bryn, believed what he wanted to, but Joseph was not easily fooled.

She set out a gray walking dress of Circassian cloth for Amy to press, along with a darker pelisse trimmed with black crape. Plain but elegant: just the sort of thing a companion to a wealthy elderly lady would wear.

She was considering bonnets when the knocker sounded, and her heart sank. Bryn?

But it was only a note from him, delivered with a lavish bouquet of flowers. He was traveling to Hampshire but had gotten a late start and would not return until Thursday evening. After his signature, he wrote, *I shall miss you.*

Delighted as she was that everything had fallen into place for her own journey, she realized she would miss him too. She sat on the edge of a chair, fingering the soft flower petals, wondering at that for a long time.

Things had been easier when she didn't like him. Her guilt was easier to bear when she had to suffer his company instead of looking forward to it. And if ever she allowed herself to care for him . . .

But she would not. Bryn was like a sweet cake. Only a fool refused to enjoy a rare treat, and only a greater fool was unable to set small pleasures aside when necessary. Soon enough she would forget the taste of him. It wasn't as though she had any choice.

Meantime, she had tomorrow. She hugged herself with glee.

Tomorrow she would see the only two people in the world she loved. The two young men she valued above all else.

Even her soul.

17

The headmaster of the Langbourne School for Young Gentlemen welcomed Clare graciously, in spite of her arrival without advance notice on a non-visiting day. Mr. Turbridge was a slender man, in his sixties she would guess, with a firm chin and kind eyes.

"Fine youngsters, Joseph and Jeremy," he observed, ushering her into a large sunny parlor. "You can be proud of them both."

"I have always been so," she replied with a smile.

He clasped his hands behind his back. "You'll be wanting a report on their progress. While you visit, I shall speak to their instructors and prepare a summary. Be assured they have both done well. From all accounts, Joseph is quite the finest scholar at Langbourne, although Jeremy's schoolwork is somewhat less, er—"

"You needn't explain." Her brows lifted. "I only hope he's not been up to his usual deviltry."

Flushing slightly, Mr. Turbridge shook his head. "Boyish pranks, but harmless. I've rarely met a child with so much energy. He's quite the favorite of the other boys, if rather trying on the patience of his teachers. They are fond of him, though. Jeremy is remarkably sweet-natured."

"I am most relieved that you understand that. He can be a scamp."

"Indeed. But he is especially kind to the smaller children. Takes them under his wing and protects them from the bullies. As I said, Miss Clare, you have reason to be proud of your brothers. They have only been here a few months, and already I foresee bright futures for them both."

Nothing could have pleased her more. Clare gave him her brightest smile, which caused him to flush even more hotly.

"I believe they are taking exercise," he said, moving toward the door. "I'll see they are cleaned up and have some refreshments brought in." He paused and turned around. "Miss Clare, we have no way to contact you, in case one of the boys becomes ill. You would wish to be informed?"

"Dear me, yes." Clare had not considered that possibility, but of course she must give the school some way to reach her. She bit her lip. Clouds was out of the question. "You may send a message to me in care of a friend." She gave the duchess's address at Grosvenor Square.

Clearly impressed, Mr. Turbridge bowed. "I shall see you again before you depart. Enjoy your visit."

When he was gone, she went to a window and gazed out over the sweeping lawns. In the distance, boys ran about chasing balls and playing tag. Their laughter and shouts floated back to her, and she pressed her cheek against the glass to hear more clearly. How long sincc she'd listened to children having a good time? Laughter had been strictly forbidden in the house after her father died.

She was not surprised that Mr. Turbridge welcomed her in such a friendly manner. The one other time she'd been here, to deliver the twins, she could offer only token payment with the promise of more to follow. Since then, she had been able to send funds to cover several years of tuition and board—thanks to Bryn. Now Joseph and Jeremy had a safe haven.

Joseph was brilliant, almost a prodigy. He might earn a scholarship to Oxford or Cambridge, and she rather expected he'd become a cleric like her father. A shiver ran up her spine. Not if her profession became known, to him or to the people who could see to his advancement. Above all, her secret must be maintained. Or was that even possible, with Bryn determined to take her out in public? Still, there was no reason for anyone to associate Clare Easton with Joseph and Jeremy Clare.

They were not her brothers by blood, although her father had given them his name. Clare had been ten years old when a young woman with wild eyes came to the small village where Terence Clare served as vicar. Widowed soon after his daughter was born, he found solace for the loss of his beloved wife in drink.

Ardis—she would never reveal her surname—was hungry and desperate the day she appeared at the church, begging the vicar to help her. She had been abandoned by the man who had promised to marry her, and her parents had cast her off.

With the impulsive kindness Clare remembered in

her father, he immediately took the woman into his home. And married her, to prevent the child she carried from being marked a bastard. By then, drinking had sapped his health, and even his sermons were seasoned with wine as he delivered them in a frail, halting voice. He died five months after the wedding, before the twins were born.

Clare, still mourning her father, was left alone with the strange, embittered woman. They moved from the vicarage to a small cottage, where the widow and the young girl were supported at the mercy of the new vicar and the kindness of the parishioners. When the infants were delivered, their mother could scarcely bear to look at them. A wet nurse fed them, and Clare did everything else. She poured out all her love on the two boys and chose their names when Ardis expressed no interest in the matter. Joseph and Jeremy were more like her own children than her brothers, although she was herself a child when they were born.

Clare hugged her waist. Her father had married Ardis, a virtual madwoman, to give the boys a name. Now she whored herself to give them a future. But she could not regret that. She had even managed to stop hating her stepmother.

Ardis was living proof that a woman could lose everything for love, including her mind. She had been a beautiful woman, with heavy blond hair and light blue eyes. The vicar had blue eyes too, and people thought it odd when the twins' eyes turned to tawny brown a year after their birth.

Ardis pretended they didn't exist, until they were active toddlers and impossible to ignore. Then the harsh discipline she visited on her stepdaughter fell on them too. It was all Clare could do to protect them.

As the years passed, Ardis withdrew more and more into her own world, becoming little more than a shadowy presence, rocking in a creaky chair with her arms clutched to her sides, reciting psalms in a dull monotone. Her death was a relief to everyone.

By then, the copper mine that supported the community was failing. With the parish no longer able to provide for them, Clare took the twins to London and sought a position as a seamstress. Even working sixteen hours a day, she could only afford two bleak rooms in a crowded, derelict neighborhood. There was little money left to feed the boys, who grew thin eating bread and the occasional meat pie.

On her day off she tutored them, and Joseph saw that Jeremy kept up with his lessons while she was working. It was dangerous for them to go outside, although Jeremy could not bear to be cooped up. She worried about them constantly.

After a year of bleak subsistence, she began to consider applying to Edna Halperth for assistance. Clare had kept everything that belonged to the mother she never knew, including her correspondence. Edna had been her mother's closest friend in childhood, although when she went to London she changed her name to Florette LaFleur and candidly admitted that she had taken up a profitable but dishonorable profession.

Strictly raised, Clare was unable to bring herself to contact Florette until a pair of drunken thugs accosted her in the street. Jeremy and Joseph rushed to help and were soundly beaten before a shopkeeper entered the fray. Joseph's arm was broken, and Jeremy had two cracked ribs.

The next morning she walked four miles to Florette's Hothouse and begged for help.

Florette immediately offered to provide anything the daughter of her childhood friend required. She made it sound as if she were in debt to Clare's mother, pleased to return the favor at last.

Clare knew better and was too proud to accept charity. She had given her plan a great deal of thought and managed to present it with scarcely a quaver in her voice. For ten thousand pounds, she would sell herself—if Florette could find a buyer.

At first, Florette protested vehemently, but then her eyes narrowed. After a long silence, she placidly agreed to Clare's proposal. She knew just the man who might be interested.

And a few days later, garbed in the blue dress and veiled hat Florette provided, Clare had waited by the door at the Hothouse for the arrival of the Earl of Caradoc. . . .

"Easter!"

She swung around to see Joseph and Jeremy at the parlor door. Her arms opened as they tore across the room for a warm hug.

After a long minute, she reluctantly let them go and stepped back to have a good look. Their sandy hair was freshly washed and sleeked back over high foreheads and golden eyes. Their blue coats were almost too tight. The twins had filled out, with good food and exercise. They were twelve years old, on the verge of manhood, but it seemed like yesterday that she'd changed their nappies.

A servant entered, carrying a tray laden with glasses of lemonade and an assortment of sandwiches, biscuits, and pastries. Predictably, Jeremy hurried to grab a strawberry tartlet.

Granted time to compose herself, Clare sat on the

sofa and sipped some lemonade while the boys, with surprisingly impeccable manners, settled across from her.

"I've missed you," she said softly.

"About time you showed up," Jeremy said with a full mouth.

Joseph regarded her with serious eyes as he drank his lemonade, while Jeremy chatted happily about learning to play cricket and ride. The school boasted a stable, and apparently he spent all his free time helping the ostlers.

"He's gone horse-mad," Joseph said when Jeremy's monologue wound down in favor of a roast beef sandwich. "Tell us how you are doing, Easter. We've heard nothing from you."

She set down her glass. "I know. And I apologize." How she hated to lie to them. Forcing a smile, she explained that she had found a good position as companion to an elderly person who was, unfortunately, somewhat eccentric. For that reason she was well paid, but certain restrictions had been imposed upon her. She could have no visitors and might not be free to visit Langbourne again for a long time. But she was content. More than that. *Happy,* with a pleasant employer, lots of books to read, and comfortable surroundings.

Joseph regarded her dubiously. "Sounds haveycavey to me. May we at least write to you?"

"Of course," she said, after a moment. "I've already given Mr. Turbridge the address. We recently moved, and things have been somewhat unsettled. But from now on I shall write to you too, every day."

"Some of the chaps have horses of their own," Jeremy said in a hopeful voice.

Joseph punched him on the shoulder. "Ask for the moon while you're at it, gudgeon. Hasn't Easter done enough for us? And she ain't even our real sister."

Eyes burning, Clare looked away. She had told them the truth about their parentage, after much interior debate, when they were old enough to understand. It seemed right that they should know, and besides, she always hated lies. Every time she told one, her heart ached.

It had become a familiar feeling.

She wanted to give Jeremy a horse. The moon, if he required it. Perhaps she could sell the necklace Bryn had given her. . . .

"I'm sorry, Easter." Jeremy reached across the table and touched her arm. "I was selfish to ask. Far as I'm concerned, you are the best sister a fellow could have."

She patted his hand. "And you are a wonderful little brother."

"Easter?" Joseph looked ashamed. "I didn't mean—"

"I know." Clare smiled at him. "You were trying to say that I owe you nothing, but that isn't so. I love you, Joseph. Nothing is more important to me than my two boys. And it makes me happy to see you in such a fine school, so in a way I'm being selfish too."

"We'll pay you back, soon as we can," Jeremy promised. "I'll study hard so I can get a good position. You'll see. Then you won't have to take care of an eccentric old aristocrat."

She suppressed a grin, imagining Bryn's reaction to that unflattering description. So often he reminded her of Jeremy—impetuous and self-absorbed but quick to repent his mistakes. Lovable rascals, the both of them. "I quite like my eccentric aristocrat," she said. "There's a wonderful library at the house, and I've been to the theater and the opera."

For the next hour she painted a colorful if inaccurate picture of her life in London, trying to assure them she had made no sacrifices on their behalf. Jeremy was delighted at her adventures and quizzed her incessantly about earls and dukes she must have met. He knew his father was an aristocrat, if Ardis had told the truth, and Clare suspected he was hoping she'd run into the man, recognize him immediately, and tell him about his two sons. Always a dreamer, Jeremy expected the impossible.

Joseph sat quietly, his brow furrowed as if suspicious of her story. He had an uncanny way of seeing past bright smiles and clever lies, perhaps because she'd had little else to offer him in the past few years. But he said nothing, if only to make things easier for her.

Dear God, how she loved them.

Too soon it was time to say goodbye. Jeremy tried to hide his sniffles behind a brave front, while Joseph squeezed her hand and unabashedly kissed her on both cheeks.

She hung out the window of the carriage to wave at them. Mr. Turbridge stood between the boys, his arms draped over their shoulders protectively, and when they were out of sight she leaned back against the squabs with a sigh.

They were in good hands. She had done the right thing.

That conviction solidified as the coach trundled toward London, her heart growing lighter with every turn of the wheels.

Ever since she had made her decision and applied to Florette for help, she had been preoccupied with what she was giving up—her reputation and her innocence in this world and her salvation in the next. Almost forgotten was the goal, the reason for everything. Seeing the boys again restored her certainty that she had taken the right road.

The only one open to her, she reflected, but so much smoother than she ever imagined. Bryn was wonderfully kind, when he needn't be. And so generous, without reward. If she left him after their first night together, the contract would be fulfilled and she could walk away, knowing the twins were safe. He had given her that right.

She gazed out the window at the placid sheep grazing beyond the whitethorn hedgerows. Perhaps one day she would have a peaceful life in the country, raising chickens and doing piecework for a village dressmaker to support herself. For most of her life that had been her dream, but now it seemed strangely uninviting. Positively dull, after Bryn.

She could hardly wait to see him again.

From now on, she would do everything in her power to please him. So long as he wanted her, or until he married, she would be the best mistress he ever had. That much, at least, she owed him, and it was all she had to give.

How to go about it was another question, but she was no longer reluctant or afraid to become his lover. Not altogether, anyway.

Deliberately, she set aside her fears. Bryn had, without knowing it, provided Joseph and Jeremy with an education, security, and a future. In return, she would devote herself to repaying the debt.

* * *

The next morning, a letter arrived from Hampshire. Bryn would return to London late Thursday afternoon and wished to escort her to the opera that evening.

A peek into the larger bedroom confirmed that the bed had been delivered while she was gone. No mirrors, she saw, except the one over the dressing table. And no platform either. Only a lovely room, done up in shades of blue, cream, and yellow, with an enormous canopied bed draped with billowy curtains.

Attila wound around her legs, rubbing his nose against her ankles. She picked him up and hugged the kitten to her breast. Tomorrow night she would sleep with Bryn in that bed.

It was time.

18

Clare was different.

Bryn saw that immediately, although he wasn't sure what had changed. Lovely as always, her hair caught up in a loose knot on top of her head, she greeted him with a sweet smile when he came into the salon at Clouds.

Gaze fixed on her face, he bowed and kissed her gloved hand. "I was bereft without you," he said.

"You were gone only three days," she replied with a laugh. "But I missed you too."

She meant it, he could tell. His heart jumped to his throat. The apprehension he always sensed in her was absent. Clare was really glad to see him. It showed in her eyes, for once unclouded with fear of what he might demand of her.

His shoulders and back, tense since he made up his mind to bed her tonight, relaxed. There would be no struggle and no resistance from her. She was ready too.

Probably because the bed had been delivered, he reflected cynically. When he returned from his trip to Hampshire with Max Peyton, he found a message from Lacey assuring him everything was fitted out at Clouds. Clare understood there was no further excuse for delay.

But she didn't seem to mind. At the least, she would lie without reluctance in his arms. He was afraid to hope for more than that.

"I have another present for you," he confessed, wondering why that made him feel guilty. "Jewels again, I'm afraid."

"I shan't like them so much as the kitten," she warned. "Attila is shut away, if you are concerned about an imminent attack."

"That rotter had better get used to me, because I expect to spend a lot of time here." He opened the silver box and held it out for her inspection. "Sapphires, Clare. I'm glad you wore blue tonight. The necklace will suit that gown."

She fingered the stones, set in gold, and turned around so he could fasten the clasp. "Thank you, Bryn. It's lovely."

Unable to resist, he placed a light kiss at her nape. To his astonishment, she leaned back against his chest. He wrapped his arms around her waist and they stood for a moment in silent communion. She smelled of lavender. He breathed deeply, savoring the fragrance and the softness of her body. Most of all, her surprising willingness to be held in his embrace.

Yes, they would make love tonight. They both knew it.

Almost, he was tempted to take her upstairs straightaway. But he stepped back and combed his fingers through his hair. "We'll hear my favorite opera tonight, princess. I have always loved Mozart."

"Then I shall love him too." She touched his cheek with one finger. "You have given me music, Bryn. I prize that gift above sapphires and gold. Perhaps even more than kittens."

Flushing, he moved toward the door. "I need to speak with Mrs. Beales for a moment."

"Be careful then. Attila is in the kitchen."

This time they went to King's Theatre. The box was smaller, if no less prominent, than the one at the Opera House, and once again Bryn had timed their arrival to coincide with the overture. He moved his chair closer to hers so their thighs almost touched. Expecting her to draw away, he was surprised when she moved closer still.

Music flooded the theater—glorious music. It pulsed in his veins as he studied her profile in the glow cast from the stage. He knew *Don Giovanni* well and had no need to look at the singers. It was more delicious by far to trace the emotions they portrayed by watching Clare's response.

Enraptured, he thought, all of them. The performers by their art, Clare by the opera, and he at the fantasy of what would happen in a few hours.

Even through the fabric of his pantaloons and the velvet of her gown, he imagined he could feel her bare leg against his own. Now and again, after a particularly splendid aria, she turned to smile at him while the audience applauded.

They shared a bottle of champagne at the interval, discussing the opera while their gazes met in a wholly different conversation. For once, Clare seemed oblivious to the attention focused on them by the curious crowd.

They existed in a world of their own, a world awash in music and the anticipation of passion. The astonishing intimacy between them was staggering to Bryn, painfully accustomed to the distance she had always maintained . . . until tonight. What had happened, in the three days he was gone, to so change her?

He thought about that as the curtains opened again. Was she rewarding him for taking up Peyton's scheme? She had told him not to do that for her sake, but he had. Without question Clare was the real reason he had agreed to it. He needed her approval. He wanted her to see him as something other than a selfish, lust-driven aristocrat who thought he could buy anything—or anyone—because he was rich and titled.

A lump congealed in his throat. He *was* selfish and lustful, to support a charity only to prove he was otherwise. Clare would see through that immediately. She'd end up not liking him any more than he liked himself at this moment.

Clare's hand reached out and he took it in his own, infinitely grateful for the slight reassurance. It occurred to him that she couldn't yet know about his arrangement with Peyton. Not a reward, then, this sudden tenderness. A bribe, perhaps? She was aware he was considering the endeavor. Did she hope to entice him into sanctity?

Mind spinning, he clutched her hand tightly and stared at the stage, seeing nothing. Clare was a vast mystery to him. He didn't understand her at all. And if he kept trying to analyze her motives, he'd only succeed in driving her away again.

For now she wanted him, or was willing to accept him for reasons of her own. He should be grateful, and he was. The rest could wait. Tonight he would make love to her, and tomorrow he would try again to figure out what he must do to make her happy.

And when he knew, he would give it to her.

In the carriage they sat close together, and his tentative kisses deepened as she welcomed them. When they arrived at Clouds there was no question that he would go upstairs with her.

A quick glance assured him that Mrs. Beales had followed his instructions. The counterpane was turned back on the bed, and he saw the edges of towels laid across the sheets to absorb Clare's virgin bleeding.

God but he was nervous. He went immediately to the table, where a decanter of wine stood beside two glasses, and poured himself a hefty draught while Clare shed her cape and hung it in the armoire.

"Would you rather I wait downstairs while you change?" he asked, past a constricted throat.

She cast him an unreadable smile. "I should like a glass of wine, Bryn. And I will require help with the buttons on my dress."

He filled another glass but left it on the table while he hurried to undo her gown. Halfway there he remembered her wine and returned to the table, emptying his own glass before offering Clare her drink.

Her eyes lit with amusement. "One would almost think you the virgin here tonight, my lord. Do relax."

He slumped onto a chair. "I don't know what's wrong with me. I've never—that is, I'm usually in control but . . . oh, hell!"

Laughing, she poured him another glass of wine,

which he seized gratefully. Then she tugged a small hassock to the chair. "Put your legs up," she invited. "I'll sit on your lap."

Soon she was nestled there, her legs on the padded armrest by his side, her back against his uplifted knees. He caught his breath.

She touched her glass lightly to his. "To our first night together."

He watched her drink, unable to move as her words sank in. "Our *first* night, Clare?" he asked warily. "Does that mean you expect there will be others?"

She looked puzzled. "Isn't that what you wanted?"

"God, yes. But our agreement was only that you would consider staying. I thought you intended to decide . . . later."

"You mean after you've bedded me?" She brushed a swatch of hair from his eyes. "Good heavens, how awkward that would be. As if I were passing judgment on what happens tonight. Unless I am mistaken, that is unlikely to be altogether pleasant. But it will not affect my decision. I plan to stay, assuming you are not terribly disappointed with me."

He felt the band of thorns, which had been wrapped around his heart since he first met her, slowly unwind and dissolve, leaving a great peace within him. As much as he had longed for their first night together, he had feared the day after, tormented by visions of waking up to find her gone.

Always, he'd been shadowed by the awareness that he bought her for only one night of reluctant compliance. Now she gave him a gift he had not dared to imagine. He wanted to tell her that, but the words froze in his throat. If she knew how much it mattered to him, she might feel entrapped. Above all things, he wanted Clare to understand that she was free to go . . . and choose to stay of her own accord.

Without doubt, he had lost his mind. Any man with sense would keep this woman by whatever devious means it required.

He gazed at her in silence for a long time, unsure what to say next. "I could never be disappointed with you," he finally managed between dry lips. "But I am greatly afraid you will not feel the same about me after your first experience. Do you know what to expect tonight?"

"More or less." She shrugged lightly. "I was raised in the country and have seen livestock mate."

He choked on a swallow of wine. "We are not cattle, my dear. Animals couple by instinct, and only when the female is ready to breed. Men and women come together for altogether different rcasons. Some of the time, anyway. Be assured that producing offspring is not why I want to make love to you."

She grinned. "I rather assumed that, after Mrs. Beales taught me any number of ways to prevent it." Her eyes clouded. "I have taken the herbal drink faithfully, every day, but if you want me to make use of the sponges, I'll need to—"

"Hush. I told you I would take care of this, in my own way. Don't give it another thought. But if you have any other questions, I shall be glad to answer them."

Nodding, she leaned back against his knees. "Actually, I do. Will you stay when you are done, or leave?"

Heat rose to his cheeks. "Does that matter?"

"I only wondered. If you stay the night, should I wake you up in the morning or let you sleep? And will you want breakfast? Because if you do, I should write a note for Mrs. Beales."

He regarded her with awe. "What the hell difference does all that make? I thought you would be concerned about . . . more intimate subjects."

"Not at all," she assured him. "You have those well in hand, and I have only to follow your lead and do what you tell me. It's the other details I'm worried about. The protocol for mistresses, if you will."

"Protocol?" His astounded expression caused her to chuckle. "Listen to me, Clare. There is no book of etiquette for lovers. We shall find our own way together. And if I have certain expectations beyond our time in bed, they can wait. Yes, I want to stay here tonight. No, don't wake me up in the morning. Unless you want to, of course. Only, be there in my arms when you do.

"Please," he added, after a moment.

"Anything you want, Bryn." She took the empty glass from his hand. "Would you like more?"

"Not wine," he said softly. "But more of you."

She bent over and set both glasses on the floor. Then, to his amazement, she wrapped her arms around his back and kissed him, her mouth open to his immediate response.

He tasted the sweet claret on her tongue and the yielding of her body. But after a long while, drugged with her kisses, he became aware she had no real desire for him. No passion. She was willing but not eager.

Take what you can, he thought. Remember that she is a virgin. This is all new for her. And she is trying.

But he could not help himself. "You don't really

want to do this. Tell me the truth, Clare. You don't really want me."

"I'm not at all sure what I feel right now," she said, after a tense pause. "But if it matters, I am glad it's you, Bryn." Her gaze lifted. "More than I can say, I'm glad it's you."

He let go a deep sigh. That ought to be enough. Certainly it was more than he had expected of their first night. And, like her, he was not sure of his own emotions. His past experiences with virgin mistresses had not prepared him for this woman. Feelings, other than sexual desire, had never been involved when he bedded any one of them. Not ever.

Now a riot of feelings hammered at him like the heels of the flamenco dancers he'd watched in Spain. He felt the rap of castanets, the soul-deep rhythm of passion thrumming in his veins.

Putting his hands on her shoulders, he turned her slightly and began to unloose the buttons on her dress. "Trust me," he breathed against the soft skin of her back. "Let this be good." His hands reached to cradle her breasts, warm and full under the soft fabric of her chemise.

Clare leaned against his chest with a wondering sigh of pleasure when his thumbs brushed her nipples.

"Take down your hair," he whispered.

She obeyed, fumbling with the pins while he continued to stroke her. When the hair cascaded over her shoulders, he helped her slip her arms from the sleeves of her dress and lowered it to her waist. Then he combed his fingers gently through her hair, parting it to kiss her nape.

"Will you come to bed with me now?" he asked huskily.

Nodding, she stood, the velvet gown pooling on the floor at her feet as she began to strip off her long gloves. She felt his gaze burning into her and heard him come to his feet. Again he lifted the hair from her neck, his fingers warm as they unclasped her necklace.

She stepped away from the dress, clad only in a nearly transparent chemise and stockings, and turned to face him. "Shall I undress you, Bryn?"

He swallowed. "Some other time, perhaps. One day you will understand what your touch does to me. For now, better we go slowly. And you must tell me if there is something I can do to make this easier for you."

She glanced around the brightly lit room. "Might we extinguish the lamps? Not if you don't want to," she added quickly.

"All but one," he conceded with a smile. "Just so I don't trip over something. I will take care of it. Anything else?"

She shook her head. "You must tell me what I can do to please you."

"I hope to *show* you, butterfly. And nothing will happen until you are ready."

Putting her hands on his shoulders, she stood on tiptoe to brush a kiss on his lips. "I am not afraid, or reluctant in any way. Please don't worry about me. Tonight is for you."

"For us," he corrected, with a smile that touched her heart.

While he lit two candles on the dressing table and extinguished the other lights, she peeled off her stockings and climbed onto the bed, sitting cross-legged with the counterpane drawn to her waist. The soft padding of towels beneath her hips was a stark reminder of the pain and bleeding to come. Closing her eyes, she listened to the sounds of Bryn undressing.

She had told him the truth, or part of it. She was not afraid of anything that would happen to her body tonight. But the sin. Oh, God, the sin of lying with him for money, no love between them, no vows to sanction what they did together. Every time she thought she had buried her guilt, it sprang up like a dusky angel at her shoulder, warning her of the consequences.

Her soul would be lost.

She had accepted that. But while there was still time to change her mind, she fought the temptation to virtue.

For Bryn, she thought with grim determination. For everything he had unwittingly done for Joseph and Jeremy, and for his kindness to her. Tonight she would think only of him, and give as much of herself as she could bear to relinquish. He would neither know nor care if she withheld pleasure from herself, in the hope of repentance and forgiveness in the future.

Sometimes even that seemed beyond her strength. Whenever he took her into his arms and kissed her, she wanted him to do more. Soon, he would. All she had to do was stop herself from wanting it.

"Clare?"

Her eyes flew open.

He stood by the bed, his naked body gilded with candlelight. The soft glow illuminated his broad shoulders and narrow waist and, most of all, the long thick phallus lifting from a shadowy place between his legs.

She gulped.

* * *

Hours later, Clare lay cradled in Bryn's arms with her head on his shoulder, listening to the soft rumble in his throat as he slept, reflecting on what had happened between them.

At the time, she had been unable to think at all.

Now, bits and pieces reassembled themselves into an experience she would never forget. Nor did she want to. It had been almost like music when he touched her and kissed her. His voice sang to her even now, the whispery words of his pleasure echoing in her heart, the thunder of his deep strokes like drums, still throbbing their rhythm between her thighs.

If there had been pain, she could not recall it. By the time he lifted himself over her, she was mindless with need for the probing hardness that thrust into an emptiness she had never felt before. Only when he filled her did she feel complete.

At the last, she almost understood why he gave so much in exchange for a few hours of passion. Whole again with him inside her, she had watched his face during the final moments. Head lifted in fierce concentration, he drove to culmination as if nothing in the universe could match the sensations he was experiencing.

For all the intensity of their physical joining, what she remembered most was Bryn's almost preternatural tenderness, as if he were creating a new world for her with no thought for himself. She could not help but be aware of his intense self-control when he led her from the sudden attack of fear when she saw his aroused manhood to near delight in taking it within her.

And after, when his breathing slowed, he had

kissed her gently, and thanked her, and asked if he hurt her.

"Not at all," she told him honestly.

He kissed her again, more deeply, and pulled himself off the bed. In the waning candlelight, she saw him move to the dressing table and wash himself. Then he returned, with a damp towel, and cleansed the place between her legs. Finally he told her to lift her hips and drew the stained towels away.

When he was settled again beside her, she went gladly into his open arms. "It was nothing like I imagined," she said, curling her arm around his waist.

"I hope that is not an insult," he responded cautiously. "But I suspect you imagined something so horrible that anything would be an improvement."

"Not . . . exactly. I just failed to understand why you wanted this so much. Now I do, in a way. It is terribly compelling, what we just did."

"Yes," he said after a moment. "And you have only begun to see why. I hope that next time you will share what I felt, Clare."

She would not, of course, but murmured something meaningless, grateful when he yawned deeply and rested his chin against her forehead. Within seconds he was asleep.

Never could she allow herself to be drawn where he wanted to lead her, for that way led to certain damnation. But perhaps, for a little while, she could give Bryn the pleasure he found with her, and repay her debt to him.

As the pale light of dawn crept into the room through the filmy curtains, her own eyes felt heavy. This once, she would probably sleep through the morning as he did, like a tree stump.

19

Dark wet streets reflected the soft glow from windows and gas lamps as Bryn rapped his cane against the wood panel. The rain had softened to a filmy drizzle, and he decided to walk the last few streets to Clouds. When the carriage shuddered to a halt he swung out, the capes of his greatcoat swirling around his shoulders.

"Go home, Jenkins," he told the driver, who sliced him a knowing grin before chucking the horses away. After fifteen years in service to the earl, Jenkins didn't credit him with enough sense to come in out of the rain, and he was on the mark tonight. Bryn tugged his curly-brimmed beaver lower on his forehead. Water dripped from tree branches, loud in the silence, as he strode past the long rows of discreet town houses.

Clare was not expecting him.

Always, he told her what time he'd come, and each day found himself setting the hour earlier. She was good company, already commanding the upper hand at piquet, although her chess remained abysmal. Sometimes he brought business papers with him and worked to the faint scratch of her needle through linen as she embroidered one of her interminable handkerchiefs.

One was in his pocket now, with Clare's idea of his monogram picked out in satin thread. He chuckled. A large C, and inside it the visage of a surly-looking bear. "Caradoc in the morning," she had told him.

Grouchy as a hibernating bear roused midwinter was what she meant.

He was a creature of late nights and later mornings. They had quarreled about that, because he expected her in bed with him when he woke up and by then she'd been stirring for hours. Reasonably, she offered to return the minute he summoned her, but it wasn't the same. He wanted to come awake with a sleepy, languorous woman in his arms. He wanted to kiss her before he opened his eyes and make love to her in warm rumpled sheets. He had refused to compromise.

Obediently sitting up against a bank of pillows while he snored next to her, Clare had embroidered a great many bears and read most of Shakespeare's plays until, on the sixth day, he gave up. She could get on about her business, and he would call her when he awakened.

That was when he discovered that compromise was not such a bad idea. He never felt her leave, and already she knew the rhythms of his sleep. Clare was always snuggled at his side when he reached for her.

He preferred quiet hours with her to any spent with his friends, and her body to any woman he'd ever enjoyed. She was intelligent and curious, and her wry sense of humor never failed to delight him even when the joke had a special barb for him. Most did. With Clare, a man could not take himself too seriously. He was surprised how relaxing that was and spent most of the time he wasn't with her wishing that he was. In every way but one, she was the perfect mistress.

When he left her yesterday, unsatisfied yet again, he had not said when he expected to return. Anger was banking inside him, building a heat that had driven him away long enough to consider how to deal with the problem. When he was with Clare, the last part of him that worked to advantage was his brain. She answered all his moods and the desires of his body before he felt them.

She gave him everything, except herself.

God knows he had tried to reach her, especially in bed. Every way he knew how—and there were a great many—he led her to the edge, only to feel her pull away. Not once had she exploded into climax. She melted into the shadows, or closed some hidden door of her own, only to emerge like a force of nature when he was beyond control. Within seconds he was aware of nothing but what she was doing to him, only a faint disappointment hovering like an imagined fragrance just as he collapsed into exhausted sleep.

Her way of calling off the wolf, he knew.

He stopped at the wrought-iron gate leading to Clouds. Wet black metal glistened in the blades of gold streaming through the fanlight over the door. A sconce must be lit in the foyer, he decided, unable to tell if Clare was waiting up for him since their bedchamber overlooked the back garden.

The hours of distance and thinking had brought him back to where he started. Clare knew a thousand ways to make herself irresistible, and one way to resist him. That had to change. He would make it change. This time, tonight, she would cross the line or he'd damn well drag her over it.

He let himself in with his key and heard a sharp hiss as he closed the door. Attila crouched on the stairs, ears back and yellow eyes gleaming with malice. God, he hated that cat! Dogs never scratched a man's boots or threw up hairballs on a man's discarded breeches. With the tip of his cane, he nudged the beast to one side and watched him streak up the stairs.

As he stepped into the bedroom, Clare set aside the book she'd been reading and leaned against the bank of pillows. His first thought was that he could see her arms. And neck, and collarbone, and the swell of her breasts. Tiny satin straps were looped over her shoulders, barely holding the transparent lace of her bodice. The negligee was the color of fresh cream, just like her skin.

He sucked in a deep breath. She had many such gowns, all gifts from him, but was always too shy to wear them. At night, she snuffed out all but one candle and drew the curtains against the morning sun. Not once, since the day he ordered her to strip for him, had he seen her body in full light.

His body surged. Without thinking, he began to peel off his coat, gaze pinned to her as she slipped from the bed and floated to him in a drift of gossamer and lace. Her thick hair billowed like smoke around her face and shoulders.

He stumbled back, sank on a chair, and began

tugging off his boots. "Stay there," he muttered, the breath hissing between his teeth. "Let me look at you."

She stopped at the foot of the bed, poised with arms at her sides, her expression unreadable.

Roughly, he jerked away the second boot. Only seconds in the room and already he was out of control. He lay back against the chair, breathing heavily, the fragment of his brain that still functioned telling him that she was leaning over to unbutton his shirt. Cool fingers skated across his shoulders, pushing starched cambric down his arms. The cloth tangled above his cuffed wrists, imprisoning him. Carefully, she untwisted the links and set him free. His shirt gone, her hands caressed his chest and moved down, pausing at the band of his breeches. Then she loosed the flap and dipped inside.

With a last grip of sanity, he clasped her fingers and pulled them away, while he could. She was bent over him, and a light fragrance of lavender wafted at the edges of his awareness.

"Are you trying to seduce me, Clare?" he managed to say.

"Would that be necessary, my lord?" Her lips curved in that secret smile all her own.

"No. But you have never . . . that is, you are always beautiful, but never more so than in that gown. Did you wear it for me?"

"Why would you think so?" she observed mischievously. "I didn't know you were coming tonight."

"You knew I couldn't stay away," he corrected, not liking the truth of that.

"I hoped you could not."

He didn't believe her. The robe was meant to please him. *She* had set out to please him, as she always did of late. But she hadn't really wanted him to come.

That should have stifled his passion, or at least taken off the edge. But she tugged him to his feet, wrapping her arms around his waist and resting her cheek against his chest. Cool fingers slipped beneath the band of his trousers, incredibly intimate although they reached only a little, to the arch of his buttocks. His mouth was smothered in a cloud of hair, and he couldn't stop his hands from running up and down the sleek lines of her back and hips and sweetly curved bottom.

He was lost. Seconds later he had peeled off his breeches and she was buried under his driving body, the filmy nightgown bunched around her waist, her legs wrapped around him. The furious completion, his back arched like a bow for the last fierce thrusts, seered him past pleasure to fire. Alone.

Collapsing over her, gasping for air, he felt his heart thundering like a racehorse just over the finish line.

Alone.

With his cheek buried against her neck, he could feel her pulse in slow, steady counterpoint to his, as if she had watched the race from a distance. Still inside her, he was aware she'd gone leagues away, to a place of her own, although one of her hands stroked his back while the other tangled in the hair at his nape.

Groaning, he flopped onto his back, not surprised when she followed, curling against him with her head resting on his shoulder. She knew he liked that. She always did what she knew he liked.

He was beginning to hate her for it.

"I'm sorry for that," he said after a while. "An

adolescent would have more finesse, but you drive me wild, Clare Easton."

"Isn't that what I'm supposed to do?"

No, not exactly. But he bloody hell didn't want to debate the subject. He wanted to show her, except that she invariably made it impossible. Still, it was early. And while his male flesh regathered itself for another effort, the rest of him would have time to draw her irrevocably to the same place she so effortlessly drove him.

"Right now," he said, "you are supposed to kiss me." Did he imagine a tiny frisson as she lifted herself over him, her breasts spilling from the slight containment of lace, teasing at his chest as she brushed his lips with her own?

"Your every wish," she murmured into his mouth, "is my command."

"In that case, you will do exactly as I tell you."

His next words were cut off as her tongue slipped between his lips, dancing across his teeth, twirling inside in a sweet invasion that sent blood racing where he wasn't ready for it to go. Her mouth was warm and sweet, like cinnamon tea.

"You need not tell me, Bryn. I already know."

He felt the scarred ridges on her palm as it settled on his chest and moved inexorably downward. And he felt himself rising up to meet her.

Not yet, he told himself, but it was too late. Her fingers closed around him, and her thumb rubbed lightly at the tip of his erection. Still moist from the first driving sex, his penis slipped deliciously between her cradling hand, swelling to the pressure of her grip as she stroked him. His back arched against the tangled sheets as he pulled her closer, deepening the kiss, mating her with his tongue and with his shaft against her hand.

He recognized male dominance rampant and yet leashed by the indescribable power of this woman. When she swung over him and lowered herself onto him, he surged inside her with nearly anguished relief. Her knees were tight around his waist, and she was supple as a willow as she moved over him, the palms of her hands braced against his chest and her head thrown back in intense concentration. He saw her with fire-rimmed eyes, molding her full breasts with his hands before seizing her hips and pulling her into his raging drive.

Not like this, his mind squealed weakly, from a distance. Exactly like this, his body demanded, until all of him was centered at a hot point of light. From even farther away than the feeble urgings of his brain, he heard himself cry out in release.

Sometime later, Bryn became aware that he was still on his back, this time softer than hot wax, with Clare once more curved at his side. She took him apart and reinvented him a hundred ways. He was helpless to stop it.

Only a fool would want to. So what if she felt nothing? He'd paid her richly enough, and would give her more. His only concern should be to keep her with him.

His brain, silent through all the time it was supposed to keep him in line, became active again as he felt Clare relaxing against him, her soft breath even with sleep. A perfect mistress. In bed, she would keep him satisfied the rest of his life. Hell, with her beauty and nearly consummate skill she could make any arrangements she liked, with him or any other healthy male.

Clearly she did not want him. His money, perhaps, and the things he gave her—the comfort of this house, the security of his protection—but not him. More and more, the conviction grew that she was working off ten thousand guineas the best way she knew how, services rendered for payment in advance. She was honorable, determined not to cheat him, bent on giving him everything he'd any right to expect. In truth, after only two weeks he considered himself in debt to her, if money for sex was what this was about.

He wasn't sure when it had stopped being that for him. Probably at the very beginning, when he determined she would want him too. It was a promise to himself, and he always kept his promises. How much of it was vanity he didn't like to consider, but he expected that unlovely trait had been the driving force.

Was he so selfish, to demand she satisfy his ego as well as his body? Showing her off in public, which she'd hated, was surely male pride, for all his disclaimers about wanting to share things with her. That was true, but early days he had flaunted her before she was ready. Maybe that was one reason she didn't like him.

There were plenty of other possible reasons, when you came down to it. Though he'd gone out of his way for her, as he had never done with any of his previous mistresses, nearly everything he tried in a effort to win her regard had backfired. The endless days and nights before he was able to bed her had made him irritable, and every bad habit he possessed, admittedly a great many, rubbed against her exactly the wrong way.

Sighing deeply, he stared at the ceiling and the shadowy candlelight dancing there. In spite of his growing frustration, they were good together. Clare had come to enjoy their outings, however public. With her peculiar grace, she endured encroaching curiosity-seekers, leaving it to him to dismiss them. She ignored the stares they invariably drew because of her beauty and his reputation. And she delighted in the plays and operas, happiest when she could lose herself in the tragedy or comedy on the stage.

They had fun together. Now and again he'd get caught up describing one of his interests, and she loved teasing him when he waxed eloquent about canals and locomotives and his particular fascination with the possibility of flying machines. He was looking forward to escorting her to a balloon ascent, fully intent on persuading her to go aloft with him. It would be magic, soaring to the skies with Clare. He could hardly wait.

Only in bed, it all crumbled. Only there, he had to face the truth that she did not desire him, was not passionate for him. And that where it most mattered, he had given her nothing. This night was worse than most, for she'd not allowed him a chance to try. He'd scarcely touched her. She had kissed him, caressed him, but not once had he felt the dampness of her welcome or stroked her to even the beginnings of pleasure.

His fingers combed through her soft hair, and he felt her stir in her sleep. Well, he'd always wanted her this way, limp and yielding, open to him. And after the two bouts of wild sexual release, surely now he had enough control of his own body to bend her to his will. He had come here tonight sworn to feel her convulse with pleasure, and damned if he'd let that promise vanish in the lassitude that threatened to overwhelm him.

He rolled over until he was on top of her, his elbows planted at her sides, and watched her eyes open sleepily.

"Bryn?"

"Oh, yes, Clare." Lowering his head, he kissed her for a long time, resting his weight on one arm as he stroked her with his right hand, reaching under the soft gown to her breasts. "Don't move until I tell you, or unless you can't help it. I want to touch you, and kiss you, and make love to you for a very long time."

He felt her nails dig, briefly, into his back, and then her hands relaxed as his tongue slid between her lips. Her mouth was musky with sleep, and he licked every part of it with moist and luxurious deliberation. I want you, he thought. I want your heart, the soul of you, the essence of you. Cradling her face with one hand, the other teasing at her nipple, he was vaguely aware she had begun to shift under the pressure of his body.

"Be still," he murmured, lifting his head for a swift breath of air. "This is for me." For you, he amended silently. If she sensed it, he would lose her. And this time he wanted to bring her to climax, devil take the reason why. Once she had experienced the same unutterable ecstasy she gave to him, there would be no turning back for her, as there was none for him. It was the surest, safest way to keep her with him. Above all else, keeping Clare was the goal.

His hand stroked the smooth lines of her leg, and his lips nibbled tiny kisses down her throat, over her shoulder, and finally to her breasts. The rough threads of lace on her gown were unimaginably intoxicating against his chin. Unhurried, he rolled his head against the soft mounds, seeking the exquisitely pebbled nipples.

Gratified, he heard a low moan deep in her throat and sucked harder, drawing more of her into his mouth. With ease, his fingers snapped one delicate satin ribbon until her breast was freed, and he laved it with his tongue between tiny bites that set her arching against him.

He wanted to touch her everywhere at once, before any part of her could escape. He tented her with his long body, the wide bow of his shoulders pressing her to the bed, his hands at once slow and anxious at her sides and smooth flanks, encompassing her with male flesh and bone, long hard fingers reaching for every curve and crevice.

There was no place she could go, no way she could evade him. He moved first to the breasts lifted to him and then to her mouth for another long, demanding kiss, while his hands molded her soft behind.

She reached for him, to pull him closer, but he pressed her arms against the bed. "Let me," he ordered, all too aware what her touch could do to him. His fingers moved to the light hair between her thighs, damp with his seed. With exquisite deliberation, he thrust a long finger into the warm, swollen lips between her legs, feeling the thick wetness there, wondering if any of it was her welcome, the fountain of her desire, or only the remnants of his own passion.

Perhaps he would know, if he tasted it. Easing himself down her body, he nestled between her thighs. She gasped, and her fingers tangled in his hair.

"Hold me," he said, "but don't stop me." Lifting her knees, he lapped gently at the unimaginably sweet softness. Him or her, it was all one now as his tongue found the hard nub of feminine joy and sucked at it while his finger slid inside her. Slick and warm and tight, her flesh closed around him even as her knees closed around his neck. With every swirl of his tongue she jerked against him, and he sent another finger into her and then a third, plunging rhythmically while he sucked her into the vortex that threatened to claim them both.

His own body twisted against the bed, his penis impossibly hard again and demanding its own release. Surging over her in one swift motion, he raised her legs over his shoulders and plunged inside, thrilling to the cry she could not contain just before his tongue flamed inside her mouth.

She was with him now, her hips flailing against the sheets, her arms curved at his armpits and her fingers clutching at his scalp, drawing him in and pulling him onward, the way he'd dreamed it could be.

And then she was gone.

In less than a flicker of an eyelash, Clare detached herself from the body that still writhed beneath him, sucking him into its depths like dry earth absorbed water. Dispassionate and passive, she slipped away, unsatisfied.

Deliberately.

With an oath, he flung himself off the bed, looking back at her from bleary eyes. She lay there, thighs spread and glistening, arms limp on the counterpane. She might as well have been on the moon for all her awareness of him.

"Damn you," he swore, groping in the dimness for his breeches. "Damn you to hell for this."

As if that got her attention when all else had failed, she sat up on her heels, the lascivious gown drooping over one bared breast where he'd torn the strap away, her hair tangled around her face. Mutely, she gazed at him in confusion.

Stuffing his legs in his pants, he grabbed for his boots and pulled them on. "This won't do, Clare!" he shouted. "What the devil are you trying to prove? That none of it is happening? That you can come out of this the virgin you were going in?"

He snatched his shirt from the carpet. "You owe me, lady." Missing the top button, he fastened the rest unevenly. "I might as well fuck a pillow."

He picked up his coat and stalked to the door, swinging around to jab a hard finger in her direction. "Get one thing straight, Clare. You are a whore, bought and paid for. A whore gives her buyer anything he wants. We both know you are holding back on me, and it isn't good enough. You cheat both of us. Refusing to feel doesn't change what you are. It just makes you bad at it."

She blinked once, gazing at him with wide, frightened eyes. Her mouth opened slightly, as if she wanted to say something, and then closed again. She wrapped her arms across her breasts.

Bryn stared at her for a last moment and slammed the door behind him.

He slammed the downstairs door, too, and stumbled into the wet streets muttering to himself, with no idea where he was going.

Sometime later, in a place he didn't recognize, he heard the shrill sound of drunken laughter and wandered inside. A gaming hell, he thought.

The air was heavy with smoke. Benumbed, he found himself seated at a green baize table with a full bottle of brandy at his elbow and cards in his hands. He reached into his pocket and pulled out a wad of banknotes folded into a gold clip.

The other faces at the table seemed very young. Adolescent fools, he thought, wondering what game they were playing. A pudgy boy with a round face introduced himself, but Bryn didn't hear his name. A thin boy was seated across from him. Ignoring the glass, he swigged brandy straight from the bottle. He dealt when it was his turn, played a card from time to time, stuffed money in his pockets when the pile in front of him grew large.

He bought drinks for the house. He bought another bottle of brandy for himself. He saw Clare, kneeling on the bed, looking at him, confused and frightened.

After a while, he saw nothing at all.

20

At the sudden roar, Bryn shot upright and looked around in confusion. Wherever he was, the place was overrun by a pack of screaming hyenas.

When he shook his head to clear it, a brigade of cavalry charged through his skull. What had hit him? He buried his face in his hands, feeling whiskers. One side of his face was wet. He glanced down at the trestle table and the pool of ale where his cheek had been.

The crowd surged forward, intent on whatever was going on in the center of the room. He could see nothing but backs and shoulders, all male, and smoke wreathing the amber light streaming from lanterns suspended overhead. The place looked as if it might once have been a stable. It smelled of animals.

He wondered if he were asleep. Having a nightmare. But the pain in his head was excruciatingly real, and the din was beyond imagining.

Groaning, he tried to stand and felt his knees give way. Falling back onto the narrow bench, he nearly toppled over and grabbed the table with both hands. God, he was thirsty. He lifted a few empty mugs and found one with an inch of warm flat ale, which he quickly swallowed.

An image flickered in his mind—his hand wrapped around a bottle . . . cards—and then it was gone. For a moment, he thought he saw feathers hanging in the smoky air. A high-pitched shriek, like a death cry, split the air and the crowd erupted into a frenzy. Bryn shut his eyes and plastered his hands over his ears.

When he looked up, a wad of money hung in front of his nose. He looked past it to a wrinkled shirt-sleeve, a limp, untied cravat, and a chubby face that seemed vaguely familiar.

"Called it again, your lordship. Damned if I can figure how you done it. Didn't think you was awake above half."

"Who the hell are you?" Bryn's tongue was furry and felt too large for his mouth.

"Ha. That's a good one." The man, barely that, dropped the notes onto the table. "Cleaned me out, and now you don't know my name." He slumped on the bench across from Bryn, his round chin fuzzed with a youthful beard, grinning widely.

"No, I don't. Where am I, and how in blazes did I get here?"

Another youngster joined them at the table, swigging heartily from a pewter mug.

"Give me that," Bryn ordered. Somewhat to his surprise, the boy handed it over immediately, wiping his mouth with the back of his hand.

"Bad stuff, m'lord," he warned the earl, "but don't 'spect anybody knows the difference by now."

It was wet, and Bryn swallowed it greedily.

"Wants to know where he is," the pudgy boy informed his friend with a laugh. "Cool as you please, like he ain't just called five of the last six fights. M'uncle was like that. Said when gentlemen leave the table, you can't tell which of 'em won or lost."

"What fights?" Just in time, Bryn remembered not to shake his head.

The fat boy laughed uproariously. "Hear that?"

His friend looked worried. "I don't think he knows, Will."

Bryn regarded him with appreciation. "That's right. I don't."

Leaning forward, the boy studied him for a moment. "Er, do you know who you are, m'lord?"

"Of course I do," he thundered, regretting it immediately. His head swam.

Will dug one elbow into his friend's ribs and tapped his forehead with a meaningful finger. "Caradoc," he whispered loudly. "Father ran mad, y'know."

In a flash, Bryn was on his feet with one fist clutching the boy's cravat in a stranglehold, dragging him across the table until the two of them were nose to nose. "You," he said chillingly, "have just made a bad mistake."

The round face seemed to swell.

"My lord!" Dimly, Bryn felt the skinny boy behind him, pounding at his shoulders. "Let him go!"

With a last hard twist at the boy's neckcloth, Bryn released his hold. "Outside, both of you," he said, trying to stay on his feet as the surge of rage dissipated, leaving him weaker than before. When he felt an arm supporting his elbow, he leaned on it with gratitude.

They came out of the overheated stable into a cool night blazing with stars. Across the courtyard stood a ramshackle inn, the doors open to a crowded hall and a taproom overflowing with noise and laughter. Curricles, coaches, and gigs were lined up outside a long narrow building. The new stable, he guessed.

This could not be London.

Cubes of baled hay were stacked by the door, and he collapsed onto one with a sigh. The two young men stood before him, looking worried. "I am not mad," he told them, enunciating every word. "But I think I must have taken a blow to my head. Will one of you kindly tell me where we are and how I got here?"

The thin boy nodded wisely. "I expect it happened last night," he said, snaring a cube of hay and settling across from the earl. "Looked none too good when you came into the Lucky Bones, m'lord. Maybe something hit you in the street. Were you robbed?"

"Couldn't have been," piped Will. "Had a wad of notes on him, even before he won all my money."

"Just tell me what happened," Bryn said through clenched teeth. "I remember going into a hell, and playing cards." And drinking. He had heard of men drinking themselves to oblivion, and the devil knew he'd wanted to forget. The last clear image he recalled was Clare, kneeling in the center of the tumbled bed, her long hair draped around her shoulders, her eyes wide with pain.

Breathing hard, he stared at the brilliant sky, dimly aware of the youngsters chattering about a mill and cockfights and wenches. Apparently, they had had a rousing good time. Ah, Clare, he thought, his eyes burning.

With effort, he wrenched his attention to the boys. "I came here with you?"

"Friday night," the thin boy said in the patient tones of one addressing a slowtop. "You, Will, and me rode out in Lambert's coach. Got rooms upstairs." He pointed to the inn. "One for you and one for the rest of us. Taking turns, we are. Lambert's up there now, with Dolly. Or Polly. Whatever her name is."

Will pulled out his watch and tried to make out the time. "I'm next, at three o'clock. Got the little red-head lined up, if I can find her."

"Damn and blast!" Bryn mauled his hair with a shaking hand. Had he, somewhere in a fog of brandy, tumbled a tavern whore? He couldn't bring himself to ask.

"You want her?" squawked Will, looking miserable. "She won't give me a toss on credit if you've changed your mind. All over you this afternoon she was, after the mill. Saw you win at odds, I expect. The girls know which ones to go for. Couldn't believe m'luck when you turned her down."

Wildly relieved, Bryn summoned a tight smile. "She's all yours, and the money to pay her with, if you'll help me get out of here. How far is London?"

"About twenty miles," put in the thin boy. "But you won't find anybody going back tonight."

Bryn struggled to his feet. "Oh, but I will. You say we came in Lambert's coach?" He had absolutely no recollection of anyone named Lambert, or the journey, or the mill, or the cockfights. "Get him. This party's over."

"M'lord," the thin boy said urgently, "we can't get him right now. If you know what I mean."

Bryn fixed him with an icy aristocratic stare. "Take me to Lambert, right now. If you know what I mean."

Minutes later, Morley Brackon and Will Fletcher stood behind the earl in the narrow hallway, waiting for Lambert to answer repeated poundings on the door. They heard muffled oaths, and the door cracked open. Lambert, a pillow clutched to his naked loins, peered blearily at them. Bryn saw a light-haired girl kneeling on the bed, a sheet pulled over her breasts, regarding them with startled eyes. Like Clare, tousled from lovemaking, mute and frightened. His heart thudded in his chest.

"Thing is, Lamby," said Fletcher, when Bryn was silent, "his lordship here wants to go home. Needs the coach, y'see."

Obviously, Lambert did not see at all. Sputtering, he dropped the pillow and bumped his head on the doorjamb when he bent over to pick it up. Behind him, the girl laughed shrilly, and the ugly sound shattered the image of Clare that had taken possession of Bryn's senses.

"I'll buy the damned coach!" he declared, reaching into his pockets. They were crammed with notes and guineas, and he dropped the lot of them on the floor. "This on account."

Lambert gazed bleakly at the small fortune cast at his feet. "Glad to sell you the coach," he stammered. "Wish I could. But it ain't mine. Belongs to m'father. He don't know I took it out, and he's like to have m'hide when I bring it home. Wouldn't care to tell him I sold the thing."

The earl, beginning to sober up, recalled that he

knew someone named Lambert. Not this boy but a stiff, cold man about fifty years old. Crandall Lambert, Lord Finchburton. "The marquess's whelp, are you?"

Wincing, the youngster nodded.

"I know your father. And I expect when he learns I had sudden need to borrow a coach, and his son was kind enough to lend me one, he'll pat you on the back for it. I'll give him a good story, Lambert, if you have the coach readied for me within the hour."

The boy looked first at the determined jaw of the earl, then at the money on the floor, and then, longingly, over his shoulder at the girl.

"Bloody hell, you idiot," Bryn snapped, "make your way home the best you can. All of you. Just get me a vehicle and some horses and a driver. Will, where's my room?"

It was three hours before the driver was found and deemed sober enough to manage the horses. Bryn took Will with him to his room, dredged a history of the long weekend he'd spent in the company of three boys nearly half his age, and then dozed for a while.

The night sky was graying to dawn when he was finally shut inside the carriage with a loaf of stale bread to settle his stomach and two jars of cool water, which he drank within the first half hour. The Black Sheep, out of the way of the main post roads, made its way by hosting weekend entertainments for youngsters hot on the town. When he was their age, Bryn reflected grimly, he had been too busy scrambling an education and making money to indulge himself.

Now, he knew what he'd missed. He wasn't sorry.

Three times he was forced to pound on the ceiling with his fist to stop the coach while he retched into the hedgerows lining the road. He'd never before drunk enough to shoot the cat, let alone passed an entire day and the better part of two nights in a mindless haze.

From what Will told him, he seemed to have functioned pretty well, at least to the point of winning bets placed on Scarface George to beat Hamfisted Harry, not to mention assorted chickens he'd favored to tear other chickens to shreds with metal claws. He'd never seen a cockfight before. Nor had he now, he thought, with a sour grin that hurt. His lips were dry, swollen, and cracked, and his head felt like a knife thrower's target, new blades piercing it with every jolt of the carriage.

He deserved it all. He deserved worse. No punishment in this life could match up to his crimes and to the guilt pounding at him.

Perhaps the boy was right—he had run mad. Only madness could account for the way he'd acted, the derisive words he'd thrown at Clare. He had savaged her.

And lost her. She would be gone by now, and he still did not know her real name or where she'd come from. She wouldn't want him to look for her, although he would, nor be glad if he found her. Which he would, eventually. Maybe she'd give him time to apologize before she slammed the door in his face.

Damned fool. Stupid, selfish, arrogant fool.

He knew she would not be there, but he directed the driver to Clouds with a misbegotten compulsion to face the scene of his crimes. The Sunday morning streets were oddly quiet. Here and there, desultory street peddlers wandered with trays of muffins and raspberries, pork pies and nosegays. A few children were out early, rolling hoops in the small parks that studded the neighborhood.

He knew the minute he entered the house that it was empty. His footsteps echoed in the hall as he stumbled upstairs to the bedchamber. The door was open, and the bed neatly made up. Clare's dressing table was bare, except for the silver-backed brush and mirror he'd given her and one yellow full-blown rose in a narrow vase.

He leaned his shoulders against the wall, arms clutched around his waist. One glance in the mirror confirmed that he looked almost worse than he felt. His eyes were red-rimmed and bloodshot, he'd two days' growth of dark beard on his face, and his clothes were bedraggled and stained with wine and ale and God knew what else.

Deliberately, he forced himself to cross the room and stare at his image. He needed to see what he was . . . what he'd become . . . and commit the picture to memory. A stranger stared back at him. Bryn suspected the real Earl of Caradoc was there in the mirror, his sins etched in the lines on his face and the guilt in his eyes.

This was the man Clare had seen. She recognized what he was from the first, before the things inside him became visible. Of course she had left him. Right now, he could scarcely believe she'd stayed with him as long as she had.

A tiny sound, like scratching, caught his attention. From the window, he thought, although it was closed and the curtains half drawn. Seeing nothing, he sighed and turned back toward the hall. Lambert's coach waited in the street, and there was no reason to stay in this place. Tomorrow he'd put Clouds up for sale. Never again would he bring a woman here.

At the door, he shot one last glance over his shoulder

at the bed, remembering Clare as she'd looked the last time he saw her. His eyes blurred.

Then something moved from behind the curtains onto the window seat, and he gazed directly into the round yellow eyes of a hostile cat. Attila bared two long fangs.

Bryn stared at him for a long time.

The cat stared back. And then, purposefully, he rolled over, lifted a black-and-white rear leg into the air, and licked himself.

Bryn crossed the room, unable to believe Clare had left her pet behind. She loved that fiendish animal. The cat ignored him, slurping noisily.

Bryn stopped a careful two feet away and looked out the window. Bright morning sunshine bathed the garden. He knew Clare had planted beds of pansies and had cultivated roses with a passion, although most everything looked brown to him. A patch of bright yellow daffodils blazed in one corner. He tugged the curtain aside so he could see them better, and his heart stopped.

In a pale blue smock, a wide-brimmed bonnet on her head, Clare knelt by a small patch of brown soil with a tray of seedlings by her side and a trowel in her hand. Unable to breathe, he saw her scoop out a tiny hole, lift a slip from the tray, and place it in the ground. She wore heavy gloves. He watched her pat the soil in place around the plant, measure a hand's breadth away, and dig another hole.

Dimly, he was aware of wet tears streaking his cheeks, and thoughtlessly he patted Attila's uplifted leg.

Sharp claws swiped at him as the cat sprang away.

It felt good. The pain in his head felt good. He

felt better than he'd ever felt in his life. Clare had not left him.

He soared out of the room, down the stairs, through the kitchen, and out the open door. Then he stopped, unable to go any closer to her.

At the sound of his arrival, Clare's head tilted and she glanced past the drooping brim of her sunbonnet. Carefully, she laid the trowel down in front of her, sank back on her heels for a moment, and then rose gracefully to her feet.

Bryn just looked at her, unable to speak. Helplessly, he lifted his hands in a mute gesture of apology.

Without hesitation, Clare walked straight up to him and wrapped her arms around his waist.

"Forgive me," she said.

21

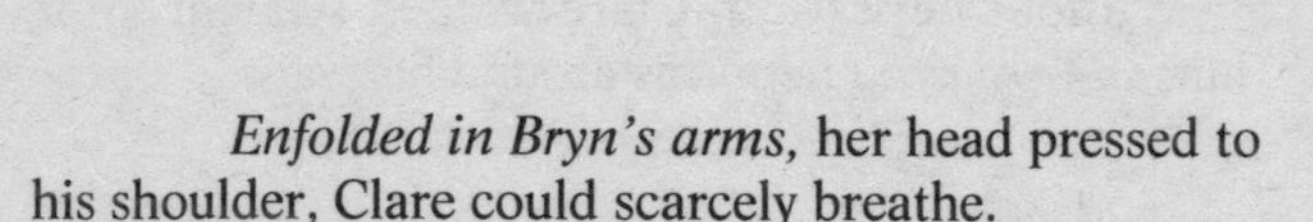

Enfolded in Bryn's arms, her head pressed to his shoulder, Clare could scarcely breathe.

"I thought you'd left me," he said again and again, crushing her against his chest as if not altogether sure she was really there. His whole body trembled.

Suddenly he set her back, gripping her shoulders hard. "Why didn't you?"

"I was not certain what you expected me to do," she confessed with a fragile smile. "Was I supposed to leave?"

"No. I . . . of course not. But I thought you would."

She bowed her head. "Then I shall, if you wish me to go."

"Good God, that's the last thing in the world I want." He seemed to realize he was shaking her, and his arms dropped heavily to his sides. "Why aren't you angry with me?"

"Angry?" Clare fingered his lapel. "I've no right."

"The devil you don't! You should be flaying me with your trowel. Planting me under the violets."

"Bryn, are you ill? Have you been injured?"

"I'm fine."

She tilted her chin, regarding him quizzically.

"All right," he muttered, "I feel rotten. But I'm not sick."

"Gut-drunk," she observed tranquilly.

He hung his head. "First time in my life."

"And last, I hope." Clare stripped off her gloves and stuffed them in her apron pocket. "To be honest, my lord, you smell like a week-old fish. I'll put on some water to heat."

He caught her as she moved past. "Clare, we need to talk."

"Yes. Later, when you've cleaned up and eaten something." She unclamped his fingers from her wrist. "I may need the trowel after all, to scrape off that grime. Did you sleep in a brewery vat last night?"

He followed her into the kitchen, seizing a heavy pot from her hands. "I'll make do with cold water for a bath." He found a smaller pan, filled it, and lit the stove. "This will be enough hot water for shaving and some tea. Clare, there's a coach out front. Will you tell the driver to go home? No, I'll do it. I need to give him a message for Finchburton."

She watched him lurch toward the hall and released a heavy sigh. Of all the things she'd imagined during the long sleepless nights, the daylight hours tormented by guilt, nothing came close to the reality.

Bryn thought she would be angry with him. He was furious with himself. But he had got everything backward, because it was all her fault.

First things first. She hurried upstairs for towels, milled soap, and his robe. While he scrubbed himself down in the kitchen, standing in a copper tub, she prepared his shaving basin and stropped his razor. Then she brewed tea, leaving him a full mug and carrying the rest to the bedchamber.

He joined her a few minutes later, the black silk robe belted around his waist and his thick hair sleek from a fierce washing. "You can take off your bonnet now," he said with a lopsided smile.

Flushing, she untied the ribbons and went back to the kitchen to fix him something to eat.

Her father had drunk himself into a stupor every night, although he made sure to do it in the privacy of his study, and never on Saturdays. Not until he'd finished crafting his Sunday sermon, with the passion of a man terrified by his own weaknesses. Most of the homilies were about forgiveness and divine mercy. She would sit with him then, and listen while he read passages aloud for her approval. But when he reached for the bottle, and he always did, she went to her bed and cried herself to sleep.

Every morning, he woke up with a headache. The housekeeper had fed him broth and crackers, she remembered. Unwrapping the cold roasted chicken Mrs. Beales had left for her luncheon, she stewed it on the stove in hot water seasoned with herbs. While the broth simmered, she cut some daffodils from the garden, arranged them in a vase, and prepared a tray. It felt good to be doing something for Bryn. Fixing things to please him.

She did not please him in bed.

He was sound asleep when she came into the room, propped up against the pillows as though he'd sat there to wait for her. His bristled chin rested on his chest. He had not managed to shave.

Clare set down the tray, took hold of his bare feet, and used all her strength to tug him down the pillows until he lay prone. Bryn asleep was senseless as a banister. His robe had tangled around his waist, baring long, darkly furred legs. Above his manhood, limp in the nest of curling hair at his groin, his stomach was flat and hard. The robe had slipped over one shoulder, baring most of his chest.

She had never truly looked at him in full light. Had never dared. After the one glimpse of him, fully erect, the night they first made love, she was careful to gaze at him only above the waist or shut her eyes. Now she looked her fill.

He is truly beautiful, she thought, wondering that she had never realized that before. Beautiful all over. Not just his face, which was remarkably handsome, or his muscular shoulders and chest, which she'd accustomed herself to seeing, but the rest of him too. A shiver swept from her scalp to her toes. Was this how he felt, when he looked at her naked body with glowing, heated eyes?

She moved to his side and pulled at the robe until it covered him to the knees. Then she fluffed a pillow under his head, stroked his cheek once with the back of her hand, and returned to her gardening.

She had begun to cultivate the herbs needed for the potion Mrs. Beales mixed up for her, the one that would prevent conception. It had seemed a good idea to grow them herself and make sure they were fresh and potent, but now it made her uncomfortable to place them one by one in the narrow patch of soil. Planting seedlings in the ground, so that Bryn could not plant his seed in her.

She knelt back, wiping her forehead with her apron. The late-morning sun was warm, and she'd forgotten to put on her bonnet again. What would it be like, to carry Bryn's child? He would be furious, of course, but once the baby was growing inside her there was nothing he could do. She could leave him before he even found out.

The idea took hold. She could never have a child legitimately. No man would marry her now. And even if there were a man forbearing enough to wed a whore, she only wanted Bryn's child.

A bastard child. It was wrong. A sin. But she was already damned, and life was so brief. How could it hurt to claim for herself what she most wanted?

Joseph and Jeremy were conceived out of wedlock too, and no one who ever met them could be sorry they were born. They were the one truly good thing their mother ever did. And God had taken care of them.

She dug her trowel into the damp earth, remembering the night Ardis told her about the twins' father. A fantasy, no doubt, spun during the endless hours the woman rocked in her chair, mumbling psalms and gazing into space. But that evening she had seemed more in touch with reality, her eyes sparkling, her face almost beautiful again.

He was a nobleman, she said, in the neighborhood to hunt with the Quorn. They met every day, in a meadow fragrant with wildflowers, where his promises filled her with dreams. But one afternoon he failed to appear and she never saw him again, although she went to that meadow every day.

After three months, her parents realized she was pregnant, something she in her ignorance had never imagined. They demanded her lover's name, but he had never told her. "We are Tristan and Isolde," he had said, "reincarnated to fulfill their destiny." Her mother and father, always cold and unfeeling, were certain she was lying to protect some tenant farmer's son and immediately disowned her.

Ardis had grown silent for a while, lost in memories, but suddenly she seized her stepdaughter's hand. Clare must never forget the boys were aristocrats, she entreated. They must be properly educated, as befitted their ancestry. That idea settled into the woman's mind, and for several months it replaced the endless recital of psalms.

"You must do it," she said over and over, in tempo with the rocking of her chair. "You must care for them when I am gone."

Clare lifted a plant from the tray and studied the delicate roots, thin as the veins in her wrist. Then she held the rosemary to her nostrils and breathed deeply. Rich earth and new life.

Joseph and Jeremy were hers now, and she had done her best for them. But dearly as she loved the boys, they were not from her own flesh, or Bryn's. If she stopped taking the herbal drink, perhaps . . .

But no. It wasn't fair to him. Always he had made clear to her that he must marry and sire an heir. Only after that might he be willing to give her a child too. It was tempting to imagine a lifetime as his mistress, making a second family for him.

She crushed the rosemary in her hand. Dear God, how quickly one sin led to another. Once set on the slippery path to hell, with nothing to lose for herself, it was so easy to forget that her wickedness would inevitably hurt others. Bryn intended to wed someone of his own class, probably Elizabeth Landry, and their marriage would have no chance for happiness while he remained unfaithful.

She suspected Bryn never considered the possibility of a happy marriage. He always spoke of his nuptials as a wearying necessity, like paying taxes. And he was selfish enough to seek his pleasures elsewhere, given the opportunity.

But she would not be the one to give him that. When her soul was consigned to hell, it would not be for the sin of adultery. She would take no one with her, especially the man she had come to love.

When she had transplanted the last herb, she went upstairs to check on him. He had rolled onto his stomach and one leg was drawn up, taking the robe with it. White bare buttocks shone against the rich blue counterpane. She bit her lip. When a man looked good even from this perspective, a woman was really in trouble.

Almost belligerently, she rearranged his robe, unable to resist touching the hard swell of his buttock. He stirred slightly and she jumped back.

Glancing at his watch on the side table, she calculated from previous experience that it would be several hours before he awoke, although considering his present condition he might well sleep the clock around. Feeling at loose ends, she wandered into the salon and picked out a book, settling comfortably on the sofa.

Halfway through *Le Morte d'Arthur,* she was startled to hear a noise from overhead. What was he doing up ahead of schedule? She had meant to change clothes and at least comb her hair before he saw her again. But it always took Bryn awhile to wake up, so she tore upstairs to make herself presentable, astonished to find him sitting up against the pillows with a plate of crackers on his lap, crunching noisily.

"Where've you been?" he demanded. "I didn't think my hands were steady enough, so I decided you had better shave me. The water must be getting cold by now."

"Well, I expect so," she said with a wry grin. "It has been sitting there for six hours."

"The devil you say!" He grabbed his watch and peered at it. "By God, it's three-thirty!"

Clare laughed, crossing to sit on the bed next to him. "So it is. You seem remarkably alert for a man who could scarcely stay on his feet this morning."

"Am I supposed to feel better?" He rubbed his forehead. "I'm not sure I do. Go away, Clare."

She had been leaning over to kiss his cheek, and pronked away like an antelope.

"The chamber pot," he explained, reddening with obvious embarrassment. "Come back in a few minutes."

With time to compose herself, Clare was cool as moss when she reentered to find him standing next to the tray munching on the last of the crackers. Somehow, the natural everyday things had taken the edge off her anxiety. She still didn't know what she was going to say to him, although the next hour was very important, but she felt almost at ease. She smiled at him.

He smiled back.

"I'm sorry," they said at the same time.

"You," he said firmly, "are not permitted to be sorry. For once I recognize that I have an apology to make, and I intend to make it. I've had little experience at humbling myself, and I'll stumble around awhile before I find the best words, so do not interrupt me while I'm looking for them."

Clare shook her head. "Please, Bryn, don't. You'll bury me under coals of fire if you apologize for something that is all my fault." He opened his mouth to object and she placed a finger across his lips. "Please."

He looked at her for a long time, and finally sat on the bed against the pillows, gesturing to a spot next to him. "You may speak first," he allowed, "and *then* I'll apologize."

Clare settled near his waist, against his lifted knees. "I too have been looking for words," she began. Her voice was scratchy with nerves, and she cleared her throat. "I understand that I have disappointed you"—he leaned up, and she placed her hand against his chest—"but truly I was trying to please you. I simply did not understand what was required of me."

His forehead wrinkled. "Clare, do you know what I want from you?"

"Not precisely. I have given it much thought since you left, though, and I shall try to do better."

He smiled. "And how, exactly, will you try?"

"I am not altogether certain. I finally decided that you would explain it to me, and then I would do whatever you say."

He shook his head. "No, you don't understand at all. I doubt this is a thing you can *try* to do better."

Her heart fluttered in her chest. "If I cannot do better, then . . . what?" For the first time in her life that she could remember, her voice squeaked.

He heard it too, because his smile widened. "You can stop fighting me. More to the point, stop fighting yourself. Clare, lovely Clare, have you ever doubted that my body wants you, or mistaken the pleasure I find when we make love?"

"Not until the last time," she said in a small voice.

"You are supposed to feel exactly the same way." The smile vanished, and he studied her somberly, tilting her chin with his hand when she looked down at her lap. "But you won't let yourself feel, Clare. And when you sense that you are responding to me, you—damn, I can't define exactly what happens. You snuff out your own fire like a candle. Sometimes you come at me like a wild woman, other times you allow me to draw you to the edge and then you . . . go away. You never let me reach you and bring you where you are meant to be."

"I know."

He looked surprised.

"But I never thought it would matter to you," she went on, twisting her head from his hand. "I see now that it does."

"Will you tell me why?" he asked softly. "Were you afraid? Is it because you don't like me and don't wish to share . . . ?" His voice faltered.

"It has nothing whatever to do with you," she said. "It is something in me, and I cannot explain it."

"*Will* not," he corrected with a sigh.

She nodded, unable to meet his eyes. "I did not expect you to come back, Bryn. But I am very glad you did."

"The same way you were glad I was to be your first lover?"

"No. For other reasons."

There was a long silence. "And that is all I am going to get from you, isn't it?" he said finally. "Not one clue, not one tiny indication of how you feel about anything."

He sounded disgruntled, but not angry. Resigned, she thought. "How can I explain," she asked, thinking her question eminently reasonable, "when I don't understand myself?"

"There is a great deal more to it than that," he told her with an edge to his voice. Then he lifted her hand and kissed her fingertips one by one. "But I can scarcely blame you, after the way I have behaved beginning to end. That is going to change, Clare, I promise you. Somehow I shall contrive to win you over, until you feel you can confide in me. Trust me."

For all her misery, Clare could not help but be amused. Bryn was always so sure he could arrange everything to his design. Even correct his own behavior, although she suspected he rarely considered that to be necessary. She leaned against his knees, relaxed for the first time in days. She could not give him what he wanted most right now, but she wanted to give him something. He still held her hand. She drew it to her lips and kissed his fingers the way he'd done to hers. Something hot flashed in his eyes.

He pulled his hand away. "No, you don't, witch," he said without rancor. "First I apologize."

"But you've done that," she murmured, toying with the folds of his silk robe. "You were angry, and whatever you said to me has already been forgotten."

His eyes narrowed. "Not by me. Nor by you, Clare Easton. And if you want an example of what you do that drives me wild, this is it. Dammit, you won't *talk* to me."

"Talk," she said grimly, "is not what you hired me for."

The silence that followed was awesome.

Bryn was taut as a bowstring. Clare's hand, resting on his throat, felt the tension in him before he released a harsh laugh.

"Good," he said. "An honest reaction. Sometimes I think the only time I ever see the real Clare is when you are angry at me. I warn you, lady, I'll take advantage of that if I must."

"It was a t-terrible thing to say," she stammered wretchedly.

"You may say anything to me, so long as you mean it. Anything at all is better than when you go away." He tapped her forehead. "In here"—his finger moved to her heart—"or here." Then he pulled her to his chest, kneading her back. "Anything is better than when you leave me."

She thought he would make love to her then. She was certain he would. And she was so afraid of disappointing him again she felt herself growing very cold.

To her surprise, he set her back and swung his long legs over the other side of the bed, burying his face in his hands. "Sweetheart, my head is killing me. And damned if I'll let you down after everything I've said. I need to clean up, and sleep this off, and pull myself together. Get home, if I can figure out a way. Dammit, don't I pay the servants in this house? Where the hell is everyone?"

"You damn well do," she said, "and they are the hell away on a perfectly proper Sunday off."

He glanced over his shoulder in blank astonishment.

"Well, you told me I could say whatever I wanted," she reminded him. "And I am trying to learn from you."

He barked a laugh and felt his head pound. "Learn this," he gritted between clenched teeth. "Never get drunk."

Clare stood and regarded him with a fond expression. "I'll send one of the stableboys from the mews to your house for a coach," she said.

"And bring me a glass—make it a jug—of water."

An hour later, with the choice of riding home in his robe or redonning the stinking clothes he'd worn for two days, Bryn decided to send over a complete wardrobe to Clouds. He expected to spend most of his time here anyway. As he kissed Clare goodbye, murmuring an apology for his scratchy beard, he realized it was the only apology she had allowed him to finish.

"We will spend all of tomorrow together," he informed her. "And we'll get an early start. I shall pick you up at ten. Dress for an outing in the country."

She handed him his ale-streaked coat. "Yes, Bryn."

"That was meant to be an invitation, not an order," he mumbled.

"I know." She gave him a full glass of water to take with him. "It will be interesting to see you awake before noon."

"Make it nine," he countered. "Hell, I'll come for you at eight."

22

Bryn made it to Clouds in Black Lightning a little after ten, head still throbbing slightly and a touch of red in his eyes, but otherwise feeling better than he had in days.

Clare met him at the door, the picture of spring in a crisp jonquil muslin dress with a scooped neck and puffed sleeves, a wide-brimmed straw bonnet tied under her chin with a jaunty yellow ribbon, and a lacy parasol.

The day was sunny and warm. Already regretting his blue broadcloth driving coat and starched collar, he decided to strip to his shirtsleeves once they reached the countryside. The grays seemed to have caught his mood, high-spirited and eager for a long hard run. Clare's arm curled around his waist as he steered through the thronged streets of midmorning London and headed for the open road.

He often drove to Richmond, or rode, because it

was increasingly hard to draw Claude Howitt to the city. One of Claude's children seemed always to be ailing, and now that Alice was about to deliver another, he refused to budge except in an emergency. Business could wait, he always said, even Caradoc's business.

Bryn didn't mind. Claude's household was like another world to him: three kids, dogs, cats, rabbits, the assorted frogs and snakes favored by the older boy, and a house that began as Alice's cottage but had been added onto so often it now stood three stories high.

Bryn's only experience with family life had been the few weeks every year he spent as a child with the close-knit Lacey clan. Of course Alice and Claude were not married, and so far as the law was concerned their children were not legitimate. But that seemed not to matter to them, nor to their neighbors and friends. Bryn had come to like the tiny village and the scattering of farms around it, to the extent that he'd bought a large stretch of land and paid the living of the curate at the small stone church of St. Didacus.

Although he'd not built a house for himself as yet, he thought that when he married, his wife and children would like a country home for the summer. By now his estate at River's End must be in ruins. He'd not been there for twenty years and had no intention of ever going back. One day he intended to plant new roots, closer to London where he felt at home, and the property at Richmond seemed a likely spot.

He recognized a long straight stretch of road ahead and let the horses go, feeling Clare's fingers dig into his side as high hedgerows thick with blackberry bushes flashed by. The horses thundered along the road, Black Lightning almost airborne behind them, its wheels scarcely touching the ground.

Clare's bonnet was blown back, secured only by the yellow ribbon against her neck, and her long hair streamed behind her. It felt like he was flying with Clare clinging to him, he her only support and anchor.

The sensation was blinding. He almost failed to see a lumbering hay wagon ahead and barely managed to pull up in time.

"My heavens," Clare said breathlessly. She let him go and tugged the bonnet over her head. "That ribbon was strangling me."

He came back to earth with a thud. The road was too narrow to pass the hay wagon, and it would be another mile before he could swing Black Lightning around. Meantime, they'd eat dust. His good mood vanished.

"What a magnificent ride," Clare said then. "I felt like a bird."

He looked over and saw wide eyes and a bright smile. What he'd thought was terror had been exhilaration.

"Damned wagon," she said, and they both laughed.

"I knew you'd like this," he declared exultantly.

"Your Black Lightning is perfectly splendid. How clever you are to have designed it."

He felt his chest swell. Wrapping his arm around her shoulder, he tried to draw her closer but the brim of her hat poked him in the cheek. One way or another, he reflected, something always kept them apart.

"Where are we going?" she asked.

He looked sideways and could see nothing but that infernal hat. "To visit a shrine," he said with heavy solemnity.

She went stiff.

Why in heaven's name was she troubled by that? "The birthplace of a celebrated rascal," he explained, and felt her relax immediately. "Attila the Cat."

Straw scraped his chin as she turned her head. "Really?"

"Claude Howitt lives down this road another two miles. With any luck, you can ingratiate yourself with that miserable feline's mother, father, and assorted siblings. Not to mention Claude's brood. He has two sons and a snot-nosed daughter by last count. Another offspring is imminent."

"Claude was the sweet man who came to the box at the opera," Clare said with pleasure. "I liked him very much." She let go of Bryn long enough to untie the ribbon and remove her hat. Then she leaned her head against his shoulder in a gesture he found heart-warmingly intimate. "What a perfect day."

"Claude and I have some business to conduct," he warned her. "At least, that's my excuse for dropping in unannounced." When she tensed he rushed on. "I often do that, Clare. Alice lets me run tame in her house, and she'll be delighted to meet you. Claude and Alice are the happiest couple I've ever known, and I have long wanted to bring you here." He reined the grays to a stop and looked down at her. "We can turn back, if you prefer."

Long lashes veiled her eyes for a moment, and then she lifted her face and smiled at him. "After the opera and Hyde Park, I expect I'll survive. Besides, I want to meet Attila's mother."

Alice, with a blond-haired moppet clutching at her skirt, welcomed Clare as if greeting a lifelong friend. The women soon withdrew to the kitchen to fix sandwiches and coffee, while the two rambunctious boys played a loud game of sheriff-and-Robin-Hood in the parlor where Bryn and Claude were trying to talk business.

When the men were served, the women and children adjourned to the barn, where Mandycat had just given birth to five more kittens. Their eyes were still closed, and their high-pitched mews as they suckled brought a smile to Clare's lips. Two of them were white with patches of black, just like Attila.

She fondled them with glee, even as several puppies rollicked at her ankles. Both women, three children, six puppies, and mother cat and kittens were thoroughly enjoying themselves when Bryn and Claude came into the barn.

Alice was draped with a sleepy three-year-old daughter, her two sons making straw men at her side. Clare had a puppy in her lap, another squirmed on her shoulder, and a tiny ball of fur was cradled between her hands.

Bryn stared at them for a long moment, never in his life more aware of the enormous power and compelling beauty of womanhood. He knew, instinctively, that this was one of those rare images that stayed with a man forever, a picture he'd be able to conjure with absolute clarity fifty years from now, if he lived so long.

Beside him, Claude smiled like a man who saw such pictures every day. He had the skill and the backing to become a successful politician or a wealthy businessman but chose instead a quiet existence in the country, ordering his life around moments like this. Bryn had always considered him likable and brilliant but indolent, a man of no ambition. Now he realized Claude Howitt was the wisest man he knew.

"No more cats," he told Clare when she held out a black-and-white handful of fur for his inspection. "Not from this lineage, anyway. You may have a puppy, if you like."

"Attila would tear a puppy to shreds," she said cheerfully, brushing straw from her skirt as she came to her feet with characteristic grace. "He likes to have his own way."

Bryn swept her a mocking bow. "Point taken. And now we must be off, because I have a surprise for you."

It was fully thirty minutes before Clare and Alice completed their goodbyes. Women, Bryn decided sourly, talked too much. And what the devil could his mistress and his friend's mistress be discussing at such length? He waited in agitation beside the curricle, Claude puffing imperturbably on his pipe, obviously accustomed to female prattle.

Finally Clare was settled beside him, chatting happily about cats and puppies while he drove at moderate speed, watching for the turnoff. Wondering if everything was ready. A few minutes later he steered onto a narrow tree-shaded lane and proceeded for about a mile before reining the grays to a halt.

Clare glanced up at him in surprise, wondering why they'd stopped in the middle of nowhere. Then, to her astonishment, a liveried footman sprang from the trees and took the horses in charge. She was still considering this wonder when Bryn swung from the curricle, came around to her side, and held out his arms. He grinned like a small boy with a snake hidden in his pocket. Positively beaming, she thought, as he took her by the waist and lifted her down. "Where are—"

"Shhh," he said.

She heard the sound of moving water and the songs of birds.

Bryn took her hand and led her to a tiny path that wound about a hundred yards. Sunlight filtered through the trees, and the sound of water grew louder. Soon he was forced to walk ahead of her, practically tugging her along as the path headed up a sloping hill.

At the top, the trees ended and a long sweep of grass, studded with wildflowers, reached to the banks of a river. An enormous blue-and-white striped pavilion, pointed at the top and open on all sides, was raised in the center of the meadow.

"Faerieland," she whispered, her eyes blurring.

"Come on," said Bryn, leading her down the hill.

Soon she could make out a table and two chairs inside the tent, resting on a thick carpet stacked with satin pillows. Two settings of the finest bone china were laid out, along with heavy silverware, delicate glasses, and a vase of flowers. Beside the table was a tripod with an ice-filled bucket and a bottle of champagne. Another table held two large straw hampers.

Bryn, hands stuffed in his pockets, watched closely as she wandered inside the tent, examining the elaborate picnic he'd arranged. Her mouth was slightly open, her head tilted to one side, her eyes wide. Finally she plucked a daffodil from the vase and held it to her breast for a moment.

Then she looked back at him and shook her head, laughing. "Only you, Bryn."

Hands still in his pockets and gaze fixed on the carpet, he stepped forward, feeling very stupid. Clare was the last woman in the world to like this sort of flamboyant display. It was a ridiculous idea.

She draped the daffodil over his left ear and rested

her hands on his shoulders. "You *are* impossible, you know," she said.

He nodded, his gaze shifting nervously to the champagne bucket.

"Where are the musicians?" she inquired mischievously.

Of course there should have been musicians. "I didn't think of that," he mumbled. "Damn."

He felt her hand on his chin and risked a look at her face. She was smiling.

"This is quite the most wonderful day of my life," she said softly. And then she kissed him.

He stood there, unable to move when her arms wrapped around him, and he heard her whisper *thank you* into his mouth, and other things he couldn't hear because of the blood pounding in his ears.

He had never been kissed like that, with a passion that wasn't sexual and was at the same time so intimate it was as if she made love to him. The earth melted under his feet.

Color was high in her cheeks when she stepped back.

He felt dazed. He probably looked it, the flower dangling across his cheek as he wrested his clenched fists from his pockets. "I forgot the music," he said, scuffing his toe on the carpet.

"Thank heavens. Are the trees swarming with servants?"

"Not one." He regathered his wits. "I thought we could serve ourselves. They'll be back to pack everything up when we are gone. Three hours at most, Clare—if you wish to stay so long."

"However did you manage all this? You must have been planning for a long time."

"Only since last night. But you are well aware I have only to give a few orders and pay the bills."

"Yes. Even so, you created magic, Bryn. We might have been set down in a tale from the *Arabian Nights.* I feel like Scheherazade."

"Still lots of Moorish things in Spain. I brought the tent home from the Peninsula. Don't know why. It took my fancy, I suppose." He busied himself uncorking the champagne and filled her glass.

"I am . . . dazzled." She sat on one of the chairs and sipped the wine appreciatively.

Bryn slouched across from her, uncertain of her mood. He wanted her to relax. Enjoy herself. He couldn't remember anything he'd wanted so much for a long time. "I bought this land years ago," he told her. "Thought one day I'd build here. A country house."

Clare looked toward the river and back up the hill, to where the trees began. "It would be a shame," she said thoughtfully, "to spoil the landscape. But how splendid to live here."

He knew at that moment exactly what he would do. This would be where he'd settle with Clare and their children, the same way Claude lived with his Alice. This would be . . . home. Tomorrow he'd begin the search for an architect.

"Bryn?"

Startled, he looked up.

"Are you hungry?" She was opening one of the hampers, her eyes rounding. "Good heavens, we could feed a regiment with all this."

"Choose what you like," he said. "The servants will eat the rest on the way home." He swallowed his champagne and refilled the glass. "Have I put you off with this extravagance?"

She looked at him over her shoulder. "Did I not make myself clear?" Seconds later she was sitting across his lap, treating him to another of those intoxicating kisses. He was almost relieved when she leaned back and brushed a swatch of hair from his forehead.

She could not help but feel his erection, rigid as an obelisk against her smooth hips. He was afraid of spoiling everything. Losing her, to the place she went when he moved inside her. For once she was pleased with him. He dared not bungle things by making love to her.

Nor did he want her to thank him—or reward him—with sex, as if he'd tried to buy her with a shiny tent and a fancy picnic.

He never meant this to be a seduction. But suddenly she was standing in front of him, tugging at his coat and drawing him down onto the satin pillows.

"You don't have to do this," he murmured.

"I want to do this," she said with conviction. "I want *you,* Bryn."

It was a thing any whore would say. He had heard it a hundred times. But Clare had never said those words. He didn't think she meant them, but he was long past where it mattered.

His hand lifted her skirt, sliding up her long leg, over her bent knee. He kissed her deeply, molding her soft thighs until his knuckles brushed the hair between her legs. He pressed higher, harder, and heard her moan.

Blessed heaven, she *did* want him. She clutched at his back, tugging at his coat and shirt, reaching under them to feel his bare flesh. He wanted her naked beneath him, the breeze cool on their hot skin, the river pulsing in their ears, so close. He wanted to be naked when his body joined with hers. But there was no time.

No time.

She knew it too. He felt her hands fumbling with his breeches and lifted himself slightly to help. For a moment he gazed down at her, and a butterfly flitted between them just before he plunged inside her with a cry of relief.

For a last moment he held still, still watching her face, cream and roses against the blue pillow, her lush hair like smoke, her eyes burning with desire. In all his life he'd never seen anything so beautiful.

"Oh, Bryn," she whispered.

He was lost in her. Wherever Clare was, he was there too, shaping himself to her body, surging in her with a fierce urgency that was soon overmastered by her own passion. And when he heard her cry out, and shake, and claw at him in stormy release, he almost betrayed her. But at the last moment he remembered to pull out, spilling his seed on the pillows before collapsing at her side.

Clare felt limp as seaweed. Pleasure washed over her in waves. When Bryn drew her into the curve of his arm she rested her cheek against his throat, and after a while they seemed to be floating together on a still ocean, at peace.

She would never repent of this day, she knew at the corners of her mind. Never confess it as a sin, kneeling on hard stone in a church, alone with her conscience and her Judge. Never be sorry.

Vaguely, she thought of Francesca and Paolo spinning in the Second Circle of Dante's Inferno among the other carnal sinners. The poet who loved Beatrice understood their transgression and forgave it as best as he could. They could not escape damnation, but even in hell they were light upon the wind, impelled by love.

"Do you ever wonder," she said into the long silence, "what price we must pay for days like this?"

"No." Bryn stroked her cheek with his finger. "Why do we live, if not for days like this?"

Clare had thought about that a great deal: *Why do we live?* She'd been taught answers. Some of them were scarred on the palms of her hands and the soles of her feet. But it seemed that she had lived to love this man, however briefly and whatever the cost. Nothing had ever seemed so clear.

Bryn rolled over her, resting on his elbows and gazing somberly into her eyes. "If you tell me you are sorry for this, I think it will kill me."

"Of course I'm not sorry. Bewildered, perhaps, and certainly amazed. But I understand now what you were trying to tell me yesterday. And the other night."

"Oh, Lord, don't bring up the other night." He buried his face against her neck.

"Nothing is what I thought it to be," she said. "Not you, nor I, nor what we just did. Part of me wants to think about it, and worry about it, but most of me doesn't want to think at all."

"You think too much, my sweet," he told her seriously. "We just made love, for the first time, I believe. Don't let anything take that away from us."

Never, she agreed silently as he kissed her. And when he entered her again, and began to move with slow, languorous, deliberate strokes, she gave herself to him with all the love burning in her heart.

Later they walked together, rumpled, redolent of wine and their lovemaking, smiling at everything and nothing. Clare took off her stockings and Bryn his boots, and they dangled their feet in the river, nibbling on the shortbread he brought along wrapped in a linen napkin. They talked about the flowers, and what colors Bryn thought things were, both disinclined to say much, afraid to break the mood. Finally they returned to the pavilion and shared a lunch of cold chicken and ham, cucumber sandwiches, wedges of cheddar cheese, and juicy peaches.

Bryn was careful to wait until her mouth was full before saying what had been on his mind all day. He'd prepared several opening statements but was horrified by what actually came out of his mouth.

"Clare, I don't want you to be my mistress any more."

She swallowed hard, choking a bit, and buried her face in her napkin. "As you w-wish," she stammered.

Her eyes were squeezed shut, and he could see no more of her face over the crumpled linen than a flushed forehead and thick eyelashes. "I want us to be lovers," he corrected hastily.

She looked up. "Are we not?"

"Certainly. Now, at least. What I mean is, I said terrible things the other night. About you being a . . . you know . . . and your duty, and so on." His tongue felt like a wet carpet. "Hell and damnation, Clare, I've come at everything all wrong from the beginning. I didn't know it at first, and the rest of the time I couldn't stop myself. But I want to start again and make things as they ought to be."

"Oh."

His throat felt raw. "You know I can never give you everything you ought to have. Not my name, nor the title. Not vows in a church." He regarded her intently. "You understand that?"

"Of course." She leaned forward, the napkin falling from her hands as she propped her elbows on the table. "Bryn, it doesn't matter if you call me lover instead of mistress. It does not change what I am."

He winced. "I'm not saying this right. You are what you were before we met—lovely and wise and compassionate. I'm the one who has changed. At least, I realize I must change and I will. Only, promise you won't leave me, Clare. I worry about that all the time."

"I will never want to leave you," she assured him.

He heard what he wanted to hear. *I will never leave you.* Distantly, he was aware that was not what she had said, but he was so happy. Happier than he had ever been, in a whole new world of happiness he'd never even imagined. It did not allow for equivocation.

He could hardly wait to make her happy, too, and give her sons and daughters conceived in the hot passion they had finally begun to share. He would have someone to talk to. Show his inventions to. All his truly close friends liked her. They'd come visit her here, in the new house he would build for her.

A few days every month he would go to London. Take care of business. Escort his wife to a party or two. Eventually see to the upbringing and education of his heir. They would want for nothing, his wife and son. He was so full of joy it enveloped the world. The universe.

He drove back to London slowly, Clare nestled in the circle of his arm, both of them silent. He expected she was reliving that afternoon in her imagination, as he was. But as they came into the city, he began to wonder if he should stay the night at Clouds.

She was sleepy with wine and her first taste of sexual pleasure, while he felt restless and exhilarated.

After considering, he decided to give her some time alone. Later, he would come back and join her in bed, if only to hold her as she slept.

Charley Cassidy ran down the stairs when Black Lightning drew up in front of the house, a worried look on his face. He took the reins while Bryn jumped out of the curricle and helped Clare alight.

At the open door, he put his hands on her shoulders, gazing intently into her eyes. "This has been the best day of my life," he said simply.

She stood on tiptoe and brushed his lips with her own. "And mine. I will never forget it, Bryn. Will you stay here tonight?"

He could tell she wanted him to, and his heart soared. "I'll be back later, but don't wait up for me if you're tired. Go to bed and I will join you there."

She kissed him again, this time with a promise he understood and could scarcely believe. She no longer pretended to want him. She truly did.

He almost floated down the front steps, so preoccupied with his own happiness that Cassidy had to pull at his sleeve to get his attention.

"I have a message for you, milord."

Charley handed him a ragged piece of paper, folded but unsealed. He scanned the note quickly, unable to make out more than a few words. He swore profoundly. Amid Lacey's indecipherable phrases were *Landry's back* and *Come to Izzy's.*

He sucked in a ragged breath. "Tell Miss Easton something important has come up and I may not make it back to Clouds tonight." Feeling suddenly lead-footed, he climbed into the curricle. "And Charley, tell her I'm sorry."

23

Robert and Isabella, grim-faced and silent, met Bryn at the door and ushered him into a parlor. There was no sign of Elizabeth, for which he was profoundly grateful. Refusing a drink, he sank onto a chair and regarded Lacey with a somber expression.

"You have become a positive nemesis," he said. "Every time we meet, you have bad news to convey. In future I shall make it a point to avoid your company."

Lacey ignored that. "Landry's in town, looking for Elizabeth, and we're pretty sure he knows where she is. Beth thinks she's seen him, skulking in the park across the street."

Bryn lifted a brow. "I presume you did the necessary reconnaissance?"

"Of sorts. Didn't want to tip that we're onto him, so we've been sending footmen on errands all day. Told them to cut through the park. No sign of anybody fitting his description, but they spotted a pair of workmen, clipping shrubs and the like. Nasty-looking brutes, from what I hear, and they pretty much stand about until someone comes past."

Probably hired thugs, Bryn reckoned. Landry must be in desperate straits, to defy him by returning to London weeks ahead of time. Desperate enough to risk everything on one last throw of the dice. "Are you sure he's back? Elizabeth could have been mistaken."

"He contacted Max Peyton this morning, begging for a loan. Peyton said he'd think about it, to keep him on a string, and went looking for you. Left a message at your house and settled in at White's, in case you showed up there. Lucky thing I ran into him and got the word, because I don't think he knows about Clouds."

"Robert sent a note," Isabella added, "and came here to warn us not to leave the house. Ever since, Beth hasn't moved from the window upstairs. She's there right now, watching out for her father and trying not to show how frightened she is. He has every legal right to take her home. I only wonder that he's not come to the door demanding we hand her over."

"As if you would." Bryn gave her a faint smile. "Landry is not one to think of applying to the law—too much chance his own crimes would come to light. I expect he'll try to get Elizabeth in his hands by other means and use her to blackmail us."

Lacey's expression hardened. "Beth won't be safe until she's married or Landry's dead. Izzy made me promise I'd wait until we talked to you, but in my opinion he ought to be shot."

"It may come to that." Bryn turned to Isabella. "You've been parading her through London the last few weeks. Any prospect of an alliance?"

She shrugged. "Beth has been accepted by the *ton* and is popular with the young men, but so far she's showed no particular interest in any one of them. And I cannot think of a family that would pay the settlement Landry will demand. She has nothing to offer in return except a sweet nature and her beauty."

"Not to mention intelligence, a sense of humor, and a hundred other things I could name." Lacey flushed. "Well, I've spent a good deal of time in her company, to help bring her into fashion, so I know what a prize she is. You won't do better for a wife, Bryn. And there's no one else who cares enough for her to buy Landry off. No one who can afford it, anyway. So what do you say? Either you marry her, or I kill him."

Isabella scowled. "For all she fears her father, I doubt that Beth would want to be the reason for his death. If you call him out, she will always feel responsible."

"So you have said a thousand times this afternoon, Izzy. I'm sick of hearing it. Landry will make trouble until he's planted in the ground, and I vote to put him there."

Bryn came to his feet. "Which means *me,* Lace, since you haven't a chance of bringing it off." He waved a hand. "No insult, but you can't shoot. And much as I'd like to put a bullet between his eyes, Izzy has the right of it."

Lacey poured himself a glass of brandy. "It seems we are back where we started a month ago. One of us calls him out, or you marry Beth."

The earl gazed at the carpet, inwardly cursing the malevolent fate that gave him the most wonderful day of his life, only to snatch it away. How could he go back to Clare, after what they had shared that afternoon, and tell her he'd become engaged to another woman a few hours later?

He felt the walls closing in around him. So many promises—to himself, to his father, to Clare, and even to Elizabeth, for whom he had unwittingly become responsible. A part of him, wholly separate from the ache in his heart, rapidly calculated profit and loss as if this nightmare were a business transaction. Already he had restored the Caradoc fortune and something of the family reputation. Wedding Elizabeth and getting a son on her would satisfy the last of his promises to Owen Talgarth. Upstairs, Elizabeth waited terrified and alone, needing his money and his power to protect her.

Could he turn his back on all that, to preserve his relationship with Clare? Given time, he might have been able to convince her to accept his legal wife and family while sharing another life, his *real* life, in a house built by the Thames where they had become lovers.

But there was no time.

He would bet everything he'd worked twenty years to acquire that Clare would vanish soon after hearing word of his betrothal. And so far, the Runners had not been able to find out her family name or where she came from. Where she might go. Almost certainly he'd lose her if he married Elizabeth. Not that he would give up, of course, and certainly he'd find her again. There was even a faint possibility he could persuade her to come back to him.

Without Clare, he would never be happy. But no one had ever promised him happiness. Blood iced in his veins. Someone would be hurt, whatever choice he made.

"Bryn?" Isabella touched his arm. "What shall we do?"

He gazed at her wearily. "Elizabeth ought to have some say in the matter, I suppose. Bring her down, will you?"

A few minutes later, Isabella ushered her guest into the salon and towed Lacey out.

For several moments, Bryn and Elizabeth gazed at each other without expression.

It occurred to him that he'd seen this young woman only twice before—once on the terrace at Lady Wetherford's house, after which he had waltzed with her, and then as she slept after a brutal beating from her father. Now he was expected to propose to her. He swallowed hard.

As if sensing his uncertainty, she gave him a brave, heart-melting smile. Admiring her poise, he led her to a sofa. Elizabeth would make any man a perfect wife, he thought. So lovely, and so controlled. He should be grateful, because he'd feel equally responsible for her were she an antidote.

"Miss Landry," he said, sitting next to her, "let me first assure you that you are in no danger. One way or another, your father will not again have an opportunity. . . ." His voice trailed off.

"To beat me?" Her gaze was steady. "It was not the first time, Lord Caradoc. But he never hurts me badly. And I am not altogether certain he is in his right mind."

Fury rose in him, at her resignation. "There is no excuse whatever for what he does to you," he said firmly. "Don't apologize for the man. The only question is how we are to proceed from here."

"Do we have a choice? He is my father. I can do nothing without his permission."

Bryn sighed. "The most obvious course may be the

best one, my dear. One day I must take a wife and provide an heir to the title. I have put that off too long and rather hoped to postpone it even longer. But it seems your needs and mine have come together at this precise moment. Would you consider marrying me?"

She gazed at him blankly. "But we don't know each other. Not at all. Dear God, why would you wish to marry *me* when you could have your pick of all the heiresses in London?"

He took her hand. "I liked you immediately, the first time we met," he said honestly. "And I've come to respect you since. You would make me a far better wife than I deserve. But there are . . . complications."

Her lips curved. "Clare Easton."

"Yes." Bryn was relieved that they could speak frankly. "I'm not certain that I am capable of loving anyone, Elizabeth. At the least, it is unlikely that I'd recognize the symptoms. But I know that life without Clare would be intolerable, and I will do everything in my power to keep her. My wife would have to accept that."

"It seems to me you know very well how it feels to be in love, my lord. Why do you not marry *her*?"

He blinked. "She is my mistress."

Elizabeth regarded him critically. "Does that matter?"

Letting go her hand, he folded his arms across his chest. "I have obligations which date from—well, about the time you were born. Whatever I feel for Clare, I must wed a woman of impeccable birth and breeding. It is a matter of promises made and thus far unkept, to my discredit."

Her gaze lowered, but Bryn caught a glint of reproach in her eyes. "Even so, you are willing to marry the daughter of a drunkard and a gambler," she said quietly.

Releasing a harsh breath, he leaned forward. "Elizabeth, you are more unlike your father than the stars are distant from the muddy ground. And if you are able to accept what little I have to offer, I will gladly meet you at the altar. You must decide if you can wed a man who will give you a home, children, and security while keeping another woman under his protection. You'll be a countess, and have money enough to satisfy every whim, but I doubt you care for that."

"I do not," she said flatly. "And in truth, my lord, you would find yourself burdened with a wife who loves another man, although I would never be unfaithful to you."

There was a short pause while that sank in. Then he came to his feet and stared at her, hands balled into fists. "Why the hell didn't you say so to start with?" Flushing, he muttered an apology for his language and began to pace the room. "That changes everything. Who is he? And where's the problem?"

"He has no money," she said in a dull voice. "He cannot afford to buy off my father, who would never consent to the marriage without an enormous settlement. And I am only seventeen, Lord Caradoc. I cannot marry without his approval."

He spun around. "Head out for Scotland and take your vows over the anvil. Why not?"

She shook her head. "I suggested that, but Rob—he would not hear of it. In his opinion I deserve better than a havey-cavey runaway marriage, as if I cared a bean for that. And he insists he cannot support a family, with no income and no prospects. He thinks I'll do better as *your* wife."

"Lacey." Bryn slapped his forehead. "By God, we're talking about Lacey. I should have known. All the signs were there, but I've been too preoccupied with my own affairs to notice."

Color flamed in her cheeks. "I told Robert I didn't mind living in the fields so long as it was with him, but he wouldn't listen. He wants me to be draped in fancy clothes and cut a tear through London society." Her voice was edged with anger. "Men are so pigheaded."

He couldn't argue with that. And suddenly the ice at his spine began to thaw. "You shall have him, Elizabeth. I'll see to it, if that is what you really want."

She looked him in the eye. "I love Robert with all my heart. And I want to be his wife, whatever the consequences."

Nodding, Bryn made rapid plans. "We'll need to be clever and spirit you out of London before your father gets wind of our scheme. Leave the details to me. For now, I suggest you go upstairs and pack your belongings while I inform Lace he is to be a bridegroom."

She studied his face, her eyes troubled. "But what if he doesn't agree? I know Robert loves me, but I was unable to convince him we should marry. What will happen when my father finds out? And what is to become of you, my lord? By your own admission, you need a wife."

Bryn laughed, feeling good for the first time since he got Lace's message. "Your prospective groom will do as I say. Your father will find himself thwarted, but by then you'll be beyond his reach. And as for me, I'll doubtless find an ambitious young woman so eager for a title and wealth that she'll ignore my liaison with Clare." He leaned forward and kissed her lightly on the cheek. "Be happy, child. I'm glad you are to be part of a family I hold dearer than my own. Now go upstairs and make yourself ready for a trip to Gretna Green."

She stood and curtseyed, blushing furiously as she hurried out of the room.

With pleasure, he watched her practically float away. Then he crossed to a window and studied his reflection in the glass. Was he in love with Clare, as Elizabeth had suggested? He had no idea. He wanted her. Perhaps he even needed her. Things had worked out for the best, he finally decided. Better he marry a woman he didn't care about at all. Elizabeth would have complicated matters, because he'd always have worried how she felt when he went to his mistress's bed.

Once Lace and Elizabeth were wed, he could concentrate on building a future with Clare. Then he would find a wife. Any well-bred girl would do. Now that he'd abandoned hope of a love match and accepted that an ideal marriage was not in the cards, he was able to proceed without delusions.

Meantime, Lacey needed a reliable source of income to support his bride. Bryn was more than willing to settle on his friend the same fortune Landry would have demanded, but he knew Robert wouldn't accept a handout. He was too proud.

"What's the verdict?" Lacey asked in a stony voice from the door. "Are you betrothed?"

"No." Bryn turned and gave him a wry grin. "But *you* are."

"What the hell does that mean?" Lacey stalked across the room, Isabella at his heels.

"Elizabeth says she all but proposed to you, and you turned her down." Bryn jabbed him in the chest with a hard finger. "I suggest you think again. Damned if I'll marry a girl my best friend wants for himself. You are on your way to Scotland, Lace, as soon as we work out the logistics."

The viscount shuffled his feet. "Don't think I haven't considered that, Bryndle, a thousand times. But I've no way to take care of her. I can barely support myself. And before you offer, I will not take your charity, not even for Beth. She wouldn't respect me if I did."

"As it happens, Lace, I am somewhat overextended in the charity department and have no intention of taking on another dependent. No, I rather suspect you'll have to work."

"W-*work?*" He looked stunned. "But I don't know how to *do* anything. Lead a cavalry charge, perhaps, but even if Boney escaped again and raised another army, I haven't the blunt to buy a commission."

Isabella laughed. "You could be a shepherd, Robbie. Surely you have wit enough for that."

Lacey turned on her. "Easy for you to say, now that you're plump in the pockets. All you had to do was marry a rich man who got himself killed in the war."

Bryn stepped between them. "Children, children. Our tempers are on edge, but let us concentrate on the problem at hand."

Lacey snorted. "You've got it all worked out, don't you? I know that smug attitude."

Bryn poured himself a glass of brandy. "In fact, I do. River's End must be restored—I promised my father I'd see to it—and you are the ideal man to take charge of the project. I like what you did at Clouds, and I'll pay you well to do the same for the Caradoc estate."

"You want to live there?" Lacey asked incredulously.

"Absolutely not." Bryn took a deep breath. Ghosts walked at River's End. He'd managed to escape everything but his memories, and he had no intention of ever setting foot in the place again. "One day my heir will claim his birthright," he said with deliberate indifference, "so I'm committed to seeing the castle brought to its former state. Better than that. Make it splendid, Lace. I expect it will take several years, and meantime you and Elizabeth can live at your own house, with your mother."

Isabella hugged him. "That's perfect, Bryndle. Mama has been too much alone, and she won't come to London however much I beg her to do so. You have found the solution to all our troubles."

He wasn't so sure of that. "Assuming Landry is watching your house," he said, "we have to get Elizabeth safely out of here without arousing his suspicions. So long as she's in my company I don't expect he'll interfere. Izzy, where could we take her tonight? Who is hosting a party?"

While she ran upstairs to check the invitations, he turned to Lacey. "For now, go to your lodgings and pack whatever you need. I'll send a servant to collect your luggage, with instructions on what to do next."

Isabella returned with a handful of cards, and he sorted through them. "The Esterhazy ball," he decided. "Landry won't be admitted there. Izzy, make sure Elizabeth is dressed for a dance, not an elopement. I'll pick the two of you up at nine o'clock."

Lacey glowered at him. "Do you intend to explain or go on snapping orders?"

"Both." Bryn put his hand on Lacey's shoulder. "So far I've only a sketchy idea how to bring this off, but in a few hours you and Elizabeth will be on your way to Scotland with Landry none the wiser. Trust me."

"Can I at least speak to her first? Make sure she really wants to do this?"

"Better we leave together, I think. Laughing, so the watchdogs suspect nothing, and *now* because I need the time to make arrangements. Come along, Lace. You'll have several hundred miles between here and Gretna to woo your bride."

24

"Do you think we were followed?" Elizabeth asked nervously as the earl's crested carriage drew up at the Esterhazy mansion.

"Possible, but unlikely." Bryn handed Isabella out of the coach and turned to help Elizabeth. "So long as you are with me, your father will make no trouble. It's what he most hopes for, after all."

With a lady on each arm, he mounted the marble steps and joined the throng waiting to pass through the receiving line. Although reasonably sure he'd accounted for every hazard, he reviewed his plan again, reflecting that he had gained some tactical experience smuggling Clare to and from Ernestine's house. On the other hand, he remembered with an interior groan, Ernie had found him out.

But this time he'd taken greater care, because the consequences of discovery were more disastrous than a scolding from the duchess.

By now Lacey was well on his way to the obscure inn where Bryn had spent the weekend. It seemed so long ago. Within the hour, Bryn and Elizabeth would make their way out the back door to the mews where a coach waited. It would carry them by a circuitous route to another unmarked coach laden with the couple's luggage. In his pocket was enough money to see Lacey to Scotland and home again. Tomorrow, Bryn would dispatch a bank draft to Heydon Manor, to get Lace started on the restoration of River's End.

He'd sent a message to Max Peyton, asking him to appear at the ball so Isabella would have someone to escort her home, and another to Princess Esterhazy, requesting that she admit Peyton.

He had decided to accompany Elizabeth to the inn and make his way back to London from there. It occurred to him that he should have told Lacey to take a horse from his own stable, because God only knew what sort of transportation that thatch-gallows had devised. Damned if he wanted to be stranded at the Black Sheep again, at the mercy of whatever ramshackle vehicle might pass by in the middle of the night.

Swearing under his breath at the oversight, he found himself face-to-face with Princess Esterhazy.

"You honor us, Lord Caradoc," she said, lifting her hand for his salute. "We have seen too little of you this season."

"I could scarcely resist what will surely be its crowning event," he said politely.

"Your Mr. Peyton is somewhere about." She lifted a curious brow. "Handsome devil, with those unusual eyes. From where did you conjure him?"

Swallowing his impatience, Bryn produced a smile.

"He is lately come from India, I believe. Thank you for inviting him, but for the rest you must quiz him yourself. I daresay he is keen to dance with his gracious hostess." Before she could pursue the interrogation, he bowed and moved on.

Just outside the ballroom, he drew the ladies aside. "Izzy, you are to stay here as long as possible. Be among the last guests to leave. By the time you return to my carriage, anybody watching this house will be hours too late figuring out that Elizabeth and I have already gone." He turned to Elizabeth, who was chewing her lower lip as she peered into the ballroom. Looking for her father, he suspected.

"I'll lead you out for a dance, my dear, in case your father has planted a spy. But I doubt there is reason for concern."

"He hasn't many friends who would be invited here," she agreed, somewhat breathlessly. "But still—"

He put a finger to her lips. "Don't worry. I shall be with you all the way, until you are delivered into Lacey's protection. You are perfectly safe."

She gazed solemnly into his eyes. "You are so kind to me, Lord Caradoc. And for no reason I can imagine. How shall I ever be able to thank you?"

He lifted a hand. "I assure you, it is my pleasure to be of service. And perhaps you can keep Lacey out of trouble. I've not managed to do so, but I expect you will. Now smile and pretend you adore me. So long as your father imagines there is hope you have snagged a rich suitor, we have bought time."

"Here you are at last." Max Peyton appeared at his shoulder, regarding the ladies with an expectant smile.

Elizabeth must be wholly besotted with Lace, Bryn thought as he performed the introductions, to be so oblivious of Peyton's dazzling smile. Isabella, on the other hand, had a look in her eyes he'd never seen before. She positively glowed as Peyton brushed his lips over her wrist.

With obvious reluctance, Max let go her hand and drew Bryn aside. "I've done some checking," he whispered. "Landry has hired any number of scoundrels to keep tabs on his daughter. Paid them with promises, I'm sure, because when he came to me this morning he was clearly at his last prayers. Keep your eyes open. I wouldn't put anything past him."

"Nor I. But there is a sword concealed in this cane, and both coaches waiting for us are manned by two armed footmen. Should there be any trouble when you take the countess home, I stowed two loaded pistols under the carriage seat."

Peyton grinned. "Quite a beauty, the Lady Isabella."

"Proceed at your own risk," Bryn warned. "She's more than a handful."

They rejoined the ladies, and after the opening minuet Bryn took Elizabeth's hand and led her down the back stairs, through the kitchen, and across a deserted alley into the mews where the first coach waited.

"No sign of trouble," said a brawny young footman as he lowered the steps. "We've watched the alley, but nobody is lurking about."

A few minutes later, they drew up on a deserted side street, where the transfer to the second coach was accomplished without incident. Bryn was almost certain they hadn't been followed, but even so he ordered the footmen to keep close watch on the road as they drove out of the city.

Elizabeth sat quietly, lost in her own thoughts for nearly an hour until the coach made a sudden turn, proceeded a short way, and came to a stop. Her gaze shot to Bryn's.

"Not to worry," he said, drawing the heavy curtains over both windows. "We'll wait here a few minutes, to make certain no one is on our trail. The footmen have shuttered the lanterns and gone back to the main road to see what passes by."

"You have thought of everything," she said in an awestruck voice.

"At the least, you may be sure that when you and Lace are on your way, there will be nothing to fear. This should be a romantic adventure, my dear, not a flight in terror. Concentrate on the road ahead, not the one behind you."

She relaxed visibly and gave him a sweet smile. "I quite like your Clare, my lord. Will you bring her to visit us?"

"Perhaps." His fingers tightened on the cane. "When you are next in London. I have no wish to go near River's End."

"Then we will come to see you."

Suddenly uncomfortable, he pulled out his watch. "Nearly two hours, I expect, before we reach the inn. Sleep if you can, Elizabeth. You've a long night ahead of you."

Twenty minutes later, a footman rapped on the panel. "One carriage," he reported, "only women inside."

Bryn pulled the curtains and nodded. "Thank you, Rafferty. Let's go on, then."

The driver soon found a place to turn around, and the coach returned to the country byroad that led to the inn.

Robert was waiting outside, an anxious look on his face. When Elizabeth alighted he rushed to take her in his arms, and Bryn turned his back while they kissed each other for what seemed like a very long time.

Finally Lacey acknowledged his presence by clearing his throat. "Er, Bryndle, the horse I hired to get here went lame two miles back. I had to walk the rest of the way. Maybe he'll be all right by tomorrow morning."

Wheeling, Bryn glared at him. "You mean I'm stuck here for the night? Dammit, Lace, why didn't you come in some sort of reliable vehicle?"

"Couldn't afford it," he replied with a shrug. "I presume you've brought money to see me to Scotland."

Bryn reached into his pocket and tossed him a leather wallet. "There's enough in here to cover post-horses and all the rest," he said crossly. "I've sent a servant ahead, to reserve rooms and secure a change of nags at proper intervals. The driver knows where to stop on the way, and you can improvise on the road home to Heydon Manor. Stay there out of my sight for several months, if you know what's good for you."

Lacey smiled at Elizabeth. "I do," he said softly. Then he shook Bryn's hand. "Sorry to leave you stranded, old man, but you're only twenty miles from London. Sooner or later you'll get home." With a grin, he helped Elizabeth into the coach and jumped in after her. "For what you've done, I owe you my life," he said out the window.

A fat lot of good that will do me, Bryn thought, as they pulled away.

The innkeeper assured him that in the morning he'd send his son to fetch a reliable mount, and meantime his lordship was welcome to the best room at the Black Sheep and a bottle of vintage port. Declining the wine, Bryn wearily mounted the stairs, suspecting from the silence and the darkened rooms that he was the only guest.

He stripped and climbed between the sheets atop a lumpy mattress, breathing a sigh of relief. Tomorrow he would confront Landry and make certain the whoreson never troubled Elizabeth again, even if that required putting a bullet through his head. One way or another this business would be settled, and he could forget everything but what mattered most to him.

Clare.

The picnic by the river seemed a lifetime ago, with all that had happened since. He buried his face in the pillow, trying to recapture the happiest hours of his life.

As the memories flooded back, they carried him into dreams where he made love to her again and again.

It was late afternoon before Bryn arrived in London. He'd forgotten to tell the innkeeper to wake him up and had slept until well past noon. After plodding twenty miles on a swaybacked mare, he was resolved that Landry could wait another day before being informed his daughter had eloped.

First, he wanted to see Clare and tell her what he'd done. She would approve, he thought. After a quick bath, shave, and change of clothes at St. James's, he set out for Clouds with a bouquet of daffodils and a sense of pleasurable anticipation.

That was quickly dashed when Charley Cassidy opened the door with a despondent look on his face. "She's gone, milord," he said.

Bryn stared at him blankly.

"Went for a walk with her maid and didn't come

home," Charley explained. "Amy came in a few minutes ago. I dunno what happened. She's with Mrs. Beales."

Bryn shoved past him, bellowing for the housekeeper.

Mrs. Beales met him in the salon, her thin lips tight. "You had better sit down," she advised.

Suddenly terrified that Landry had somehow made off with Clare, Bryn grabbed the woman by the shoulders and shook her. "What the hell is going on?"

Pulling away, she pointed to a chair.

After a moment, he muttered an oath and dropped obediently onto the cushion. "Tell me. And make it fast."

She folded her arms. "This afternoon Miss Easton said she wished to take her kitten for an outing in the park. She appeared somewhat unsettled, although I didn't know why at the time. Her maid went with her and has just now returned. It seems that Miss Easton hired a hackney a few blocks from here and instructed Amy to occupy herself for several hours before coming home. I was questioning her when you arrived."

"That's all she knows? Clare got in a hack and disappeared?"

"This may explain why." She crossed to a table, picked up a newspaper, and tossed it to him. "Miss Easton was reading it during lunch."

He caught the paper in midair. It was folded open, and he saw coffee stains on the page. He scanned rapidly until he encountered his own name.

The Earl of Caradoc is honored to announce his betrothal to the Honorable Elizabeth Landry, daughter of Lord Landry.

"I'll tear the bastard to pieces and feed him to the goats," Bryn swore, crushing the paper in his hands.

"You might have told her," Mrs. Beales said acidly. "Not left her to read it in the *Times.*"

He threw the housekeeper a scathing look. "It's all a humbug. Landry planted this item to force my hand. And it might have worked, devil take him, but he was too late. Last night, with my assistance and blessing, Elizabeth eloped with Robert Lacey."

Her face softened. "Ought to have known you would never serve the young lady such a turn. Sorry I jumped to conclusions, milord. Will you be wishing to speak with Amy now?"

He nodded, slumping in the chair with his forearms on his knees as Mrs. Beales left the room. If only he'd thought to send Clare a message, telling her what he was about. But he had been wrapped up in plans for the elopement and had expected to be at Clouds before morning to explain in person.

It was easy to imagine how she felt. After the picnic, he'd promised to spend the night with her and then dispatched Charley to tell her something had come up. When she read the notice in the *Times,* she doubtless assumed that the "something" was a proposal to Elizabeth.

He knew Clare thought him selfish and manipulative. Which he was. And it certainly looked as if he had seized the perfect opportunity to secure the Talgarth line, confident his mistress would not leave him after what they shared in that silken pavilion beside the river. She must think he had staged the elaborate display only to win her over before arranging his marriage to another woman.

Clare had no reason to trust him, because he gave her none. He never confided in her. For that matter, he never confided in anyone. What he felt was none of their business, and other people could take him or leave him—so long as they didn't get in his way.

He released a painful breath. That was not the case with Clare, but he was not in the habit of explaining himself. Or of confronting his own feelings at all, let alone finding words to describe them.

"Milord?"

Looking up, he saw Clare's maid standing in the doorway, wringing her skirt with both hands. She was pale as candle wax.

"Come in, child," he said gruffly. "I won't eat you."

Amy advanced two short steps, her gaze focused on the floor. "I knowed it was wrong," she blurted. "But she made me promise not to come back here before five o'clock. And I never thought she was going away permanent like. All she had was her reticule and the basket with her cat. Maybe she's just payin' a visit."

"Perhaps." He stood and saw her flinch. "None of this is your fault, girl. I only want to know if you heard Miss Easton tell the coachman her destination."

Looking miserable, she shook her head. "No, milord. She said as how I oughter visit me mum, who's been ailin', and I took off down the street right away."

"Can you think of anything she said that might help us find her?"

"She was awful quiet," Amy replied. "She don't talk much anyway, though she's real friendly, but today it was like she was somewhere else." She shuffled her feet. "You'll be wantin' me to pack up now, I 'spect."

He waved a hand. "Certainly not. Miss Easton will be returning to Clouds, and meantime you can stay with your mother. Your wages will continue to be paid."

Color returned to her cheeks as she curtseyed. "Thank you, milord. I know you'll find her. Didn't seem to me she wanted to go. Her eyes was unhappy."

"What was she wearing?" he snapped, just as Amy reached the door.

She turned around. "A blue dress, and a hat with a veil. I remember her pulling it over her face when she got into the hack."

Clare had left in the same clothing she wore when she first came to Clouds. It seemed to him a declaration of sorts, her way of closing the circle. Dismissing the maid, Bryn headed upstairs.

When he entered the larger bedroom he immediately saw a folded sheet of vellum on the bed but could not bring himself to look at it right away. Instead he examined her jewelry cases, unsurprised to find every necklace and bracelet and set of earbobs intact. The enormous armoire was crammed with clothing. She had taken nothing, except that damned cat.

Little fool. He remembered Clare telling him the ten thousand guineas he gave her were already spent, to repay some sort of debt. How was she to live?

Finally, with shaking hands, he picked up the letter.

Dear Bryn,

You will be angry that I have gone in this fashion. Please do not blame Amy or turn her off without a reference.

May I wish you happy? Elizabeth is lovely and brave. You could not have chosen better, and she is the most fortunate of women to have you.

I wish I had the courage to face you and say goodbye, but it is better that we not see each other again. You must devote yourself to your wife and to the children she will give you. To me, you were generous and kind beyond anything I deserved. Yesterday was the most beautiful day of my life, and I shall never forget it. Or you. Always, you will be in my prayers.

Clare

Her lovely handwriting had faltered near the end, and he knew she had left a thousand things unsaid.

As he had, all the time he was with her.

He sat on the edge of the bed, head bowed, for a long while, seeing her again as he had the first time, poised on the marble steps at Florette's Hothouse in her blue dress and veil. Remembering the first time she slept in his arms, wrapped in that tent of a nightgown. Kneeling, almost naked, on this same bed when he accused her of failing him. Of not doing her job, as a whore, to at least pretend he satisfied her.

He saw her at the Opera House, lost in the music. At the theater, clutching his hand when Laertes's poison-tipped sword cut Hamlet down. He felt the bite of her tongue when she raked him over the coals and savored again her deft, subtle wit.

And he could almost feel her in his arms again, on the satin pillows by the river, afire with passion for the first time. While he imagined, also for the first time, the possibility of falling in love.

Carefully, he folded the letter and put it in his pocket. He would find her and bring her home if he had to crawl across every square inch of England on his hands and knees. But where to start?

At the beginning, his instinct told him. Only

Florette knew anything about Clare . . . where she had come from and where she might go. The problem was, he didn't know where Florette had gone either.

Coming to his feet, he resolved to find out.

Rose welcomed the Earl of Caradoc to the Hothouse with a false smile and a malicious gleam in her eyes.

She despised him, Bryn knew, although they had met only a few times, and briefly. He followed her into the salon, noticing that she'd redecorated it to suit her abysmal taste. In shades of red, he imagined, to match her name, although most everything looked brown to him. So did the dress she barely wore, two quarter-moon curves of nipple showing at the bodice.

"Trolling for another virgin mistress?" she inquired slyly. "Or dare I hope you have finally condescended to pay for a toss upstairs?"

Biting back the setdown she deserved, he produced an amiable smile. "Neither, at the moment. But be assured I will apply to you when I require either service. Meantime, I have need of Florette's address."

Her eyes narrowed. "Had Florette wanted you to know her direction, she'd have provided it."

"She promised to do so," he said honestly, "but it must have slipped her mind. Now a matter of some urgency has arisen, and she would wish to know the details."

Rose tossed her head. "How vexing for you, since I am not at liberty to disclose her whereabouts. Florette would not sign over the deed until I gave my word to that effect. And even a whore, Lord Caradoc, must honor her word."

He remembered Clare telling him the same thing, a

lifetime ago. But Rose was cut from different cloth. "How much?" he asked bluntly. "I'll pay well for the information."

He saw the flash of greed in her eyes before she turned away. Calculating the price, no doubt, trying to figure out how badly he wanted the information.

After a long silence, she walked to the door and opened it. "You must apply elsewhere," she said with obvious reluctance, and a touch of satisfaction at thwarting him. "Florette took me off the streets, and thanks to her I now own the finest house of pleasure in London. I'll not betray her confidence."

Squaring his shoulders, he crossed the room and stopped directly in front of her. "Such loyalty does you credit, Rose. Will you at least send her a letter on my behalf? Naturally I'd compensate you for the favor."

Her smile became positively malevolent. "Since you have refused, all these years, to buy what I was selling, I will not accommodate you now in any fashion. Good night, Lord Caradoc."

It was a clear dismissal. Fingers itching to wring her neck, he bowed curtly and returned to his carriage, directing the coachman to Isabella's house.

Izzy, dressed for a night on the town, greeted him with a flurry of questions. After assuring her that Lacey and Elizabeth were safely on their way, he lowered himself onto a chair and combed his fingers through his hair.

"Clare's run away," he said dully. "She saw the notice in the *Times* and thinks I mean to marry the chit myself."

"Good God, Bryndle. Didn't you let her know about the elopement?"

"Everything happened too fast. I thought Landry had set himself to get hold of Elizabeth and use her to bring me around. But he had another card up his sleeve, one I failed to anticipate. It never occurred to me to send word to Clare."

"Nor to me," she admitted with a frown. "I read the announcement this morning and laughed to think how humiliated Landry would be when the truth came out. But surely all we have to do is tell Clare what happened. She'll understand."

"If we can find her. I've had Runners tracing her background since we first met, and they've come up with precisely nothing. It's as if she materialized from thin air. I have no idea where she came from or where she's gone. Izzy, do you know anything that would help?"

"No." She looked thoughtful. "But Ernie might. The three of us have had lunch at her house several times in the last three weeks."

He raised his head. "Indeed?" Mrs. Beales had told him about Ernestine's visit to Clouds while he was on his travels with Max Peyton and said that Clare had spent the next day in her company, but he could never bring himself to quiz either of them about it. Clare had seemed so much happier when he returned, even welcomed him to her bed. If Ernestine had accepted her and influenced her new attitude, so much the better. And he'd been in no hurry to face the duchess again.

Now he was, heading for the door at full speed.

"I'm coming with you," Isabella said as she grabbed her cape.

* * *

Ernestine Fitzwalter gazed solemnly at the earl through her round-rimmed spectacles. She had never seen Bryn like this, humbled and desperate. But while her heart went out to him, there was nothing she could do.

She had given her word.

By now, several letters had come to her house, addressed to Easter Clare. She had sent them over to Clouds, noting the awkward penmanship on some and the neat, precise handwriting on others. Two individuals wrote to her, from the Langbourne School for Young Gentlemen. Clare had confessed to giving the address at Grosvenor Square to her "friends" and begged forgiveness for the impertinence.

Of course she had interrogated the driver who took Clare to Berkhamsted. He described the pair of sandy-haired boys waving goodbye when they drove away . . . too old to be Clare's children, which had been her first thought, but surely related in some way.

Over the luncheons they shared, she had discovered a bit more. Clare insisted she had no living family, and Ernestine believed her. But for some reason those two boys were important to her, and wherever she'd gone she would stay in contact with them.

Yes, Ernestine thought with a sigh, she knew a great deal about the earl's mistress, including her real name. "Caradoc, I have promised the young woman not to reveal anything she confided in me," she said brusquely. "Miss Easton has favored me with her trust, and I cannot betray it."

"Devil take it, is everyone in London sworn to secrecy? I thought she might have gone to stay with Florette, but Rose won't tell me where that is. Now you have apparently joined this conspiracy of silence. Doesn't anybody understand that Clare would want to know the truth? That it will make all the difference?"

"Yes, Brynmore, I do," she said kindly. "And I hope you find her. Knowing your tenacity, I expect you will. But when she returns, I'd not have her think the people she considers her friends have turned against her. She is too much alone, in spirit, already."

He lifted troubled eyes to her face. "What am I to do, Ernie, if you won't help me?"

"I have an idea," Isabella put in. "The day we met, Clare asked me to deliver an envelope to a messenger waiting at a post house just outside London." Before Bryn could ask, she shook her head. "I too swore not to say anything, but perhaps I could go there tomorrow and ask a few questions."

"Just tell me the name of the inn, Izzy, or who the letter was addressed to. The Runners can take it from there."

She sighed. "I cannot. Like Ernie, I promised. But if the innkeeper knows anything—"

He threw up his hands. "Useless, the both of you. Why the hell are you more loyal to Clare than to me? Especially when you are hurting her by not telling me what you know."

Ernestine leaned back in her chair. "Nothing is stopping us from trying to find the young lady ourselves," she observed placidly. "I suggest you continue the search in your own way, while Isabella and I pursue other avenues. If you think Clare will come back to you once she knows the whole story, it doesn't matter which of us reaches her first."

"And you must make sure the newspapers publish

a correction to Landry's announcement," Isabella reminded him. "She might see that and come back of her own accord."

After a few beats, he nodded and came to his feet. "I must rely on you, then. For now, Landry should be informed that all his hopes are dashed, and I shall take great pleasure in doing so. Izzy, the coach can drop me at St. James's Street and take you wherever you are headed."

"Lady Sefton's rout," she said. "Mr. Peyton is meeting me there." When he lifted a brow, she laughed. "I promise to make an early night of it and head out for that post house first thing in the morning."

When they were gone, Ernestine Fitzwalter summoned her own carriage and directed her driver to the Hothouse, suspecting that Clare had indeed taken refuge with Florette.

She had ways Caradoc had never thought of to get this Rose person to talk. Before the evening was out, a coach would be dispatched to bring Clare back to London.

25

Clare huddled against the wooden panel as the coach sped along the road, Attila sleeping peacefully in the basket on her lap. By her side, a fat woman grated the air with her snores. The two men sitting opposite her were playing at cards, flipping the pasteboards on the leather squabs, scarcely able to see in the dim light from the lantern. Occasionally they disputed the score and voices rose, only to die down again.

She leaned her head back and closed her eyes, wishing it had been possible to stay the night at the Bull and Cock. The host, who remembered her, had offered a room, although the inn was crowded. But she didn't dare turn down the chance to continue her journey when a stage bound for East Sussex pulled in to change horses.

Besides, Isabella knew about the post house, and Bryn could track her there.

She was not altogether certain why she'd run away without facing him. It was cowardly, but the wicked temptation to stay might well have overcome her resistance. Bryn had a way of breaking through all her defenses, leading her to places she had promised herself not to go.

She was so weak. Dear God, she had meant to spend only one night with him, but he coaxed her into another and yet another until she began to dream of a lifetime with him. Of having his children. Even before the exquisite pleasure he gave her on the silken pillows by the river, she had found him nearly irresistible.

But adultery was a fence she refused to cross. Almost from the beginning she had known he would marry Elizabeth. She ought to be glad he'd found a wife who deserved him. Elizabeth would make him happy. She was beautiful and intelligent. She would appreciate Bryn's virtues and tolerate his faults.

The stage drew up at an inn to change horses, and Clare alighted to use the necessary. Then she let Attila out of his basket to relieve himself and run about. The cat never failed to come to her when she called. He was generally sweet and good-natured, and she often wondered why he had taken Bryn into such dislike.

But she had disliked him too, when they first met. How long ago it seemed, the day he regarded her with aristocratic insolence from the street in front of Florette's Hothouse. And the next morning, when he ordered her to strip for him: she had loathed him then.

She loved him now.

With a sigh, she summoned Attila, returned him to the basket, and reentered the coach. Florette had bought a small house in Hastings and given her the address before leaving London. Clare was to come to her if ever she needed a place to stay.

And she did, for a little while. With Joseph and Jeremy in good hands, *their* futures assured, she had only her own future to consider. Eventually, she would carve a life for herself and be independent. Slipping her hand under the lid of the basket, she stroked Attila's head and heard him purr.

Few women were so fortunate, she decided, as the coach rumbled through the night. Bryn had given her memories to last a lifetime. She had experienced passion, and the joy of loving a complex, difficult, wonderful man. When the pain dissipated, as it eventually would, she could begin to make reparation for her sins.

Repentance, if it ever came, would be much more difficult.

Bryn carved his way through the crowded gaming room at White's, his gaze fixed murderously on his quarry.

Landry sat with his back to the door, tossing dice at a large round table. With a vicious swipe, Bryn kicked the chair from under him and the baron tumbled to the carpet. He barely had time to roll over before his neckcloth was seized in a strong hand.

Bryn twisted the cravat, dragging Landry to his knees. "You," he said icily, "have caused me a great deal of trouble. Now you will answer for it."

Someone tugged at his arm. "You are choking him, my lord."

Bryn threw the man off, his eyes never leaving Landry's red, sputtering face. "I would call you out here and now, if not for your daughter. Elizabeth is halfway to Scotland, on her way to marry Viscount Heydon, and I'd not have her begin the honeymoon forced to pretend mourning for a father who beat her."

A low murmur rumbled through the crowd of observers, quickly silenced as Bryn spoke again.

"You are quite done up, Landry. No rich son-in-law, despite your efforts to acquire one by planting a false notice in the *Times.* Heydon hasn't a feather to fly with, so you cannot rely on him to cover your debts. And if you had wings, you could not get to them in time to stop the wedding.

"Only one question remains. Will you manage to escape England before your creditors have you thrown into Fleet or before I change my mind and cut out your liver with a dull knife?" He lifted Landry off his knees, dangling him in the air like gallows bait. "You're a gambling man. Care to place a bet?"

Choking, Landry flailed helplessly in the earl's iron grip.

Two men seized Bryn's elbows, and another tried to loosen his fingers from the baron's neckcloth. "You are killing him!" one of them shouted.

With disgust, Bryn released Landry and shoved him to the floor. "Get him out of here before I finish the job."

As a pair of footmen hauled the baron away, the onlookers found their voices. Bryn scarcely heard them, blood pounding in his ears like artillery fire. Someone put a glass in his hand, and he drank the brandy in a single swallow, every muscle in his body taut with rage.

He should have killed Landry while he had the chance. Every instinct told him that. The certainty was so strong he moved forward, but two men blocked his path.

"Not worth the trouble," Alvanley said.

"You'd have to leave the country," Pennington reminded him. "Sure you want to do that?"

With effort, Bryn focused on their concerned faces, swearing under his breath. They were right, of course. He had to find Clare.

Alvanley steered him back to the table, pushed him into a chair, and reached for the dice. "Good time to pluck you, Caradoc, while you ain't seeing straight."

Why not? he thought bleakly. He could do nothing useful in the middle of this hellish night, except get filthy drunk and stay busy enough to forget about Clare for a few hours.

He glanced up at the circle of men gathered around the baize-covered table and managed a wry grin. "I'll take on all comers, no limit. Someone get me a bottle of cognac."

Several hours later, he'd no idea how many, he made his way into the nearly deserted street. It had begun to drizzle, and he welcomed the cool mist against his forehead and cheeks. Vaguely aware he had won rather a lot of money, he reflected that virtual oblivion seemed to bring him luck at gaming tables and cockfights.

Turning the wrong way, he found himself at Pall Mall instead of King Street. A hackney driver, huddled in his cloak, looked up hopefully, but he shook his head. St James's Square was only a few streets away, and he wanted to walk. Clear his head and make plans for tomorrow morning.

Bow Street first, to hire every Runner not otherwise engaged and any others he could bribe away from prior commitments to join the search for Clare Easton. Then he'd find Izzy and see if she had learned anything at that post house. Lost in thought, he passed the turn at George Street and had to back-track. It had begun to rain in earnest, and he could barely see two feet ahead of him.

Dimly recognizing the circular park in the middle of St. James's Square, he crossed the road to follow the gaslit walk to his house. The square was eerily silent, except for the dull pounding of rain and his own heels clicking on the pavement.

Where was she? What was Clare doing at this moment? He closed his eyes briefly, imagining her in the rain, cold and lost, as lonely as he felt right now. She hadn't wanted to leave, he was certain. But only yesterday, for the first time, had she really wanted to stay. Before, she had done so because she felt she owed it to him, but everything had changed in those few hours by the river.

Then Landry drove her away with his lies.

Blinded by the rain, Bryn plodded ahead, his mind spinning. Clare would come back to him, once she knew the truth. All he had to do was find her. And then he would do everything in his power to keep her.

From the park to his left, on the other side of the wrought-iron fence, he heard a noise. He turned, trying to see through the water clumping his eyelashes.

"Caradoc!" Giles Landry stumbled through a gate onto the sidewalk, waving a pistol. "Got you now."

Bryn took a step back as the baron materialized in front of him. In the wavering gaslight, Landry's eyes glittered with malice.

"Figured you to do right by Eliz'beth," he muttered, holding the gun between both hands to keep it steady. "But you shuffled her off to Heydon. Had her first, I'd wager. Everybody knows how you favor the virgins. Ruined her and me. Time you paid for that."

"I never touched your daughter, Landry." Without a weapon, aware he was confronting a madman, Bryn held out his arms in a gesture of submission and schooled his voice. "This is about money. You need it, and I have it. We can come to terms."

"Think I'd trust you now?" Landry snorted. "You'll give me fine words while this gun is pointed at your heart, but the minute I let you walk away you'll be scheming to get rid of me without a payoff."

"Maybe not. Think about it. I can afford your price, whatever it is, and what you really want is to get away without any more trouble." Bryn had to force the conciliating words between his teeth. "I know when I'm beaten, Landry. You win. Everyone in London knows I'm a man of my word, and you can count on me to honor it. Besides, how will it help you to kill me? You'll never get away with it, after what happened at White's."

"What the hell do I care?" Landry slurred. "Like you said, I'm done up. Nothing to lose. And damned if I'll take the word of Owen Talgarth's son. He was a lying son of a bitch, and so are you. You'll destroy me sooner or later, Caradoc, but if I'm going down I'm taking you with me." He lifted the pistol. "Rot in hell!"

Before he could move, Bryn saw a flash and something slammed him hard in the chest. Then his head struck the pavement and the world went black.

26

Dark.

So dark. He felt heavy, encased in stone. But he was floating, too, in the black void. He thought he must be in a tunnel, somewhere underground, but there were sounds. Like voices, and not always, but sometimes he heard them. Or imagined he did.

Clare's voice. He must have had dreamed that. She was gone.

Now he was gone too. He didn't know where. Under the ground, cold as marble, floating. . . .

It came again, the soft voice. Her voice. She said his name.

He tried to move toward the sound, straining against the bonds that held him. *Wait,* he called, but he couldn't open his mouth. Could not move.

He had to reach her. She would leave again. With all his strength, he pulled against the weight chaining him to the darkness. And pain swept through him, so intense he could only flee from it, deeper into the black tunnel.

"I think he moved his hand," Clare told Dr. Winslow urgently. "The right one. It lifted a bit, and the fingers curved."

Dr. Winslow looked down at the pale, limp hand resting on the blanket. "You may have imagined it, Miss Easton. Too many hours in this room. Better you get some sleep now, and let someone else sit with him for a time." When she looked mutinous, he signed and took the earl's pulse. "Slow and thready. He only grows weaker. Unless he rouses enough to take some nourishment, there is no hope."

"You said two days ago that he could not last more than a few hours, but he's still alive. Don't you dare give up on him. Don't you dare!" Flushing hotly, she touched his arm in a gesture of apology. "Forgive me. I know you will not give up. And it is a great comfort to us all that you have stayed here every night and come by so often during the day."

"Her grace was most insistent," he said, "although there has been little I could do since removing the bullet. He lost too much blood, lying there in the rain God knows how long before someone found him. But he survived the operation, and moving his fingers is a good sign."

Clare knew he didn't believe she'd seen it and was only trying to reassure her. But she smiled at him and agreed to let Isabella stay with the earl while she got some sleep.

Dr. Winslow picked up his bag. "I can tell you only

the truth, Miss Easton, because you would not settle for less. That he has endured this long surprises me, but he is growing weaker. Even so, the will to live often produces miracles. I have seen that happen, in cases where all my experience indicated the patient was lost. And Lord Caradoc has a powerful incentive to recover, knowing that you are here waiting for him."

But he did not know, she thought miserably as the doctor took his leave. Bryn knew only that she had run away from him. Misjudged him. Trusted a few lines in a newspaper instead of the man who created a paradise by the river only to please her. And gave himself, in a way she could not mistake, when they made love under that silken canopy.

She had let him down. Been gone when he most needed her. If the duchess had not convinced someone at the Hothouse to reveal Florette's address and gone for her, Bryn might have died before she could make amends.

Clare lowered herself onto the chair beside him and took hold of the hand that had moved. She had apologized, over and over, for not believing in him. Begged him to open his eyes and forgive her. But he lay still as a corpse, only the slight rise and fall of his chest and the raspy sound of his breath assuring her he still lived. She was afraid to take her eyes off him even for a moment, lest he die without her knowing it.

Four days since he was shot, and two since her return, but not once had he moved until a few minutes ago. Someone was always with him, watching for any sign of improvement. Isabella and the duchess spelled her from time to time and sometimes sat with her by the bed, talking to him.

She could not bear the silence, especially at night.

In long rambling monologues she told Bryn stories, sometimes made up but more often incidents from her own life. Not the bad things—he didn't need to hear those—but she shared with him her joy when Joseph and Jeremy were born. She led him through their infancy and childhood and recounted nearly all of Jeremy's madcap adventures. They were so alike, Bryn and Jeremy. She could see them together, hurtling down the road in Bryn's curricle, testing how fast Black Lightning could really go.

Sometimes she prayed, or tried to. It seemed futile, for surely God's ears were closed to the pleas of a whore unless they were prayers of repentance. And she was beyond repentance now. If Bryn lived, and wanted her again, she would stay. More than that, she would revel in her sin. Enjoy to the fullest every minute they were together, now that she knew how precious life could be.

The only thing she had not done, in the endless hours gazing at his bloodless face and sunken cheeks, was cry. All her tears must have been spent years ago. She felt hard and empty, scarcely a woman at all if she could not weep for him.

She touched his forehead. So cold, like his hand. *Oh, God,* she thought. *Please. He only tried to help Elizabeth. How can You punish him for that?*

Isabella came into the room, her gaze focused on Bryn's still face. "Dr. Winslow said you ought to rest now."

Clare looked at her blankly for a moment and then shook her head. "Give me a little more time, if you will. I thought I saw him move."

"The doctor told me." Isabella looked skeptical. "I've had a good rest and will keep careful watch while you do the same. If he moves again, I promise to call you immediately."

"No." Clare lifted her chin. "One hour, and then I'll go to bed. Have some broth sent up. He requires nourishment, the doctor said. I'll try to feed him."

"My dear, he's hardly been able to take water."

They would open his mouth forcefully, at regular intervals, and dribble moisture from a sponge between his lips. But most of it ran down his face.

"I'll try again," Clare said in a determined voice. "Watching and waiting has accomplished nothing. He is slipping away, bit by bit. We must pull him back, whatever it takes."

Isabella nodded. "I'll see to the broth and relieve you in an hour. Unless you'd like me to stay with you now?"

"Thank you, but no. If I fail, you can have a go at him." She managed a wan smile. "If Bryn has any sense, he'll come about before the duchess takes her turn."

When the door closed, Clare sat forward on the chair and gripped Bryn's hand between her own. "Now you listen to me, Caradoc," she said loudly. "Wake up! I mean it! It's past time you stopped this nonsense. In all creation there was never a man could sleep the way you do."

She went on in similar fashion for half an hour, practically shouting at him, with no response. He never stirred, and his hand remained icy cold and limp.

No use, she thought in despair, even as she continued to rail at him. He was past reaching, more in God's arms than her own.

Give him back, she begged. *I'll do anything. Whatever You want. Let him live and I promise never to sin with him again. Don't let him die like this, thinking he is alone. Allow me one chance to tell him that he was loved, and then I'll go away.*

She became aware that her eyes were burning and felt a hot tear streak down her face. Then another, and another, until she could no longer see his face. Still she clutched his hand, pressing it to her cheek, pleading without words to the God of her father, the God of love and forgiveness her father had believed in, the God she'd nearly forgotten after all the years listening to Ardis preach to her of hellfire and damnation.

He heard the voice again. It seemed he'd been trying forever to leave this dark place and follow the sound to where it led, but each time he got close, almost there, the pain overwhelmed him. So much easier to let go, sink back and down, not fight. For all his striving, the darkness gripped him ever more tightly. He was so cold, unbearably weary. Even for Clare, he could not do it.

He dreamed colors. Bright yellows and vivid blues. Colors he'd never seen before. They spiraled around him, making pictures that dissolved into new pictures. He dreamed a daffodil that became a rose, a tree that melted into a river. He rode a black horse that turned to white and became transparent when it left the ground. He was flying, on the horse and then alone, over the turquoise sea to the snowy mountains and ever higher until he passed the sun. Stars like diamonds whizzed by him, their glow brighter than the darkness, which dissolved into blinding, glorious light.

Clare. *Light.*

He reached for her.

* * *

"Bryn!"

She was sure of it. He had squeezed her hand. She kissed his fingers, wet with her tears, and felt them move against her lips. "Bryn," she said again, her voice raw. "Wake up, my love."

Letting go his hand, she gripped his shoulders. "Do you hear me? Wake up!" Not caring if it hurt, she shook him hard and thought she heard a groan. "Dammit, Caradoc, open your eyes."

His lashes fluttered.

"Yes. Oh, God, yes," she whispered, shaking him again.

This time she could practically feel him struggle to obey. "Do it, Bryn! You can do it. Look at me!" Tears dripped from her chin onto his face, onto his closed eyelids.

And they opened. Only for a moment at first, but longer the next time, and longer still until he gazed at her.

"Do you know me?" she asked breathlessly.

He nodded slightly, and she saw his lips trying to move. Grabbing for the sponge, she moistened them. His tongue licked out and she wet the sponge again, this time squeezing it into his open mouth.

All the while he gazed up at her, choking at first on the liquid but finally able to swallow a bit. Again and again she dripped water into his mouth, lifting his head with one hand to help him drink.

After a while he lay back, shaking his head weakly. But his eyes stayed open, fixed on her face, as she moved away long enough to pull the bell rope. Then she sat on the bed and leaned over him, stroking his damp hair from his forehead, massaging his scalp, as if that would help him stay alert.

"Isabella is bringing some soup," she said practically. "You must stay awake and drink it, Bryn. I won't let you go to sleep again, even if I have to send for the duchess to bully you. And she'll do it, you know."

His lips curved slightly, and she wanted to jump for joy. He'd come back, however tentatively, and she would not let him get away.

A footman knocked at the door and peered in, the fearful expression on his young face showing that he expected the worst.

Clare smiled at him over her shoulder. "Lord Caradoc has awakened," she said, pleased to see his immediate delight at the news. "Will you summon Dr. Winslow, and ask Lady Isabella to hurry with that broth?"

"Yes, Miss Easton." He bowed, and then addressed the earl. "Good to have you back, milord. Damned if it ain't." Blushing furiously, he hurried away.

"See?" Clare rubbed Bryn's temples. "Everybody is happy you have decided to get well."

He licked cracked lips, trying to form a word. "You?" he finally managed in a whisper.

"Me most of all," she assured him.

Bryn was a terrible patient.

Or so everyone kept telling him, although he considered his demands perfectly reasonable. But it appeared he was no longer master in his own house, so few of his orders were obeyed. He asked for roast beef and received endless mugs of broth. The very servants he dismissed for serving him bowls of tasteless pap served up the same foul concoctions at his next meal.

He was in considerable pain. The doctor recommended he not take laudanum, at least until he'd recovered more strength, and with that Bryn agreed. But he saw no reason he shouldn't numb himself with cognac. After endless wrangling, he was allowed one glass of port after dinner.

As his frustration mounted, so did his temper. And Clare met him with equal obduracy. She'd become a veritable martinet, directing the household—and him—with an iron will.

And when he called her to account, she immediately agreed to return to Clouds. In fact, she would rather do so now that he was out of danger. It was unseemly for the earl's mistress to be in residence at his home, and the duchess would be more than pleased to take over.

That threat was more than enough to keep him on good behavior for almost a full day. He wanted Clare with him all the time and even tried to convince her to sleep by his side in the enormous canopied bed. She refused, but she always sat with him late into the night, when the pain was worst.

He was never left alone in the room, not since he seized a rare moment of privacy to try out his legs. They'd given way three paces from the bed, where a footman found him curled on the rug, drenched in blood because the fall had reopened his wound.

In spite of that setback he continued to improve, and after a week Clare allowed him to receive visitors other than Isabella and Ernestine. First to call was the magistrate, anxious to question him about his assailant.

Bryn had already decided to lie about that.

"Common footpads," he told Mr. Peebles. "They came at me in the dark, and it was raining. Can't describe them, and doubt I could identify the men if they were standing in front of me now."

The magistrate scribbled in his notebook, clearly unsatisfied. "Didn't rob you," he pointed out. "And you was carrying a lot of blunt."

Bryn had wondered about that. Landry must have lost his mind altogether, to bolt without taking the money. "I was a trifle bosky at the time," he confessed, "and remember little of the encounter. Likely I objected with my fists, and one of the robbers pulled the trigger. They must have run off, figuring someone heard the shot."

"Mebbe." Mr. Peebles lifted a brow. "But you were seen to leave your club a little after three o'clock, and I've walked the distance to where you were found. A journey of ten minutes at most, even in the rain and foxed. You were not discovered until two hours later."

Bryn shrugged, painfully. "No accounting for it. They had plenty of time to pick my pockets but failed to do so. Chances are they panicked. I hit my head, you know, when I fell. Most everything that happened is a blur."

"We can only hope you recall more, when your health is restored." Mr. Peebles regarded him closely. "Apparently you were engaged in a quarrel earlier that evening, with—"

"Giles Landry. What of it?"

"It seems rather coincidental that you were struck down shortly after. We thought it advisable to ask the baron a few questions concerning his whereabouts, but he has disappeared."

"I'm not surprised," Bryn said indifferently. "It's no secret Landry hoped I would marry his daughter and pay off his debts. That failing, he has no doubt fled his creditors, but that is irrelevant to your investigation. I'd have recognized him, were he one of the men who attacked me."

"Very good, milord." Mr. Peebles closed his notebook. "You will let us know if something else comes to mind?"

"Certainly."

When he was gone, Bryn lapsed against the bank of pillows with a sigh. He'd no intention of dragging Elizabeth's father through the courts. That would shame her, and her new husband, and eventually their children. Besides, Landry was far from the reach of British justice by now, assuming he'd dredged up enough money to buy his way back across the Channel. And if he remained in England or ever came back, Bryn would find him and exact justice of his own.

The next day, he discovered that would not be necessary.

Max Peyton was permitted to call—for ten minutes only, because Clare insisted Bryn was still too weak to take up matters of business. But Peyton had not come about business.

"Landry's dead," he said, the moment they were alone. "Thought you'd want to know."

"How?" Bryn regarded him angrily. "If you've taken this out of my hands—"

"Damnedest thing," Max interrupted. "The man had the audacity to apply again to me for a stake. Enough to leave the country and keep him going for a while. Sent a note and offered to sign his house over to me, rundown hovel that it is. I agreed to meet him at a gin hole in the rookery."

"*You* killed him? Bloody hell, Peyton. Too many people involved in this mess as it is."

"Not I," Max protested. "All I did was accept the deed in exchange for a sheaf of banknotes. Oh, and I happened to mention that fact to five or six rather large brutes on my way out. From the racket, I expect they went after him like a pack of wolves. His body will turn up one of these days."

Bryn stared at him in amazement.

"Past time you were free of the ungodly baron," Peyton observed tranquilly. "He nearly managed to dispatch you, and where would I be if he came back to finish the job? I need your backing for my schools, Caradoc. You needn't feel responsible for the man's fortunate demise. Besides, I knew you wouldn't turn him over to the courts. This matter could only be handled by unorthodox means, and with you laid up—"

"How do you know he's dead?" Bryn interrupted.

"I know." Peyton came to his feet. "Mind you, the most difficult task is yours. His daughter must be informed, and I leave it to you to invent a story suitable for her ears. Naturally the house will be transferred to her. The deed will have mysteriously disappeared, so she will inherit as a matter of course."

Bryn was grateful and furious. He resented Peyton's interference, which implied he was incapable of handling his own affairs. But he could almost hear Clare's voice, reminding him that all his efforts to keep Landry under control had failed. "You are a ruthless man," he said with mingled respect and irritation.

"More so than you, Caradoc," Peyton replied urbanely. "And to think you once accused me of aspiring to canonization." He crossed to the door and glanced back over his shoulder. "Had Landry killed you, I'd have torn him apart with my own two hands."

Bryn thought about those words, and the indecipherable look in those tawny eyes, for a long time. Probably Max referred to his investment in their trading venture, which would have come to nothing if he'd died.

Or perhaps Bryn had somehow made another friend.

27

"About time you showed up."

Bryn gave Florette a sour look as she entered the bedchamber. After returning to London with Clare, she had moved into Clouds while his recovery was in doubt but adamantly refused to visit until he sent a message demanding her appearance.

"It is not the thing," she said calmly, "for me to be here at all. Where are your wits, Caradoc?"

He regarded her with interest as she settled on a chair beside the bed. She had let her hair go gray and left off using kohl at her eyes and paint on her lips and cheeks. In a simple high-necked walking dress and unadorned bonnet, she might have been a tradesman's wife or a country widow. There was no trace of the flamboyant faux-Frenchwoman he'd known for twenty years.

"You courtesans are damned high sticklers," he said irritably. "You'll take an earl to your bed but won't set foot in his house. It's been all I could do to keep Clare here at St. James's."

Florette set a corked bottle on the night table. "Maude Beales sent this over. It's a restorative potion, and you are to take a spoonful three times a day."

"The devil I will." He grimaced. "Women hovering over me every time I look up, telling me to eat this or drink that. Witches, the lot of you."

"I see you are back to your old self again," she observed caustically. "A shame, that, but even a grumpy Caradoc is better than no Caradoc at all. Now that you are recovered, I can return to Hastings and tend my cabbages."

"East Sussex," he observed dryly, "is rather a long way from the Loire Valley. Are you at last to be honest with me, Flo? Perhaps even tell me your real name?"

"Edna Halperth," she said with a grin. "Too pedestrian for a high-flyer, don't you think? Florette LaFleur had a much better ring to it. In Hastings I am plain Mrs. Edna Halperth, but I'd rather you address me as you always have, for old time's sake."

He pulled himself straighter against the bank of pillows, muttering an oath when the nightshirt and robe tangled under his buttocks. Among the many things he despised about being confined to bed was having to wear a nightshirt, even the one Clare had embroidered at the neck with tiny bears while she sat with him.

"Florette it is," he agreed, looking her in the eye. "And if you are about to take yourself off again, let us speak plainly to one another, *for old time's sake.* Why did Clare go into hiding just because she thought I was to be married? She knows I intend to, one of these days. And she ought to have known I would tell her myself, not leave her to read about it in the newspaper."

"She realizes that now. And is sorry she mistrusted you."

"Yes." He waved a hand. "She has told me so a hundred times. But the point is, she hared off to Sussex for no good reason. I'd have expected her to ring a peal over me after seeing that notice, and not blamed her for doing so. But even if it were true, if I *had* betrothed myself to Elizabeth Landry, what difference would it make?"

"Apparently a great deal, to Clare." After a long moment, Florette released a sigh. "I'll not tell you anything you ought to discover for yourself, except this one thing, because you are clearly too dull-witted even to conceive of the idea. She will not stay with you once you are married."

"Why the hell not?" He glowered at her. "These arrangements are common. Almost necessary, with alliances made to join titles and secure fortunes even if the husband and wife can scarcely abide one another. Most every man I know keeps a mistress—or chases widows and opera dancers. And nearly every woman takes a lover, once she has given her husband an heir."

Florette gave him a scathing look. "*Common?* Perhaps, in your circle of friends. But Clare is anything but common, and by now you ought to have realized it. You disappoint me, Caradoc. I'd not have entrusted her to you had I known you would persist in your stubborn assurance that you can have everything you want, regardless of the cost to others."

Swallowing hard, he sank a few inches down the pillows. Apparently he was at fault, but he didn't understand why. Clare had sold herself to him, proving she was not constrained by moral rectitude. And he was certain, or nearly so, that she wanted to stay with him.

Why should a marriage of convenience, with perfect understanding on everyone's part, change that?

The wound in his chest seemed to be on fire again. Probably because it was near his heart, which had begun to pound furiously. "Tell me what it will cost her, if I marry," he said between his teeth. "I intend to give Clare everything she could possibly want. Make a home for us, and be with her except when I have obligations elsewhere. Those will be few. Secondary. What has she to lose?"

"That you must ask *her,*" Flo said gravely. "It is past time the two of you became acquainted outside the bedchamber."

"She won't talk to me." He twisted a fold of blanket between his fingers. "Whenever I try, she closes up like an oyster."

Flo came to her feet. "Try harder. And while you're at it, think about what you want the most, because more than a little compromise will be necessary. On both parts," she added, leaning over to plant a kiss on his cheek. "Clare is a match for you in every way, including bullheaded obstinacy, and I only wish I could stay to watch the fireworks. But my garden needs tending, so I must go home. Besides, I am under strict orders not to tire you. You have my address, now, and are welcome to visit any time you like."

"I will, and soon," he promised. "With Clare."

"Nothing would please me more." Flo gave him a sardonic glance from the door. "By the way, I stopped off at the Hothouse yesterday to see how things are going on. Rose told me you came by and that you were an arrogant, overbearing son of a bitch."

"But you knew that already," he said as she blew him a kiss and swept into the hall.

What a woman, he thought when the door closed behind her. If not for Florette, he'd never have met Clare. She knew exactly what she was about, bringing them together. Unfortunately, she'd left the rest up to him, and he had piled one mistake on top of another. Nearly died before having a chance to set things right.

The time for secrets was past, he resolved. Tonight, he would force Clare to tell him the truth: about herself, and what she wanted, and why she left him.

With a groan, he reached for the bottle Mrs. Beales had sent, pulled out the cork, and managed to swallow a mouthful of the foul-tasting brew. He was going to need a restorative and a great deal of luck, when he next confronted his mistress.

His beloved, he corrected mentally. Damn it all, Rose had the right of things. He *was* arrogant and overbearing. He should be concerned with Clare's needs, not his own.

As punishment, he swigged another draught from the bottle and lay back to plan a conciliatory, humble approach. Think of what you most want, Flo had told him. Hell, that was easy.

He wanted Clare.

Clare saw immediately that Bryn was stronger after his visit with Florette. Certainly in better humor. Even Dr. Winslow's poking and prodding an hour later failed to annoy him, and for the first time he was permitted a dinner he could actually chew.

"A bit more wine will be acceptable," the doctor had told her, and with some pleasure she carried a decanter of port to Bryn's room that evening. He insisted she drink with him, and because she was overjoyed to see him doing so well, she agreed.

He sat up against the mahogany headboard, pillows stuffed behind his back, cradling his third glass of port.

"Who is Jeremy?" he asked suddenly.

Her gaze flew from the handkerchief she was embroidering to his face.

"I've begun remembering a few things," he explained. "Not a great deal, but when I was unconscious I kept hearing your voice. Mostly I could not make out the words, although I'm certain you said that name many times. And another, which I cannot recall."

"Joseph," she said softly. "Jeremy and Joseph."

"Ah."

When he failed to speak again, she returned her attention to her embroidery, but the bear's ear wound up rather a long way from its head. Flo had lectured her, harshly, about the need to tell Bryn the truth about herself. And she knew she must, but she didn't know how to begin. Most of all, she worried that he would pity her because she had traded her body for the twins' schooling. Or feel guilty because he took advantage of her desperation, even though he had no way of knowing what she was about.

She wanted to wait until he was stronger. Why burden him with confidences now, while his health should be the only consideration? But she was only making excuses, a voice in her head insisted. Putting off the inevitable. Bryn's strength was not in question. Only her own.

With deliberation, she put the embroidery hoop aside and folded her hands in her lap. Bryn was looking at her, his gaze warm and open.

"Tell me," he said quietly.

And she did, from the beginning, faltering at first and then in a rush, to get it over with before she lost her courage. He interrupted only once.

"Ardis is the one who put the scars on your hands and feet?"

She hadn't meant to tell him that, but she nodded. "I doubt she was ever in her right mind, after her lover abandoned her. When I was old enough to understand, I forgave her everything she did to me—and to the boys. She was cast off by her parents, and even when she found someone to protect her—my father—he died a few months later."

"Leaving you to care for a madwoman and a pair of infants. Dear God, Clare." His voice was filled with wonder. "I never imagined."

"How could you?" She produced a smile. "And it was not such a trial, you know. Joseph and Jeremy are more than worth any sacrifice we made on their behalf. Including you, Bryn, because they have a chance at a good life thanks to your generosity. I only wish you could meet them, but that is not possible. If they suspected that I—" Unable to finish the thought, she curled her arms around her waist. "They must never know."

"Of course not." He held out a hand. "Come here, Clare."

After a moment, she moved onto the bed next to him, resting her head on his shoulder. "My name is Easter," she whispered against his neck. "Easter Clare."

She felt him chuckle, although he tried hard to suppress it. "Because you were born on Easter Sunday?"

"My birthday is in October." She toyed with a button on his nightshirt. "Lamentably, Father took a fancy to the name. I have always loathed it."

"Clare suits you. May I continue to call you that, or would you prefer—"

"Clare," she said swiftly. "Please. Changing my name has been the only part of this masquerade I enjoyed. And for the twins' sake, it is better that only you and Florette know my real identity."

"Have no fear I will betray your secrets, butterfly. I am only glad you have confided in me."

"At last, you mean." She sat back. "Lying has been the least of my sins, although I hated every untruth even as I spoke it. But there seemed to be no choice. I never expected things to become so . . . complicated."

"One night and you'd be gone," he said with a faint smile.

She nodded. "But then I met Lady Isabella, and Elizabeth Landry, and the duchess. And Robert Lacey and Charley Cassidy and Mrs. Beales. Every moment I feared I would betray myself. And always, by lying, I was betraying the friendship they offered me. It would have been a great deal easier if people had not been so kind."

Especially you, she thought, in the long silence that followed. He was regarding her with an expression unlike any she had ever seen. She didn't know how to interpret the look in his eyes, focused so closely on her face, or the muscle ticking in his jaw.

Finally he spoke, his voice barely a whisper. "What a nightmare this has been for you. I never knew. Never suspected, although I should have. Florette thought I would, when she gave you into my hands, but I have failed you."

"Indeed you have not," she said, with a return of spirit. "After our first two encounters, you have been wonderful to me. How absurd, to blame yourself for believing what I wanted you to believe. We did not begin well, Bryn, but above all things I hope we can part as friends."

"*Part?*" He seized her hand. "We are only just now finding each other. Dammit, Clare, the past is irrelevant, except that I have a great deal to account for. And I will make a future so bright that you will forget what you have endured all these years. Already I've been planning. We'll build a house by the river where we had the picnic. You can call on Alice, come to London whenever you like, and visit Joseph and Jeremy at their school. I'll see them admitted to Oxford or Cambridge, whichever they prefer. Eventually they will learn that we are living together, but by then they will be worldly enough to understand. Men always understand these arrangements. And they will never know you first came to me for their sake."

If only it were so easy. She could not help but smile at his blind self-assurance, although her heart was breaking. As always, Bryn assumed he could bend the universe to his will. How could she tell him?

"What's wrong?" he asked, squeezing her fingers. "Nothing has changed, except that I will deal better with you than I have done."

"Oh, Bryn." She closed her eyes. "I have made a promise. One I cannot set aside, however much I long to revoke it. When you are well again, I must leave you."

The glass in his hand shattered. He looked down, to the spattering of port wine on the sheets and his nightshirt, mingling with the blood dripping from his hand.

With a gasp, Clare jumped up and hurried to the bell rope.

"Don't," he said from a constricted throat. "Not yet."

She gave him an exasperated look and pulled the tasseled cord. "Hold still, Bryn. There are bits of glass all over the bed."

Minutes later the bedchamber swarmed with servants. The top sheet, blanket, and counterpane were carefully removed, and two large footmen helped Bryn to a chair. Clare directed them to stand nearby, holding Argand lamps so she could see to tend the cuts on his hand. Two large trays were set on a table beside him, with basins, cups, towels, gauze, and other things he had dimly heard her request from the maids.

After rinsing the blood away, she studied the wounds intently, her bottom lip clamped between her teeth. "I see a few splinters of glass. Try not to move while I draw them out."

Moving was definitely beyond his power. He could scarcely breath as her words echoed in his head: *I must leave you.*

He watched in a daze as she worked. Now and again she soaked his hand in a basin of fresh water before dipping tweezers into a cup of brandy and plucking nearly invisible pieces of the wineglass from his flesh. After a while, she began to press his palm and fingers with the pad of her thumb. "Tell me if you feel anything," she instructed.

Twice he nodded, and she went back to work with the tweezers. Finally she washed his hand in soapy water, rinsed it well, and drizzled brandy over the wounds until the cup was empty. He felt nothing, except the pain in his heart.

After applying salve, Clare wrapped the hand in

gauze and came to her feet. "That should do it. The footmen will help you change into a clean nightshirt." She picked up one of thc trays and moved to the door, followed by the maids.

"Come back," he managed to say between dry lips.

"Yes. When you are settled in bed."

A few minutes later, stretched on his back between fresh sheets, he watched the footmen extinguish all the lights except for one lamp on the night table. As the room grew dim, it seemed they were snuffing, one by one, his hopes and dreams.

I must leave you.

He didn't hear the servants depart. The darkness closed around him, crushing his chest, driving the air from his lungs. How was he to live without Clare? The finality in her voice had been unmistakable. She was determined to go, for some reason that had nothing to do with him.

Even if she explained, and he was not certain she would, no words from him would change her mind. She had made a promise, one she could not set aside. And he well understood what it was to be bound by honor to a course that led nowhere. How impossible it was to turn back.

"Bryn?" She came into the room and closed the door behind her.

"I'm awake. Come here, Clare. We have to talk."

"I know." She lowered herself on a chair at his side and lifted the bandaged hand. "Does it hurt?"

"Attila did worse damage." In the soft glow of the lamp, her long hair loose around her shoulders, she had never looked more beautiful. He felt the effort it cost her to smile at him.

"You must take better care of yourself. Now we

have only one unscarred hand between the two of us. I ought to scold you for being so clumsy with that glass."

"How did you expect me to react? You said you were leaving me. For God's sake, why? I don't understand."

She lowered her head. "It seems that you do. It is precisely for God's sake that I must go."

"That makes no sense whatever," he said, after a beat. "This is between you and me."

"I only wish that were true. And I shall try to explain, Bryn, although I don't expect you will be persuaded that I have no other choice."

"I am already convinced you believe it to be true," he said quietly. "Don't be afraid to tell me how you feel. I'll not object or interrupt."

Nodding, she folded her hands in her lap. "You know that my father was a man of faith. From the cradle, I was taught the Commandments and schooled to believe as he did. Even when my stepmother twisted those principles into a rigid discipline that had little to do with true religion, I never lost my own faith.

"But when I became your mistress, I fell from grace. I knew that and accepted the consequences, although there was still hope I'd be forgiven if I spent the rest of my life repenting and making reparation. That was my intent, until I began to take pleasure in my sin. I never meant to. You remember how I fought it—and you."

He winced, remembering all too well.

"At the end, I could not help myself," she confided. "I came to want you more than salvation and was sure I would never regret our time together, although it meant burning in hell for eternity."

He wanted to protest but swallowed his words.

Clare was, for once, speaking from her heart. And his own heart ached as he began to realize the incalculable pain she had kept hidden from him all these weeks. She was a vicar's daughter, driven to sell herself at the risk of her soul for the sons of a madwoman who'd tortured her. The interior struggle with her exacting conscience had torn her apart.

At that moment, he'd have willingly consigned his own black soul to the devil if she could be spared one instant of her torment. A poor bargain, he reflected darkly. Already firmly in Lucifer's grasp, he had nothing to offer any of the Powers that ruled an afterlife he'd never believed in.

She was speaking again, in a low monotone. "You were dying, Bryn. I felt you slipping away, so far away that nothing could bring you back except a miracle. I prayed so hard, knowing I had no right to pray, and still you grew weaker. Sometimes I thought you had ceased to breathe altogether.

"And then I promised God that if He let you live I would never sin with you again. I knew it was a futile prayer, since I was lost already, but immediately the words were said you squeezed my hand. Opened your eyes. For some reason, that vow made all the difference. Do you understand that I have given my word and must honor it?"

He stared at her in blank astonishment before remembering that moments ago he'd thought to do the same thing—make a bargain with God, or Satan if need be, for Clare's sake. With *anyone* having power to alter reality to suit his own wishes. But he had not truly believed that possible.

Clare did.

Now that he understood the depth of her religious

conviction, he could not blame her. But she was wrong. She had to be, because he would not give her up for a promise she made under duress. No god worth his salt would hold her to it.

Releasing a long breath, he took hold of her hand. "Do you honestly think the Almighty bargains with his creatures for their lives and souls? Clare, listen to me. I recall very little of what happened after I was shot, except the sound of your voice. I kept trying to reach it, but whenever I got close the pain turned me away."

He drew her fingers to his lips, wanting her to feel his words as he spoke them.

"The last moments before I awoke are very clear. The temptation to give up was nearly overwhelming, and I'm fairly certain I would have done so, if not for your voice and the assurance you were there, waiting for me. I cannot believe any god would be so cruel as to lead me back to you, only to snatch you away because of a promise you made out of desperation. I won't believe in a god who plays games like that, pitting us against each other for his own amusement. And neither should you."

She was quiet for a long time, her eyes closed. Then the tip of her forefinger stroked his taut lips. "Perhaps you are right, Bryn. I don't know what God has in mind, and I cannot imagine He is toying with us. But I promised. Surely He expects me to—"

He cut her off with a foul oath. And immediately apologized. "Forgive me. I know very well what it is to be entangled in promises, and how it feels when they suddenly make no sense at all."

"What shall we do, then?" she murmured. "We can never be happy with each other under these circumstances."

"There is a solution," he said forcefully. "What we need is time, to figure out what it is. For the foreseeable future you are in no danger of sinning with me, since I can barely lift my head, let alone anything else. And when I regain my strength, I won't try to seduce you. Stay with me, Clare, and promise you won't run away again until we find an answer."

Her lips curved. "You are so sure of yourself. It never fails to astound me. I'll make no more promises, because I'm very unsure of myself at the moment. But so long as we are not lovers, I have no reason to leave you." Her voice grew soft. "Nor do I want to."

"Well enough, then," he said, wishing she would kiss him. To his astonishment she did, lightly, no more than a brush of her lips across his, but the tiny gesture gave him hope.

"Sleep now," she instructed, coming to her feet and moving with a determined stride to the door. "This has been a long and difficult day, and we are both tired. I'll join you for breakfast."

He lay awake for several hours after she'd gone, reflecting on the things she had revealed about herself and what she had endured while he selfishly pursued his own goals, oblivious to her silent anguish. Only one thing seemed clear, as exhaustion took possession of his senses.

He must go home and face the past that still haunted him, the ghosts who had set him on a collision course with any hope of a future with Clare.

And she must go with him, because he lacked the strength to confront them alone.

28

Two weeks later, Clare and Bryn set out for River's End.

She was glad to be on the road at last. Bryn had been impossible the last few days, sometimes brooding, other times chafing at the restrictions imposed on him by the doctor. In general, a royal pain in the backside.

She knew he was unhappy, as was she, but by silent agreement they never discussed her departure. Instead, they quarreled incessantly about how much he was permitted to drink, why she must remain at St. James's instead of moving back to Clouds, and her refusal to accept the expensive jewelry he requisitioned from Clark and Sons. A new parcel arrived every afternoon, containing diamonds and rubies and emeralds enough to support her in comfort for the rest of her life.

She could not bear to look at his gifts, although

she loved him all the more for wanting to take care of her—and angered him with her determination to preserve her independence. Was she not already indebted beyond her power to repay him?

They kept hurting each other, without wanting to.

Sometimes she wanted to disappear again and make a clean end, but he would find her. She intended to settle in Hastings. The seaside town had become a popular summer resort, and Florette knew of an excellent modiste who would be glad to employ her. With a job and a place to live until she could afford a cottage of her own, one close enough to visit the twins, there was no reason to stay in London now that Bryn was recovered.

She had agreed to accompany him to the Caradoc estate only because of the little he'd told her about his childhood there. There must be compelling reasons why he had not gone back for twenty years, although he refused to speak of them. And when he begged her, with uncharacteristic humility, to make the journey, she could not refuse.

Heydon Manor, a few miles north of River's End, was a pleasant and unpretentious country house surrounded by well-tended gardens. Robert and Elizabeth waited by the circular drive to welcome them, along with the viscount's mother, Lady Dorinda Lacey, who rushed to hug Bryn the moment he stepped out of the carriage.

Almost immediately Clare felt at home, despite one awkward moment when they were shown to a single bedroom.

Since the day he first awoke, Bryn had wanted to sleep with her. After learning of her vow, he swore he'd not touch her sexually, although he still wanted to hold her in his arms.

She believed him but did not trust herself and finally told him so. He had been inordinately pleased by her confession.

Separate rooms had been reserved at the inns where they stopped, and he seemed content to hold her hand in the carriage and kiss her cheek when they said good night. But when they were ushered into the bedchamber at Heydon Manor, Bryn saw the distressed look on her face and drew Lacey aside. A few minutes later she was escorted to a room of her own.

Dinner was informal, everyone talking at once, catching up on the news. Robert described, in high good humor, the adventures he and Elizabeth encountered on the road to Gretna Green. Bryn sketched, briefly, his encounter with the thugs who shot him, passing over his near brush with death. Lady Dorinda asked about Isabella and Ernestine.

Through it all, Clare smiled often and said nothing. She could not help but envy Robert and Elizabeth, so obviously happy together, and kept sneaking glances at Bryn, lounging in his chair beside her. What would it be like, to love him freely and openly? Without shame?

Once, she had thought it difficult to go to his bed. Once, she could imagine nothing worse than damning herself irretrievably because she wanted to be there. Now she understood those torments were nothing compared to the agony of saying goodbye for the last time.

When the ladies withdrew, leaving the men to their port and cigars, Bryn turned to Lacey with a serious expression. "Elizabeth's father is dead," he said flatly. "We must decide how to tell her."

"He was the one who shot you, of course." Lacey swirled the wine in his glass. "Any fool could figure that out, except, apparently, the magistrate. Yes, a report of your near demise made it all the way to the local news rag. I assume you lied to protect Beth, but how did Landry meet his end? You were in no condition to see to it."

Bryn regarded his friend with new respect. He had thought to gloss over the truth, but changed his mind and outlined the details, omitting only Max Peyton's name. A reliable source had assured him that Landry was butchered at a gin mill and that his body would probably wash up on the banks of the Thames.

"I don't want Elizabeth to know her father put a bullet in me," he finished. "She already feels indebted to me, and guilty because he tried to force a marriage between us. Why is it, Lace, that victims take responsibility for the people who hurt them? Why do they protect the whoresons?"

"Why, for that matter, do you insist on protecting Beth? Tell you what, old sod. She's stronger, in her way, than you or I will ever be. And she would want to know the truth. I'll be the one to tell her, though. It will be easier, coming from me."

Nodding, Bryn refilled his glass. "I haven't told Clare, so make sure Elizabeth understands that."

Lacey frowned at him. "Damned stupid, if you ask me. Women don't like being lied to."

"Clare and I have enough problems as it is," Bryn said curtly. "Have you made any progress at the estate?"

"Not to speak of. Still on my honeymoon, you know, and I never dreamed you'd swoop down for an inspection. Last week I hired workmen to sweep out the cobwebs and cart away the rotted furniture, but the place is a shambles. Hell, Bryn, what do you expect to see?"

"Hell is precisely what I expect to see. Don't worry, Lace. This is by way of a pilgrimage, not an inspection.

I'm looking for the part of me I left at River's End, and a few answers."

The viscount regarded him sternly. "The answers are perfectly clear. Thing is, you're not asking the right questions."

Bryn gazed moodily into his glass of wine. "At this point I'm ready to listen to any advice, even yours. So what are the questions?"

Lacey propped his elbows on the table. "Only one, really. Why are you hell-bent to live out your father's life instead of your own?"

Bryn's head shot up. "I'm not doing that."

"No? Well, not his real life, of course. Just the one he ought to have lived, the one without the gaming and whoring."

"And what the devil is wrong with declining to lose my fortune at the tables or kill myself with diseased women? You came a damned sight closer to both than I ever did, before you met Elizabeth."

"Point taken," Lacey said with a grin. "Thing is, you've gone to extremes in the other direction. Oh, you're no saint—far from it—but you just plain don't *see,* Bryndle. Your mind is like your eyes, only a few colors you can take in. The others you are missing altogether, and one of them is named Clare."

"You know nothing about Clare and me." Bryn gave him a scorching look. "Stay out of this, Lace."

"I intend to. But you did ask, so I'll give you a last piece of advice. Tell her everything, from the beginning. Let her know who you are and how you got that way."

"You think that will make a difference? She has troubles of her own, ones that have nothing to do with me. Except they mean she cannot—" He waved a hand. "Knowing me better won't change that."

"She might help you know yourself. Anyway, that's the best I can do. Honesty. Try it." Lacey came to his feet. "One other thing. Last time you were at River's End, plotting out the rest of your life, you were fifteen years old. You ain't too smart now, old boy. What in blazes did you know back then?"

Mounted in front of Bryn on a large bay horse, Clare regarded the derelict house with amazement. It was part medieval castle, part Tudor mansion, with bits and pieces of architectural styles tacked on here and there over the centuries.

The crenellated stone walls had been torn down in front but still surrounded the house on three sides, as if the Talgarths had turned their backs on Wales. Ivy covered much of the house, and weeds had taken over the gardens.

Bryn swung down and helped her alight. "The place is a mess," he warned.

"I can see that. Robert will bring it to life again, or as much as he can until someone makes it a home."

"That won't happen for many years, Clare." He led her up the steps to the unlocked door, which creaked when he pushed it open. "I want it restored for my heir, and to give Lace a job he can handle. I've no intention of living here myself."

Aware of the bitterness in his voice, she only nodded and followed him inside.

The smell of damp stone and moldy wood nearly overpowered her. In the wide hall, stained paper curled away from the walls, which were hung with faded portraits, the figures nearly unrecognizable beneath decades of dust and grime. Empty niches and barren pedestals gave bleak testimony to better days.

"The original fortress was constructed in the eleventh century," he said. "Not much is left of it, except the great hall and the defensive walls."

She trailed him through an enormous arched doorway into a massive room, the stone walls blackened by smoke except where tapestries had previously hung. At the far end of the hall a veritable medieval arsenal was arrayed behind a platform that once held, she suspected, the table of honor at lavish banquets. There were crossbows and spears, pikes and maces, broadswords and long knives of all sorts. Two fireplaces, one on either side of the room, were tall enough for Bryn to stand in.

From overhead, she heard the rustle of birds nesting on the heavy wooden beams that crisscrossed the ceiling.

"It was not always so desolate," Bryn said quietly. "When my father came home from his travels with a horde of friends in his wake, the hall was filled with music and laughter. I used to watch through one of the peepholes and imagine myself sitting there"—he pointed to the platform—"in his chair. He was like the king of a glittering court, always the center of attention. I wanted to be like that. Like him."

He laughed, the sound echoing hollowly in the vast room.

"A child's dream, built—like all dreams—on quicksand. Is anything ever the way we think it is, Clare? Or want it to be?"

She gazed at him helplessly, but he didn't appear to expect an answer. He had begun to wander around the hall, lost in his memories. "Would you rather be alone?" she asked after a while.

He spun on his heels. "God, no. If you can bear my company and this house, I need you with me. We won't stay long. There is only one other room I want to see."

She held out her arms. "As long as it takes, Bryn."

With a swift stride, he crossed the room and seized her hand. "Come upstairs, then. And thank you. I would sooner not face this alone."

The sheer size and odd configuration of the manor became apparent as he led her to a wide staircase and then down a seemingly endless hall that turned first to the right and then the left before dead-ending at a wide doorway. The door itself hung drunkenly from one hinge and made a groaning sound when he pushed it open.

"My father's chamber," he said without expression. "He died in that bed."

Only the carved wooden frame and canopy remained. Against one wall stood a heavy armoire, and a side table ran almost the length of the other. There were no chairs, no carpeting, no other furniture. Her eyes were drawn to a large painting, the sole touch of color in the room although it badly needed cleaning.

Still holding her hand, Bryn moved to stand in front of the portrait.

She gasped. The hair was powdered, but the blue eyes and forceful chin were more than familiar. "That could be you!"

"Owen Talgarth, sixteenth Earl of Caradoc. Whenever I look into a mirror, I see him. Or rather, I see this picture. He looked nothing like it the last few years."

"When he was ill," she said, gripping Bryn's fingers tightly. Even through her gloves and his, they felt cold. "Will it help to tell me what happened?"

He shrugged. "Lacey said I should, although I cannot think how it will change anything. I'm not even sure why I brought you here, or why I came myself. Can you work an exorcism, Clare? Rid me of these demons?"

"I can listen," she said simply.

And she did, for nearly an hour as he spoke in a flat, emotionless voice. With growing horror, she followed him through the years when he had idolized his father to the loneliness of mother and child when the earl abandoned them in favor of his own pleasures, and finally to the destruction of everything Bryn had believed in.

He looked at the portrait as he told the story, as if addressing Owen Talgarth instead of her. And she looked at his face, reading the pain he tried to conceal as he skimmed over the worst details, making little of his own ordeal.

It was a long moment before she realized he'd stopped speaking. He had been describing the last night before his father sank into unconsciousness and seemed unable to continue.

Finally he tore his gaze from the painting and looked at her. "I might have forgiven him anything, Clare. I wanted to. But he killed my mother."

Her heart gave a lurch. "Oh, God, Bryn. He murdered her?"

"He might as well have done. She contracted the pox from him, or that's my guess. He was sick from it when he came home for a few months but seemed to recover. The disease comes and goes for a time, and then it stays. I suspect he knew he was dying when he took off again for one last mad grab at life, gambling away what remained of his fortune—and left his wife to confront her illness alone. She could not. One day she walked into the river, and her body was found a few miles away. Everyone called it an accident, but I heard the whispers."

His voice hardened.

"The hell of it is, he loved her. And she thought he walked on air. But love was never enough for him. He had everything that ought to matter, and he wanted more. At the end, he had nothing at all."

"Except you," she murmured.

"A skinny boy still trying to hold on to his illusions," he said mockingly. "I had the senseless notion that I could change everything, make it all go away, if I became what he ought to have been. I promised myself I would. But I've accomplished exactly nothing." He gestured at the gloomy chamber. "The estate is a ruin. There is no heir. All I have done is make money and spend it on my own indulgences."

"Harmless indulgences," she reminded him gently. "You earned your fortune and have not gambled it away. There will be a legacy for your children when you marry. You are not your father, Bryn. And any debt you ever owed was paid during the years you cared for him."

He mustered a faint smile. "It occurs to me that we both spent our childhood in much the same way, me tending a father blind and insane from his disease, you nursing a madwoman who left two children for you to raise alone. But I have failed my obligations, while you—"

"Have also failed," she said bluntly. "Joseph and Jeremy would be ashamed to know what I have done."

He put his hands on her shoulders. "Only if they are fools. You are the bravest individual I have ever met, and they would agree." His grip tightened. "I'd have given you the money, Clare, without obligation, had you told me the truth from the beginning."

Tears burned her eyes. "I expect you would have, now that I know you. But I didn't, not then. And even so, I would have been too proud and stubborn to accept."

"It appears that we share any number of vices," he observed.

She leaned against his chest, grateful when his arms wrapped around her because her knees had buckled. "Yes," she whispered to his lapel. "But you saved me, while I have given you so very little. And have sworn to give you no more. It isn't fair, Bryn. You deserve better." Crying in earnest, she lifted her gaze to his face. "What are we to do?"

He regarded her gravely. "The last thing my father said to me, the last thing that made sense, was *Do what you want.* And so I have, for the most part, although I watched him suffer the consequences of that philosophy. If I was careful about money and women, it was only because I feared to die as he did, impoverished and insane. But now I am beginning to understand that I never learned how to live, until I met you. We belong together, Clare. Can you not see that?"

Her throat tightened. "I have promised otherwise, in exchange for your life."

"And you honestly believe God will hold you to that?" He shook his head. "I am not convinced that your vow of future chastity and my recovery are related."

"Perhaps not," she admitted. "But don't you see? It is a matter of personal integrity. You have spent twenty years haunted by promises made on behalf of a father who betrayed you in every way. How can I turn my back on a promise made to God?"

He rested his cheek against hers. "You cannot, princess. You would never be happy with me if you did." After a moment, he stepped back and took her hand. "I have found what I was looking for. Now let me show you what is beautiful about River's End."

He led her outside and up a stone stairway to the narrow walk along the fortress walls.

She caught her breath. The view was spectacular. In the distance, a ridge of mountains lifted to the blue sky. Where they fell off to a valley lush with trees, a river curled like a silver ribbon, sunlight flashing off the water.

"The Black Mountains," he said. "Between them and the river Honddu, you can just make out the remains of Offa's Dyke. It runs all the way from the north coast to Chepstow. For a long time the dike marked the border between England and Wales, although the territory was often disputed. The first Earl of Caradoc built on this promontory at William the Conqueror's behest, to hold off the barbarians, although I suspect the Normans did more harm to England than the Welsh." He grinned. "I rather lean to the west, because Welshmen are such lovers of music."

"How beautiful this is, Bryn," she said in an awed voice. "No wonder you want to preserve it."

"The village of Talgarth is located across those mountains," he told her. "I have no doubt my ancestors tended pigs and herded sheep there, until some ambitious young rogue betrayed his heritage and fought on the winning side. If Harold had prevailed against the Conqueror, I would be a peasant instead of an earl."

She chuckled. "Unimaginable. No shepherd was ever so arrogant."

"Nor any earl," he said seriously, "with so little reason." He put his hands on her cheeks, gazing resolutely into her eyes. "Marry me, Clare."

She blinked. He was out of his mind to even suggest it. "You cannot mean that. What a crackbrained notion!"

"I have never meant anything more. You promised not to sin with me, but if we are married there *is* no sin. You can keep your meaningless vow to God and we will both be happy. It is the obvious answer. And don't try to tell me otherwise, because I know you want me almost as much as I want you."

Stepping back, she squared her shoulders. "And what of your own vow, to marry well with a woman of your own class? Don't be absurd, Bryn. I am the daughter of a country vicar, ineligible even had I not turned whore. You are not thinking clearly."

His hands tightened to fists. "On the contrary. I am thinking clearly for the first time in my life. And if I ever again hear you refer to yourself as a whore, I will take you over my knee. You became my mistress for reasons the whole world would applaud, and even your strict God has already forgiven you. Now put an end to this charade and be my wife."

She took a deep breath. "No, I will not. No."

Bryn regarded her with a stunned expression. "Why the hell not?"

"At this moment," Clare said slowly, "you think it a perfect solution. But when we leave here, and you've had time to consider, you will know otherwise."

"I *have* considered. Listen to me, princess. Lots of men marry their mistresses—Charles Fox for one—

and nobody that mattered gave a damn. Prinny tried to marry Maria Fitzherbert. The Duke of Clarence had ten little FitzClarences by Mrs. Jordan. These things are forgiven and forgotten."

"Bryn, I don't know how to live among people who dishonor their marriage vows and breed children who will carry the stigma of being born out of wedlock all their lives. What little taste I've had of aristocratic disregard for fidelity only convinces me that I want no part of it. A careless nobleman took his pleasure with Ardis and left her pregnant and alone. I doubt he has ever given her a second thought, and he doesn't even know he fathered two wonderful boys."

"What is all that to the point? You and I will be married, Clare. Our children will be legitimate. I shall always be faithful to you."

She drew herself up. "I believe you mean that. And I also believe you would come to regret allying yourself with a woman of common birth who sold herself for money. You cannot change overnight, Bryn, and would despise yourself for setting aside the promises you made years ago. They would come back to haunt us both. I won't let you do it."

"By God, Clare, how can you be so bullheaded? I was wrong before, and now I'm right. If I can change, so can you."

She regarded him somberly. "I have done a great many things I ought not. Even enjoyed them, to my shame. But I will not take advantage of your impulsive whim. And you *are* impulsive, you know, with a lamentable tendency to fly off the handle. If it is any comfort, I care enough for you to save you from yourself."

"Thank you very much," he said sarcastically. "As if I am not perfectly capable of directing my own life."

"Exactly." She dredged a smile from the pain that nearly overwhelmed her. "We will speak no more of this, Bryn. I'll not marry you, and if you importune me I shall leave immediately. Better we part as friends, don't you think?"

He gave her a shadowed look. "Better we not part at all. But I'll say no more on the subject. It will take more than words to dig you out of the cave you are hiding in. I know that, because I have been holed up in a place much like it for twenty years." Tilting her chin with his hand, he directed her attention to the Black Mountains. "All barriers can be crossed, butterfly, and even the deepest well is open to the sky."

Having no idea what he meant, she took his arm. "I'd as soon go back to London, if you are ready."

His eyes were clouded. "Tomorrow morning. I'm finished here."

Clare began to make preparations to leave.

When they arrived in London she moved back to Clouds, surprised that Bryn offered no objections. In spite of his promise, she had rather expected him to try and change her mind. But he seemed to have lost interest in marrying her, or even in keeping her close by.

For that matter, he was strangely indifferent to her plans for the future, although she tried to discuss them on the trip home. For the most part quiet and reflective, he listened politely, nodded, and soon changed the subject. Beyond insisting that she remain in the city for a performance of his favorite opera, scheduled a week away, he appeared ready to say goodbye.

Even so, he kept her busy while they awaited *The Magic Flute,* and took her on a last whirlwind tour of London. They went to Vauxhall Gardens and the Tower, Westminster Abbey and Astley's Royal Amphitheatre, and one afternoon he staunchly endured an excursion to the Royal Academy so she could enjoy the paintings.

Every day he brought her a new book, but no more jewelry, thank the Lord. She had agreed to take everything he'd given her, because she knew it would hurt him if she did not. Again, he hadn't seemed to care. "Whatever you like," was all he said.

She was puzzled by this new mood. He was so unlike the Bryn she had come to know, although they both enjoyed the excursions and laughed a great deal. She ought to be relieved that their parting would be amicable, and grateful for the happy memories he was building for her.

Instead, she lay awake at night in the small bedroom where she first stayed at Clouds, wrestling with her own demons. Bryn now realized, as she had done immediately, that a marriage between them was impossible. But some mean-spirited part of her wished he had fought the idea a little harder.

Foolish, of course. If he wooed her or tried to seduce her, she would have no choice but to turn him away. It was only female vanity that longed for some hint that their final parting was as difficult for him as for her.

But how could it be? She loved him.

He did not love her.

He still desired her, though. She saw it in his eyes and recognized the strict discipline he imposed on himself when they were together. But desire was not the same thing as love. She had no right to expect him to share her feelings and took care not to show her own.

Saturday night would be their last together. On Sunday, his carriage would take her to Hastings and it would all be over. A new life awaited her. She tried to look ahead, gathering her courage, bracing herself for the pain.

But Friday night, when he brought her home from the theater, Bryn announced a change of plans. Alice had given birth to a daughter, and her christening was to be Saturday afternoon. Claude wanted him to stand as godfather, so instead of the opera they would go to Richmond for the ceremony. The child was to be named Emily Clare, so naturally Alice expected Clare to attend.

"You only just found this out?" she protested angrily.

"I have known for several days," he said in a calm voice. "I feared your over-strict conscience might lead you to fret about going into a church, so I didn't tell you. Perhaps we'll make it back to London for the opera, perhaps not. But I could not tell Claude and Alice that we plan to separate just when they are so happy."

"Of course not," she said, after a moment. "I shall be glad to see them one more time. You understand I must still leave for Hastings on Sunday?"

He shrugged. "Whatever you decide. Be ready at ten o'clock tomorrow morning, and wear something blue. It is how I want to remember you." He brushed his lips across her cheek and moved to the door. "And Clare," he said over his shoulder, "leave your hair down. Please."

29

When they arrived just after noon, Clare saw a number of carriages lined up alongside the tiny church of St. Didacus. A towheaded urchin scurried over to take the reins, and Bryn swung her down from Black Lightning.

"You look beautiful," he said, his hands warm on her waist as he held her close for a last private moment. "That dress suits you."

As he had requested, she wore a pale blue gown, the sprig muslin picked out in darker blue. When he picked her up at Clouds he asked her to leave off her pelisse, and again she obeyed. Whatever he wanted, on their last day together, she would give him.

"Surely we are late," she observed. "Everyone is already inside."

"They won't start without us," he assured her. "Can you smile? This is supposed to be a happy occasion."

With effort, she obliged him, unutterably nervous for some reason. Her discomfort grew when he untied the ribbon at her neck and lifted away her bonnet, tossing it into the curricle.

"I want to see your face, Clare. Indulge me." His fingers stroked her hair, lifting it, spreading it over her shoulders.

At the moment, gazing into his eyes, she could deny him nothing. And when he took her hand, drawing her toward the church, she stumbled only once. To see Claude and Alice with their new child was almost more than she could bear, knowing such joy would never be hers. She only hoped she was strong enough not to cry.

As they stepped into the church, she saw Lady Isabella standing by the open door leading into the nave, holding a bouquet of daffodils tied with white satin ribbon.

"About time," said the countess. "I was beginning to worry. What kept you?"

"Clare wouldn't let me drive fast," Bryn replied with a laugh. "Too much traffic. For some reason, she doesn't think I know what I'm doing."

"In general she would be right, but not this time." Isabella turned to Clare and held out the bouquet. "This is for you."

Dazed, Clare accepted the flowers and looked past Isabella, into the church. The bouquet slipped from her fingers. Everyone she knew was there.

In the rear pews were Charley Cassidy, Maude Beales, Amy, and Lyle Hendly, the chef. Next to him stood Florette. She recognized Bryn's valet and other servants from the house at St. James's Square.

Closer to the front, Claude held the hand of a still

very pregnant Alice. Their three children waved a greeting.

Elizabeth Laçey, with Lady Dorinda at her side, gave her a bright smile. Robert was standing by the communion rail near the altar.

And in the front pew, one on either side of Ernestine Fitzwalter, were Joseph and Jeremy. They looked dignified and proud.

Bryn picked up the bouquet and held it out to her, his eyes glowing. "You cannot have imagined I'd let you get away so easily, butterfly. This is our wedding day."

She regarded him for a long moment, aghast at what he had done. And then she slapped him.

"The hell it is!"

Dumbfounded, Bryn watched her stride with firm purpose out the door.

"Oh, my," Isabella murmured.

He handed her the bouquet. "A case of last-minute bridal jitters. Tell the vicar there will be a slight delay."

Clare had stopped at the end of the churchyard path, beside the village's main street, apparently considering what to do next. Her back was straight, and her hands opened and closed to fists as if she wanted to hit him again.

He approached carefully, halting a few feet away. "I believe you violated sanctuary by attacking me in a church, princess."

He heard an oath no vicar's daughter ought to know. And then she swung around and advanced on him with murder in her eyes.

"You think this is *funny?* Of all the contemptible, arrogant, high-handed things you have ever done, this is the most outrageous! How could you? How *dare* you?"

With fortitude, he held his ground. "I would dare anything for you," he said simply, "even your temper. You gave me no choice, Clare. Damned if I'll let your noble but misguided notion about what's best for me get in the way of what I want."

"And Caradoc must always have what he wants, by whatever means." She glowered at him. "Do you realize what you have done?"

"Certainly. I invited our friends to a wedding, procured a special license, and arranged for an alfresco reception where we had our picnic by the river. You do remember that?" He was pleased to see her blush.

"And neglected to inform the bride," she said in a blistering voice. "Because you knew I would never agree."

He waved a hand. "I allowed for that possibility, yes. You are a remarkably obstinate woman, my dear, and I figured a surprise attack was the only way to catch you off guard long enough to see reason. There was even a slight chance you'd think it vastly romantic."

"I think it vastly harebrained." She caught her breath. "And cruel, Bryn. What about Joseph and Jeremy? Dear God, how could you bring them here. Now they know—"

"What the duchess told them," he said calmly. "Fortunately, she knew where they attended school, from the letters they sent you. She picked them up yesterday, and they spent last night at her house. From her account, the boys are delighted that you are to be a countess, although Joseph required assurance that I deserve you. Ernie had considerable difficulty convincing him.

"As for Jeremy, he was impressed by my fortune and I understand that he plans to hit me up for a horse.

Both of them assume that we met under proper circumstances and that I fell madly in love with you." He put his hands on her shoulders. "That last part is true."

She blinked. "You *love* me?"

He spoke past a heavy lump in his throat. "I have never said so, sweet Clare, but only because I didn't know it. Like all the colors I cannot see, love never seemed possible for me. It destroyed my mother, was ravaged by my father, and eluded me for thirty-five years. I failed to recognize it. Now I do."

"Oh." She backed away, biting at her lower lip. "But that only makes everything more difficult."

"I fail to see how. A man who loves you wants to marry you. And you are not indifferent to me. I am vain enough to think this now, although you had good reason to despise me for a long time. But that changed. You know it did."

"Yes," she admitted in a low voice. "But don't you see? If I didn't care for you, I would marry you in an instant."

He shook his head. "Female logic. God help England if women ever get the vote. Until this moment, I thought you prodigiously wise, but now I wonder."

"Of *course* I want the security, Bryn. I want everything you can give to me and the twins. Even the horse for Jeremy. More than that, I want to be with you. But most of all I want you to have a wife worthy of your position, because you will never be happy until the name of Caradoc is spoken with respect. That will not happen if you marry your mistress."

"On the contrary." He moved a step closer, relieved that she did not retreat, and tangled his fingers in her hair. "I expect us to be the envy of the *ton,* once the scandal is forgotten. And it will be, Clare, sooner than you think. By the time our daughters are presented, no one will even remember my own peculiar reputation, let alone that you occasionally appeared with me in public before our betrothal was announced. To the devil with what anyone thinks. We can weather any storm, so long as we are together."

"You make it sound so easy," she said despondently.

"And so it is." He dropped to one knee. "Marry me, butterfly. Tell me yes."

"No. I cannot." Her gaze lifted from his face, focusing on something behind him. "Do get up, Bryn. Everyone is staring at us."

"Marry me," he repeated.

"They've all come out of the church!"

He shrugged. "Say yes or I'll go onto two knees." When she failed to reply, he did. "Next I'll kiss your feet. Marry me."

"*Bryn!*"

Wrapping his fingers around her ankle, he leaned forward.

"Bloody hell!" She clutched at his hair. "*Yes,* you wretched man. Yes. I will marry you. Only stand up. You are making a fool of yourself."

Surging to his feet, he grabbed her by the waist and swung her around. "I often do," he said with a laugh. "Get used to it."

"I already am," she blazed. "Put me down!"

"Not yet." He lifted her into his arms and kissed her deeply, glorying in her immediate response. From the church steps came the sound of applause.

"You have made me the happiest man in England," he murmured against her lips. "Make that the world. I love you, Easter Clare."

She sucked in a deep breath. "And I love you too, Bryn."

"Oh, God." His arms dropped to his sides.

Clare landed on her backside in the dirt.

He looked down at her with a dazed expression on his face. "Truly? I hoped someday you would, a long time from now, when I'd become the man you ought to have. And I am determined to do so, my love, whatever it requires. I promise."

"To start with, you could help me up," she said in a disgruntled voice.

Cursing himself, he lifted her to her feet and gave her a lopsided smile of apology. "Obviously I have a long way to go."

"You will do well enough as you are, Caradoc. I am none too perfect myself. But while I love you with all my heart, don't imagine I have forgiven you for this monstrous deception. When the celebration is over and the guests have gone, I fully intend to call you to account."

He pretended to shiver in terror. "Surely you won't scold me on our wedding night? Let us call a truce until tomorrow morning. Then you can rake me through the coals."

"Tomorrow *afternoon,*" she corrected. "I want you fully awake for my lecture, and you are insensible before midday. You'll not escape lightly, bear."

"But I have all night to change your mind," he reminded her. "Now come along, because the vicar grows almost as impatient as I am."

Hand in hand, they moved to the church door as the wedding guests filtered inside ahead of them with wide smiles on their faces.

All except Jeremy, who had wandered over to

examine Black Lightning, more fascinated by Bryn's curricle than the sight of two grown-ups kissing each other. Finally realizing that everyone had disappeared, he raced down the aisle behind the bride and groom.

Robert Lacey beckoned him forward before he could slide into a pew and handed him the ring. "You can be best man," he whispered.

The duchess pushed Joseph into the aisle. "Go stand by your sister. They will want you both beside them."

It was a nearly perfect wedding, until the bride said, "I, Easter Wilhelmina, take you—"

At which point the groom dissolved in laughter. "Wilhelmina?" he choked.

She glared at him. "Wilhelmina. Get used to it, *Bryndle*."

AVAILABLE NOW

Alone in a Crowd by Georgia Bockoven

After a terrible accident, country music sensation Cole Webster must undergo reconstructive surgery which gives him temporary anonymity. Before he can reveal his true identity, Cole loses his heart to Holly, a beautiful woman who values her privacy above all else. Cole must come to terms with who he is and what he's looking for in life before he can find love and true happiness.

Destiny Awaits by Suzanne Elizabeth

When wealthy and spoiled Tess Harper was transported back in time to Kansas, 1885, it didn't take her long to find trouble. Captivating farmer Joseph Maguire agreed to bail her out on one condition–that she live with him and care for his two orphaned nieces. Despite the hardships of prairie life, Tess soon realized that this love of a lifetime was to be her destiny.

Broken Vows by Donna Grove

To Rachel Girard, nothing was more important than her family's cattle ranch, which would one day be hers. But when her father declared she must take a husband or lose her birthright, Rachel offered footloose bounty hunter Caleb Delaney a fortune if he'd marry her–then leave her! Cal knew he'd be a fool to refuse, but he would soon wonder if a life without Rachel was worth anything at all.

Lady in Blue by Lynn Kerstan

A delightful, sexy romance set in the Regency period. Wealthy and powerful Brynmore Talgarth never wanted a wife, despite pressure to restore the family's reputation by marrying well. But once he met young, destitute, and beautiful Clare Easton, an indecent proposal led the way to a love neither knew could exist.

The Long Road Home by Mary Alice Monroe

Bankrupt and alone after her financier husband dies, Nora MacKenzie's life is shattered. After fleeing to a sheep farm in Vermont, she meets up with the mysterious C. W. Friendship soon blossoms into love, but C. W. is keeping some dangerous secrets that could destroy them both.

Winter Bride by Teresa Southwick

Wyoming rancher Matt Decker needed a wife. His mother sent him Eliza Jones, the young woman who had adored Matt when they were children. Eliza was anxious to start a new life out west, but the last thing Matt wanted was to marry someone to whom he might become emotionally attached.

COMING SOON

Evensong by Candace Camp

A tale of love and deception in medieval England from the incomparable Candace Camp. When Aline was offered a fortune to impersonate a noble lady, the beautiful dancing girl thought it worth the risk. Then, in the arms of the handsome knight she was to deceive, she realized she chanced not just her life, but her heart.

Once Upon a Pirate by Nancy Block

When Zoe Dunham inadvertently plunges into the past, landing on the deck of a pirate ship, she thinks her ex-husband has finally gone insane and has kidnapped her under the persona of his infamous pirate ancestor, to whom he bears a strong resemblance. But sexy Black Jack Alexander is all too real and Zoe must now come to terms with the heartbreak of her divorce *and* her curious romp through time.

Angel's Aura by Brenda Jernigan

In the sleepy town of Martinsboro, North Carolina, local health club hunk Manly Richards turns up dead and all fingers point to Angel Larue, the married muscleman's latest love-on-the-side. Of course, housewife and part-time reporter Barbara Upchurch knows her sister is no killer, but she must convince the police of Angel's innocence while the real culprit is out there making sure Barbara's snooping days are numbered!

The Lost Goddess by Patricia Simpson

Cursed by an ancient Egyptian cult, Asheris was doomed to immortal torment until Karissa's fiery desire freed him. Now they must put their love to the ultimate test and challenge dark forces to save the life of their young daughter Julia, whose strange psychic powers have placed her in grave danger. A spellbinding novel from "one of the premier writers of supernatural romance." —*Romantic Times*

Fire and Water by Mary Spencer

On the run in the Sierra Nevadas, Mariette Call tried to figure out why her murdered husband's journals were so important to a politician back east. She and dashing Federal Marshal Matthew Kagan, sent along to protect her, manage to elude their pursuers and also discover a deep passion for each other.

Hearts of the Storm by Pamela Willis

Josie Campbell could put a bullet through a man's hat at a hundred yards with as much skill as she could nurse a fugitive slave baby back to health. She vowed never to belong to any man—until magnetic Clint McCarter rode into town. But the black clouds of the Civil War were gathering, and there was little time for love unless Clint and Josie could find happiness at the heart of the storm.

Harper Monogram **The Mark of Distinctive Women's Fiction**